NICOLA UPSON

Stanley
and
Elsie

DUCKWORTH

First published in the United Kingdom by Duckworth in 2019

Duckworth, an imprint of Prelude Books Ltd
13 Carrington Road, Richmond,
TW10 5AA, United Kingdom
www.preludebooks.co.uk

For bulk and special sales please contact
info@preludebooks.co.uk

Extracts from the writings of Stanley Spencer are used by kind
permission of The Estate of Stanley Spencer.

A catalogue record for this book is available
from the British Library

ISBN 978-0-7156-5368-5
1 3 5 7 9 10 8 6 4 2

For Mandy

Inky scratches, all with love

It's absurd, and he knows it. Off to war in a straw hat and an old summer suit.

He looks at himself in the mirror – detached, appraising – and wonders why his eyes fail him. Try as he might, he can't reconcile the man who stands in front of him with the setting he knows so well. Something has changed, something intangible. It's as if a stranger has entered the room, and, for the sake of all he loves, he turns to leave before it can be for ever tainted.

Nothing acknowledges his going. The bed is already made, its canopy carefully straightened, and his bible sits open on a small wooden table in the corner. In the peace of the early morning, he takes courage from the room's ordinariness: the ugly chest of drawers and marble-topped washstand; the clutter of odd china which has gathered there over the years, exiled piece by piece from other parts of the house. The familiar sounds of the day hold him back: piano music from the drawing room as his father's ten o'clock pupil wrestles with the subtleties of Bach; a faint murmuring in the attic which he once believed to be the voice of an angel. In a moment, he must leave them all behind and go downstairs, knowing from experience where to tread to avoid the telltale creaks and sighs; his first act of cowardice in this war, it seems, is to betray his family – sneaking away like a criminal when they would want to wish him well.

The unfinished painting sits reproachfully on a makeshift easel, placed squarely between the window and the bed. He puts his bag down to tidy the paints and straighten the brushes, resisting the temptation to pick one up. The bare wooden floorboards are speckled with blues and browns, a constant source of frustration to an otherwise good-tempered maid. He kneels to scrape at the paint with his thumbnail, then thinks better of it, knowing instinctively that this time she will leave it there. The painting pleases him: a figure standing on Cookham Bridge beneath a cloud-scarred sky that seems a natural extension of the one outside his window. The figure stares out of the canvas and into the wind, preoccupied by something which the painting can only hint at – himself, perhaps, sensing the intrusion of war. The white of the lower canvas shines in the morning light, clean and full of possibility. Already he can see where the picture will take him. The river, the boatyard, the swans in the foreground – all are as real as if he has actually painted them, but he has run out of time and the painting will have to wait. With a sigh, he takes the canvas from the easel and turns it, mute, to face the wall.

I

'We blew about for five years like a couple of rooks in that cottage in the field by the railway cutting.'

Stanley Spencer

1

Elsie leant the mirror against the bed and looked back over her shoulder to check the seams on her stockings. 'Bloody hell! I don't believe it!'

'Watch your language, girl. You might be after a job with an artist, but I won't have you bringing that sort of talk home with you.'

Elsie blushed and swore again, this time under her breath; she hadn't noticed her mother standing in the doorway. 'How can this skirt have mud on it? I haven't put a foot outside. If Tom's been messing with my things again when I told him not to, I'll do more than swear.'

'You can't blame your brother for every bit of dirt in the house, and it's hardly the end of the world. Come downstairs when you're ready and I'll scrub it off for you.'

Her mother left her to it, and Elsie wondered for the thousandth time if boys were saints in every family, or just in hers. She hung the mirror back on its hook above the fireplace and brushed her hair, wondering if a dash of lipstick would give the wrong impression. Her reflection stared back at her from the glass – round faced and healthy looking, brown eyes set under well-defined brows and a mouth that seemed always on the verge of a smile, no matter how angry she felt. It was an ordinary face, pleasant at best, and there was no point in trying to pretend otherwise. Artist or not, he would have to take her as he found her. She took her best coat from the back of the door, where it perched like a guest's across a bulge of winter clothing. It was always the same when she came home: she felt like a lodger in her own room – which, of course, she was.

She went downstairs and was touched to see her family gathered round the kitchen table to see her off. Her father lingered unconvincingly over tying his boot laces, late for the fields but determined not to miss her departure, and her youngest sister jumped down from her chair with a squeal and thrust a folded piece of paper into her hands. Elsie looked down at the picture, a child's rose-tinted view of a maid at work in a busy kitchen. 'You'll be an artist yourself one day, Lily,' she said fondly, ruffling her hair. 'If I get the job, I'll put in a good word for you.'

Lily beamed and Elsie gave herself up to the mercy of her mother's clothes brush. 'What's he painting, this man you're going to work for?' Tom asked through a mouthful of bread.

'*Might* be going to work for. It depends if he likes me or not. And he's painting the walls of a chapel.'

'Why?'

'To remember someone who died in the war.'

'Can't he make do with a headstone like the rest of us?'

The thought was uttered with the naïve insolence of a twelve-year-old, but Elsie caught the smile of approval on her father's face, and she couldn't blame him; ten years on from the end of the war, it seemed a waste to spend so much on the dead when times were hard for the living. 'That's not for Mr Spencer to say, is it? He's just doing a job like the rest of us.'

Elsie heard her mother give a snort of disbelief, but the mud was a stubborn adversary and there was only room for one enemy at a time. 'Is that where you're going, then?' Tom continued, his curiosity apparently inexhaustible. 'To the chapel?'

'No, of course not. The Spencers are staying on a farm in the village until their own house is finished. I'm going to see them there. Mrs Spencer, anyway. I probably won't set eyes on him.'

'So they're having a house built specially?' her mother muttered, half in envy, half in admiration. 'They've done well for themselves, I must say.'

Elsie smiled. 'So will I if they take me on. A new house, with all mod cons. I can put my feet up.'

'If that's the case, there's plenty of washing here to keep you busy. There – good as new.' She gave the skirt a final brush for luck and watched as Elsie sat down by the stove to put her gaiters on. 'You're not going on that motorbike, surely? You'll be covered in mud from head to toe, and what sort of impression will that make?'

'Of course I'm taking the bike. How else am I going to get there?'

She saw her mother nod to her father, and he cleared his throat. 'You know I got a bit extra at Christmas, love. Your mother and I thought you could get the bus.' He took some coins out of his pocket and gave them to her. 'The roads are icy at this time of year and you know how your mother frets. There's a bus at half-past, and you'll catch it if we get a move on. I'll walk you to the end of the road.'

It was a long speech by her father's standards, and Elsie acknowledged it with a squeeze of his hand, colluding in the household myth that it was her mother who worried most about the children. She found her bag and checked that her references were safe, then followed her father out into the lane. The weak February sun was doing its best to burn the frost away, but the road was still white in all but the most exposed places and their footsteps sounded hollow in the chill quiet of the morning. They walked in comfortable silence, preoccupied by her pending absence. She knew her father hated it when any of them left home. He would happily keep all his children by his side if the walls of their cottage could take a family of fourteen, but her own feelings were more complicated – a mixture of sadness, fear and hope. As they waited by the village sign, she sensed that there was something he wanted to say, but it took the stutter of an engine in the distance to bring him to the point. 'You will be careful, love, won't you?' he said, staring at his boots. 'You hear things about these artist types. They're not like us. Promise me you'll look after yourself.'

'I'm twenty-two, Dad,' she said, trying to keep the irritation out of her voice. 'I know how to behave.'

'It's not you I'm worried about.'

He took off his cap to scratch his head, and Elsie noticed that he had finally begun to look his age. It occurred to her now that their lives never really allowed them time to look at each other properly, beyond the habits of their daily routines, and she realised with a shock that the image of her parents she carried in her mind was no longer borne out by reality. 'I'll be careful, Dad,' she said, more gently this time. 'I promise. And anyway, Mr Spencer's got a wife and a young baby. They're just an ordinary family, and the only thing that'll interest him about me is my cooking. Other than that, I doubt he'll give me the time of day.'

That brought a smile, but as she paid her fare and waved to him from the window, he looked less convinced than ever. She had come and gone to this job and that for years, but his concerns made today's departure more intense than usual and Elsie was relieved when the bus left the village and pulled out into the open countryside. It was the first spring-like day of the year and she moved to the seats that the sun favoured most, enjoying nine miles of being at no one's beck and call.

In no time at all, Burghclere was signposted. Elsie looked in vain for the chapel that had brought her here, but the only grand building on the main street seemed to be the church itself. The bus dropped her by its gates and she watched it disappear around the bend, nervous now and already mourning the journey's brief interlude from real life. Palmers Hill Farm was off the beaten track, well away from the heart of the village, and she was glad of the directions that had come with the letter of appointment. A laurel hedge flourished on either side of the farm gate, flanking a carriage driveway with a pond in the centre, and Elsie hesitated, unsure of whether to announce herself at the main entrance or look for a path to the back door; after a moment or two, she decided on the latter, worried in case anyone from the house should see her dithering.

Her knock was answered quickly by a woman with a small child in her arms. Mrs Spencer was older than Elsie had expected, but she had an open face and a welcoming smile and seemed relieved to see her. 'I'm Elsie Munday, Mrs Spencer. I've come for the interview. I hope I'm not too early?'

'Not at all, Miss Munday, and I'm delighted you're here, but I'm not Mrs Spencer.' She wiped her free hand on her apron and held it out. 'Pleased to meet you. My name's Mrs Foster. The Spencers are staying with us.'

'Oh, of course. I'm sorry. I should have thought.'

'No matter. It's an easy mistake to make when I've got my hands full like this.' She smiled and bounced the child up and down in her arms, receiving a giggle in response. 'We've just been making a stew, haven't we, little one? Come inside, Miss Munday. It's a beautiful day, but the air's still spiteful and you don't want to be out in it long.' She ushered her visitor into a large kitchen with a glorious smell of cooking and Elsie found herself wishing already that this was the house she had come to work in. 'Your last place was at Selborne, I hear?'

'That's right. I've been there for three years, but the family are moving away and it's too far for me to go with them.'

'Ah well, you'll find this a bit different – a new house and just you to run it. But the Spencers are a nice couple and I'll be sorry to see them go. There's never a dull moment.' She smiled, but moved on before Elsie could pluck up the courage to ask what she meant. 'Neither of them could remember what time they'd asked you to come, but it's good that you're here now because you'll be able to meet them both. Mr Spencer will be in from the chapel for his lunch soon. I've no idea where Mrs Spencer is, but I'll see if I can find her if you'll take charge of this one for a minute? She's as good as gold, but if you have any trouble, just take her round the front to see the ducks. I won't be long.'

She disappeared further into the house, leaving Elsie to look round the kitchen. It was packed with furniture, collected – she guessed – over several generations, and such a contrast to her own home, where any precious space was taken by people rather than things. Painting was obviously hungry work: a long, scrubbed table was laden with mounds of thickly cut bread and two plates of butter, and there was a large dish of jam and another of cheese. The centre-piece was a fruitcake left over from Christmas, worn down to a quarter of its original size. Above her head, the beams were studded with brass of every shape and form, and Elsie shuddered, thinking of the hours it must take to make them shine so brightly. If nothing else, a new house would surely mean less brass to clean; it was the job she hated most, knowing that every breath in the room simply brought closer the time when she would have to do it all again.

The toddler in her arms began to squirm and Elsie resorted to the advice she had been given. The stables and outbuildings at the front of the farm were built from the same red brick as the house, but had fared less well over the years and seemed to be held together by nothing but ivy. Elsie set the child down by the pond and held her hand as she chattered with the ducks, wondering if Mrs Foster's attitude implied that the job was all but hers and surprised by how badly she wanted it. As she played with the little girl, she heard wheels on the gravel behind her and turned to see a man riding unsteadily towards the front door on a lady's bicycle. He changed direction when he noticed her, almost losing control of the bicycle in the process, and came to an abrupt halt a couple of yards short of the pond. The child gave a squeal of delight, Elsie and the ducks now completely forgotten, and her father let the bicycle fall to the ground as he swung her up on to his shoulders.

'I absolutely loathe the wretched thing,' he said, giving the front wheel an amiable kick, 'but I can't walk to the chapel and back three times a day. I'd have no time left to paint.' The wheel spun uselessly in the air, and Elsie noticed that the bicycle basket was a jackdaw's nest of old newspapers, broken pencils and balls of string. 'I'm Stanley Spencer,' he added, although the splashes of paint on his jacket had told her as much, 'and you must be our new maid. I see you and Shirin are already the best of friends.'

His voice was light, dancing over the words and reminding Elsie of a teacher she had liked at school. 'We seem to be getting on all right so far, sir. And Shirin's a lovely name.'

'Isn't it? A friend of ours suggested it. It's Persian – it means "sweet".'

'Then it's found the right home. I'm Elsie and I dread to think what that means. Elsie Munday.'

Stanley smiled. He was a slight man, with only an inch or two's advantage over her own five foot, but his face was strong and hand-some, with intelligent eyes and a sensitive mouth – beautiful, Elsie might have said, if it didn't imply a femininity which was not at all what she meant. 'Very pleased to meet you, Elsie Munday,' he said, unwinding his hair – already unruly – from Shirin's playful fingers. 'Does Mrs Spencer know you're here? She'll be delighted. Having you with us will give her the chance to get back to some painting.'

From what Elsie had seen so far, his wife wasn't much troubled by cooking or childcare, but she kept her thoughts to herself. 'Is Mrs Spencer an artist as well, then?' she asked.

'Oh yes. A lot of people will tell you that she's a better painter than I am.'

'And is she?'

The words were out before she had a chance to consider how rude they were, but Stanley only grinned. 'She could be, if she took it seriously enough. Come on, let's go and have some lunch. I've been painting tea urns all morning and it's thirsty work.'

He left the bicycle on the ground and headed back to the house, carrying Shirin in his arms and talking to her all the way. By the time they reached the kitchen, Mrs Foster had company and Elsie looked with interest at the woman who was obviously intending to employ her. Hilda Spencer was striking rather than beautiful, with a mass of auburn hair, tied loosely in a bun at the nape of her neck. In repose, her expression was naturally stern, but she brightened at seeing her husband and her words of greeting to Elsie were brief but gracious. By now, an extra place had been laid at the table and Elsie hovered awkwardly by it, unsure of whether she would offend more by behaving as a guest or as a maid in someone else's kitchen; in the end, she did what came naturally and went over to the range to help. While Mrs Foster ladled out bowlfuls of chicken and vegetable stew, Elsie made tea in the large brown pot that stood waiting on the side.

Stanley chattered away throughout the meal, picking over one topic and then another like a rook scavenging a newly ploughed field; Hilda said little, speaking only to correct or contradict her husband. Elsie watched them both, relieved to have no part in the conversation and fascinated by how easily they retreated into each other, oblivious to anyone else in the room. Occasionally she caught Mrs Foster's eye and the farmer's wife gave her a wry smile, clearly more than used to being a casual observer at her own dinner table. There was a pause in the monologue as the bowls were cleared away and Elsie took advantage of it, realising by now that if there was to be any sort of formal discussion it would be up to her to introduce it. 'I've brought references, Mrs Spencer,' she said, reaching into her bag. 'There's a letter here from the cook at Selborne.'

'That's lovely, Elsie. Thank you.' Hilda took the envelope and slid it unopened behind a platter on the dresser, where it was likely to remain until somebody dusted the crockery.

'And if there's anything you'd like to ask me? Anything about my work?'

'Where's your suitcase?' Stanley demanded, spreading a hunk of bread thickly with butter and adding a spoonful of jam to the side of his plate. 'I didn't see it in the hallway.'

'My suitcase?' Elsie stared at him, bewildered.

'Yes. Surely you're not coming to us empty-handed?'

'No, of course not, but I'd understood that this was just an interview. I didn't realise you wanted me to start straight away.'

'Oh, you must. Chapel View is shipshape and we're moving in at the weekend. It's a marvellous house and Hilda's designed most of it, haven't you, ducky?'

'Yes, but it's the garden I'm most looking forward to,' Hilda said, and it was the first time that Elsie had seen her truly animated. Even as she looked directly across the table, though, her eyes were distant, as if something important in her life remained stubbornly out of reach. 'We must have lots of flowers and I intend to grow all our vegetables, Elsie, so you'll have to tell me what you like. It's the one thing I've missed in Hampstead – being out in the open air.' Elsie nodded, trying to match her enthusiasm, but the longer the conversation went on, the harder it was to raise the questions that concerned her most. Eventually, even Hilda noticed her hesitation. 'Is something wrong, Elsie?'

'No, Mrs Spencer, not wrong, exactly. It's just that…'

'Yes?'

'Well, we haven't discussed terms yet, so I'm not sure where I stand.'

'Terms?'

The Spencers looked at her blankly and Elsie felt herself blush. 'That's right,' she said, deciding to be blunt. 'What will my wages be?'

'Oh, I see! Do you know, I hadn't thought. You must forgive us. We've never had a maid of our own before – my mother always dealt with that sort of thing.'

'What do you normally get?' her husband asked.

'At my last place they paid me thirty pounds a year, but I was a kitchen maid there and a general's not quite the same thing.'

'I see.'

The conversation floundered in an awkward silence, and it was left to the one person in the room with no direct interest to save it. 'I think forty pounds a year would be about right,' Mrs Foster said, stifling a smile. 'How does that sound, Miss Munday? All found, obviously.'

'That would be perfectly all right, if it suits Mrs Spencer?'

Hilda nodded and Stanley leapt up from the table. 'Splendid! So you'll be with us at the weekend?'

'I think Miss Munday might need more time than that,' Mrs Foster said diplomatically. 'She'll have to work out her notice first.'

'It's two weeks, so I could start on the twenty-third.'

'The twenty-third of February it is. That's our wedding anniversary and we'll have been married three years. You'll be my gift to Hilda.' He kissed his wife and daughter, and took a scarf from the back of the door. 'I'd better get going. I'll walk you into the village, Elsie Munday. You can have a look at the chapel.'

Elsie would rather have seen the house she was going to work in, but it seemed rude to object and she gathered her things together, worried now about getting home late. The Spencers wandered through to the hall, and Elsie paused to thank her host. 'That was a lovely meal, Mrs Foster. I've obviously got high standards to live up to.'

'Oh, they're no trouble and you'll soon get used to their ways. I'll miss them when they've gone, especially the little one. Come and see me when you've settled in, Miss Munday. And you know where I am if you need anything.'

Elsie went outside and found her new employer reunited with his bicycle, impatient to be off; there was no sign of Mrs Spencer. 'What's a tea urn doing in a war painting?' she asked, keen to show some interest in his work as they walked back up the track to the road.

The question came out more flippantly than she had intended, but he didn't seem to mind. 'I don't want them to look like war paintings, Elsie. I want them to look like heaven.' She could have argued that the same question applied, but she waited for him to explain, having learnt from the conversation over lunch that he needed no prompting to talk. 'The army wouldn't have me at first because of my height, so I joined up as a medical orderly and they sent me to a war hospital in Bristol. I spent my days emptying bedpans, cleaning bathrooms and scraping frostbite off the patients' feet.'

'It's not for me to say, Mr Spencer, but that doesn't sound very heavenly. I'm not surprised you needed a cup of tea.'

Stanley barely smiled, too intent on his meaning to brook interruption. 'Even during the war, you could hold on to some sort of hope. It was noble, you know, the way those men talked to each other about ordinary, homely things – their families or their gardens and the vegetables they were growing. Some of them had horrific injuries, but they managed to find peace in the most mundane events. When you're faced with hell, you have to redeem it in some way, don't you?'

'I suppose so.'

'Well, that's what I do when I paint. Even the crucifixion was a happy scene when the old masters painted it.'

That was easy to say when the nails were hammered into other hands, Elsie thought. 'Didn't you fight?' she asked, then quickly softened the question, hating the note of judgement in her own voice. 'I mean, did you stay at that hospital for the whole war?'

'Just the first few months. After that I went overseas and served with the Field Ambulance in Macedonia. When the army stopped being so fussy, I joined the Royal Berkshires and fought on the front line.'

Elsie nodded. 'My oldest brother was over there, but he never talks about it. He used to leave the room whenever my ma brought it up. I can't imagine him living through it all over again like you're doing. There must be things you'd rather forget.'

'I've certainly dug more graves than I wanted to.' They walked over the crossroads and Elsie noticed that Stanley's face – so expressive up to now – was impossible to read. She tried to think of something new to talk about, something less personal. If he chose to paint over the war, that was his business and it wasn't her place to question it, but he surprised her by adding: 'I honestly think the worst part of the whole business was leaving home. I've always hated it. It wasn't what I was going to that frightened me, it was what I would miss by being away. You must know how that feels.'

'You get used to it when you've done it as often as I have.'

'But the first time?'

She paused, remembering the shock of arriving in a strange house when she was barely fourteen, lying awake at night and longing for the sounds of home and the grudging warmth of her sister's body in their tiny bed. It was more than fear, more than loneliness, but nothing had hurt her as much as her first visit home, when the talk around the dinner table had moved on without her, and her younger sister had rolled as easily into Elsie's place as a pebble coming to rest on a beach. 'You're right,' she said, quickening the pace. 'It's hard to leave what you love.'

'That's why you have to take it with you. Wherever I was during the war, I could go for a walk round Cookham in my mind. I put all the things I loved about it into my work and having something familiar gave me the strength to make a home anywhere. That's the wonderful thing about painting. It goes to prepare a place for you.'

'I thought that was Christ.'

'Is there a difference?' There was no answer to that, at least not one that she knew, and they walked on in silence. The best part of the day was gone, and the sky had grown sullen and petulant. Above their heads, a criss-cross of branches stood out bare and black against the grey afternoon. 'What do you think about when you're scrubbing floors?' Stanley asked suddenly.

Elsie frowned, wondering if he was making fun of her, but there was no hint of teasing in his eyes. 'Oh, I don't know,' she said. 'The last film I went to see. The boy I went to see it with.'

'One boy in particular?'

'Not especially. A few of them seem to like me. I'm a good dancer.'

'Are you? I'm a terrible dancer. But what I was trying to explain is that the jobs I dreaded most turned out to have a different meaning. When I was down on my hands and knees, scrubbing floors until I thought I'd never stand up again, I had the most splendid ideas. In the end, whenever I picked up that brush and felt the soap on my hands, it was almost like going to church. Bathtubs, laundry, your tea urns – they all stood for something more important. So that was *my* war. There'd be no point in trying to paint anybody else's.'

They had reached the junction by the church and Elsie looked up at the tower, anxious to find out if it was as late as she feared. Spencer carried on without her, heading left towards the railway bridge. 'Come on,' he said, turning back when he noticed her lagging behind. 'I want to show you the chapel.'

Elsie hesitated, worried that she had missed her bus home. 'I'm sorry, Mr Spencer, but I don't think I've got time today. Perhaps I could see it when I come for good?'

He seemed irritated rather than offended by her refusal, like a child whose plans had been spoilt. 'All right. It's probably best if you don't hold me up. I'm losing the light and I need to get on.' He hopped on to the bicycle and rode off, calling back over his shoulder: 'See you in a fortnight, Elsie Munday.'

2

Elsie picked up Shirin and sat her in the kitchen drawer while she finished cooking the breakfast. The child giggled and stretched out her hand, and Elsie obliged her with her current toy of choice – a clothes peg from the washing line that hung above the range. 'There you are, sweet pea. See what you can do with that one.' Shirin took the gift and earnestly set about trapping as many tea towels as possible in its grip. Elsie smiled at her concentration, a two-year-old version of her father's. She stood back, wiping her hands on a cloth that had so far escaped attention, and looked round the kitchen with satisfaction. The floor was swept, the table laid, and the coffee percolator waited in its tin of water, next to a saucepan of milk.

Not every room at Chapel View lifted Elsie's heart in quite the same way. Three weeks into her new position, and well over a month since the Spencers first moved in, corners of the house were still piled with boxes, unpacked at random as particular items were needed, and no amount of gentle probing on her part had brought forth any direction as to where everything might go. Her days were a similar jumble of cooking, cleaning and guesswork, teasing out one person's preferences and balancing them against the other's, with Shirin the only member of the household whose needs and good nature stayed constant. Still, she felt at home. The cottage was isolated, but her room was comfortable and she had soon got over the awkwardness of living in such close proximity to a newly married couple. The Spencers treated her well, and there was no doubt in Elsie's mind that she would be allowed to run the house her way, if only because her employers showed so little interest in offering an alternative.

Above her, a bedroom door opened and Stanley pounded heavily down the stairs, gaining in energy what he lacked in stature. Elsie looked at him with a mixture of weariness and amusement, noting the same clothes as yesterday and the day before, the wild, hedgerow hair which had only a passing acquaintance with a comb. 'I feel like I'm back in the army when you shake your head at me like that,' he said, dropping a sheaf of drawings on to the kitchen table. 'There was a sergeant major who could put the fear of God into me, but I wasn't paying him.'

Elsie could easily have retorted that her weekly pay was a little late, but an absent-mindedness with money was another feature of the Spencer household with which she was already familiar. 'I've got my own war on with your ironing,' she said instead. 'And at the moment I'm losing the battle.' He grinned and sat down by the range to put his shoes on while she poured him a cup of tea. 'Does Mrs Spencer want a tray again this morning?'

'Yes, she's writing her Christian Science letters. I've no idea what she finds to say every day, but it makes her happy.' He lifted Shirin out of her drawer and sat down at the table with the child on his lap. 'Get my breakfast first, though, will you? I'm late and I've got a lot to do.'

She did as he asked, then moved the drawings carefully to one side to make room on the table for a tray. The picture on top caught her eye, a pencil drawing of a woman's face, so vivid that she felt as if they had met. Stanley noticed her interest and waved his knife at the pile. 'Have a look at the others,' he said through a mouthful of toast. 'Tell me what you think.'

Elsie turned the sketches over one by one, looking at a series of unknown faces, punctuated every now and then by a vase of flowers or a drawing of Shirin as a baby. She was still trying to think of something interesting to say when she found herself staring at a full-length portrait of a naked man. His face was in profile, looking back over his shoulder as if he were about to turn and walk away, but it was obviously a younger Stanley and she felt her cheeks grow hot, knowing that he was watching her. Quickly, she covered the drawing with another and left the rest of the pile unexplored. 'I like this one,' she said, holding up a harmless picture of narcissi. 'They're my mum's favourite flowers.'

'Beautiful, aren't they?' He appraised the drawing again through her eyes, oblivious to any embarrassment.

'Yes. You've got it just right. I can almost smell them.'

'Oh, it's not mine, it's Hilda's. She drew those flowers three days after Shirin was born. I remember her telling me that they expressed the joy she felt. All those drawings are hers.' He smiled at her surprise and Elsie sensed that she had simultaneously passed a test and walked into a trap. 'Listen, Elsie, will you do something for me? Try and encourage Hilda to work while you're here with her. I'll have lunch at the chapel to give her some peace and quiet.'

Elsie hesitated, reluctant to reverse the normal order of things by finding things for her employer to do; more selfishly, she thought of the boxes that badly needed Hilda's attention if the household was ever to run smoothly. 'I'll do my best,' she agreed cautiously, 'but the house is new and she's still settling in. I don't know anything about painting, but perhaps Mrs Spencer will find it easier when she feels a bit more at home. It's different for you. You've been working at the chapel for nearly a year now.'

'Yes, but home's nothing to do with a house, is it? Her *work* should be her home.'

Or her family, Elsie thought, but she saw little point in arguing, even if she had felt confident enough to do so. 'I'll make you some sandwiches to take,' she offered.

'I haven't got time for that. Bring them to me later.'

He slammed the back door without a goodbye, leaving Elsie and Shirin to stare at each other across the table. 'Well, that's Daddy off to work,' Elsie said brightly. 'Shall we see what Mummy's got in store for us?'

The Spencers' bedroom was at the front of the house, one of the rooms that gave Chapel View its name. Elsie knocked and put the tray down on the bed, which was all but obscured by a snowfall of paper; ink marched across the pages like the scratchings of a bird in winter, and Hilda barely glanced up. 'Thanks, Elsie. Was that Mr Spencer leaving?'

'Yes. He's staying out all day today.' She collected a trail of clothes from the floor and returned them, neatly folded, to the chair. From the window, she could see Stanley making his way across the field to the railway cutting, his impatience evident in his walk. She watched until he disappeared down the bank, taking his customary shortcut to the chapel, then turned back to the bed. 'Is there anything else I can get you?'

The only response was a heavy sigh. Hilda pushed the tray away untouched and threw the covers aside, sending the letters scattering to the floor. 'I know how important this project is to him, but I do so want it to be over.' She took a dressing gown from the back of the door and joined Elsie by the window. 'I was horrified when we came here for the first time. It all seemed so small and empty, the sort of place you'd get lost in by accident but never mean to come to. I know the Behrends have been good to us, paying for the chapel and the house, and Stanley couldn't ask for better patrons. I just wish they lived somewhere else.' She smiled sadly. 'I miss Hampstead, Elsie. I can't wait to go back when he's finished.'

It was the first time that Hilda had shared a confidence, although Elsie had overheard enough conversations between husband and wife to know that she wasn't happy. 'I suppose it must be a shock when you're used to something more lively,' she said. 'I've never been further than Newbury.'

'Right now, Newbury would be heaven.' Hilda sighed again and poured some coffee. 'I suppose I'm being silly. We've got a nice house and we're better off than we've ever been…'

'But Mr Spencer's got a purpose and you haven't.'

'Yes, that's exactly it. I miss being someone in my own right rather than just Mrs Stanley Spencer.'

'Perhaps you should start painting again. It might take you out of yourself.'

Hilda frowned, and the brief moment of intimacy between them vanished as suddenly as it had come. 'It didn't take him long to get you on side, did it?'

It had been a clumsy attempt, and Elsie cursed herself for introducing the subject at all. She had no wish to take sides when she was already fond of them both, and as far as she could see, neither husband nor wife needed any help from her in getting their own way – they both stood their ground and did exactly what they wanted. 'I'm sorry, Mrs Spencer,' she said, 'but if it's any consolation, I've upset Mr Spencer as well. I told him you'd paint when you were ready.'

'Did you now?' She smiled grudgingly. 'Well, you're quite right, Elsie, and I'm certainly not in the mood for it yet.'

'Not even if the alternative is helping Shirin and me clear the boxes in the hallway?'

'Those damned boxes! I thought by ignoring them I could pretend we weren't staying, but there's so much to do in that chapel. We could be here for years.'

'All the more reason to get it sorted. Would it help if I made a start without you? If I put things in the wrong place, you can always change them.'

'Oh, put them where you like. Would you really do that? I'd be so grateful.' Elsie nodded, amused that a simple willingness to do her job could be met with such appreciation. 'In that case, I'll spend the day in the garden,' Hilda said with genuine enthusiasm. 'Call me if you need me.'

***

28

By lunchtime, Elsie had succeeded in reducing the pile of living room boxes to half its size. She cut cheese for sandwiches, wondering why the prospect of a visit to the chapel should make her so nervous. Stanley hadn't asked her again since the day of their meeting, and she had soon learnt that he was quick to see a slight where none was intended, particularly when it concerned his work. She packed a flask and some fruit and set out across the field, following the flattened path that had begun to mark his daily trips back and forth. Rooks blew about in the trees by the railway cutting, their glossy black plumage less striking now against the polish of new leaves, and she watched them playing as she walked. In the distance, a whistle sounded and a thin pencil line of steam grew more defined as a train drew closer, picking up speed out of the station. Elsie waited for it to go past, covering her ears against the roar which sometimes shook the walls of their cottage in the night, then climbed carefully down the grass bank, across the tracks and up the other side.

A narrow thicket filled with primroses divided the cutting from the neighbouring field. She pushed open the gate that led to the chapel grounds and paused, trying to see more in the building than the unappealing, featureless red brick that had so disappointed her when she first set eyes on it – but any hint of beauty or spirituality still eluded her. The chapel itself was an oblong box, with a roof that seemed in two minds whether to pitch or lie flat, and a cross had been perched on top like an afterthought. The front wall was dominated by three long, plain-glass windows, dropping down to double wooden doors, and it was flanked on each side by a small almshouse, built to give a home to veterans but as yet unoccupied. Today, the sun drew a pleasant rosy hue from the bricks, but the building still looked like the entrance to a cemetery. In her mind, Elsie had imagined a grander, more church-like setting for Stanley's paintings. All his talk of heaven had conjured up the age-old, shared traditions that underpinned her own sense of what was sacred, but this building had no past and no community, none of the richness and mystery that her own beliefs had been raised on.

The only God she could picture residing in this bland, symmetrical building wore a pinstriped suit.

She lingered outside for a moment, reluctant to leave the light of the afternoon behind. The front of the building was laid to lawn, with young apple trees planted at the road end and the path to the entrance broken halfway down by a well. The hum of a bumble bee accompanied her to the door – the quintessential sound of summer, teased from a March day by an over-generous sun. Close up, the polished oak panelling had already weathered a little and the wood felt pleasantly warm to her touch. She pushed the door open, surprised by how solid and heavy it was.

Inside, the chapel was smaller than she had expected, with no more than ten yards between her and the back wall. Each of the long sides was divided into recessed panels, four arches above four rectangles, separated by a dado rail, and so far four of the spaces held a finished painting. Stanley stood with his back to her in the middle of the floor, an oblong canvas on the easel in front of him. He turned around when he heard her and raised his brush in greeting. 'Throw those doors open, will you? The sun's moving round to the side now and I need all the light I can get.'

Elsie put her basket down on the step and pushed each door back as far as it would go, allowing the sun to venture further over the threshold. A visitors' book sat on a table just inside the door and she picked up the pen. 'You don't have to sign in,' Stanley called when he saw what she was doing. 'You're family.'

His words pleased her, but she carried on anyway. 'I want to do it. One day, when you're famous, I want them to know I was here.'

'You don't think I'm famous already?'

She grinned. 'I'd never heard of you.' The pages of the book were filled with names and she flicked back through them, noticing how out of place her own careful script looked next to the more flamboyant signatures. 'You've had plenty of visitors, haven't you?' she said. 'It's a wonder you get anything done.'

'It keeps the Behrends happy. They like to invite their friends over to see the chapel. Anyone who visits Grey House gets forwarded here like a letter.'

'Then I hope you tidy up.' The area near the easel was littered with jam jars, one still with its original contents, the others collecting knives or paintbrushes, and in all her life Elsie had never seen so much paper, scrunched up in balls on the floor, piled high on chairs or pinned to the blank walls. She had expected to see tubs of paint and other materials, but surprisingly little of the clutter seemed connected to Stanley's work: half a loaf of bread, long past its best, sat with a stack of dirty plates on a table where the altar would be; a battered old copy of *Huckleberry Finn* lay half open in a nest of scarves and gloves; and one of Shirin's favourite toys – a rabbit with a missing ear which Elsie had spent hours scouring the house for – was perched on a stepladder, left behind on the child's last visit to see her father. 'I'm not sure that Flopsy will make quite the right impression on the Behrends' friends,' she said, putting the toy in her basket.

He winked. 'The artist at work. All part of the show. Isn't Shirin with you?'

'No. She's helping her mother plant potatoes.'

'Good. They'll enjoy that.'

There was no hint of his earlier resentment, and Elsie was relieved to be spared the task of defending Hilda's preference for the garden. She shivered as the chill of the chapel interior took hold. The tentative spring day was no match for the walls and flagstones, which held the damp of a long winter, and the stove that Stanley had placed close to his easel was even less effective with an open door. 'Here you are,' she said, handing over a packet of sandwiches and a flask. 'I should have brought you a hot water bottle. It's freezing in here.'

'Wait until you see it in the depths of winter. This is positively cosy.' He took the lunch eagerly and poured some tea. 'Elsie, you're an angel. Have a cup with me.'

'No, save it for later. You'll need it if you're staying the afternoon, and there's nothing worse than trying to work when you're cold.'

'You're right,' he said, settling down on a rung of the stepladder to unwrap the greaseproof parcel. 'I'd much rather be hungry than cold.' He looked expectantly at her as he ate, waiting for her verdict. 'Well? What do you think of my holy box?'

'It's coming on,' she said, managing to sound less doubtful than she felt. The paintings he had completed so far were all on the north wall, and Elsie guessed that the work in progress was destined for the last empty rectangular panel on that side. The close grouping of colour only served to emphasise how much work was still to be done; she counted eleven more recesses waiting to be filled, and the volume of sketches pinned to the vast altar wall suggested that much of this, too, was to be painted. The scale of the project boded well for her own future, but she understood now why Hilda's spirits were so low. 'It's nice to see it taking shape,' she added, conscious that he was hoping for something more, 'but wouldn't you rather have a proper studio to paint in? I thought artists were particular about where they worked.'

'Perhaps the famous ones are,' he said dryly, 'but it's never bothered me. I've always worked where I could.' He got up and went over to the easel, picking up a pencil and making the tiniest of alterations. 'It was difficult at first, before I left home. I shared a room with my brother and there was never enough space for us both to paint. We'd be carting half-finished pictures round the house, waiting for a corner of the dining table.'

'I reckon that's why I've never been much of an artist. There was no room to move round our table when I was growing up.' She spoke without resentment, having a sudden pang of nostalgia for the familiarity of her own kitchen, the room she seemed to have spent most of her waking life in. In her mind, she saw her mother standing by the range and heard the rhythms of chatter and silence that seemed to govern their days, and she wondered if she would ever have that sense of belonging again.

Stanley seemed to follow her thoughts. 'We wouldn't have had it any other way, though, would we? There was no harm in it.'

'Just a lot of smudged pictures.'

He laughed, and Elsie noticed how much younger he looked when his face was relaxed and not preoccupied with the solution of a problem that only he could see. 'In the end, I found other places to work. You've seen my big painting, the Cookham Resurrection?' She shook her head. 'No? I'll show you a picture of it. But I painted that in a small room in Hampstead when Hilda and I were courting. I used to wait for a glimpse of her across the Heath, and all those moments are in that painting: the way she walked and what she wore, the joy I felt when she came into the room. Whenever she left, the picture changed, as if she'd taken something of it with her. If I'd had my way, it would have stayed there forever, a part of Hilda and me.' He paused to pour more tea, and Elsie wondered if he realised how different he sounded when he was talking *about* Hilda rather than *to* her. 'That's why the chapel means so much. The pictures will always be here, where they were painted and where they belong. All I need is the peace to work on them.'

She took the hint and bent to pick up her basket. 'I'll leave you to it, then.'

'No, Elsie, I didn't mean that.' He caught her arm. 'Stay and talk to me for a bit. Have one of these. You've made enough for an army.' He held out the parcel and she took a sandwich. 'Peace and solitude aren't always the same thing. What I'm talking about is peace in here, peace of the soul.'

She wanted to ask where he found his peace, but was afraid of not understanding the answer. 'Peace to work at war?' she said instead.

'Something like that.'

Except it wasn't war, not in the sense that she had expected. She walked over to look closely at the paintings for the first time, taking in the muted colours which seemed to reflect the reddish browns of the chapel's wooden ceiling, the ordinary figures doing ordinary things. For once, Stanley remained silent, giving her time to think about what she saw, and after a moment or two she realised that he had begun to work again: behind her, the chapel was so quiet that she could hear the faint, rhythmic sound of his brush against the canvas. Less self-conscious now, she examined the paintings one by one, beginning with the scene closest to her. A man in a blue shirt and white apron lay on his stomach in a corridor, scrubbing the floor with a wide, circular motion. The look of concentration on his face was so intense that he seemed oblivious to the men around him: one was stepping over him; another – rounding the corner quickly – struggled clumsily with a tray of bread. The lathery patterns on the floor were painted so vividly that Elsie could almost smell the soap. One half of the canvas was in shadow and the overall effect – drab and claustrophobic – depressed her. A figure on the left of the picture who looked like Stanley stared back at her in wonder, as bewildered by his surroundings as she was. 'Is this the hospital you told me about?' she asked.

'Beaufort? That's right. Or the Bristol Lunatic Asylum, as was.' He stopped what he was doing again and came over, standing close enough for her to smell the turpentine on his hands.

'And is he a soldier?' Elsie looked at the prone man's khaki trousers and puttees, trying to reconcile them with the menial task he was absorbed in.

'Sometimes I think of him as a soldier. Sometimes he's an orderly, and sometimes he's one of the lunatics.' His expression grew more serious as he continued. 'I liked those men,' he said. 'Actually, I envied them.' She was about to ask why, but he moved on to another part of the painting. 'There was a figure here, too, originally, but I painted him out. I don't often do that, but the picture was too busy.'

The outline remained, a faint, ghostly presence in an otherwise tangible world. 'Is that supposed to be you?' Elsie asked, pointing back to the left-hand side.

'All my figures are me. I put myself where I want to be.'

'Scrubbing floors or lugging tea urns?' she questioned, glancing at the various scenarios that Stanley had chosen to paint.

'It had to be done and I never really disliked it. And there must have been a meaning to it all, or why would I remember it so clearly?'

Elsie had given a lot of thought to her first conversation with Stanley, but she hadn't yet managed to find the spiritual reward for domestic work that he seemed convinced was there; perhaps it would come to her in later life, when she didn't have so much of it ahead of her. She looked up at the single arched painting, the only picture to be set outside; after the intensity of the corridors, it was a relief to see the profusion of flowering rhododendron. 'I like that one,' she said, nodding towards the gaggle of soldiers on a bus, comparing bullet holes in their helmets. 'It reminds me of village days out.'

'That's the men arriving at Beaufort for the first time. I want visitors to the chapel to feel as if they're leaving the sunshine behind and coming into a dark, unknown world, just like those men did.'

Elsie stood back and looked round, trying to imagine how the building would feel when Stanley's work was done. Her eye caught a plaque on the wall over the door, and she read aloud the dedication: 'To the memory of Harry Willoughby Sandham. Is that Mrs Behrend's brother?' Stanley nodded. 'What happened to him?'

'He died of a ruptured spleen after several bouts of malaria. Caught it out in Salonika – lots of us did – but he died at home after he was demobbed so they wouldn't put his name on the memorial. Poor Hal. Bloody awful, isn't it?'

'Yes, it is. It must have been terrible for his family to get him back only to lose him again.'

'I meant the plaque. All that baroque and gold nonsense. It's completely out of character with the rest of the chapel, but the Behrends made the arrangements. I had no say in it.'

Elsie could see nothing unreasonable in the Behrends' modest claim on the chapel they had paid for, but she kept her thoughts to herself. She looked back at the north wall, wondering what Harry Sandham would make of these quiet, gentle scenes.

'There's something heroic in the everyday, don't you think?' Stanley said, and she nodded. She had never really thought about it before, but this faith in the order of domestic life was common among men who had fought, as if it were the one thing that still made sense. '*Nil sine labore*.' He read the plaque's Latin inscription with a soft, almost tender reverence.

'What does that mean?'

'Nothing without labour. Speaking of which...'

He finished the last sandwich and screwed the greaseproof paper into a ball, sending it scuttling after the others on the floor. Elsie collected her things and waited, curious to see how he worked. He stood close to the easel, using the smallest of brushes to fill the top left-hand corner with a rose-coloured paint that struck a more cheerful note than the other pictures. 'Do you always start there?' she asked.

'Usually. It saves me getting my sleeve in the paint.'

She wondered why he bothered to take such a precaution when nothing else about his clothing was afforded the same care; she always knew the colours he was working in by the shirts she had to wash. The painting was in its early stages, but the canvas had been divided into squares and a detailed pencil drawing – copied from a smaller sketch on the floor – told Elsie that it was another domestic scene, set in a laundry this time, with men sorting piles of sheets while a nurse in a starched white cap stood at a table with her back to the room. Stanley worked patiently, obviously sure of what he was doing because he never stepped back to look, and Elsie tried to calculate how long it would take that tiny brush to cover these vast, bare walls. 'Are all the pictures going to be of the hospital?' she asked.

'Oh no. You see the long stretches above the arches?'

'You're not painting those as well?'

'Of course I am. They'll be panoramic scenes of life in the camps. Tents on the hillside, washing by the riverbed, that sort of thing. The east wall is for the resurrection, and that will be in Macedonia, too. The landscape there was extraordinary.'

He started to expand the vision, fiddling all the time with his paintbrush, and Elsie listened, understanding very little of what he meant but caught up in his excitement. 'This isn't really about Mrs Behrend's brother, is it?' she said when he had finished. 'It's about you.'

It was an observation, not a criticism, but she worried that he might take it the wrong way; instead, he simply looked pleased. 'It's just the beginning, Elsie. I want to do another building when this is finished, filled with paintings of the people I love. Hilda will have her own chapel, and Shirin, and Ma and Pa and the people from Cookham. You'll be there, too. Wait and see.'

He smiled at her, and although he meant nothing by the promise, she felt awkward and had to look away. 'I'd better be getting back,' she said, stooping to collect some of the rubbish from the floor. '*Nil sine labore* and all that.'

Her pronunciation was barely recognisable, but he laughed. 'I'll see you back at the house. Tell Hilda I won't be late.'

3

The air was filled with the sharp, staccato cry of blackbirds at dusk as Elsie returned to Chapel View, still in high spirits from her afternoon off. She slowed the motorcycle at the end of the road and listened to the shifting patchwork of sound as each bird bid farewell to the day, delighting in the melancholy of an early summer's evening with all the enthusiasm of someone whose life has always been happy.

The bike was a cast-off from one of her brothers, abandoned when he joined the navy, and she had taken possession of it quickly before her mother could justify an instinct that women – or at least ladies – didn't ride anything with an engine. She left it at the gate, pleased to have made most of the journey in daylight. As she neared the house, the birdsong was replaced by the sound of a piano. Stanley had a talent for music that seemed almost as natural as his painting, and although Elsie didn't recognise much of what he played, she had quickly learnt to read his mood by the tone of whatever was coming from the keys. Tonight, he was cheerful. The lamps were lit, the curtains still wide open and she could see the family through the sitting room window. Stanley had his back to her at the piano and Shirin sat on the stool next to him, eagerly contributing notes from a tune that existed only in her head. Hilda was perched on the arm of a chair, sorting through a pile of sheet music which threatened to slip from her lap at any moment; she wore a brown velvet dress, long and loose-fitting, and her head was bowed in concentration, allowing the firelight to emphasise the rich red shades of her hair. Eventually she found the piece of music she was looking for and stood up, letting the unwanted sheets fall to the floor. She placed it on the piano, her hand resting lightly on Stanley's shoulder, and Elsie watched, enjoying a rare opportunity to observe the family while no one was conscious of her presence. She was just marvelling at how deceptively ordinary they looked when Shirin turned to the window and waved.

'How was the film?' Hilda called as Elsie took her coat off in the hallway. 'Did Lillian Gish get her man?'

'Of a fashion. It was more complicated than usual.'

'Let me guess. Lots of lingering looks to the camera and hardship borne stoically before a triumphant happy ending?' Stanley grinned and looked her up and down. 'You should wear blue more often, Elsie. It suits you.'

'Yes, it does.' Hilda patted the chair next to the fire. 'Come and tell us what happened. It'll save us going to see it.'

Elsie sat down and, with Shirin's help, began to remove her gaiters. 'Well,' she said, aware that she had a captive audience, 'Miss Gish plays a poor girl called Letty who goes to stay on her cousin's ranch. She has three marriage proposals so they toss a coin for her...'

'Sounds like you and your brother,' Hilda interrupted, giving Stanley a wry smile. 'Did I ever tell you, Elsie? They were both keen on me. One beautiful summer's day, Gilbert took me to Cookham and punted me over the river to see Stanley, and I had to choose between them then and there.'

'You know how to put a girl on the spot, don't you?' Elsie said, shaking her head in disapproval. She began to tidy the sheet music on the floor, imagining the Spencer brothers side by side in front of Hilda. 'Thank goodness it wasn't a hundred years ago. You'd have been at each other with pistols.'

'It was all perfectly amicable,' Stanley insisted. 'Gilbert was very gracious about it. The Spencers don't hold grudges.' He must have caught the look that passed between Elsie and Hilda, because he added: 'Not within the family, at least. Gil has a very forgiving nature. He even turned up during our honeymoon. Hilda invited him. I'm still not sure why.'

'I thought you'd be pleased to see him.'

'At any other time, perhaps, but I stupidly assumed we'd spend our honeymoon alone. Anyway, carry on, Elsie. I'm worried about Miss Gish.'

'Where was I?'

'They were tossing a coin for Letty.'

'Oh, yes. Well, she throws her lot in with one of them,' Elsie explained, pleased to get back to firmer ground, 'and after a bit of a carry-on with some horses and a gun, they all live happily ever after.' She pulled Shirin on to her knee, gently distracting her from the teaspoon she had been using to sprinkle coal dust on to the rug. 'I'm not sure I've done it justice, but you three seem to be having a nice evening.'

'We are. Stanley's finished another painting, so we've been celebrating.'

'The laundry picture's done?'

He nodded. 'That's five in place now. Only fourteen to go.'

Hilda lifted her eyes to the heavens, but she seemed more relaxed than usual. 'I think it's the best one yet. It's got so much more energy.'

If Stanley noticed his wife's implicit criticism of the four preceding paintings, he didn't seem to mind. 'I can't wait to see it,' Elsie said, genuinely excited. Each new picture told her something more about Stanley, and she had come to think of the chapel paintings as pieces in a private jigsaw, which – when completed – would explain a view of the world that she still struggled to understand. 'I'll put the kettle on. All that ranch dust has made me thirsty.'

She went through to the kitchen, gratified to see that there was very little left of the pie she had made for supper. She cut herself a slice and ate it while the kettle boiled, then took the tray through to the sitting room. 'They're beautiful,' she said, nodding to a vase of blue hyacinths which had appeared on the table in her absence, filling the room with their scent. A piece of paper about the size of a postcard was propped up against the vase, and she looked admiringly at the sensitive detail which celebrated the perfection of each bell-shaped flower. The picture was inscribed to Hilda, and Elsie had no doubt that it meant more to her than any of her husband's more famous paintings. 'There's nothing quite as special as the first flowers from a garden,' she said, struck by how thoughtful Stanley could be when he tried. She rarely felt like an intruder at Chapel View, but tonight she was keen to leave the couple to themselves. 'Do you want me to put Shirin to bed on my way up?' she asked.

'That would be lovely, but have your tea first.'

'I'll take it upstairs. If I don't write a letter home soon, Ma will be sending out a search party.' Elsie said goodnight and took Shirin to the nursery, tucking her in amid the usual protestations. 'If you're a good girl and go to sleep, I'll take you to see Daddy's new painting in the morning.' It was a cheap bargain, but effective, and within a few minutes Elsie was closing the door gently behind her.

She crossed the landing to her own room. The house was quiet except for the occasional rustle of someone making up the fire or moving through to the kitchen, and as she lay on her bed, writing the chatty, reassuring weekly letter, she was struck more than usual by their isolation. She had found it hard to get used to a home in which the idiosyncrasies of age were entirely absent; the modern rooms which made her life easier during the day seemed strange and alien at night, and she longed for a stirring in the timbers or the creaking of a floorboard, but there was nothing – only the cry of some unlucky creature fallen prey to a fox in the woods. She read for a while to distract herself from the silence, then put down her magazine and turned out the light.

The late-night mail train usually thundered past before the Spencers turned in, but tonight they were early. Elsie listened as the familiar routine was played out: soft footsteps going to check on Shirin, the click of a latch, then the gentle creak of springs as first one and then the other climbed into bed. They talked for a while, and although the murmur of voices was low and indistinct, she could hear enough to know that it was Stanley who had most to say. The faint haze of light vanished from the landing as a lamp was extinguished, and Elsie pulled the blankets higher over her head as the slow, rhythmic knocking of the bedpost against the wall betrayed the only sliver of privacy that remained between them. To her surprise, the light quickly reappeared and she heard voices again, angry this time, followed by the slamming of the bedroom door and Stanley's footsteps on the stairs. She held her breath and waited, but Hilda made no attempt to follow.

Across the landing, Shirin began to cry. Elsie wrapped herself in a dressing gown and left her room, making enough noise to let Hilda know that the child was cared for. She stayed in the nursery for a long time, wondering where Stanley had gone and hoping that the crisis would blow over. When she was sure that Shirin was sound asleep again, she tiptoed out on to the landing just as Stanley was climbing the stairs. He had left the lights on in the hallway and she could see that his eyes were red and puffy. 'Is Shirin all right?' he asked. She nodded, and he went back to his room, now in darkness, without another word.

4

The next morning, Elsie went out to the back yard to fetch the laundry, relieved to be free of the house. She was learning to predict the pattern of life at Chapel View, governed as it was by the rhythms of Stanley's work, and she had already begun to dread the fallow period between his finishing one painting and starting another. Sometimes it was a day or two, sometimes a week, but he hung around at home, sketching or writing long letters, disrupting Shirin's routine and generally getting under her feet. Worst of all, his restlessness seemed to feed his irritation with Hilda, and the couple pecked and sniped at each other until Elsie itched to bang their heads together and leave them to fend for themselves.

The warm air was pleasant on her face, but the sun had dried the linen too efficiently and now she would have to wet it again before ironing. Impatiently, she dropped the peg basket on to the floor and began to hum as she heard Stanley open the kitchen door and follow her outside, hoping to deter him from beginning a conversation. Instead, he sat with his back against the sun-drenched wall, shielding his eyes and watching intently as she took the feet of a row of stockings in her hand and unpegged them one by one, throwing them over her shoulder before moving on to the pillowcases. 'Why in heaven do you want to waste your time on me?' she asked as he opened his sketchbook. 'Don't you have a chapel to be getting on with? There was still a lot to do last time I looked.'

He said nothing, absorbed only in the page, and Elsie wondered if he'd even heard. She worked her way to the end of the line, gathering an armful of linen that smelt of summer and reminded her of childhood Mondays, when all the hedges in their garden would be draped with starched white sheets. 'Because you enjoy life,' Stanley said, getting up to open the door for her. She looked at him, confused. 'That's why I love to draw you. The world delights you. It's in everything you do.' It was ironic that he should make such an observation on a morning which had repeatedly tried her patience, and she laughed, immediately proving his point. 'You see? I wish Hilda had your appetite for life. I wish she had just one ounce of your vitality or your joy, instead of spoiling everything the way she does.'

Elsie glanced nervously up at the house, wondering if his words would carry to the open bedroom window. 'I'm sure that's not—'

'I don't know what Hilda wants. I give her all the best bits of myself, all the things that she could never find in anybody else, but I might as well be throwing scraps to the wind.' His voice grew louder and Elsie tried to lead him inside, where the tirade could be muffled. 'She won't even let me make love to her at the moment, and what am I supposed to—'

'Please don't, Mr Spencer,' Elsie said, embarrassed enough to interrupt him. In two months, she had had to revise all her old ideas about a servant's place, and quickly learnt that treading on eggshells got her nowhere with the Spencers. They respected her for speaking her mind, and both of them had shared confidences which she would, in the past, have considered to be none of her business – but she couldn't allow herself to be put in an impossible situation by discussing things of which she had no knowledge, and on which she certainly wasn't entitled to hold an opinion. 'Your marriage is private,' she said firmly. 'You shouldn't be talking to me like this.'

'Why not? I can trust you, can't I?'

He had missed the point, as he often did, but there was no sense in trying to explain. 'It's too personal,' she insisted, refusing to be drawn any further. 'And it's Mrs Spencer you should be talking to, not me.'

5

Time alone at Chapel View was rare, and Elsie wouldn't have chosen to devote a peaceful July morning to cleaning the flues, but she and the kitchen range had developed an uneasy understanding and she had no intention of relinquishing the upper hand. By ten o'clock, Stanley was safely at the chapel and Hilda had left to have coffee with Mary Behrend, taking Shirin with her. Elsie covered the floor with a sheet, then took a long-handled rake and began to work on the corners of the oven. Handful after handful of soot rewarded her, and within seconds her arms were black to the elbows. She was just breathing a sigh of relief that no one was at home to see her when Stanley rushed in through the back door, catching his foot on the dust sheet and sending a cloud of soot billowing further into the room. 'What's the matter?' she asked.

'I need a sponge.'

'As you can see, I'm not baking this morning,' Elsie said, her relief quickly replaced by irritation.

'Don't be silly. I mean a bathroom sponge. I've stood there for an hour trying to remember what they look like, but I need one in front of me. Go and get it for me, will you?' She paused, waiting for the logic of the request to catch up with her, and he scowled impatiently. 'Don't bother. I'll go myself.'

He disappeared upstairs and returned a few minutes later with the sponge, a mirror and his head covered in shampoo. 'Wouldn't it have been easier to wash your hair before breakfast?' Elsie asked, trying not to laugh.

'I'm going back to the chapel,' he said, summoning as much dignity as he could, 'but I meant to tell you that the men are building the scaffold for the resurrection wall today and I need to keep an eye on them—'

Before he could finish, Hilda walked back into the kitchen, flushed from the sun and slightly out of breath. She set Shirin down next to the soot, much to the child's delight, and glanced at her husband, taking his appearance in her stride. 'I'm sorry, Elsie, but I forgot to tell you – my mother's coming for lunch on Sunday.'

'That's all we need,' Stanley muttered under his breath, and Elsie had to agree; she had never met Mrs Carline, but had heard enough about her to know that two days' notice left her very little time to get the house up to the standard that would be expected.

'I don't know if she'll be staying overnight,' Hilda continued, ignoring the intervention, 'so you'll need to make sure we've got enough clean laundry, just in case. Now, I must go,' she insisted, as if it were Elsie who was holding her up. 'I don't want to keep Mary waiting.'

She left, ineffectually brushing at the smuts on Shirin's clean dress, and Stanley followed her to the door. 'As I was saying, I won't be able to leave the builders on their own in case they do something diabolical, so bring us lunch, will you? There are three of them, so pack plenty.'

'All right, but at least let me get you a towel before you go. You're dripping everywhere.'

'There's no time. I need to paint a soldier washing his hair while this still looks fresh. I'll see you later.'

****

His mood hadn't improved by lunchtime, and Elsie only had to take one look at the chaos in the chapel to know that the lunch she brought was welcome but a woman in the way was not. Stanley was belligerently trying to work as the builders constructed their scaffold around him, his hair lank and matted from shampoo which hadn't been properly rinsed. The sponge lay discarded on the floor, its outline now perfectly sketched in a Beaufort bathroom scene, and Elsie picked it up to return it to its rightful place.

The chapel's sparse, cool interior was pleasant at the height of summer and she left it reluctantly. As she opened the gate to the cottage, she heard the determined ring of a spade against dry soil and saw that Hilda was back from the Behrends' and out in the garden. She had changed into an old pair of trousers and a short-sleeved blouse which offered little protection against the sun, and her arms were already flushed pink. 'You're working hard,' Elsie said. 'Was a life of leisure with the Behrends too much for you?'

Hilda smiled and wiped the sweat from her forehead. 'Something like that.' She stretched, trying to rub the stiffness from her back. 'I thought if I exhausted myself physically, I might manage to sleep through Stanley's late-night tirades. He won't mind if there's no one to answer back. In fact, he'd prefer it.'

It was said half in jest and Elsie smiled, but she knew what Hilda meant; sometimes she could hear Stanley talking long into the early hours, and while the disturbed nights seemed to have no ill effects on his energy, his wife looked pale and drawn. 'Shall I put the kettle on?'

'I thought you'd never ask.'

Elsie left her to her digging, returning twenty minutes later with the tea, some cold lemonade, and a bowl of salad, bread and hard-boiled eggs. 'Time for a break,' she said firmly. Shirin was having a picnic with Flopsy in the shade of an apple tree, and Elsie gave them each a drink, admiring the makeshift spread – a carrot, a radish and an empty snail shell – with all the enthusiasm that was expected of her. 'Do Mr Spencer and Mrs Carline get on?' she asked, pouring the tea.

Hilda nodded. 'Stanley and my family are as thick as thieves. He was friends with my brothers long before I knew him. That's how we met.' She deftly shelled one of the eggs and dipped the end in salt. 'I often think he married the Carline family, not just me. Why?'

'He didn't seem terribly pleased that she was coming.'

'Oh, don't take any notice of that. He'll moan until she's walking up the garden path, then enjoy every minute of it and complain when she's gone.' She caught Shirin's hand just in time to save her from the shock of a whole radish. 'I know they're pretty, darling, but you won't like them. Trust me.' Shirin turned her attention to the lettuce and Hilda relaxed. 'Stanley's a creature of habit. You know that as well as I do by now. Sometimes I love him for it. Sometimes it drives me to distraction.'

She drained her cup and resumed her digging, and Elsie looked admiringly at the steadily growing strip of fine, root-free soil. 'You certainly know what you're doing with that spade,' she observed as she began to pick some peas for dinner. 'My father would be proud of you.'

'Some things stay with you. I was in the land army during the war.'

'I didn't know that.'

'Why would you? It was a lifetime ago.'

There was a wistful note in her voice, and Elsie was struck by how vivid and alive Stanley's war was in comparison with his wife's. It had never occurred to her to ask how Hilda had spent those years, but in many ways her service must have been similar to Stanley's at Beaufort: no heroics and no limelight, just menial, repetitive tasks that needed to be done. 'Where did they send you?' she asked.

'To a village in Suffolk called Wangford.' She bent down to drag a handful of stubborn thistles from the soil. 'I've never felt so free as I did then, not even at art school. I lived in a tiny caravan with a friend of mine. We signed up together, although we didn't know one end of a cow from another.' Hilda smiled, remembering. 'All those dark winter mornings! The farmer used to knock on the caravan door, and we'd drag ourselves out of bed. I must have done half the work in my sleep.'

Her words seemed in part an attempt to convince herself that the memory was real, and Elsie looked at Hilda with a new respect. She had been a child herself when war broke out, but she knew how hard her father had worked on the land and recalled very clearly his frequent, bitter claim that some of the men would be glad to sign up for a rest. He had wanted to fight but was already too old, and she had thanked God every day for that accident of birth, not really understanding the reality of what she was thanking Him for, but obeying an eight-year-old's instinct for the horror that lurked in a grown-up world. 'It must have been a shock after what you were used to,' she said, 'but it sounds like you quite enjoyed yourselves.'

'I remember feeling very alive,' Hilda said. She left her fork in the ground and sat down on the bench by the vegetable garden. 'It was all so extreme, I suppose. Hot days in the fields, or up to my knees in a ditch of freezing water.' She smiled, suddenly embarrassed. 'Listen to me, telling you about a farming life when you were born to it. I played at it for a couple of years, that's all. We tried hard, but it was the best of a bad job.'

'You can't play at farm work. I bet the men you worked with didn't cut you any slack, not if they were like my father.' She handed Hilda the colander of peas to shell and moved to the next row. 'I'm no better than you. I don't know half of what my mother's had to put up with. When I think about it, she's given me the hardest gift of all – the choice not to be like her. All my sisters have gone into service or shop work, and even the boys look for something different. We live on the land but we're not part of it like our parents were, and when I marry, I won't be looking for a farmer to sweep me off my feet.'

Hilda laughed. 'I remember going home for the weekend and I couldn't get the dirt from under my fingernails. I'll never forget the look on my mother's face as I poured the tea.'

'I reckon you must have seen as much mud as the men in those fields,' Elsie said, serious for a moment.

'Probably, but that's all it was – mud. Nothing like what Stanley saw. Don't let those hospital scenes fool you, Elsie. He had a terrible time when he got out there.' The sound of a whistle reached them from the station, lazy and half-hearted, and Hilda waited for the train to go past. 'You hear talk of men being changed by the fighting, don't you?' Elsie nodded. 'I never knew Stanley before the war—'

'So you knew what you were getting.'

'Yes, but I often wish I *had* known him earlier. All this work at the chapel – he's trying to rediscover who he was and I've no idea how to help him because I don't know the man he's looking for. Every picture he paints seems to take him further away from me.'

'Have you said anything to him?'

She shook her head. 'No. I don't want to get in the way of what he wants, but sometimes it feels like he's blaming me for not being part of that past life in Cookham, as if our marriage is another obstacle to who he wants to be.'

Elsie understood what Hilda meant, but she had lived with the couple long enough to know that they were as bad as each other. Like the furrows in that Suffolk field, they ploughed through life in a straight and stubborn course, each oddly accepting of selfishness in the other. 'Giving Mr Spencer *everything* he wants might not be the best thing – for either of you.'

The suggestion of compromise was acknowledged with a smile, but nothing more. 'It's funny you should ask me about Wangford,' Hilda said, changing the subject. 'I've been thinking about it lately. It's where Stanley and I were married and had our honeymoon. I wondered if we should take Shirin there for a holiday.'

'I'm sure she'd love it. What's it like?'

Hilda began to describe a pretty village, edged by marshland and fields leading down to the sea, then stopped. 'Wait, I can do better than that. Come with me.' She headed down the garden, and Elsie scooped up Shirin and followed. The summer house was still home to the crates and suitcases that had lain untouched since Hilda told her to put them there in the spring. At the very back, turned to the wall and protected by a dust sheet, stood a small group of canvases, and Elsie waited while Hilda found the one she was looking for. 'This is Wangford,' she said. 'That's the farmhouse we stayed at.' The long panorama was painted in muted shades of green and brown, with a dark line of trees that showed the untidiness of late winter. A cart track wound past the house, leading the eye to a plume of smoke from an invisible train, and Elsie looked with interest at the unassuming red-brick cottage in which the Spencers had begun their married life. 'I thought we'd never get there. Stanley broke off the engagement six times before we made it up the aisle.'

'Why did you put up with that?'

'Because I love him.' Her voice held a hint of the weariness she sometimes used when Shirin asked a question that was too easy. 'Stanley says something, and the world doesn't look quite as it did before – you must see that?' Elsie nodded. 'We could have a break in the autumn, I suppose, before he gets too engrossed in the altar wall. I'd like Shirin to see where we were happy.'

The past tense hung in the air between them. Elsie was tempted to say something about the dangers of trying to go back in time when it was the present that needed sorting, but what was common sense to her might have sounded glib or disrespectful, and she kept her counsel. 'Are you really that unhappy here?' she asked, watching as Shirin opened a suitcase that contained Hilda's redundant paints and brushes.

'Not all the time. Sometimes there's a perfect afternoon like today. Sometimes we go for a walk or laugh at the same thing or sit in bed and talk, but then it's over. Stanley sees something more in those times than I do. For him, they're part of some grand spiritual plan; for me, they're just fleeting moments that never last long enough, and I can't stitch them into anything bigger, no matter how hard I try.'

She began to slide the canvas back into its shroud, signalling the end of the conversation. 'Would you like me to clean this place up?' Elsie asked. 'It seems a shame to put your things away again now they're out, and it wouldn't take much to make it nice.'

Hilda smiled at her transparency, but she did at least consider the offer before refusing it. 'Perhaps one day, but not just yet. I'll think about it, though. I promise.'

6

'Surely your mother isn't coming again already?'

Hilda looked up from the letter she was reading. 'What do you mean? Her last visit was weeks ago. And anyway, why shouldn't she come as often as she wants to?'

Elsie glanced at Stanley as she removed his empty plate. The expression of horror on his face would have amused her had she not come to recognise it as the first sign of an impending row. 'It might be weeks but it feels like yesterday,' he said petulantly. 'I wouldn't mind, but you become a Carline again the minute she walks through the door. No one ever really leaves that clan.'

'Don't be so ridiculous. Only you would regard a mother coming to visit her daughter as a gathering of the clans.'

'You know what I mean. No one is ever quite good enough when two Carlines get together.' He waited, but Hilda had returned to her post and her lack of attention irritated him. Elsie stacked the plates and brushed the cloth down, hoping that a well-aimed shower of crumbs might be enough to encourage the couple to leave the table and take their trouble elsewhere, but neither of them seemed in a hurry. Stanley poured himself another cup of tea and watched as she carried the dishes through to the kitchen. 'One of the loonies at Beaufort used to clear the tables with a trolley,' he called after her. 'He'd push it down the row and sweep the plates on to it with his arm.'

'You must have got through a lot of china,' Elsie said, returning with a broom and setting it down in what she hoped was a meaningful fashion.

Stanley moved a chair back for her, oblivious to the hint. 'Nothing ever got broken. It was all asylum stuff. Cheap tin plates and everything blunted and dulled until it was harmless.'

'I know how that feels.'

Hilda's retort was the red rag her husband had been waiting for. 'What have you got to complain about?' he demanded. 'Elsie does everything round the house and you make it as difficult as possible, staying in bed all morning, then taking Shirin for a walk when lunch is about to be served.' Elsie tried to catch Hilda's eye, wishing that Stanley wouldn't continually use her as a weapon in his marriage. His partiality towards her was beginning to erode the trust that had built steadily between the two women, and she had noticed recently that Hilda confided in her less often. Accustomed all her life to female company, Elsie missed the solidarity of those conversations, which had softened the absence of her mother and sisters; moreover, Hilda's growing sense of isolation made her increasingly withdrawn and Elsie knew that this would do her more harm than good. 'There's nothing to stop you doing whatever you like,' Stanley continued, 'so if you're feeling dull, you've only got yourself to blame.'

'But there's nothing *to* do, stuck out here in the middle of nowhere. I'm going out of my mind with boredom while you're in your precious chapel, and you won't even have a few days off to take your family to the seaside. Do it for Shirin if you won't do it for me. She needs stimulation, too.'

'Why do you always think you know better than other people what's good for them? It must be lovely to be so certain of everything.'

'Of course I know. I'm her mother.'

'When it suits you.' The nudge of a broom at Stanley's feet was usually enough to get him away from the table, but today

Elsie used the ploy in vain. He glared at her and she retreated to the kitchen, pleased to put a wall between herself and the hurt in Hilda's eyes. 'I don't understand why you feel the need to chase about all over the place,' he continued. 'And anyway, I haven't got time for holidays. Have you seen the size of that altar wall?'

'You should have thought of that when you designed it. Why can't you be content just to paint, Stan? You're good enough. What are you trying to prove to yourself with these schemes that go on for years and eat away at our lives?'

'You've never understood those big pictures. Instead of simply supporting me like a wife should, you're continually asking me to justify myself.' Elsie went to push the kitchen door to, but there was no shutting out the force of the argument. Through the gap, she saw Stanley gesture to the picture of the hyacinth which stood in pride of place on the mantelpiece. 'You set more store by that sketch than anything I've done that's meaningful. I only did it to fill the time when I was bored. There's nothing of me in it.'

'Perhaps that's why I like it so much. And has it ever occurred to you to think about what *other* people need? What might make *them* happy? Life's one big picture as far as you're concerned. You put yourself at the centre of it and paint the rest of us around you, hoping we'll stay where you want us to. But real people are different. Real people live and breathe and change, and not only at the stroke of a brush.'

'Don't they just? You're certainly not the woman I married. You should have wanted to paint more than ever after we met, but on the contrary. You set out to be everything I love least: tired and listless and dull. The only things that cheer you up are gardening and sewing, and anyone can do those. You have a talent, Hilda, and I bend over backwards to encourage you, but you refuse to paint just to spite me. Perhaps I should pretend to hate the idea of your doing any proper work. You'd start straight away.'

'I didn't know our marriage rested solely on my wanting to paint.' It was said with a note of finality, and Elsie saw Hilda reach for the pad of paper that was never far from her lap.

'What are you doing?' Stanley asked. 'Writing to your Christian Scientists again? No wonder you're not interested in any of my ideas when you can look down on the rest of the world from that pedestal. The view must be splendid.'

'Actually, I'm writing to Jas. I'm going to tell him what the issues are between us and let him decide which of us has the bigger grievance.'

'Jas? Well then, if you're going to requisition one of our friends, he shall hear my side of things, too.' Stanley jumped up and rummaged through the bureau. 'Elsie!' he called, when he couldn't find what he wanted. 'Bring me something to write on. My wife seems to have the monopoly on notepaper.'

Elsie did as she was asked, fetching the Basildon Bond from the drawer where it was always kept, then stared in astonishment as Stanley and Hilda sat opposite each other at the dining room table, pouring out their grudges to the same unsuspecting victim. She busied herself with the washing-up, relieved to have a few moments of peace and quiet. After half an hour, she heard voices again, more measured this time, and realised that each party in the dispute was reading aloud to the other. Shaking her head in disbelief, she went outside to chop some kindling, taking her frustrations out on a bundle of sticks that had done her no harm. When she returned, the dining room was empty and Stanley and Hilda had disappeared. All that remained of the argument was a pair of envelopes propped against a vase of chrysanthemums, addressed to the same man in two different hands and left for her to post.

7

November was a week old before it offered a dry day. Elsie had always hated the bleak, featureless mornings which marked the passage from autumn to winter, but this year the rain seemed to fall with a biblical gusto, soaking the fields around the cottage and darkening the landscape almost beyond recognition. Even when the downpour stopped, the air was filled with the constant drip of water from trees and rooftops. The house was swathed in laundry, overflowing the washing lines by the range and filling every room with the smell of soap, and the gloom drove Stanley home early from the chapel each day, shaking the rain from his hat, his clothes soaked from the short walk. As he warmed himself by the fire, drinking tea and talking of the progress he had made on the altar wall, steam rose gently from his sodden jacket like a spirit leaving its body.

The morning when the clouds finally relented felt as precious as the first day of spring. Elsie walked slowly to the chapel, noticing that the blackthorn now drew a line of burnt charcoal along the roadside, its branches spiked and tangled like curls of barbed wire. If possible, the building looked bleaker than ever in winter, its façade no longer softened by the sun. Inside, a vast section of scaffolding covered the altar wall, obscuring all but a few feet of canvas near the ceiling, and Elsie wondered for the thousandth time how Stanley managed to paint anything when his feet were so far from firm ground. The chapel seemed empty in the grudging November light, but his voice drifted down to her from the scaffold's highest platform and she saw him perched in the corner, reading a book with a blanket wrapped around his shoulders. 'Hard at it, I see,' she said. 'Be careful you don't overdo it.'

He grinned and raised his hands in a gesture of helplessness. 'I've run out of burnt umber. I can't do another thing until the midday train gets in.' The art supplies for the chapel were ordered from London and arrived at the station every few weeks to be carried over by a horse and cart from the neighbouring farm. She had gone with Stanley once or twice to collect them and was fascinated by his easy rapport with the labourers who helped him. The respect they gave him had nothing to do with his painting – she doubted that they were aware of his celebrity, or that it would have impressed them if they had been. But when he was with them, he became again the village boy that she had pieced together from all his talk of Cookham; he seemed genuinely interested in their lives, and they loved him for it.

She held up her basket. 'I've brought your post and a hot water bottle. Shall I leave them down here?'

'No, bring them up.'

'You want me to come up there?'

She stared at him in disbelief but he simply nodded, daring her to do as he asked. 'Call yourself a country girl? It's just like climbing a tree.'

'You won't be saying that when I'm on crutches and you're fetching your own coal in.'

'Come on.'

Elsie had lived too long with brothers to refuse a challenge. She tucked the letters and hot water bottle inside her coat, then began to climb the first of three short ladders that formed a zig-zag path to the top of the scaffold, feeling oddly like the little girl whose favourite hiding place had been a barn loft on the farm where her father worked. It was strictly out of bounds, a place of danger where discarded tools with rusty spikes stood like instruments of medieval torture in the corner, but her fear of getting into trouble was no match for the sense of freedom and adventure that she felt whenever she climbed that ladder. She had lain up there for hours, watching motes of dust play in a shaft of sunlight and listening to the men at work outside, returning home as late as she dared. One hot August afternoon she had fallen asleep among the straw and woke an hour later in her father's arms, drowsy and sure of her punishment, but all he did was smile and wink, and nothing was ever said to her mother. It was the first secret she could ever remember having, and she realised when she was older that he had always known where she was.

Now, as then, she concentrated on the next rung of the ladder, never once looking back. When she was safely in reach, Stanley took her arm and pulled her up on to the platform. 'See? Nothing to it.'

She took a moment to steady herself, then dared to look around. The platform was three feet wide and ran from wall to wall, with a strip of wire netting stretched along the front in case Stanley forgot himself and stepped back from his work. What little room existed was made more perilous by the clutter of materials; the debris that usually surrounded Stanley when he worked had simply been elevated, and the planks were an obstacle course of paints, palettes and brushes, interspersed with a stool, a small stepladder and a few home comforts. Elsie glanced down into the chapel, enjoying the peculiar sense of perspective that the vantage point gave her. From here, the completed paintings along the right-hand wall looked like distant windows into another world, where people went about their lives oblivious to her gaze. 'Well, you wanted heaven,' she said, standing as far back from the edge as she could without touching the painted wall. 'We're certainly high enough.'

'Isn't it marvellous? You get a sense of what the whole thing will be like when it's finished.' Elsie looked again at the right-hand side, now half-filled with images, and understood for the first time the pattern that Stanley had repeatedly tried to explain to her. The bottom row of four rectangular paintings showed lonely figures absorbed in dreary tasks. The colours were muted, the faces expressionless, and taken as a whole they seemed to represent a claustrophobic underworld of cramped rooms, dark corridors and bleak grey stone – hell, for want of a better word. By contrast, the completed arches on the next level were full of light and colour, and to look at them was like coming out into the air. These paintings teemed with people, and she wondered if it was too simplistic to see the transition as one of loneliness to a sense of purpose and belonging. 'I love watching over them all,' he said affectionately. 'It must be how God feels. Did you bring any tea?'

She laughed, familiar by now with the way in which he could move from one plane to another without acknowledging a difference. 'There's a flask down there in the basket. You can fetch it.'

He shinned down the ladders, making it look easy, and Elsie picked up the book that he had left open on the stool. 'Who's Desmond?' she called after him, reading the inscription on the title page.

'An angel with a beard. He appeared one day when I was scrubbing the floors at Beaufort, and he befriended me when I most needed it.' Stanley poured some tea, giving the clean cup to Elsie and wiping over a used tin mug for himself. 'He introduced me to things I'd never read. That copy of St Augustine's *Confessions* was the first book he gave me.'

Elsie flicked through the pages and found a series of prayers and reflections on God, life and morality. 'Looks a bit thin on plot if you ask me.'

'It's full of lust, sin, grief and redemption. What more do you want?'

'Boy meets girl and a happy ending. Is that too much to ask?'

Perhaps she imagined it, but his smile seemed wistful. 'I don't suppose so. But this little book kept me going in that hospital.'

'What's so special about it?'

'There's a passage about serving God through ordinary things. "Ever busy, yet ever at rest. Gathering yet never needing, bearing, filling, guarding, creating, nourishing, perfecting, seeking though thou hast no lack." As soon as I read that, I knew why I was there. It was all a service to God, even if I wasn't fighting.'

'Perhaps that's how Mrs Spencer feels when she's doing those things you say anyone can do. Perhaps she finds a meaning in those.'

His face clouded. 'Don't be silly. It's not the same thing.'

'Isn't it? You draw me in the garden picking sprouts, but you ignore the fact that she grew them in the first place. What's the difference?'

'Hilda's better than that. She doesn't need to make sacrifices.'

The slight was water off a duck's back, and Elsie had learnt that the best way to deal with Stanley's more petulant outbursts was to ignore them. She ran her fingers down the spine of the book, finding its battered cover more poignant than its contents; it had, quite literally, been through the wars with Stanley, and its scars moved her. 'Did Desmond come back?' she asked.

'He didn't fight. He was excused on medical grounds and became a priest.' He took a small pile of photographs from the pages of another book and handed one to Elsie. 'We drifted apart after the war, but I always felt I could share my doubts with him.'

'You had doubts? About your faith?' Elsie looked at him, surprised.

'Had. Have.' He shuffled through the pack of photographs, and Elsie caught glimpses of men in uniform and hospital beds. 'I wish sometimes that I could share Hilda's certainties. She's convinced that she's much closer to God than I am, and she's probably right.'

Elsie took the pictures from his hand and looked at the one on top, interested to see the hospital she had heard so much about. The ward was full, its beds pushed close together, with men standing round the edges or perched awkwardly on chairs. Some of them had bandages over their eyes, others nursed broken limbs, but all wore that same shy half-smile, caught somewhere between pride and guilt. Stanley stood slightly apart from everyone, fading into the background at the very edge of the photograph. His face was unmistakeable, but Elsie was touched to see that he had written 'me' just above it – another attempt, perhaps, to validate his service. She pointed to two soldiers standing next to each other, whose names were also scribbled above their heads. 'Were they friends of yours?'

'Yes, and the chap who was taking the photograph. He died shortly afterwards. They gave him an injection of strychnine for rheumatic fever and he was gone the next morning.' Stanley shook his head in disbelief, and Elsie wondered how the randomness of death could still surprise him after all he had seen. 'It was a wretched thing, to die in that terrible place. I wish I could have helped him.'

'At least he was buried at home,' Elsie said. 'No comfort to him, but it must have meant the world to his family.'

'Yes, you're right. We buried so many out there, our side and theirs.' He stood and encouraged her to face the back wall, his hands resting lightly on her shoulders. 'It's for them, this Resurrection. They'll all be here eventually.' The top of the painting was at eye level now, grey sky falling to a smoky hillside, with a pencil line of trees and a pack of mules and sleeping soldiers. 'They'll come into a world of peace,' he said. 'That *was* the point, after all.'

Elsie looked down, peering through the gaps in the scaffold to the unpainted wall below. It was impossible to guess at the finished picture, but she could see glimpses of what was to come – squares marked out in pencil and lightly sketched figures, all faint and ghostly in the shadows, waiting patiently for the new life they were promised. 'Why don't you ever talk to Mrs Spencer like this?' she asked quietly.

For once, he didn't snap back but seemed to contemplate the question. He drew a breath to speak, but she heard the chapel door open and another voice drifted up to them. 'Hello? Are you there, Stanley?'

Elsie stepped hurriedly away from him. 'It's the Behrends,' she whispered. 'They sent a message to say they'd drop in but I forgot to tell you. Sorry.'

Mary Behrend looked up in surprise as Elsie descended from the scaffolding, but she was too polite to comment. 'We thought we'd come and see how you were getting on,' she said, smiling and kissing Stanley. 'I hope this isn't an awkward time?'

'It's your chapel, Mary. You must come whenever you like. Is Louis with you?'

'Yes. He's fetching something from the car.'

'Good. There's another arch gone up since you were last here and I've made a start on the east wall.'

'So I see. How splendid!' Elsie tidied up while Stanley showed his patron what her money was paying for. She liked Mary Behrend, and found it amusing that Stanley's benefactor always behaved as if *he* were the one doing *her* a favour, an impression he never went to any great lengths to dispel.

Mr Behrend arrived a few minutes later, carrying a large box tied with ribbon. 'For Shirin's birthday next week,' he said with a wink, 'but she doesn't have to wait if she doesn't want to. Did you get the dado business sorted, Mary?'

'No, dear, not yet.' Elsie looked curiously at Mrs Behrend, wondering why she sounded nervous. 'I thought *you* might want to ask Stanley about it.'

Her husband frowned, but Stanley was oblivious to any awkwardness. 'We were talking about the new pictures,' he said. 'Come and have a look.'

Louis Behrend did as he was told, studiously avoiding his wife's eye. 'What does Hilda think of it all?' he asked. 'She's the best critic I've met.'

'Oh, she's pleased with how it's going,' Stanley said vaguely. 'She particularly likes *Sorting the Laundry* and *Ablutions*.'

Behrend lifted his glasses and peered closely at the most recent painting, the one of soldiers washing in the bathroom at Beaufort.

'I know that cleanliness is next to godliness, Stanley, but not too next, eh?'

Stanley laughed, although Elsie wasn't entirely sure that the comment had been made in jest. 'What about the dado?' he asked. 'There's not a problem is there?'

The couple hesitated, each waiting for the other to speak, but chivalry won out in the end. 'We were having a word with Pearson the other day,' Behrend began, and Elsie recognised the name of the chapel's architect; she had heard it often at Chapel View, usually prefaced by another word which she would not have wanted to repeat in company. 'He asked us to suggest… well, to ask, if you thought it might be not an idea to go back and have another look at the original design for…'

Elsie turned away to hide a smile when she saw the look of indignation on Stanley's face. 'Absolutely not,' he said, before Louis Behrend had even finished his sentence. 'It would be completely wrong, as I've already explained.' The Behrends looked at each other and Elsie saw Mary give her husband a shrug. 'I'd have to rethink the whole scheme if you're going to insist on—'

'No, no.' Mary held up her hand. 'We're not insisting on anything, Stanley. We wouldn't dream of it. We just promised Mr Pearson we'd mention it when we saw you, but I'll tell him it's out of the question. And I'm sure the new mouldings won't be much more expensive, will they, dear?'

'Not in the scheme of things,' Behrend said, with a note of resignation in his voice. 'Perhaps he can take the old ones back.'

'Excellent idea! Now that's settled, would you like to come back to Chapel View for some lunch?'

'Oh no, we wouldn't dream of imposing.'

'It's not an imposition at all. Elsie can rustle something up and Hilda would love to see you.'

Stanley beamed at Elsie, who felt obliged to consolidate the invitation. 'It's really no trouble,' she said, mentally running through the larder to see what would stretch. 'I'll go back now and get it ready.'

8

The suitcases lay open on the bed in the spare room and Elsie wrestled with the one nearest to her, leaning down heavily on the lid while Hilda tried to fasten it. 'Ducky?' Stanley's voice called up the stairs, clipped and impatient. 'What on earth are you doing? We need to go.' He waited in vain for an answer, then came up to see for himself, staring in frustration at the disorder. 'For goodness sake, ducky, I packed those cases last night. Why have you opened them again?'

'I was checking we'd got everything.'

'Of course we have. Elsie and I made sure of that, precisely so we wouldn't have this last-minute panic.'

'So where are the socks I asked you to rinse through for Shirin?' Hilda's irritation was obvious, and Elsie winced. 'I can't see them anywhere.'

'They're downstairs, drying by the fire. Elsie can send them on. I've packed plenty of clean ones.'

'Elsie's got enough to do for her own Christmas. Go and fetch the socks.'

'But they're soaking wet!'

'Then wrap them in a towel. And put a clean shirt on. You can't turn up at Downshire Hill like that.'

Stanley stormed out and Elsie closed the rest of the cases in silence. She picked one up to take it downstairs, but Hilda caught her arm. 'Wait a minute, I've got something for you.' She disappeared to her own room and returned a few seconds later with an envelope, looking so awkward that Elsie wondered if she was about to be given her notice. 'Sorry it's not wrapped,' Hilda said, 'but I thought you might like it.'

Elsie tore the seal and looked at her present, a beautiful pencil drawing of Shirin. In her hair, she wore the ribbons that her grandmother had given her the week before, but Elsie would have known the sketch was recent without such telltale signs; the child was at an age where her features seemed to change by the day, and Hilda had captured perfectly the expression of wry amusement that occasionally passed across her face, a tolerance for adult failings which was way beyond her years. 'I don't know what to say,' Elsie murmured, taken aback by the gift.

'Shirin worships you and I know how much you love her.' She stood at Elsie's shoulder and they looked at the picture together. 'She won't stay like that for long. It's nice to have a moment to hold on to.'

'Thank you,' Elsie said. 'I don't know what to be more pleased by – the picture itself, or the fact that you've drawn it.'

'I *did* enjoy myself while I was doing it,' Hilda admitted, as if confessing to the most shameful of habits. 'But this is our secret, at least for now.'

9

Elsie's Christmases at home were so familiar, so rooted in moments of shared joy, that each year felt as if she were reliving an old memory rather than creating something new. She slipped easily into the morning muddle: the clamour to wash and dress while her brothers resisted clean shirts; nervous glances at the clock and anguished protests as new toys were left behind; the chaotic departure for church while her mother remained in the warmth and peace of the kitchen. For as long as Elsie could remember, no one had been allowed to help with Christmas dinner; the meal was treated with reverence – her ma's gift to the family – and to tamper would have been like offering to paint a corner of the chapel. She fetched her hat and coat from the bedroom at the back of the house, falling in with the ever-changing sleeping arrangements that marked the comings and goings of her siblings. Each time she came home, it was as if the cottage had been picked up and tossed by the wind, its contents falling into an arrangement that confused and disorientated her, and there was scarcely any point in getting used to it.

The day was seasonal, with a sharp frost that broke the monotony of the ploughed fields around the village. Her father – a churchman all his life – had left early to ring the morning peal and the bells echoed in the taut winter air, punctuated occasionally by the sound of ice being broken on water troughs, thin and distant, like glass shattering in another room. St Mary's had borrowed from the world outside to compensate for her own inadequacies:

armfuls of holly brought colour to the faded altar cloths, and a host of voices – willing, if not heavenly – conspired to make the creaks and sighs of the organ less evident than usual. Elsie joined in heartily, first with the carols and then with the gossip, swapping news with the women among the gravestones and laughing with the lads who wore mistletoe in their caps as an excuse to try their luck.

The kids raced each other up and down the lane back to their cottage, and Elsie fell into step beside her father. 'You look happy, love,' he said, smiling at her.

'I like Christmas. You know that.'

'It's more than that, though. I noticed it when you were home before. You've found a place that suits you this time.'

Elsie nodded, wondering how to explain to her father the freedom and sense of possibility that life with the Spencers now gave her. In the end, she decided that to be too specific about the reasons for her happiness would only worry him, so she said simply: 'They're good to me, and their little girl's a joy.'

'You'll be thinking about one of your own before you know it.'

Elsie laughed, but it was true: in recent weeks, her growing fondness for Shirin had led her to think about a family of her own. 'There's plenty of time for that,' she said.

'Well, don't leave it too long. I'm not getting any younger, and your mother and me don't want to miss out on our grandchildren.'

Back at home, the smell of roast beef wafted through the kitchen. She hugged two of her older sisters, stragglers who had returned home for lunch while she was at church, then took her place at the dinner table, extended now at either end to make room for the husbands and wives who had joined the family in recent years. Elsie was one of fourteen children, the oldest still unmarried, and for the first time she felt self-conscious of her single life, as if she were outgrowing it. When the meal was over and the extra table leaves packed away in one of the sheds, where they would remain until Easter, the youngest children settled on the floor to build elaborate houses from a new pack of cards and her mother lit the lamps. Elsie knelt down by the tree, remembering that she had not yet handed over the gifts that Stanley and Hilda had sent for her parents. They were the only presents left, except for two small parcels which were placed carefully by the tree for babies who had died. The gifts were never unwrapped, but Elsie could tell from their shape that they were different each year. She had no idea what happened to the old ones; perhaps they were reassigned to the living children the following Christmas, tiny hand-me-downs from a brother and sister they would never know, but who remained an integral part of the family.

'These are for you,' she said, handing a bottle to her father and something flat and rectangular to her mother. 'They're from Mr and Mrs Spencer.'

'That was good of them. There was no need.' Her mother unwrapped the drawing, which Stanley had gone to the trouble of framing, and Elsie had to smile at the bewildered expression on her face. 'That's very thoughtful,' she said, glancing wistfully at her husband's port. 'But why's he drawn you in your working clothes?'

Elsie shrugged. 'He doesn't often see me in furs,' she said, more sarcastically than she intended. 'I'm always in my apron when he's sketching.'

'Does he draw you a lot, then?' her mother asked, making no effort to hide her surprise.

'Now and again. He says he likes the way I do things.'

'Does he indeed?' Her sister Phyllis winked at her and looked over their mother's shoulder, joggling her baby in her arms. 'He's given you very good legs. I'd like to meet this Mr Spencer.'

Elsie glared at her, knowing that their parents needed no encouragement to revisit their concerns about the morals of artists – or lack of them, as they saw it. 'You can if you like,' she said. 'Mrs Spencer said at the start that I could have family to stay.' She smiled at her mother in what she hoped was a nothing-to-hide sort of way, then turned back to Phyllis. 'I dare say he'll draw you, too, if you stand still long enough. He'll have to work harder on your legs, though. God gave me mine, and they don't need improving on.'

Phyllis threw a cushion good-naturedly across the room, catching the house of cards as she did so, and the tension was lost in the cries of indignation from the floor. Within minutes, the drawing lay forgotten under a chair, and Elsie doubted very much that it would ever find a place on the wall. 'Do you really have to go back on Wednesday, Else?' her mother asked, when the kids had been pacified with a barley sugar. 'You said they were away until new year.'

'They are, but I've got to have the house ready and there's plenty to do before they come back. I never have time to do anything properly when they're under my feet.'

'She'll have had more than enough of us by then, Edie,' her father said with a twinkle, pulling his boots on. 'I'd better go and see to the animals. Who's coming to help?' Two young hands shot up and he ruffled their hair, waiting while they struggled into their coats. 'It's nice to have you back with us, love,' he said on his way out. 'Just for a bit.'

Elsie stood up to draw the curtains and watched as the three figures walked across the yard in the half-light. Birds pecking over the scraps from dinner scattered as her father headed towards the stable, whistling softly and accompanied by Tom and Lily, each proudly swinging a hurricane lamp. She had done the same thing many times herself on Christmas day, finding the peculiar magic of the season in the animals' contentment and the simplicity of the scene, but it was *their* turn now, and while part of her envied them that childlike sense of excitement which could never be recaptured, something else spoke to her of a different sort of expectation, a different sort of hope.

10

It was just after five o'clock on New Year's Eve when she got back to Chapel View, but the gloom of a day which had never truly been light made it feel much later. Elsie closed the gate behind her and looked up at the house, surprised to see a faint glimmer from the Spencers' bedroom window. She walked around to the back, the key ready in her hand, but the door was unlocked and a trail of mud and dead leaves ran across the kitchen floor. No one was supposed to be here for another three days and she hesitated, wondering what she would do if a tramp or burglar had got in while the house was empty, but she knew she had secured all the doors and there was no sign of a broken window. She put her case down and called out. 'Hello? Mrs Spencer, is that you?' There was no answer, so she went to the staircase, picking up a poker from the hearth on the way. The nursery was just as she had left it, with none of the joyful clutter that should have marked Shirin's return, and suddenly Elsie's mind took a darker turn. What if something had happened while they were away? Caring little now about intruders, she crossed the landing and knocked on the Spencers' door.

Stanley was sitting up in bed, fully dressed with his muddy shoes discarded on the floor and an army blanket over his knees. The sheets were covered in notepaper, and he was so engrossed in his task that he barely looked up. 'I thought you weren't back until tomorrow,' he said.

'I wasn't, but the weather looked bad overnight and I wanted to make sure of getting here.' He nodded, but offered no further comment. 'Where's Mrs Spencer?'

'Still in Hampstead with Shirin.'

'But they're all right? Shirin's not ill?'

'Oh no, they're perfectly all right. In fact, I'd go as far as to say that Mrs Spencer is blooming, back in the bosom of her family.' He gestured to the letter. 'I was just writing to her about that very thing.'

Elsie's heart stopped racing, but the panic over Shirin was soon replaced by the thought of what her mother would say if she could see her now, alone in the house with a man and standing at his bedroom door. 'Wouldn't it have been easier to stay where you were and talk to her?' she said.

'I can't think when I'm with her. I get all muddled, and she says the same. We lead each other off on tangents and forget what we wanted to say.'

'I think they call that a conversation. I've heard it's quite common in some houses.' He smiled, but looked sadder than ever. 'You'll destroy that love of yours with all these letters,' she said quietly. 'It's not good for you to be apart. Grudges get worse at a distance.'

'She told me at Christmas that she's always more herself when she's not with me,' Stanley admitted. 'It's just the opposite for me. I knew the first time I met her that she was the one.'

'That's not what she tells me,' Elsie said wryly. 'She says you broke off your engagement so many times that she didn't know if she was coming or going.'

'She told you that?' Elsie nodded. 'Does she talk about me often?'

'You're not the only one who bends my ear.'

'I'm sorry.'

'It's all right. I've got two of them. Have you had anything to eat?'

He shook his head. 'I haven't been back long and I came straight up here.'

'Then I'll get the kitchen up and running and see what I can do.'

He followed her downstairs, and watched while she lit the range and filled the kettle. 'Here, give that to me. It'll be quicker.' He took the kettle from her and grabbed a bundle of dry sticks from the fire basket, then carried everything next door to the sitting room. There was a hook above the open fireplace, and as soon as he put a match to the wood, the kettle disappeared in the flames. The house was cold and inhospitable, even though it had only been shut up for a week, and the glow in the hearth was welcome. 'I used to love camp life,' Stanley said, as the kettle began to boil. 'Those early mornings when everything was so ordinary. The smell of bacon, and nothing more threatening than a dog scavenging by the food tins. You could almost believe in peace.' He stared into the flames and Elsie waited for him to continue, realising suddenly how precious these moments had become to her; no one else spoke to her like this, and she had begun to hoard the images in her mind as greedily as a collector would cover a wall. 'Then it all began again and there was no getting away from it.'

The lid of the kettle rattled in protest as water spilled into the grate, and Elsie used a cloth to remove it from the fire. 'Time for tea,' she said. 'I brought some food back with me. There's plenty for two.' She laid out bread, cheese and Christmas cake on a tray, while Stanley wrestled with a jar of pickles which refused to surrender its lid. 'Just as well you didn't have to live on gherkins during the war,' she said, laughing at his frustration. 'You'd have starved and saved the enemy a lot of trouble.' She stuck two forks in the cork and used an old knife pushed through the prongs to ease the lid off. 'There. Let's eat next door. It's cheerier.'

They took their time over the meal and Elsie chatted about her Christmas, sensing that Stanley had no wish to reminisce about his. 'Did your parents like the drawing?' he asked.

'They loved it,' she lied. 'The only thing that got more attention was a magic set Tom had from Ma and Pa. He drove us up the wall. I could cheerfully have made it disappear myself by Boxing Day.'

Stanley smiled. 'My brother Horace used to do magic. We boys would all be in one big bed together and he'd start chanting and blowing the candles out. Just when we were about to give up, he'd dive down the bed and produce a dead frog or a bird's feather.'

'I bet he'd hidden them earlier.'

'There was a hole in the mattress at the bottom of the bed and he just put his hand through, but we were happy to believe him and he was actually very good. He did it professionally for a while.' Stanley got up and rummaged through a drawer. 'This is his advertisement.'

Elsie took the piece of paper – kept, she suspected, for the sketch on the back rather than out of respect for Horace's conjuring skills – and looked down at a dark-haired man with a moustache, dressed in white tie and brandishing a perfectly fanned pack of cards. 'Did Horace teach you any magic? Something useful, like how to finish a chapel in a week.'

'He was very tight-lipped about it, but I picked up a thing or two.'

'Show me.'

'What have you got in your pocket?'

'Nothing.'

'Are you sure about that?'

'Of course I am.' She put her hand in the pocket of her apron to prove it, and took out a beautiful silver pendant on a chain. 'How did that get there?' she asked in astonishment.

He said nothing, just tapped his nose with his forefinger. 'Keep it,' he said, as she held it out to him.

'I couldn't. It's far too precious.'

'I want you to have it,' he insisted. 'It'll suit you. Let me put it on.' He leant forward to fasten the necklace and Elsie felt herself redden. 'It isn't real silver. Pa bought it for Ma at a fair one year. I'm not sure how I came to have it, but it's only worth a couple of shillings.' It wasn't the value that made the gift special, but Elsie didn't know how to explain that without sounding sentimental. 'Tell me about *your* family,' he said, stoking up the fire. 'Where do you fit in?'

'Seven of fourteen.'

'Lucky, then.'

'Well, strictly speaking I was number eight. I had a twin but she died. They thought I was going the same way for a while. The midwife said I wouldn't last the day, but I proved her wrong. Ma takes great delight in telling me I was stubborn from the day I was born.' Stanley looked at her with interest, encouraging her to go on, but she hesitated. She rarely talked about the loss of her sister, even at home. The anger at being cheated of something so precious before she was aware of it had only grown worse with age; it was like having a perpetual question hanging over her life, one that could never be answered. 'I often wonder why I got to live and not her,' she admitted, 'but something you said made me think. That zest for life you're always talking about – perhaps that's down to her. Perhaps I'm living for us both.'

He nodded, as if the thought made perfect sense. 'It's hard to lose a sibling. Worse for our parents, I suppose, but it changes you.'

'Harder still if you grew up together,' she said. 'Two of my sisters died at birth, but at least I hadn't grown to love them.' Elsie knew the first news that had greeted Stanley on his return from war was the death of his brother, Sydney, killed in one of the last German counter-attacks. She guessed that they had been close, because Stanley – usually so vocal about everything – was uncharacteristically quiet on the subject, and now was no different. He changed the subject and they talked long into the evening, chatting easily about their families and their early lives, pausing only as the clock drew close to midnight.

'I wonder what she's doing now?' Stanley said. 'You know, Elsie, I can't bear to think of Hilda being miserable, but I'm the one who causes her the most suffering.'

'And the most happiness.'

'Do you think so?' She nodded. 'When I'm alone, all I want is to be with her. Then I see her and all that certainty dissolves, like some sort of mirage.'

Elsie's hand strayed to the pendant around her neck. 'You can't summon people up when it suits you and make them disappear when it doesn't,' she said. 'It's not fair on Hilda, and it's certainly not fair on Shirin. You've got to make a decision and stick to it. What do you want?'

In the distance, across the fields, she heard the bells from the church bidding the old year a solemn farewell; there was a pause, then a new, more joyful peal rang out into the night. She got up to open the window and let the sound fill the silence in the room, and Stanley stood with her, so close that she could feel his breath on the back of her neck. 'Happy new year, Elsie,' he said softly, and for a moment she thought he was going to kiss her, but he simply turned and left the room. She stood there for a long time after the bells had died away, relishing the cold, clean air, trying to reconcile herself to the knowledge that the kiss was something she had wanted rather than feared.

11

'Where are you off to?' Stanley asked as Elsie took her coat from the peg in the hall.

'Just out for a walk, unless there's something you want?'

'No, but if you hang on a minute I'll come with you. It's a nice evening.'

Elsie busied herself in the kitchen, putting away the tea things while she waited for him to find his jacket and change his shoes. She had been looking forward to an hour to herself and tried not to resent the change of plan. In these past few weeks, her evenings had ceased to be her own. Hilda's absence had become a habit which neither she nor Stanley seemed inclined to break, and the longer she stayed away, the more Elsie struggled to make sense of her own situation, caught in a no man's land between servant and something indefinably more – companion to a man who was not her husband and desperately missing a little girl who was not hers to miss. Her repeated encouragements to Stanley to visit Hampstead fell on deaf ears and eventually she gave up, but her position nagged at her conscience and she knew something had to change.

Stanley appeared in the doorway, oblivious as usual to any reservations on her part. 'Come on,' he said impatiently. 'Let's go while we've still got the daylight.'

Her mood lifted as they walked out into the lane, turning right to follow the railway cutting until they reached Ox Drove, where a narrow cart track – pockmarked with deep holes and other scars of winter – ran through bracken-covered strips of woodland. The evening was chilly, but the sun lingered, as if caught in the branches of the trees, and Elsie looked up at the tiny buds which promised a new year. The colours were more pronounced now, and after a few false starts she finally allowed herself to trust in this prologue to spring. 'I love this part of the year,' Stanley said, pausing to admire the deep-purple wood of an alder tree. 'Everything's biding its time, then suddenly the woods are on fire.'

Elsie listened as he talked about the places he loved, seeing them through his eyes as clearly as if she had grown up there herself. 'Don't you ever want to paint something beautiful for a change?' she asked. Stanley smiled and she felt foolish, just as she had when they first met and she had ventured a question that seemed too basic for him to take seriously. 'I mean something from the world you live in now,' she added, determined not to let him get away with a simple dismissal. 'Something that you fought *for* rather than the fighting itself. Wouldn't that be a better tribute?'

This time, Elsie was gratified to see that he thought carefully before answering. 'When I was out in Macedonia, I never thought I'd come back,' he said eventually. 'I don't think any of us did. So when I got on that boat and sailed home, it was like being born again. I remember crossing the Channel at night and seeing the lighthouse on the Isle of Wight. I knew I'd want to paint that moment – the sense of escaping death and emerging into a better world.'

'The Resurrection.'

'Exactly. But it's not enough to paint the lighthouse. No one would understand what it meant.' He pointed upwards, encouraging her to look at the branches. 'I could paint those trees and, yes, they might be beautiful, but that alone wouldn't convey the joy of them. And the paintings in the chapel are the same. A world of peace is nothing without the soldiers emerging into it. It's just an empty landscape.'

'One of these days I'll know what you're talking about.'

He grinned. 'I hope you'll understand when you see the finished wall. And I will paint some landscapes while I'm here. They sell well, and we need a car.'

'How long *will* you be here?' The question came out before she could stop it, a symptom of the uncertainties that hung over her future.

'As long as it takes.'

'But what if Mrs Spencer doesn't come back?'

'She'll come back.' He quickened his pace, although the tone of his voice would have been enough to deter her from pursuing the subject, and Elsie struggled to keep up. 'Remind me to go and see Mr Head,' he said, prompted by the outline of the builder's workshop on the brow of a distant hill. 'I'll be ready for them to move the scaffolding in a few weeks.'

'Are you nervous?'

'Why would I be nervous?'

'Seeing the whole wall for the first time. You've been working on it for months. You must wonder how it's going to look.'

'I know exactly how it will look. I might have painted it in sections, but it's been complete in my mind all along.' There was no arrogance in the claim, just a straightforward faith in his endeavours. She envied him his confidence, and was about to say so when he stopped and held up his hand. 'Listen! I'm sure that was a nightjar.'

'It can't have been. They won't be back for another month.' But there it was, the strange purring trill that filled the Drove at dusk as soon as the birds returned. The call was unmistakeable, like the whirr of an old-fashioned spinning wheel, and Elsie listened as it rose and fell against the breeze.

'I love it when they're here,' Stanley said, his voice almost a whisper. 'They look so homely in the trees. It reminds me of our room, when I'm waiting for Hilda to get into bed.' The chirring stopped and they watched as a shadowy form took off from an oak tree. Its lichen-grey plumage was a perfect match for the deepening dusk, and Elsie soon lost sight of it. 'Perhaps their coming early is a good sign,' Stanley said. 'Perhaps it means Hilda will come home.' The bird's ghostlike disappearance seemed to endorse his superstitious optimism, and Elsie didn't argue as they left the path and crossed the field towards the church. 'Why does she *always* find excuses to stay away?'

'Her brother's death was such a shock and she needs to take care of her mother,' Elsie said, exasperated by his lack of sympathy for the Carlines' sudden bereavement. 'I'd hardly call that an excuse. I'd do the same myself.'

'And the two months before that?'

'I don't know, Mr Spencer. Why don't you go and ask *her* instead of expecting me to have all the answers?' She stopped, forcing him to turn and look at her. 'We can't go on like this. It's not right.'

'What do you mean?' He stared at her in such genuine bewilderment that for a moment Elsie doubted her own judgement. 'We get on, don't we?' he said. 'We're alike, you and I. We know what we want and we don't get in each other's way.'

'But think of how it must look.'

'Why on earth does that matter?'

Stanley's naivety about the most fundamental things charmed and infuriated Elsie in equal measure. 'What do you imagine Mrs Behrend thought the other day when she called in unexpectedly and found us hot and bothered on the landing while your wife and child are away?'

'We were moving a chest of drawers!'

'I know that, but she didn't.' Elsie tried to control her anger, honest enough to know that it stemmed not from Mary Behrend's interpretation of their relationship, but from her own confused feelings. 'And *she's* a nice lady, so what are the others saying behind my back?'

'You're being ridiculous.'

'That's easy for you to say. It's never the man they gossip about. You won't be looking for another job in a few months or years or however long it takes you to finish that chapel. And anyway, you're an artist. You're entitled to behave badly.'

'But we're not behaving badly.'

'I need to move out and get a room in the village.'

'You can't move out.'

'Of course I can. You pay me to cook your meals and wash your clothes, and I can still do that if I live down the road.'

'But it's more than that. I need you.'

'Well you shouldn't!' She felt the tears prick at her eyes and stopped before any more words could give them free rein. Without waiting to hear what Stanley had to say, she walked quickly past him and headed back towards the house, longing for the sanctuary of her room. At the narrowest part of the road, she stood to one side to let a taxi pass, but thought nothing of it until she turned into Pound Lane and noticed that the lights were on in Chapel View.

She paused at the gate, giving Stanley a chance to catch up. 'Hilda's back,' he said quietly, half-afraid to believe his own words. 'Elsie, she's back.'

Shirin chose that moment to break free of the house and rush down the path to greet her father. 'Daddy!' she squealed, holding out her arms to be picked up. 'Daddy, we're home!' Stanley ruffled her hair as he walked past her into the hallway, and the look of hurt and disappointment on the little girl's face was more than Elsie could bear. She picked her up and swung her round, then held her close, breathing in the faint scent of talcum powder mixed with Hilda's perfume, a strange blurring of adult and child which seemed suddenly appropriate to a girl forced to grow up before her time. Through the open front door, Elsie saw Stanley and Hilda embracing by the stairs. The bright-red poppies on Hilda's skirt stood out against the wallpaper's more muted patterns, fixing the scene in Elsie's mind, and she watched as the couple looked tenderly at each other, wondering how long their joy would last. She hung back, reluctant to interrupt, but Shirin was not to be denied again; she squirmed to be put down and Elsie let her run inside, where she clung to her mother's legs, content to be an outsider in the family reunion.

'You see?' Stanley said, noticing her in the doorway. 'I told you everything would be all right. I knew that bird was a sign.'

'Yes, you did. Welcome back, Mrs Spencer. It's nice to see you.'

'You too, Elsie. And thank you for looking after everything while I've been away.'

If Hilda found anything strange in her husband's return to the house with the maid at dusk, she didn't say so, and, at Shirin's instigation, Elsie allowed herself to be drawn awkwardly into the embrace. 'Why didn't you let us know you were coming?' Stanley demanded. 'We could have made proper arrangements.'

'I only decided this morning. I got your letter, and it seemed silly to stay away if we were both thinking the same way and wanting the same things. We should at least try to sort this out, shouldn't we?'

Elsie went through to the kitchen to put the kettle on, then scooped up Shirin in her arms. 'Right, my girl, let's get you off to bed and leave Mummy and Daddy to talk.' Tired from her journey, Shirin could only manage a perfunctory objection and Elsie soon had her changed and tucked up in the nursery. 'Can we stay here now?' she asked as Elsie sat down on the bed with a story book. 'I don't want to go away again.'

'Yes, sweet pea, of course you can stay. Things have been a bit difficult for the grown-ups lately, but this is your home and it's where you belong.'

'Do you promise?'

Elsie kissed her on the forehead, realising how much she had missed her. 'Cross my heart,' she said, hoping for both their sakes that it was a promise she could keep.

12

Elsie sat with the Behrends' maid, Rose, on the grass outside the chapel, waiting while the completed altar wall was viewed for the first time. 'They've been in there a long time,' Rose said doubtfully. 'I can't work out if that's good or bad. I hope they're not making him repaint it.'

'*Nobody* makes him repaint things, especially not the people who are paying for them. If they don't like it, he'll be busy telling them why they're wrong.'

Rose smiled and watched as Elsie gently discouraged Shirin from picking tiny apples off the low-hanging branches of a nearby tree. 'You're good with her,' she said. 'I can't do a thing with the Behrends' two, not now they've grown up a bit. Little devils they are, especially George.'

'He's at that awkward age.'

'He's that all right. I heard him ask his father the other day if there'd be any money left for him when the chapel was finished.' She smiled and raised her face to the June sun. 'Mind you, he's got a point. They're well off but they're not made of money. There'll be some that knock them for being extravagant.'

'They've already started, from what Mr Spencer says.' Elsie looked at her friend, wondering whether or not to confide in her. They had known each other for a long time, and it was Rose who had tipped her off about the job with the Spencers in the first place; she knew the village as well as anyone and had an enviable ear for gossip. 'Can I ask you something?'

'Course you can.'

'And you'll tell me the truth?'

Rose pretended to think about it, then smiled. 'You know me. I wasn't born with an ounce of tact, so spit it out.'

'Do people talk about me? The Behrends and their friends, I mean.'

'All the time. If I hear one more peep about your apple cobbler or how nicely you keep the floors polished, I'll bow out and let you get on with it.'

'I didn't mean that.'

'So what did you mean?' Rose stared at her intently, all joking gone, and Elsie hesitated. 'What's the matter, Else? You haven't been yourself lately, and it's not like you to let things get on top of you.'

Bored suddenly of the apples, Shirin began to show a predatory interest in a butterfly, and Elsie pulled her firmly on to her lap. 'I suppose I've been worrying about what people might think – all that time I was here alone with him.'

'Why? Nothing went on, did it? He didn't take advantage?'

'Of course he didn't, but you know what people are like. I daren't tell my mother that Mrs Spencer was away. I had to keep remembering to mention her in my letters.'

'Well *I* haven't heard anything, and you know I don't miss much.'

'Not even from the Behrends?'

'No, not a whisper. Mind you, they're so nice I don't think it would occur to them to think ill of anybody.' Elsie tried to feel reassured, but her efforts were obviously unconvincing because Rose leant over and squeezed her hand. 'Is there something you're not telling me?' She waited for an answer, and then, when none was forthcoming, supplied it herself. 'Elsie Munday, have you taken a fancy to Mr Spencer? Well I never! You have, haven't you?'

Elsie blushed. 'It's not like that. He's just a bit different. We talk and it's nice, but there's nothing in it.'

'Be careful. You know where talk can lead.'

'I'm not stupid, Rose. They're a lovely family and I'm fond of them all. But even if I weren't, I don't think Mr Spencer would so much as look at another woman. When he's not with Mrs Spencer, all he does is talk about her. She's the only woman he's ever loved.'

'He told you that?' Elsie nodded. 'Blimey, you do talk. What else has he said?'

Before she was forced to choose between indiscretion and disappointing her friend, Stanley emerged from the chapel, followed by the Behrends. Mary Behrend had a handkerchief in her hand and was obviously moved by what she had seen. 'It must mean a lot to have her brother remembered after all this time,' Elsie said. 'I can't imagine how I'd feel if I lost one of mine and his sacrifice wasn't even marked.'

'Mmm. This is her way of making amends, I suppose.'

Elsie looked at Rose in surprise. 'What's she got to make amends for? It's not her fault they wouldn't put his name on the memorials.'

'Oh, I don't mean that. Don't you know what happened?'

'Mr Spencer said he had malaria, but because he died at home they wouldn't add him to the list.'

'Well, that's half the story. Poor bastard had a ruptured spleen – that probably *was* the malaria – and they say Mrs Behrend gave him a nip of brandy. She was only trying to help but it finished him off, apparently. She's never forgiven herself. Someone told me it was ages before she'd even have his name mentioned.'

'Is that true?' Elsie asked, looking at her in horror.

Rose shrugged. 'It's what I've heard. Don't say anything, though. I'm not sure if the Spencers know.'

'That poor woman. She's always been so kind. It's just not fair, is it?' They watched as the Behrends said goodbye to Stanley, a warm handshake and a kiss signifying their gratitude.

'Life's not,' Rose said cheerfully, getting up and brushing the dust off her skirt. 'That's my cue to get going. We're off to Newbury to buy George some new clothes. He's going to stay with a friend this summer and it can't come a day too soon.' She kissed Elsie on the cheek. 'I'll see you Thursday afternoon. Are we still on for the pictures?'

Elsie nodded. 'We can go on the bike again now I've got some new spark plugs. It'll be quicker than the bus.'

'If we must.' Rose made a face. 'Nothing like arriving in style. And in the meantime, stop worrying.'

She met the Behrends by their car, while Elsie took Shirin's hand and walked over to Stanley. 'You got away with it, then?'

He smiled. 'They love it.'

'I'm pleased for you. I'll go and get the lunch on to celebrate.'

'Don't you want to look at the wall first? I'd like you to see it. Let me take Shirin home and tell Hilda the good news while you go inside. I'll only be gone a minute.'

Elsie agreed, glad to have a few precious moments to look at the painting without distractions. She knew how much the *Resurrection* wall meant to Stanley, and desperately wanted to understand it. Half-anxious, half-excited, she went inside, deliberately keeping her eyes on the floor until she had closed the door behind her and shut out the rest of the world. Even so, nothing could have prepared her for what she saw. The far wall had always dominated the small chapel, even when it was bare, but its presence now was remarkable – a moving, whirling cacophony of people and images, dizzying in its detail. What struck her first was the multitude of white wooden crosses which covered the landscape. In keeping with the rest of the chapel, the crosses were strangely domestic: some resembled the picket fencing at Chapel View; others were squared together to form picture frames for individual faces, creating a series of miniature portraits and reminding Elsie of the photographs that sat on every sideboard in every home. All over the painting, soldiers were emerging from their graves, shaking hands with their colleagues or performing the everyday tasks of war – rolling puttees, cleaning buttons, cutting barbed wire. The line of fields and hills against the sky was familiar to her as the countryside around Burghclere, but still it seemed alien, as if the colour had been drained from the world and replaced by muted browns, whites and greys. In parts it was almost sepia, and Elsie – an outsider, who could never really know – understood for the first time how war must bleed the beauty from a landscape.

It was hard to distinguish the detail at the top of the painting from where she stood, and she was glad to have seen it first from the scaffolding: the tiny figures under sleeping bags and the resting mules; the bricks that Stanley had complained about every night when he came home – as monotonous, he said, as doing the sky in a jigsaw. She lowered her gaze to the centre of the wall, where a pair of white mules lay on the ground, still harnessed to a waggon. The animals were twisting their necks to stare back at a small seated figure, dressed in white and receiving crosses. With a shock, Elsie realised that this seemingly insignificant man, placed so high in the picture that he could hardly be seen, was Christ.

The scaffolding had been moved to the left-hand side of the chapel, ready for Stanley to begin work on the panoramic scene which would run across the arched canvases. Elsie walked past it to look more closely at the lower part of *The Resurrection*, which had a different feel to the rest of the painting. There was a splash of greenery in the corner, and the detail of it was so realistic that it appeared to be growing out of the vestry door, crawling upwards to engulf the scorched, barren earth above. The figures here were larger, with pale skin that hinted at the death they had left behind, and Elsie shivered. As she stood there, the sun emerged from a cloud and quickly disappeared again, and the changing light through the window behind her created a strange effect on the painting, an illusion of movement which was not unlike the flickering images of a cinema screen. One or two of the soldiers' faces were obscured by the crosses they carried, and she found that frustrating, as if there would always be a part of this painting – a part of these men – that she could never know.

She wanted to cry, although she would have found it hard to say why. The painting was an extraordinary piece of work. If much of its significance passed her by, it still possessed a raw, emotional power that spoke to her without the need for further explanation, and she knew that no matter how often she visited or what Stanley chose to paint on the remaining walls, nothing would affect her like this. For the first time since she had known it, the chapel felt sacred.

'Well?' Elsie had been too absorbed in her thoughts to notice Stanley coming in quietly behind her. She turned round and he nodded, satisfied, when he saw the tears in her eyes. 'You don't have to say anything. That's the answer I wanted.' He walked over to stand beside her, his footsteps unusually loud on the flagstones, and she waited for him to speak. 'I've buried so many people, Elsie. I've lost too much to believe that death is the end.'

His words echoed something he had said at their very first meeting. Back then, he was being flippant, deflecting her question about the war with an aggressive matter-of-factness which lots of men used when they thought they could never be understood; now, he spoke them as a sort of confession, asking not for forgiveness but for solidarity, an endorsement of his faith. 'There's no fear,' she said, looking again at the faces and the clasped hands which seemed to stand for so much more than a simple handshake. 'You see the painting and you think it's still a battlefield, then you realise that they're happy. They want to be there.'

Stanley seemed pleased. 'It's all we longed for, that feeling of being at home. See here?' He pointed to a man who stood framed between two crosses. 'It's as if he's standing in the doorway of his house at the end of the day, looking at the street he loves. And these chaps at the bottom – once the altar table's in, it'll look like they're having a chat over dinner.' He stood back and smiled, still seeing new things in his own painting. 'I'm very fond of peace. That's what I wanted to give them.'

'I like the mules.'

'So do I. I don't know how anyone can say they don't have a place in the afterlife. They've just as much right to be there as we have.'

'Who said they hadn't?'

'The Bishop of Guildford. Sometimes religion has very little to do with Christ.'

'You haven't exactly given him a starring role yourself. Blink and you miss him.'

'But he's there. That's what matters.'

'Those mules on the right don't look like they've been resurrected. Why's that?'

He glanced sharply at her. 'What do you mean?'

She pointed to the top right-hand corner. 'The ones in the compound. They've got their heads lowered like they don't belong there.' He stared at them, frowning, and Elsie could tell that the effect she saw was not the one he had intended. 'There must be a lot of memories here,' she said, trying to imagine the impact the painting would have on those who had actually shared Stanley's experiences. 'Good and bad.'

'Yes, there are.' He scratched his head, as he often did when he was thinking. 'The soldiers used to say that every day was a day nearer to peace. I feel that here, when I work. This chapel, these paintings – they're how I'll find the person I've lost.'

'And who is that?'

He avoided the question, choosing instead to tidy some paints away, and Elsie wondered how someone so open and willing to talk could still be so hard to know. It was frustrating, like the figures in the painting, and she wanted to tell him to take the cross away from his face but she doubted that he ever would. 'You're probably right about the mules,' he said, glancing back at the wall. 'It's too late to change them now, though.'

89

13

The house that Stanley had rented in Cookham that summer was small but pretty, an end terrace in a row of cottages near the school. Elsie pulled back the flowered curtains in her bedroom and looked out across the garden to a patchwork of crumbling red brick and colour-washed stone, the walls and paths and out-houses which stood as hidden secrets in most English high streets. The cross-country journey from Burghclere had been anything but calm, and her first impressions of the village were muted by relief at simply getting there – but still she had noticed how self-contained Cookham seemed, just a few streets, bordered by grassland and water meadows, all nestled in a bend of the River Thames. The mood was of harmony and contentment, a nonchalant, take-me-or-leave-me attitude, and Elsie wondered how easy it would be for a stranger to peel back the layers and find the village that Stanley talked of with such love.

She went downstairs and found the family declaring its priorities for the three-week stay by unpacking what was most important: Stanley and Hilda were storing sketchbooks, paints and canvases in a sunny front room, and Shirin had transformed the kitchen into a makeshift library, covering the floor with a pile of storybooks from which she refused to be parted. Two suitcases of clothes stood abandoned in the hallway, and Elsie picked one up. 'I'll get you settled in,' she said. 'Then we can have tea.'

Hilda smiled. 'Thanks, Elsie. Is your room all right?'

'It's lovely.' She watched the couple for a moment from the stairs, still getting used to the peace, then set about making them at home in the main bedroom. When she came back down, Stanley was putting on his jacket.

'I'm off to see how Annie is,' he said. 'I'm sure Percy's exaggerating when he says she can't cope on her own at Fernlea, but I need to check for myself.'

Hilda touched his arm. 'Do you want me to come with you?'

'It's best if I go on my own. You stay here with Shirin.'

'All right. Give your sister my love.'

'I won't be long.'

'Shall I move the car while you're gone?' Hilda called after him. 'We did rather ditch it.'

Stanley paused but didn't turn around. 'I'm sure the car will be perfectly fine where it is,' he said through gritted teeth, then closed the door firmly behind him.

Hilda and Elsie looked at each other and burst out laughing. 'I hope he can't hear us,' Hilda said, helpless to stop. 'He'd be so cross. I suppose he'll get the hang of it eventually.'

'Of course he will. Driving can be difficult at first and it's a big car. Anyway,' she added without conviction, 'that delivery van was going far too fast.'

'I suppose it was. Still, the look on Stanley's face was priceless. He does so hate being bad at something, and I can't interfere while he's so set on proving he can do it.' She opened the front door and walked out to the gate. 'I might just straighten it up so there's more room to get past. Do you think he'd notice?' Elsie raised an eyebrow. 'Yes, of course he'd notice. I'll leave it where it is. We don't want to start with a row.'

'That's probably best.' Elsie peered down the street to where the shiny new Clyno saloon sat at an awkward angle to the pavement. 'I was thinking that me and Shirin might get the train back, though.'

Hilda laughed, and absent-mindedly began to deadhead the roses in the front garden. 'It's so nice to get away together, even if it is only to Cookham. Shops on the doorstep, cafés and hotels. I'd quite forgotten what that was like.'

'Have you spent much time here?'

'We came more often when Stanley's father was still alive. Shirin was the apple of his eye, although he terrified her. I think it was the beard.' She knelt to some geraniums in pots and Elsie watched her, envious of the instinctive understanding that her hands possessed for anything that flowered; it might have been her imagination, but it seemed to Elsie that plants grew taller and stronger for Hilda. 'Stanley took it hard when his father died.'

'How long has he been gone?'

'Eighteen months or so. He died in the January of twenty-eight, just before you came to us. There was that terrible outbreak of flu, so Stan couldn't even go to the funeral. We haven't been back here much since then.'

'It seems a nice place.'

'Yes, it's nice.' There was a note of qualification in her voice and Elsie waited for her to expand. 'I just can't find it in me to love it the way Stanley does, and that's always been an issue between us. I suppose it's because I wasn't born here, but to me it's just like a hundred other villages. I don't see Christ walking through the streets like he does.' Neither did Elsie, but she understood how the ties of a happy childhood continued to pull, particularly in a place which seemed to stand still. 'I hope Annie *is* all right,' Hilda added. 'They were always close, and it would break Stan's heart to see Fernlea with no Spencers living there.'

'Didn't Annie ever leave home?'

'Only for a while. She spent some time abroad when Horace and his wife were here, even got engaged for a bit, but it didn't come to anything. It was a shame for her, because it made her the obvious choice when someone had to be here to look after their parents. Now she's in her fifties and it's too late. Stanley feels it badly. Annie was just as talented as the boys, but she never had a chance to pursue any of that.'

'She paints as well?'

'No, she's a musician. Most of the family are. Stan and Gil are the odd ones out, although both of them play well. Stan always said that Annie could have made a career out of her music if she'd been allowed to study like her brothers. But you know what it's like – we girls have to take care of the home, unless we can find a way out.'

Elsie tried and failed to imagine Hilda as the capable daughter taking over the reins of her mother's Hampstead household, and couldn't help feeling that Mrs Carline had had a lucky escape. The thought of Stanley's sister alone in the family home, surrounded by a past which had destroyed any hope of a future, knowing that it was too late to make a life of her own, moved Elsie, but part of her sympathy was born of selfishness: as the oldest unmarried daughter, and with a life steeped in service to others, it was not inconceivable that Annie's fate might one day be her own.

She fetched Shirin and took her outside to play with her mother, then began to make preparations for their evening meal. After a while, she heard the click of the back gate and Stanley opened the door into the kitchen, visibly upset. He wiped his feet diligently on the mat, a thing he never did, and Elsie knew that he was trying to avoid her eye. 'How did you get on?' she asked gently. 'Was Miss Spencer pleased to see you?'

'She's in a terrible way,' he said, and she noticed that his voice was flat and empty, without any of the musical notes that she so loved; the only other time that she had heard him speak like this was during the darkest time of Hilda's absence. 'I don't know what to do. The house is in such a state. There's filth everywhere, and she's not taking care of herself. She can't go on living like that. I'll have to sort the house out while I'm here.'

'I'll help you.'

'You don't have to do that. It's my responsibility.'

'I know I don't have to, but where's the sense in you taking a fortnight over it when it'll be done in a couple of days with two of us? You've got a family here expecting a holiday, and *all* of you need that.' He nodded. 'So that's agreed?' Still he hesitated, and Elsie realised suddenly that his reluctance to let her help stemmed in part from shame; he didn't want her to see the home that he had talked about so lovingly in its present state, as if it would invalidate everything he had told her of his childhood. 'There's no disgrace in needing a bit of looking after,' she said. 'We all come to that in the end.'

'Do we?' He smiled sadly. 'Thank you. I don't know what to say.'

'That's a first.' She took his jacket and hung it in the hallway. 'Hilda and Shirin are out the front. Go and see them. Dinner won't be long.'

He did as he was told, but turned back at the kitchen door. 'Horace has pawned all Pa's clothes,' he said bitterly. 'God knows what else he might have taken. It's impossible to tell when the whole house looks like it's been ransacked. Why didn't I check on her more often?'

'Don't be hard on yourself. You're a big family, and it's not just down to you. I know your Pa meant a lot to you, but he's gone now and they're only things. It's Annie who matters, and you *can* do something for her.' She ushered him out from under her feet. 'Right now, though, you should be spending time in the sun with your wife and daughter. Don't forget how much you missed *them* when they went away.'

14

The pavements of Cookham seemed to soak up the heat of the sun and throw it back at twice its strength. Elsie paused outside the forge, switching her basket from one arm to the other, then set off down the high street at a leisurely pace, keen to take everything in. As Hilda had said, the bustle of the village on a weekday morning was a far cry from the emptiness of Burghclere, and the contrast was welcome, but the first thing that struck her was how tight-knit everything seemed. After the open space of the Moor and the meadows down to the river, the main thoroughfare felt narrower than it really was, throwing together a harmonious jumble of shops and houses. Gentlemen lifted their hats as she passed but the women looked probingly at her, instinctively curious about a stranger in their midst, and Elsie was more grateful than ever for the remoteness of Burghclere during Hilda's long absence; Cookham, she imagined, would have had a rather different attitude to Stanley's domestic arrangements.

Fernlea, his family home, was halfway down the high street and she lingered outside, pretending to admire a beautiful mauve hibiscus which had somehow flourished in an otherwise neglected front garden. The house was one of a pair of three-storey villas, identical except for a Virginia creeper which covered one more enthusiastically than the other, and separated from the road by cast iron railings and a privet hedge. A brass plate hung loosely on the gate, tarnished and dirty, but Elsie could just make out the words

'William Spencer, Organist of St Nicholas, Hedsor' engraved on it, and the sense of pride left over from older, happier days moved her. A small passage ran down the side of the building, past a neat little ivy-clad cottage, and she was tempted to use it to see what she could of the back of the house, but decency stopped her. Instead, she turned and crossed the street to Ovey's Farm, remembering the name from Stanley's tales of painting in the barn there. She had never taken him literally when he talked of the farm across the road, assuming that he meant somewhere on the outskirts of the village, but there it was, incongruous in the middle of the high street, with a group of cows standing sociably by the gate. Smiling to herself, Elsie took a last look at Fernlea, but the smile faded to something more awkward as she noticed a woman sitting at one of the first-floor windows, staring blankly out into the street. It was hard to say how much her first impressions of Annie Spencer were influenced by what she already knew, but the face at the window looked lost, deep in the shadows even on the sunniest of days.

She moved on, following the hastily sketched map that Stanley had left for her. The lane leading down to the river wound gently round to the right, flanked on either side by the soft, red-brick walls that seemed to define so much of the village. She crossed the bridge and saw Hilda first, sitting on the bank with her sketchbook on her knees. Her head – protected from the sun by a cloche hat that Stanley had bought her earlier in the summer – was bowed low in concentration, and Elsie was pleased to see that her enthusiasm for her work grew stronger by the day. The grass around her was littered with pencils and discarded pieces of paper, while Stanley stood in the shade a few yards further downriver, surrounded in much the same way by the tools of his trade. Shirin kept an egalitarian distance between her parents, as absorbed in her picture book as they were in their work. She waved when she noticed Elsie and ran across the grass to meet her, finishing the manoeuvre with a tumble over a tuft of grass which sparked a look of indignation so like her father's that Elsie had to stifle a smile. 'I saw it move,' she said, gathering the child up in her free arm. 'You didn't fall, you were tripped.' Shirin giggled and Elsie carried her over to Hilda. 'I've brought tea and lemonade,' she said, setting the basket down and returning Stanley's greeting. 'One was hot and one was cold when I left the cottage, but I dare say they're meeting somewhere in the middle by now.'

Curious, she tried to steal a glance at Hilda's drawing, but the sketchbook had already been closed. 'Thanks, Elsie. I'll have lemonade.'

'Tea for me. It's more refreshing.' Stanley threw himself down on the grass next to Shirin and pinched her cheeks. 'Is there anything to eat? I'm famished.'

'The last of the seed cake's in that tin,' Elsie said, pouring the drinks.

'I hate seed cake. I told you that.'

'Only after I'd baked it.' She handed the tin to Hilda and winked at Shirin. 'And there are some chocolate biscuits, but they're not for grown-ups. If someone asks nicely, perhaps we could make an exception.' Shirin put her finger to her chin and pretended to think, then broke a biscuit in two and handed the smaller part to her father. 'I thought you might like a picnic out here for your lunch,' Elsie continued. 'It's a lovely day, and it would save you having to pack up your things. Seems a shame to stop working when you're just getting settled.'

'No need to go to that trouble. We're all going out to lunch. There's a tearoom in the high street that I used to love.'

'All right, if you're sure?'

Stanley nodded. 'It's gone eleven now. Wait here while we finish up and we can all go together.'

Elsie did as she was asked, playing I spy with Shirin as she listened to the distant sounds of children swimming in the weir. When they were ready, she helped Hilda and Stanley pack up their things and the family walked back to the high street. The Copper Kettle Tearoom was set back from the road, close to Fernlea, and Elsie looked up at the house as they passed but there was no sign of Annie at the window; Stanley, she noticed, stared resolutely ahead. A bell rang pleasantly as they went inside, and the woman behind the counter nodded and smiled when Stanley gestured to the table by the window. She was tall and attractive, with a magazine glamour that seemed strangely out of place amid the café's old-fashioned charm; looking at her slender figure and perfect cheekbones, Elsie doubted that she had ever so much as sniffed a cake, let alone baked one. Instinctively, she smoothed her hair and straightened her blouse.

The woman came over to them, and Elsie noticed with some satisfaction that she was older than she had seemed at first, much nearer the Spencers' age than her own. 'I'm afraid I'm only holding the fort today,' she said apologetically. 'Mrs Buckpitt's away, so I can't offer you the usual menu – just salads, sandwiches and cakes. If you want something hot, I could probably manage a muffin.'

Hilda smiled. 'Sandwiches would be perfect. Perhaps you could bring us a selection, with some tea? And I think Shirin *would* like a muffin, if it's not too much trouble.'

'No trouble at all.'

'Make that two, then,' Stanley said, 'and plenty of jam. Mrs Buckpitt's all right, I hope?'

'Oh yes. Just visiting her sister.'

She disappeared into the kitchen, walking with such mannequin perfection that Elsie half-expected to see a price tag hanging from the back of her dress. 'That'll be why there's no smell of cooking,' she said, giving up the cushion from her own chair to allow Shirin a better view of the table. 'I wouldn't want someone like that looking after *my* kitchen, I must say.'

Hilda laughed at the disapproval in her voice. 'I'm sure the poor woman's doing her best. Not all of us can live up to your standards when it comes to home baking. I should know.'

They chatted while they waited for their food, and Stanley seemed to find a name or an anecdote for most of the people who walked past. 'You must be local?' the woman said as she put a tea tray down in the middle of the table. 'I don't remember seeing you here before, though.'

'I grew up in Cookham,' Stanley explained, 'but I left just after the war and we don't get back as often as we should. And you?'

'Quite similar, really. My father was in the army and we moved around a lot when I was young, so I was only here for a year or two. Then my friend and I were looking for somewhere to live that was close to London, and I remembered Cookham. It was one of the few places I was happy in.'

Stanley's smile was warm now, rather than polite, and Elsie noticed that an affection for his beloved village had captured his interest far more effectively than simple good looks. She braced herself for a long conversation in which neither she nor Hilda would be required to take much part, but they were saved by a smell of burning from the kitchen. 'Oh, damn,' the woman said, suddenly remembering the muffins. 'I'm so sorry. Please excuse me.' Elsie listened for the sound of scraping, fearing for Shirin's lunch, but muffins must have been in good supply that day because when they finally appeared they were a perfect pale gold. Sandwiches followed, artfully arranged on the plate but without much substance, and Elsie hoped for Mrs Buckpitt's sake that her sister wouldn't keep her long. The tea shop began to empty as the lunch hour drew to a close, and the woman was too busy issuing bills to continue the conversation she had started, but she glanced over to their table once or twice, apparently interested in the sketchbooks that Stanley had leant against a table leg.

'Stanley Spencer! I thought it was you. It *is* good to see you back here.' A new arrival stopped by Stanley's chair and held out his hand. 'I was so sorry when we lost your father,' he said. 'The village isn't the same without him.'

Stanley shook his head. 'No, it isn't. Thank you, Mr Gould. Gil told me how kind everyone was.'

'At least he lived to see how well you've done for yourself. A picture in the Tate Gallery! He was so proud of that.'

'I'm pleased to hear it. Pa always wanted the best for his children.'

'Annie's not so good these days, though.' Mr Gould paused, waiting for Stanley to say something, then added: 'The wife's been round to Fernlea a couple of times to see if there's anything she can do, but there was no answer.'

Elsie looked at Stanley's face, realising that the state of the house must have been one of the main topics of conversation in the village for months. She wanted to say something to help him, but it wasn't her place and Hilda seemed too preoccupied with her own thoughts to notice his embarrassment. 'Annie lives a quiet life,' he said eventually. 'That's why we're here, to make sure she's all right, so please thank your wife for her concern but tell her not to worry.'

He had effectively closed down the conversation, and after a few half-hearted generalities Mr Gould took his seat. They finished the sandwiches, and the woman came over to collect their empty plates. 'I hope you don't mind my asking,' she said, 'but are you the *artist* Stanley Spencer?'

He nodded absent-mindedly, dabbing at the jam on Shirin's dress while she cheerfully replaced twice what he had managed to remove. 'That's right.'

'How wonderful! They talked of you so often when I was at the Slade, but I never dreamt you were from Cookham.'

Stanley stopped what he was doing and looked at her. 'You were at the Slade?'

'That's right, at the end of the war.'

'Around the same time as Hilda, then. You don't remember each other?'

Hilda shook her head and held out her hand. 'No, I'm afraid not, but very pleased to meet you, Miss…?'

'Preece. Patricia Preece.' Stanley pulled a chair over from the next table and Patricia Preece sat down, much to the annoyance of a couple who had asked for more tea. 'I walked past your *Nativity* every day on the way to class. Dorothy and I – that's my friend, Dorothy Hepworth – we both so admired that painting.'

100

'What did you like about it?' Stanley asked, unable to take a compliment without interrogating it.

Patricia thought for a moment, and Elsie wondered if she was genuinely trying to remember or simply choosing the words which she thought would most please Stanley. 'There was something poetic about it,' she said at last. 'Something sensitive and very human. We both thought it was interesting that you arranged the painting around a man and a woman, and made the baby in the manger almost incidental. Such an original way of looking at things.'

Stanley nodded, as if Patricia had passed some sort of test, while Shirin seemed to have more in common with the overlooked baby Jesus; bored with grown-up talk and feeling a little neglected herself, she sought attention by knocking over the pepper pot, and Elsie hurriedly pulled her on to her lap.

'Do you still paint?' Hilda asked.

'Oh yes, we both do. We had a studio in Gower Street for a while, then we spent four years in Paris and how could you not paint there? There's something wonderful about the light, we thought. Paris is the most exciting city in the world, don't you think?'

'I don't know it very well,' Hilda said. 'Stanley doesn't hold with the French influence.'

'I don't see that Paris can offer anything Cookham can't,' he said, a little huffily. 'Or any other city for that matter.'

'I do envy you that time,' Hilda said longingly. 'My brothers were in Paris, and they came back so full of ideas. It must have been wonderful.'

'It was. We stayed in a boarding house full of students, and they took us out every evening. Painting all day and dancing all night. It was our idea of heaven.'

Elsie couldn't help but notice how often the words 'we' and 'our' slipped into Patricia's conversation, and she wondered if the mysterious Dorothy could possibly be as annoying as her friend. In her opinion, Paris had had a lucky escape. 'I'm surprised you came back,' Hilda said wistfully. 'It sounds idyllic.'

'We missed our friends and Dorothy needed to see her family more often. We travelled round for a while, then decided to settle here. It suits us – handy for going up to town and, as I said, I was happy here the first time. Dorothy's father was kind enough to arrange a mortgage on a house for us. You must know Moor Thatch? We've been there a couple of years now.'

'How strange that we should have been in Cookham at the same time,' Stanley said, 'both loving the place but oblivious to each other. Where did you live?'

'In Mill Lane. My father rented one of those houses leading down to the river.'

'Ah, the posh end. We were in the high street, at Fernlea.'

'And we used to shop at the grocery stores just opposite! Your father was the old man in the dressing gown? How quaint.'

Elsie stared at Stanley but he seemed oblivious to the insult. The couple hoping for tea had given up on the idea and now stood purposefully at the counter, waiting to pay. 'I'd better get on,' Patricia said reluctantly. 'Can I tempt you with anything else? Mrs Buckpitt's seed cake is second to none.'

Elsie and Hilda laughed in unison, and Patricia looked at them curiously. 'No, thank you,' Stanley said, reaching for his wallet. 'Just the bill.'

'I'd love to see your work,' Hilda said when their account was settled, and as she never said anything just because it was expected of her, Elsie assumed that she meant it. 'And Miss Hepworth's, too.'

'My pictures are poor things next to Dorothy's,' Patricia admitted. 'She was brought to the Slade by Professor Tonks himself, and she had her first painting at the Academy when she was eighteen. Still, there might be something of mine you like. Augustus John has bought one or two pieces, and he was kind enough to mention me in an article on women painters that he wrote last year. Did you read it?'

'Hilda was in it,' Stanley said, when it became obvious that she wasn't going to say so herself.

At least Patricia had the decency to look embarrassed. 'Why don't you come back to Moor Thatch now?' she suggested. 'I'm about to close up here and Dorothy would love to meet you. We've obviously got so much in common. Do come.'

Stanley looked at Hilda, who nodded, and they waited while Patricia fetched her things, locked the Copper Kettle's front door and posted the keys through the letterbox. As they walked up the street towards the war memorial, Stanley and Hilda paused to help Shirin with her shoelaces and Elsie fell awkwardly into step with Patricia. 'Is your house nearby?' she asked, if only to break the silence.

'Just over there. Its name rather gives it away.'

She pointed to a thatched cottage on Cookham Moor, and Elsie felt foolish. The house was white with small leaded windows – a larger, romanticised version of the homes that country people really lived in, surrounded by well-kept gardens of a good size. She had noticed it often but thought nothing of it; today, it seemed to dominate the entrance to the village. 'It's pretty,' she said. 'It must be one of the oldest cottages here.'

Patricia laughed and the sound was sweet but strangely unsettling, like a music box beginning to wind down. 'Gracious, no,' she said. 'It was only built a couple of years before we bought it. It's all *faux*, my dear. I've got dresses older than that house.' She stopped at the junction with School Lane, waiting for Stanley and Hilda to catch up. 'You're welcome to come too, of course. I'm sure Connie would love to meet you. She's just started charring for us, so a friend in the village would be nice.'

Elsie counted to three before answering, but still the words came out more brusquely than she had intended. 'That's very kind, but I've got plenty to do in my own kitchen.' She collected Shirin's toys and the sketching materials from Stanley and Hilda, then headed home, glancing back only once, but the family had already disappeared into the cottage overlooking the Moor.

15

Stanley prevaricated about Fernlea, using every excuse he could think of to avoid what awaited him there, and eventually Elsie had to bully him into it. 'Imagine how much better you'll feel when you've done something about it,' she said, taking advantage of a morning when Hilda had decided to catch up on her letters. 'Apart from anything else, it'll stop people talking.'

This was her trump card. An hour later they were standing outside the house, staring at the peeling paintwork on the windowsills and the feathery long grass which grew around an old tin trunk, incongruously dumped in the front garden. 'Gil always said it was architecture to confess to, not boast about,' Stanley said, touching the gate affectionately. 'These hinges will need oiling.'

Elsie looked at him impatiently. 'That's like saying a starving man needs a napkin. I can think of more pressing things than a creaky gate. Come on, let's go inside.'

He put his key in the door and called up the stairs. 'It's only me, Annie. I've come to tidy the house a bit.'

The hall smelt musty, even from the front step. Through the open doorway, Elsie saw a woman appear on the first-floor landing, her face gaunt in the shadows. Her long hair was straggly and unkempt, neither worn loose nor properly tied, and she seemed uncertain and afraid. 'Those people came in and moved things again,' she said, taking her brother's reassurance as an accusation.

'I don't know who they are, but they leave things in such a mess. There's nothing I can do.'

Annie's words made no sense, but her voice was strong and surprisingly young – musical, like her brother's. Elsie looked at Stanley and he shook his head, warning her not to contradict anything she was told. 'Well, they're gone now and there's no harm done. We'll soon get things looking shipshape again.' He stood aside to let Elsie into the hallway. 'I've brought a friend of mine to help. This is Elsie. She looks after Hilda and me, and she's come to give us a hand.'

Elsie noted the forced cheerfulness in his voice and took the same tack. 'It's lovely to meet you, Miss Spencer,' she said brightly, as Annie came cautiously down the stairs. 'I've heard a lot about you.' The hand that took hers was pitifully frail, with skin as dry as parchment. Close up, Annie's clothes smelt of dirt and neglect, of a dignity long forgotten, and it was as much as Elsie could do not to hold her breath. 'I've brought some tea things,' she said, holding up a bag. 'Shall we put the kettle on? I'll do it if you'll show me where it is.'

She put her arm round the older woman's shoulders and led her gently down the hallway to the kitchen. There was nowhere to sit, and a quick glance round made it obvious that spending much time in this room was unlikely to lift anybody's spirits. 'Why don't you go into the garden and I'll bring it out to you?' she suggested. 'It's a beautiful day.' Annie looked doubtful, but the morning sun was persuasive and Elsie watched, pleased, as she sat in an old wooden chair and lifted her face to its warmth. The state of the kitchen depressed her, and she doubted that they would even scratch the surface of the chaos in the time allotted to the task, but a more analytical assessment showed that much of their work consisted in simply throwing things away – rotting vegetables, bread that had turned a vivid shade of blue, pans which were far beyond cleaning. Once the debris had been cleared, it wouldn't take her long to scrub the floor and make the room functional again.

She took the tea and some cake outside, then followed the sound of a piano to the drawing room at the front of the house. Here, the walls were damp and in a terrible state, but Elsie suspected that the room had never been much-used, even when the children had all been at home: it reeked of lace-ridden special occasions, those awkward, once-a-year teas which would have been so much more joyful if held in the parts of the house that were actually lived in. To her surprise, the paintings on the walls were reproductions and she wondered why – in a family of two artists – the Spencer walls were still full of depressing old pictures by other people. 'Annie's in the garden having tea,' she said, as Stanley closed the lid on the piano. 'She seems happy enough. I'll bring more food and some clean clothes round later. She might feel more like looking after herself when everything else is nice again.'

'Thanks, Elsie.' He squeezed her hand gratefully and looked at the cup she had brought his tea in, a souvenir from Queen Victoria's Diamond Jubilee. 'This takes me back,' he said. 'Gil and I were at the head of the Cookham procession, and Pa was so proud. It's been in the cupboard for more than thirty years.'

'And there's food there with it that's nearly as old. That kitchen needs a right good clear out.'

Stanley's face clouded. 'Percy's right, isn't he? Annie can't stay here on her own. She might just about manage somewhere smaller, like Cliveden View.'

'Where's that?'

'Out of the village, just past the railway station. Grandpa built that, too. My grandmother retired there after he died.'

'He was obviously handy with a brick, your grandfather,' she said, and Stanley smiled. 'What will happen to Fernlea if Annie does leave?'

He shrugged. 'It'll have to be sold.'

The thought made him more depressed than ever, and Elsie knew that if anything useful was to be done she would have to take charge. 'Go into the kitchen and sort out everything that needs throwing away,' she said firmly. 'You can talk to Annie while you're working. She looks like she could do with a bit of ordinary conversation and you've never been shy of that. For heaven's sake be ruthless, though. Don't let her hoard things she'll never use. I'll make a start in the bedrooms. Where's the mop and bucket?'

He directed her to the cupboard under the stairs. 'Gil and I used to dig about in here for hours,' he said, as she passed out a broom, a scrubbing brush and a pile of old rags which would do for floor cloths. 'Somehow all that family junk seemed much more entertaining than the toys we were given.' He filled a bucket with hot water from the kettle, and absent-mindedly brushed some cobwebs off Elsie's dress. 'Curiosity's more dangerous as an adult, though. Perhaps the things you wish for aren't always the things you need.'

Wondering what he meant, she climbed the stairs and saw that there were two main bedrooms off the landing, while another door led up to the attic. Perhaps Stanley's dithering was contagious, but the bedroom where Annie obviously slept seemed too private, so she decided to start next door. This room was lighter and more cheerful, the first in which she could actually feel some of the warmth that Stanley always conjured up when talking of his childhood home. It was filled with simple furniture – a large double bed, a washstand, a wooden card table and a chest of drawers whose surface doubled as a bookshelf – and Elsie recognised enough of the books Stanley loved to know that the room must be the one he had shared with his brothers. She began to work, carefully lifting each book and odd memento, and as she wiped away the grime and dust, ingrained over years, she had the strange certainty that she was revealing something precious. It brought to mind her conversation with Hilda in the garden at Burghclere, and she wondered – if Hilda were here now, peeling back the layers of her husband's life – would she find the understanding she sought?

She got down on her hands and knees and began to scrub the wooden boards, absorbed in her thoughts. After a while, she heard footsteps bounding up the stairs and Stanley put his head round the door. 'I'm popping across the road for some bleach,' he said. 'That kitchen floor needs more than hot water.'

'Righto, but give me a hand with this first.' Together, they pushed the furniture by the window over to the side of the room and Elsie took up her brush again. 'The bleach?' she said as Stanley stood staring at the floor. 'I can't have you getting under my feet when we've got so much to do.'

Ignoring her, he knelt down and ran his fingers across the floorboards, where she could just make out faint splashes of blue and brown paint. 'They're still here,' he said. 'Don't get rid of them, will you?'

'Not if you don't want me to.'

He smiled, guessing from her tone that she required an explanation. 'They're from the painting I was working on when I went to war. I left them there for luck. As long as that painting stood against the wall on the other side of the bed, there was a chance that I'd be spared to finish it. I couldn't even begin to explain how I felt when I walked back into this room and turned it round, and there we were, looking at each other again. It was a miracle.'

He spoke of the painting as most men would a lover. 'What was it of?'

'Cookham Bridge, with the boatyard in the foreground. Almost the same view that Hilda's painting now, but set during swan-upping.'

'It must have been hard to leave it unfinished,' she said, knowing how intensely Stanley worked on a painting once it was begun.

'It was worse towards the end. I could hardly ask to be excused the big offensive while I nipped home to finish my work, but don't think it didn't cross my mind.' He touched the paint one last time, then stood up. 'The Behrends bought the picture eventually. You should ask to see it when you call on Rose.'

Elsie had noticed that Stanley's enthusiasm for talking about his paintings dwindled as time passed, and she wondered if he would ever dismiss *The Resurrection* in such a way; she imagined him talking to someone in London – 'you should go and see it if you're ever in Burghclere' – and the thought saddened her. 'You haven't taken many of your things,' she said, watching him as he looked round the room, assessing what had changed.

'No, I never got round to it. There wasn't room in Hampstead, and there doesn't seem much sense in filling Chapel View when it's only temporary.' He took a copy of *The Pickwick Papers* from the shelf. 'Pa started the Cookham Library, you know. He made a few pounds from some poetry and used the money to buy these so that people could borrow them from our front room.' The book looked as good as new, and he smiled. 'No one ever came, but at least he tried.'

'What was your father like?'

It was a vague question, but Stanley considered it carefully. 'He couldn't bear a minute to be wasted, and everything interested him – everything, and everybody. He could never understand people who weren't fascinated by the world, and he wanted to wring out every ounce of it.'

'Like father, like son.'

'I hope so. I've never met anyone with such a sense of wonder at the world.' Stanley's description of William Spencer sounded very different from the caricature that Patricia Preece had painted, and Elsie said so. 'You have to know someone, though, don't you?' he countered. 'We're all a bit odd on the outside.' He walked over to the table by the bed and opened the enormous family bible, and Elsie saw that a long list of names had been written on the flyleaf. 'Look how many of us there are,' Stanley said, 'and now there's only Annie left in Cookham. I thought we'd *always* be here.' He was quiet for a moment, then qualified the phrase. 'I thought *I'd* always be here.'

'You're not far away.'

The words sounded trite and Stanley dismissed them. 'It's not the same as being here. Patricia said that to me yesterday, and she was right.'

Elsie wasn't aware that Stanley had seen Patricia again, but she said nothing. Sensing that he wanted time alone in the room, she finished the floor quickly and collected her things. 'Why don't I fetch the bleach? Then I'll start on Annie's room, and you can get on with the kitchen when you're ready.'

He nodded, but followed her downstairs almost immediately, as if being left with the past was too big a risk. Annie was still outside, dozing in the sun, and Stanley stood at the window, watching her. 'It was Annie who encouraged me to draw,' he said. 'She taught us in the little school at the bottom of next door's garden, and she could see I felt a bit of a dunce during lessons, so she made me concentrate on what I was good at.'

'Do you remember your first picture?'

'It was a song thrush. I was very proud of it.' He smiled, thinking back. 'She gave everything up for us. There was no money for a professional nurse by the time Gil and I came along, and Ma relied on her. I think that must be my earliest memory: Annie putting us to bed each night. We'd go to sleep to the sound of her viola. She was as talented as the rest of us, but everything she loved had to wait for a few snatched minutes at the fag end of the day. No wonder she's bitter.'

'Are you sure she is?'

'Wouldn't you be?'

'Perhaps, but all I see is a woman who's lost her purpose. Stop feeling guilty and think about her.' He looked at her, surprised, but she didn't see the need to temper her words; Stanley responded well to straight talking and his tendency to put himself at the centre of any emotion was the thing about him that she could tolerate least. 'You're doing what you can for her now. That's what matters.'

'It is, isn't it?' He turned away from the window, having apparently resolved something in his own mind. 'We'll need to spend more time here, just to keep an eye on her. And I must get on with the chapel. We can't start to think about moving back properly until that's finished.'

'Moving back here?' Elsie asked before she could stop herself. 'Will Mrs Spencer be happy with that?'

'Of course. Why shouldn't she be?' He took his keys from the table and headed for the hallway. 'We'll *all* be happy here. You'll have to come too, of course. We couldn't manage without you now.'

The front door closed and she watched him cross the road to the stores, surprised to find that the long-awaited promise of a future with the Spencers wasn't quite as reassuring as she had expected.

16

The holiday extended to four weeks, then five, and it was decided that the Carlines would join them for the last few days, staying in a house near the river. Stanley and Hilda left early one morning to collect them, and Shirin – excited at the prospect of a visit from her uncle and grandmother – insisted on going as well, leaving Elsie to enjoy her peace and quiet. She cleaned the cottage from top to bottom, baked enough food to keep Annie going for the next few days, then settled down in the sunny courtyard garden to write a letter home. Before she knew it, the morning had slipped through her fingers and the distant sound of the church clock sent her hurrying to the high street before the shops closed for their half day.

She dropped the food off at Fernlea, pleased to see that the kitchen was still tidy, and crossed the road to McKay's. There was a delivery van parked outside and she tried to recall where she had seen it before, then recognised it as the vehicle which had overtaken them on their way here, nearly forcing Stanley into the ditch. The driver was standing at the counter, chatting, and Elsie noticed him watching her as she browsed the shelves. The shop had its own special smell, an enticing blend of coffee, cheese and home-cured ham, and she took her time, relishing the luxury of choice. When she had what she needed, she took her basket to the till, hoping that the delivery man might finish his conversation and leave, but he seemed in no hurry.

'Afternoon, Miss Munday,' the grocer said. 'How are you today? And Mr and Mrs Spencer?'

'Very well, thank you.' Elsie had soon learnt that her connection to Stanley earned her a warm welcome in the high street, partly from loyalty to an old Cookham family and partly from the notoriety that came with his fame. 'And you?'

'Not so bad. Can I get you anything else?'

'Half a pound of bacon and some tea, please.' She looked meaningfully at her companion by the counter. 'If I'm not interrupting anything.'

'Course you're not. Ken here was just idling away the time on his way back to Maidenhead.'

'Ken here' grinned at her, and she noticed that it transformed an otherwise ordinary face into something more memorable. He reminded her of a homely Gary Cooper, not bad looking if you liked that sort of thing. 'Ken Beckford,' he said with a wink. 'Pleased to meet you. It's obviously true what they say about Monday's child. Must be my lucky day.'

Elsie suppressed a smile and gave him a look which she hoped implied a weary familiarity with that particular joke. 'Perhaps if you idled less and set out for Maidenhead in good time, the rest of us might be safer on the roads,' she said, satisfied to see that the comment wrong-footed him. 'Do you remember the car you nearly ran into the ditch a few weeks ago? You're lucky I'm still here to take a compliment.'

Ken Beckford took his teasing good-naturedly, and Elsie liked him all the more for it. 'It's whoever was driving needs to be reported,' he said with a laugh, 'pootling along at ten miles an hour. Mind you, if I'd known there was precious cargo on board, I'd have been more careful. The least I can do to make amends is carry your shopping home.' He picked up her basket, giving Elsie no chance to refuse his offer even if she had wanted to. She paid for her groceries and led the way out of the shop. 'Where do you live?' he asked, shielding his eyes from the midday sun.

'Malt House Cottages, just off School Lane, but we're only there for the summer. Mr Spencer has a sister in Cookham who needed help with the house, so he's brought the family here for a painting holiday.'

'A whole summer of decorating? Doesn't sound like much of a holiday to me.'

Elsie threw back her head and laughed. 'Not that sort of painting! Mr Spencer's an artist. He's got pictures in posh London galleries.' Ken turned scarlet with embarrassment, and Elsie felt sorry for him. 'It's my fault for not explaining properly,' she said. 'How were you supposed to know?' They were nearly at the war memorial and Elsie slowed down, reluctant to give up his company so soon 'There's never a dull moment with the Spencers,' she said, 'so it's nice to have a bit of ordinary, humdrum conversation for a change.' This time it was her turn to look embarrassed. 'I didn't mean…'

'I'll take it as a compliment. So where do they live the rest of the time? Not too far away, I hope.'

'Burghclere. Mr Spencer's painting a chapel there.'

'Of course he is.'

Elsie laughed and began to explain, but she was distracted by a lorry coming down School Lane from the Maidenhead end. It was towing a large maroon car and, as it drew closer, she could just make out the Spencers and the Carlines squashed into the front seat next to the driver. 'Oh dear, that's them,' she said in horror. 'What on earth's happened?'

'At least you can't blame *me* this time.'

The lorry pulled into the kerb and everyone got out. 'Thank God they're not hurt,' Elsie said, relieved to see Shirin in her mother's arms. They watched as Hilda helped a visibly shaken Mrs Carline to the gate while Stanley oversaw the unloading of the car. 'He looks furious, doesn't he?'

'That's one word for it.'

As if to prove her point, Stanley delivered a healthy kick to one of the rear tyres. 'You can drive the bloody thing from now on,' he shouted at Hilda as he stormed past her into the house. 'I never wanted it in the first place.'

'I'd better go,' Elsie said. 'It's going to be a difficult afternoon.'

She went to take her basket, but Ken held on to it. 'Would you like to come out with me one night next week?' he asked. 'We could go to the pictures or have a bite to eat.'

'I won't be here. We're leaving on Monday.'

'That doesn't matter. Burghclere's not so far in the scheme of things.'

'I don't suppose it is, the way you drive.'

He smiled. 'Is that a yes?'

'All right then.'

She took her shopping and headed for the house. 'Where will I find you?' Ken called after her. 'I don't even know your first name.'

Elsie turned and winked at him. 'It's Elsie, and you'll find me if you want to.'

17

Moor Thatch sat quietly in the evening sunshine as the village put the finishing touches to its day. A few stragglers still idled on the Moor, but most of the Saturday bustle had died down and people were moving inside. Soon a light or two would appear in the windows of the Crown Hotel, and even Elsie – who stubbornly clung to summer each year – had to admit that the nights were drawing in. She stopped a few doors down, by the crooked cottage on the corner of the lane, and took the note out of her bag. Left to her own devices, she would have slipped it through Patricia Preece's letterbox and fled, but Stanley had insisted that she wait for an answer so she opened the gate and followed the path round to the front porch, trying not to stare too overtly in case she was being watched; in any case, the dark leaded windows were impenetrable without help from a light inside. The door was made of heavy oak and studded with iron, more fitting in a remote Elizabethan manor house than a village green cottage, and Elsie felt less sure of her welcome than ever. Reluctantly, she lifted her hand to the knocker.

The door was opened by a mousy little thing and Elsie announced herself. 'I've come from the Spencers,' she said, feeling almost indecently vigorous next to the timid bag of nerves who scuttled round Moor Thatch. 'They've sent a note for Miss Preece and Miss Hepworth, and they'd appreciate an answer tonight.' She held out the note, but the girl had already disappeared, and

Elsie was left looking into a surprisingly small hallway with lots of rooms leading off it.

The help returned almost immediately and Elsie was shown through to the sitting room. It was surprisingly light, with views to the Moor and a pretty rear garden as well as two smaller windows to the side; the room was tasteful but not ostentatious, with comfortable furniture and a number of expensive-looking vases and figurines which would surely strike the fear of God into anyone who had to dust them. Dorothy Hepworth stood by a red-brick fireplace, a short, heavily built woman with light-brown hair parted at the side and smoothed to her head. She wore a fawn-coloured skirt and cardigan, neat but dowdy and far too old for her, chosen – or so Elsie thought – to help her fade into the background. Patricia sat in a chair by the window with a shawl around her shoulders, her dress a more vivid shade of the greens beyond the glass. She looked at her visitor, waiting for her to speak, and Elsie wondered if it was churlish of her to note with satisfaction that Patricia had a slight cast in her left eye, one small imperfection in an otherwise flawless face. 'The Spencers and the Carlines are having a picnic in Bellrope Meadow tomorrow,' she said, seeing little point in waiting while her hosts read through the letter. 'It'll be their last day in Cookham, and they'd very much like you both to join them.'

She glanced at Dorothy, just in time to see a mixture of annoyance and relief pass across her face, but Patricia simply smiled. 'We'd love to come,' she said, without any consultation. 'What time should we be there?'

'It's all in the note.' Elsie placed the envelope on the mantelpiece next to the service bell. 'I'll tell Mr and Mrs Spencer to expect you.'

The house was still empty when she got back. Stanley and Shirin were out with Mrs Carline, and Hilda had been gone all afternoon, keen to finish the painting she was working on before they left the village. The air had grown chilly, and Elsie took a cardigan from

Hilda's wardrobe and walked down to the river to see if there was anything else she needed. The tables on the Ferry hotel's lawns were busy, and she paused under the bridge as she saw Hilda working just beyond the boatyard. She watched unseen for several minutes, noticing how content Hilda seemed; the restlessness that had been so much a part of her was entirely gone now, replaced by a new sense of purpose in both her work and her family. At last, she looked up from the canvas.

'That's kind of you,' she said, beckoning Elsie over. 'I hadn't realised how cold I was.' She stood to put the cardigan on, still looking appraisingly at the painting. 'Are the Preeces coming tomorrow?'

The term was an easy plural that Stanley had adopted for the couple, although it implied a unity which certainly hadn't been evident during Elsie's brief visit. 'Yes, they said they would.'

'Good. I can't make my mind up about Dorothy, but Patricia seems nice and it's useful for Stanley to have someone to talk to who hasn't heard it all before.' She glanced conspiratorially at Elsie. 'It takes the strain off the rest of us.'

Elsie nodded, although she couldn't share Hilda's enthusiasm for the other women's company. 'How's the painting coming along?' she asked, changing the subject. 'Will you finish it before we leave?'

'I think I just have. Come and look.'

Elsie walked round to the other side of the easel. The painting was stunning, a tapestry of rich greens and browns dominated by Cookham Bridge and the lush trees beyond, their colours somehow intensified in the reflections on the water. In the foreground, wooden punts fanned out from Turk's boatyard while swans gathered by the bank, and a black dog stared impatiently back along the river path, waiting for an unseen figure to appear. On the bridge itself, a young child gazed down on the scene through the elaborate ironwork while her mother stood aside to allow some horses to pass, their carts piled high with sacks. The whole picture spoke of a remarkable serenity, and it seemed to Elsie to capture perfectly the leisurely peace of late summer, the happiness of the past few weeks. 'It's beautiful,' she said, unable to take her eyes from it. 'Really beautiful.'

'Do you think so?'

'Yes, I do.' It struck her, looking at the canvas, that there was something very different about Hilda's attitude to the figures in her landscapes. When Stanley painted people, it was as if they were joyfully connected to their surroundings, be it the stark brown corridors of Beaufort or a street in his beloved Cookham, but the figures on the bridge seemed incidental to the scene. Stanley had spent much of the holiday working on a picture of the old Tarry Stone which stood at the head of the high street. It was important to the village, apparently, but Elsie couldn't understand why anyone would want a painting of it, no matter how cleverly he had captured the stone's texture. There was something missing in that deserted background of his, something human, whereas Hilda's painting would have been just as complete had the bridge been empty. She couldn't analyse it any further, and she struggled to understand exactly what she meant, but she knew somehow that this was at the heart of the conflict in their marriage. 'I do love it,' she said, realising that she had been quiet for a long time. 'You'd never be far from here if you had this to look at.'

Hilda looked pleased. 'I hope Stanley will like it. He loves this view.' She paused, suddenly unsure of herself. 'Elsie, there's something I want to tell you, but you have to promise to keep it to yourself. I don't want to talk to Stan about it until I'm absolutely certain.' Elsie nodded and braced herself, waiting for an awkward question about how Stanley spent his afternoons or what she thought of his liking for Patricia. 'I think Shirin's going to have a little brother or sister.'

The announcement was so at odds with what Elsie had been expecting that it took her a moment to catch up. 'What? But that's wonderful news!'

'Do you think so? I was so happy at first. It seemed like a miracle, but then…'

She tailed off, and Elsie tried to make sense of the conflicting expressions in her face. 'But then what?'

'But then I started to think about the last time. I don't know what Stanley will say. I'm afraid he won't be pleased.'

'Why not? He *loves* Shirin.'

'Of course he does. I didn't mean that he wouldn't love another baby, but it was difficult between *us* after Shirin was born. I didn't have any energy and I didn't want to work…'

'Lots of women feel like that after they've had a little one.'

'But they're not married to Stanley Spencer.' She gave a half-hearted smile. 'He hates it when I'm not painting, you know that. It nearly destroyed us, but this summer has been different. I'm starting to work again, and Stanley and I – well…' She put a hand on her belly and blushed. 'We're obviously getting on again, better than we ever have. I don't want to lose that. I can't go through those terrible times again.'

'But things are different now. If you and Mr Spencer are happier, you'll cope better. And the second baby isn't such a shock as the first, or so my mother always says. You'll be more prepared, and you'll have your family round you. Shirin will love having someone to boss about.'

'She will, won't she?'

'And I'll do whatever I can.'

'Thank you,' Hilda said. 'I can't tell you what a difference that makes, but promise me you won't say anything about the baby, not even to my mother. I don't want everyone to start making a fuss, just in case I'm wrong.'

'Mrs Carline and I aren't exactly on heart-to-heart terms. I've never known anyone to speak so little and say so much.' Hilda laughed, and Elsie noticed how it transformed her face: some women were attractive whatever their mood, others couldn't be helped by the broadest of smiles, but Hilda was one of those people whose beauty was as tied to her emotions as the moon to the tides. 'I don't think you're wrong, though, do you?' she said.

Hilda shook her head. 'No, I don't. Oh, it's such a relief to think that it might be all right. Perhaps another child will give Stanley the incentive he needs to finish the chapel, then we can all move back to London and find a proper family home. You'll love Hampstead, Elsie. It's so full of life.'

It was the second time in a week that Elsie's permanence with the Spencers had been taken for granted, and she wondered which version of her future would come to fruition. She smiled at Hilda, masking her concerns, and hoped that she would never have to choose.

18

Elsie had worried that they might be testing the patience of the season by planning a picnic in the third week of September, but Sunday dawned bright and cheerful. She got up earlier than usual to prepare the food, and moved around the kitchen as quietly as possible, trying not to wake an already over-excited Shirin. By eight o'clock, everything was ready and she added freshly cut sandwiches, salad and hard-boiled eggs to the dishes she had made in advance. There was far too much, but the one thing she had missed while working for the Spencers was the grander cooking that a big house required; anything left over would always find a home at Fernlea.

After breakfast, Stanley and his brother-in-law went ahead to choose a spot, then Mrs Carline and Shirin were stationed to guard the belongings as a series of trips to and from the houses was made, transporting picnic baskets, chairs, blankets and umbrellas. Bellrope Meadow was a long, wedge-shaped stretch of land between the church and the river, popular with families after the morning service. The grass was a delicate pale yellow, exhausted from months of heat, and the strongest colours came from summer dresses as people sat around in their Sunday best, talking or looking at the river. The church tower peeped through tall chestnut trees, and Elsie followed the line of the village away to the left, pleased by her familiarity with a place she had grown fond of; downriver, she could just see Cookham Bridge, and she wondered if Hilda had shown Stanley her painting yet, or whether it would be saved as a gift to go with her news, a symbol of her determination not to let another child come between them.

When the food had been safely transported, she sat down at the edge of the group and chatted with Doris, the maid who had come with the Carlines from Hampstead. She was a nice woman, easy to talk to, and Elsie took advantage of the gaps in their conversation to study Hilda's family more closely. Mrs Carline must have been in her sixties but she seemed older, trapped in an earlier era by her preference for heavy skirts and hats which threw her face into shadow. Richard was younger than Hilda by six or seven years but he had her features: a well-defined jaw, full mouth and heavy-lidded, deep-brown eyes. As a family, they talked incessantly, speaking over each other and changing the subject at random, and she wondered if it was the solitary nature of their painting that made them behave like this in company, a welcome release from hours spent in silent contemplation of their own imaginations. Stanley held his own but had to fight for the limelight, and Elsie tried to imagine what it might have been like if the two families had met while the parents were in their heyday – the Spencers with their untutored eccentricities, the Carlines with their intellect and fiercely held opinions. It was not a household in which she would have gladly worked.

There were three other men in the party, visiting from London for the day. As the buzz of conversation grew louder, fuelled by good food and wine, she noticed the Preeces coming through the gate from the churchyard. Patricia looked shy and uncertain, while Dorothy had the air of someone who would rather be elsewhere. Stanley jumped up when he saw them and met them halfway across the grass, and Hilda kissed them both. 'I'm so glad you could come,' she said. 'Here, let me introduce you.' Patricia and Dorothy shook hands with everyone, and their introduction to Mrs Carline reeked so much of a court presentation to the old queen that Elsie half expected them to curtsey. She handed more food around, watching with interest as Patricia lost some of her apprehensiveness and took her share of the conversation, which was almost exclusively about art. By contrast, Dorothy said very little.

'Dick wrote a piece on the chapel for *The Studio* magazine last year,' Stanley said, helping himself to more bread and passing the basket to Patricia.

Richard smiled and turned to the new arrivals, giving them the full benefit of his boyish good looks. 'Have you been to look at the paintings?'

'Not yet,' Patricia said. 'Stanley's promised to show us round as soon as he's back. I expect there's a lot of press interest in the project?'

Stanley shook his head. 'Not really. The Behrends don't want a fuss.'

Patricia looked surprised. 'But surely you can't be happy with that?'

'Why not?'

'Because it's years of work. You must want all that effort to get you somewhere?' Stanley shrugged and Elsie noticed that Hilda was looking at Patricia with a new interest. 'Aren't you worried about being so isolated from the mainstream, especially after all the publicity you had for the Tate *Resurrection*? You shouldn't hide yourself away painting something that no one will see.'

Elsie looked round, noticing that most of the party was in agreement with Patricia; only Stanley seemed to take issue with her. 'The Behrends are paying the bills,' he said. 'As long as they don't interfere, they can be as private as they like.'

'Oh, for a generous patron and the luxury of painting what doesn't sell.' Patricia smiled to take the edge off her words. 'You're a lucky man and I'm only jealous. Dorothy and I have to take what we can get. Portraits, still lifes, landscapes if we're lucky.'

'There's nothing wrong with that,' Hilda said. 'Our father was much the same. He trained in Paris, then set up a studio in

124

the Fulham Road and took any commission he could to earn a living.'

'But he had a family to keep,' Mrs Carline added. 'Then he had a picture accepted by the Academy.' There was a real pride in her voice and Elsie listened with interest. She knew little about Hilda's father, except that he had died suddenly while the family was in Italy, but she had always got the impression of a solid family man, who – very much like Stanley's father – had wanted his children to succeed in whatever made them happy. 'He always had work after that,' Mrs Carline continued. 'You should come to Hampstead and see the house. Lots of his pictures are still there – his and the children's.'

'And yours, Mother.'

'You paint as well, Mrs Carline?'

The question was Dorothy's, the first time that she had taken part in the conversation. 'What else could I do in this family?' Mrs Carline said, holding up her hands, and everyone laughed.

'It must have been wonderful to have such encouragement,' Patricia said wistfully.

'It wasn't quite as rosy as it sounds,' Hilda admitted. 'I'm sure our father would have chosen less precarious paths for us, but we beat him down eventually.'

'What about your parents, Miss Preece?' Richard asked. 'Did they encourage you?'

'Oh please, call me Patricia. No, I'm afraid not. My father was a lieutenant-colonel in the Welch Fusiliers and Dorothy's parents are in the woollen industry. Neither of us had any encouragement before art school, and since then we've encouraged each other.'

'I could introduce you to some galleries next time you're in town, if that would help?' Richard offered. 'Between us, we've got a number of useful contacts. You too, of course, Miss Hepworth.'

Patricia smiled, and Elsie felt an unexpected wave of gratitude to Hilda's brother for distracting her from Stanley. 'That would be very kind of you,' Patricia said, looking at Dorothy. 'We'd both appreciate it.'

'More tea?' There was a clipped tone to Stanley's voice as he put himself between the Preeces and Richard Carline, waving the flask like a weapon. He had been very much the outsider in the preceding conversation, even more so than Dorothy, and he seemed determined to make up ground. 'Patricia was in Cookham before the war,' he said, sitting down next to her. 'It's extraordinary how many memories we both have of that time.' They began to talk about the village, going over some of the ground that they had first discussed in the Copper Kettle, and Elsie was struck by how much significance Stanley gave to what was, in effect, a coincidence; in his mind, it seemed to give him and Patricia a history which they didn't actually have. It was strange, she thought; usually he resented anyone taking an interest in Cookham, as if the glories of the village were his alone to celebrate, but he was more than happy to share them with Patricia.

If Richard noticed Stanley's resentment, it only served to spur him on. Sensing that his offer of an introduction to valuable London galleries had disposed Patricia kindly in his favour, he suggested a walk and was graciously accepted. 'That would be lovely, wouldn't it, Dorothy?' she said, standing up and brushing some grass from her dress. Elsie could see from Richard's face that he hadn't intended to extend the invitation, but he recovered well. Was Dorothy used to being Patrica's afterthought, she wondered, the unnamed lodger in the 'Preece' household?

'She might be right about the chapel, Stan,' Hilda said when they had gone. 'Perhaps you should talk to Mary about it.'

'I wish you'd call me Stanley,' he said irritably, watching the trio walk off across the grass. 'You know I hate my name being shortened.'

'I don't know anything of the sort,' Hilda said, compounding her original sin by laughing. She resumed her conversation with her mother, and Elsie took advantage of the lull in the picnic to clear away the empty dishes. She packed them into one of the hampers and walked back to the cottage, glad of some time to herself. Hilda's words from yesterday weighed heavily on her, even though they had been meant reassuringly; having sampled a small taste of Hampstead life, she sincerely doubted that she would ever come to love or even tolerate it, and this, coupled with an instinctive feeling that a city was not for her, made her worry about her future more than ever. She felt at home in Cookham, and not all of its charms were connected to the Spencers. Her meeting with Ken might come to nothing, but she had thought about him often and the memory of his smile as she waved goodbye had lingered. She would be disappointed if he didn't look her up in Burghclere as he had promised.

By the time she got back to Bellrope Meadow, the walkers had rejoined the picnic. Richard was sitting with his family and friends again, while Stanley held court with Patricia and Dorothy, talking about the chapel. There was no sign of Doris, and Elsie guessed that she had returned to the Carlines' lodgings in the high street to pack for their departure the following day. She slowed her pace, feeling awkward about where to sit and who to talk to, but Shirin came to her rescue by summoning her to look at the drawing she had made. She lifted the little girl on to her lap, chattering away to her while keeping half an ear on the conversation that Hilda was having with her brother. 'They seem *very* close, though, don't you think?' Richard said, and Elsie glanced nervously towards Patricia and Stanley, wondering what Hilda would say.

'Of course they are. They've known each other for years.'

'Mmm, so I gather.' Elsie breathed out, realising that she had misread the comment, but the rest of the conversation made no sense to her. 'That wasn't quite what I meant,' Richard continued. 'It seems to me that they've brought a little too much of the Paris lifestyle back with them. You can take the girls out of the Left Bank...' Hilda's reply was lost in a squeal from Shirin as a grasshopper chose that moment to land on her leg. Elsie brushed the insect off, trying to work out what the words meant; there was a smirk in Richard's voice that worried her and she couldn't shake off the conviction that Stanley was making a fool of himself. At least they were leaving tomorrow. Back at the chapel, absorbed in his work and with a new baby on the way, things might settle down.

'That was a wonderful picnic, Elsie,' Hilda said, passing her mother the last of the salmon parcels. 'Will you take a photograph of us all before we clear away?'

'Of course I will.' Elsie took the camera and listened while Hilda explained how it worked. Years later, she found she didn't need to look at the physical photograph to bring its composition to mind: Hilda at the edge of the group, shielded by her mother, while Stanley knelt between Patricia and Dorothy, staring back at his wife as if seeing her for the first time; and Shirin in the middle of it all, holding a toy fishing net and smiling up at the lens, oblivious to the frailties of the adult world around her.

19

Stanley was restless in the days that followed their return to Burghclere. His moods ebbed and flowed, irritable one moment and exuberant the next, and Elsie had never known him to be so impatient with his work. He seemed unable to cope with the isolation of the chapel and was forever popping back to the house on one pretext or another, as if Cookham had reawakened a sociable side of his nature that he now couldn't live without. He talked constantly of Patricia Preece to anyone who would listen, and it wouldn't have surprised her to learn that the painted soldiers on the chapel walls were regularly treated to a monologue on Patricia's charms.

She glanced up at the kitchen clock, knowing that if she didn't soon head Stanley off with a flask and something to eat, he would be back at the table, getting in her way. She gave the copper pan she was holding a final polish, then cut some bread and cheese and hurried out across the field to the railway cutting. It was a bright day but cold, with a clear, keen air that Elsie found exhilarating. She crossed the track and climbed the bank on the other side, noticing that the hedgerows teemed with creatures foraging for the end of summer.

She paused at the open door, familiar now with the way that *The Resurrection* ambushed her emotions and still not immune to its power. Stanley stood with his back to her, where light from the windows fell naturally on to his canvas. He was working on one of the arched paintings and seemed at last to be making good progress. She knocked and he waved his hand without turning around. 'I hope you've brought plenty. I could eat a hayrick.'

'How do you know who it is?' she asked. 'Didn't your mother ever tell you not to take a girl for granted?'

'My mother told me lots of things, but I don't remember that being one of them. Anyway, I prefer to think of it as having faith.' This time he did turn around, and beamed when he saw the basket. 'And you never let me down. Hilda isn't doing too much, is she? She needs her rest now.'

Other than showing a solicitous concern for Hilda's health, Stanley didn't seem much altered by the news that they were to have another child. Elsie's congratulations had been warmly received, but in much the same way as he would have welcomed a favourable comment on his paintings, and she wondered if Hilda's concerns were unfounded or if she had simply found a way to reassure him. 'Mrs Spencer's upstairs writing her letters,' she said, 'so there's nothing to worry about there.'

'That's a matter of opinion,' Stanley muttered. 'A few more hard-earned pounds waved off to Christian Science.'

Peace had reigned in the Spencer household for several months. The only real issue that remained between them was Hilda's reliance on her Christian Science practitioners, to whom she would sometimes send the money that Stanley had given her for clothes or housekeeping. As the person who had to shop with what was left, Elsie could understand his objections, although she supposed it was little different to passing the plate round in church. She said nothing on the subject, knowing that Stanley was perfectly capable of voicing his own grievances. 'I'll pour you some tea,' she offered. He took a handkerchief out of his pocket to wipe round an old mug, but she stopped him. 'No need for that. I've brought you a clean one.'

She poured the tea into the jubilee mug and he stared at her in delight. 'You brought it back?'

Elsie nodded. 'It was only gathering dust with Annie. And I pinched this for you as well.' She handed over the brass plate from Fernlea's gate, with his father's name now polished and gleaming. 'It practically fell off in my hand. I thought it might help you feel more at home while you're here.'

He got up and hugged her. 'Elsie, you're a wonder! How do you always know what I need before I do?'

She shrugged. 'I suppose I just think about what I'd want myself.' He propped the small gold rectangle against his easel, and Elsie looked closely for the first time at the half-finished picture. 'Where's this one going? Up there?'

She nodded to the remaining empty space on the north wall, but Stanley shook his head. 'No, I'm putting a kit inspection there. This one's called *Reveille*. It's for the other side of the altar.'

'On the home straight, then.' The first painting on the south side was set in a bell-shaped tent which perfectly suited the arch of the canvas. Three soldiers were dressing under mosquito nets suspended from rings in the tent's roof, and Elsie moved closer to get the full effect of the fine mesh netting which seemed to billow out from the canvas. She had no idea how a paintbrush could create something so real, but she understood now why Stanley's progress had seemed slow: this must have taken an age. The man on the left was emerging fully clothed from his net, but there was something exposed and vulnerable about the bare skin of his hand. As if to emphasise the danger, his fingers pointed upwards to a sinister swarm of mosquitoes gathered at the top of the tent. 'You had malaria, didn't you?' she said.

'Yes, several times.'

'Was it terrible?'

'Some bouts were worse than others. You never knew when it was going to hit you, so you never felt truly safe. It could lie dormant for months and recur at any time, like it did with Mary's brother Hal.' He finished his tea and came to look at the picture with her. 'I'm going to set one of the small panels along this side in a malaria ward. I remember how cosy it was. That was the worst part: being ill so far from home, and wondering if you'd come through it. That and the guilt.'

'Why guilt?'

'Because you're not fighting or doing what you were sent there to do.'

Elsie nodded, still fascinated by the way in which the mosquito nets obscured the men underneath. The soft webs of material made the figures pale and ghostly, like spirits ascending to heaven, and to Elsie's eyes the link between one life and the next was much more obvious here than in the actual Resurrection. On the right-hand side – drawn in but yet to be painted – a more robust man sat shaving in the corner, while another group of soldiers looked on through the open tent flap.

'They're coming to tell their friends the war's over,' Stanley said, pointing to the pencilled figures. He turned the easel around so that the canvas was more in line with where it would eventually sit. 'See? If you imagine it when it's in position, they're looking towards *The Resurrection*, just like the soldier in the opposite painting. The pictures talk to each other. It's as if the sergeant over there is standing on the dugout, listening to what the chaps in the tent have got to say.'

If it occasionally seemed to Elsie that Stanley painted scenes at random, she had no doubt now that there was a design to the chapel which went much deeper than a simple ordering of events. She remembered him telling her once that he painted things as God had created them – landscape first, people last – and now he had explained the altar paintings, their arrangement seemed just as logical. She realised that she had never really taken much notice of the final arched picture on the north wall. It had been painted in the dark days of the previous winter, when she didn't often visit the chapel, and in any case it wasn't a painting that pushed itself forward: its colours were muted, and although it shared the beiges and browns of *The Resurrection*, it was dwarfed by the altar painting's size. Soldiers stood in trenches with their equipment laid out ready on the side of the dugout, waiting for the order from their sergeant. Their bodies looked weary, their faces anxious and uncertain, and it was the only painting so far to hint at the fear and tension of war. Coils of barbed wire encroached from the top of the canvas, like the most ominous of black skies, and yet the figure in the foreground to whom Stanley pointed – the one looking back at *The Resurrection* – seemed calm and at peace. 'What's his name?' she asked.

'Challoner, but we called him Challenger because it seemed to suit him. He was a splendid chap, so very brave.' She looked again at the soldier – turning his pith helmet in his hands, his sergeant's uniform camouflaged with fronds of fern – and wondered why the familiar accolades which tripped so readily off thousands of tongues sounded new and sincere when Stanley used them. 'Whenever there was a night of heavy shelling, he'd lie on the parapet while we stood shaking in the trenches. All the men loved him.'

There was a sadness in his voice which already answered her question, but she asked it anyway. 'What happened to him?'

'He was killed in action in Salonika. We buried him just as we remembered him on that parapet – on his side, defiant and watching over us.' With a sigh, he turned the easel back to where it had stood originally. 'Painting that picture brought it all back. I hadn't intended it to be so bleak, but it was terrifying – that moment at dawn when we were called from the trenches, expecting an attack. I used to wonder what it would be like if we came out one morning and found that it was over.'

'It happened eventually, I suppose.'

'Not for Challenger, but I can give it to him here.'

In the distance, Elsie heard a car door closing, followed by footsteps on the path outside, and Mary Behrend appeared in the doorway. 'Ah Stanley, I've found you. I dropped by a couple of times yesterday but there was no one here.'

Stanley showed no sign of guilt at having been caught absent without leave. 'What can I do for you, Mary?' he asked.

'I wanted to invite you and Hilda to lunch on Saturday. Ottoline Morrell's coming for the day and she's very much hoping you'll show her the chapel in the afternoon.'

'I can't I'm afraid. I'll be in Cookham.'

'But you've only just come back.'

Stanley shrugged. 'There are things I need to keep an eye on. I'll be going more regularly from now on.'

'Not too often, I hope.' She spoke lightly, but Elsie saw her glance anxiously at the blank walls. 'There's still a lot of work to do.'

'Isn't there?' He said it with enthusiasm, as if the words represented an opportunity rather than a concern. 'I've been thinking about the side walls. We're going to have a camp scene on the north wall, as you know, but I thought we could also have some men carrying stones to build a road. If I include a row of tents about two-thirds of the way along, each scene will have its own identity.' He was gesturing at the space above the arches as he spoke and Elsie had no doubt that the picture was already there in his mind, fully formed on the wall like a still from a film.

Stanley carried on, outlining his plans for the south wall, but Mary Behrend wasn't listening. Elsie watched as she walked over to the new painting and stared at it. She raised her hand, and for a moment Elsie thought that she was going to touch the canvas, but her fingers hovered an inch or two away from it, where Stanley had painted the gathering of mosquitoes. There was an expression of such intense sadness on her face that Elsie had to look away, reluctant to intrude on a private grief; she couldn't begin to imagine what personal torment Mary Behrend went through whenever she thought of her brother's death. 'They're the only weapons you've painted,' she said quietly. 'So far, in the whole of the chapel, those mosquitoes are the only things that can kill.'

'What?' Stanley looked at his patron in surprise, then understood what she meant. 'Yes,' he said. 'Yes, I suppose they are.' He went to stand next to her, and they looked at the painting in silence. '"He that loseth his life for my sake shall save it",' Stanley said eventually. 'I felt that very strongly when I was out there. We all did. And I feel it now, whenever I'm here. I couldn't do this if I didn't.'

She nodded but didn't seem particularly reassured by his words, and Elsie wondered if they had brought Stanley any comfort when his brother Sydney died. Mrs Behrend pulled herself together and picked up her bag. 'Well, it's a shame about Saturday but do let me know if your plans for the weekend change. Ottoline would be thrilled to see you.' She smiled and nodded a goodbye to Elsie. 'But if you really can't come, Louis and I will show her round and you'll have to rely on us to do you justice.'

A flicker of annoyance passed across Stanley's face, and Elsie thought that he was going to say something; she had often heard him insist that the work spoke for itself. Wisely, he chose to keep quiet and only said goodbye. Elsie waited until she heard the car start, then said: 'This woman sounds important. Can't you go to Cookham another weekend?'

Stanley's reserves of patience were never generous, and Mary Behrend had exhausted them all. 'Not you as well,' he said, throwing up his hands in exasperation. 'First Hilda, then Mary and now you. I thought you *wanted* me to pay more attention to Annie.'

'It's not Annie you're going for, though, is it?'

He looked at her defiantly. 'What are you trying to say, Elsie? And remind me again why it's your place to say it?'

Elsie knew that she had already overstepped the mark, but she pressed on regardless. 'Invite Miss Preece here on Saturday if you must see her.'

Stanley went back to the easel and picked up his brush, effectively dismissing her. She saw the muscles tighten in his face as he tried to control his anger. 'I need to get on. I'll be back for supper at six and I don't want to be disturbed again until then.'

20

It was only a matter of time before Patricia returned one of Stanley's frequent visits to Cookham. 'The Preeces are coming today,' he announced one morning at breakfast. 'Will you bring them over when they get here?'

Elsie looked at him in horror. 'Why are they coming here? Can't they go straight to the chapel?'

'They might want to freshen up after the journey and you can make them a cup of tea. I said you'd meet their train, but Patricia thinks they can find their own way.'

Was there no end to the woman's talents? Elsie thought. Art, charm and walking three hundred yards without a chaperone. Stanley frowned at her, clearly reading her thoughts, and she chose a more constructive argument. 'The workmen are coming to mend the grate today, Mr Spencer. It'll be chaos.'

'How was I supposed to know that?'

'Because you called them in yourself! Last week, remember? When we had smoke coming out of the skirting board?'

'Ah yes. Well, it can't be changed now and I'm sure Patricia and Dorothy won't mind.'

'That's all right, then,' Elsie muttered under her breath, her temper made worse by a niggling indigestion. 'There's Shirin to think about, too,' she added, tickling the little girl's chin. 'Mrs Spencer won't be back from Hampstead until this afternoon.'

'Yes, I know.' He wiped the last piece of bread round his plate and stood up. 'You'll cope, Elsie. You always do. And don't worry about lunch. Mary's invited us to Grey House.'

He left and she cleared away after him, hoping that if the kitchen was already tidy, the workmen would be more inclined to keep it that way. It was a folly of optimism, and within minutes of their arrival they were making themselves thoroughly at home. 'Let me move the clothes line away from the range,' Elsie said, as they dumped their tools on to the hearthrug. 'You don't want that in your way while you're trying to work.'

'Don't bother, love,' said the one called Oliver, cheerfully wrenching the fender off to get a better look at the job. He was obviously in charge, an older man with a military-style moustache and brushes bulging from the pocket of his apron. 'We've worked round worse than a few wet socks.'

To prove the point, his workmate ducked underneath the clothes line and began to grout out the cement, half disappearing up the chimney like an unseasonal Santa Claus. The damp socks lay neatly across his back, a child's pair in blue and an adult's in red, as if father and daughter were tiptoeing guiltily from the room, and Elsie wished that she could follow. Feeling unusually helpless in her own kitchen, she watched as Oliver held the saw level with the mantel-piece and carefully examined its teeth, wondering what on earth he intended to use it for. 'Would you like a cup of tea?' she asked, resigned to a difficult morning, and then, when he looked doubt-fully at the stove: 'It's all right. I can boil the water next door.'

She hung the kettle over some sticks in the dining room grate, as Stanley had at new year, and waited for it to boil. When she returned with the tray, Shirin seemed to have been hired as a second apprentice and was obviously in her element. Spurred on by the activity around her, she had picked up one of Elsie's gaiters and was holding it straight out in front of her, copying Oliver's intent examination of the saw. As the workmen surrounded themselves with a circle of nails, screws and obscure bits of metal, Shirin found her own equivalent in the basket of clothes pegs which she emptied on to the floor. She was absorbed in attaching them at regular intervals to the gaiter, and Elsie had to smile as she handed out the tea. She sank down on a kitchen chair, bending to collect the pegs that Shirin had discarded, but the pain in her side left her short of breath and slightly nauseous. She tried to recall what she had eaten and hoped that Stanley wasn't suffering in the same way; he wouldn't thank her for putting him out of action on the day that Patricia came to call.

The work gathered pace and with it the noise, a clamour of hammering and whistling which grew in intensity until Elsie could barely hear herself think. Shirin possessed a child's innate talent for absorbing dirt from the safest of distances, and her face was soon black with dust; only when Elsie tried to wipe the smudges away with her hand did she realise that it was a case of the pot calling the kettle black. Shirin giggled and allowed herself to be carried over to the sink, but Elsie hadn't got far with making either of them more respectable when she heard a voice outside. 'Hello? Is anybody there?' The back door had been left ajar, and Patricia put her head round and smiled apologetically. 'Sorry to turn up unannounced. We did knock at the front but there was no answer, and we were beginning to wonder if we'd got the wrong house.'

If only, Elsie thought. She wiped her hands on a tea cloth, realising from the horrified look on Patricia's face that both she and the kitchen must present quite some spectacle. 'I'm sorry, Miss Preece, but we weren't expecting you so early.' It wasn't the most gracious of welcomes, but it had the advantage of being honest. 'Do come in.'

'If you're sure it's safe.'

The comment was spoken lightly, but Elsie noticed that Patricia was careful not to touch anything as she came into the kitchen, and she didn't blame her; the outfit – a dark velvet skirt, topped with a silk knit jumper in a vulnerable cream – looked expensive. Dorothy followed behind, dressed in a simple navy trouser suit, and the two would have made an odd-looking pair were it not for a united look of disdain which settled the argument of their clothes. 'I'll take you through to the sitting room and bring you some tea,' Elsie offered. 'I can't say it's peaceful, but at least you'll be away from the mess.'

'No, don't bother,' Patricia said, putting her hand on Elsie's arm. She smiled again, aware that such a swift refusal might have seemed rude. 'Please don't go to any trouble. You're obviously busy and we had coffee at Newbury. We could just go straight to the chapel if that's convenient? Or I'm sure we can find our own way if you'll point us in the right direction?'

Elsie hid her relief well. She looked at Shirin, torn between a need to stay with her and a curiosity to see the Preeces' reaction to Stanley's work, and it was Oliver who came to her rescue. 'Leave the little one here if you like. She'll be safe enough, and we'll keep her happy. I've quite forgotten what it's like to have one that age at home, so it'll be a treat. What d'you say, bright eyes?'

Shirin nodded eagerly and the matter was settled. Grateful for some air, Elsie showed her guests out of the house and into the lane, although it was hard to say who was leading whom: Dorothy struck out at a brisk pace, as if she wanted the day to be over as soon as possible, and Patricia kept up well, skilfully avoiding the potholes. Elsie trailed after them like a balloon on a string until they reached the road, then she turned right and made polite conversation about the weather until they reached the chapel gate. Their response to the building itself was much the same as hers had been. 'Oh,' said Patricia flatly. 'Is that it? I was expecting something…'

She tailed off and Elsie helped her out. 'Something more like a chapel?'

'Yes. Or at least less like a crematorium.'

'It's different inside.' A low October sun threw its light at a gentler angle, but it held its strength and Elsie was pleased not to be taking them there on a cloudy day, when the paintings could seem dull and mute. The doors were wide open and she went in first, more interested than usual to see what impression the chapel would make on its visitors. 'Miss Preece and Miss Hepworth are here,' she said, standing back to watch.

Stanley was leaning his *Reveille* picture against the wall, gauging how it would look when it was lifted into place. He left the canvas and sprang across the floor to greet them, kissing Patricia and offering his hand to Dorothy. The gesture was formal and oddly out of character – shaking hands was something he rarely did, even with men he was meeting for the first time – and Elsie wondered if it seemed as unnatural to the women as it did to her. 'Well?' he demanded, before either of them had had a chance to look round. 'What do you think?'

Elsie watched Patricia and Dorothy scanning the walls, trying to make sense of the paintings as a multitude of figures scurried before their eyes. The chapel was a lot to take in and she tried to imagine what her own response would have been had she not had Stanley to explain each picture to her as it was finished. 'It's very inventive,' Patricia said eventually, glancing at Dorothy for support. 'And what a scale to work on!' She walked over to the north wall and looked at the lower panels. 'Personally I find the colours jar a little, and it doesn't seem as poetic as your earlier work. Is the blandness deliberate? Or is it something that the Behrends asked for?'

It was hard to say which would offend Stanley more: the criticism of his work or the idea that he would paint to order. Elsie looked anxiously at him, waiting for the explosion, but his response was surprisingly mild. 'Isn't that what peace is sometimes? A succession of bland moments? We have to cherish them, though, otherwise what was the point of fighting for them?'

She smiled to herself and collected a few of the dirty cups to wash, happy to be the unseen help while it allowed her to eavesdrop on the conversation. 'I like the way you've used the crosses,' Dorothy said, looking up at the altar wall. 'It's ingenious, and it gives such an unusual structure to the painting.'

Stanley seemed pleased. 'They hold it up, don't they? It was going to be barbed wire originally, but there was something not quite right about it.' He walked closer to the painting, encouraging his guests to do the same. 'The crosses were an accident really,' he admitted. 'When I was painting the Tate *Resurrection*, I used to take a mount and put it over different parts of the canvas to make pictures within pictures. I bet you've both done the same thing with your own paintings?'

Dorothy nodded. 'But hardly on this scale, as Patricia said.' She stared thoughtfully at the pattern of white crosses, genuinely interested in the effect they created. 'Wherever you start, they lead your eye to the mules. It's cleverly done.'

'The mules *are* very striking,' Patricia said.

It was a simplistic comment, similar to something that Elsie had said herself and hardly worthy of another artist, but Stanley gave it as much consideration as Dorothy's more perceptive observations. 'And the figure lying between them,' he added eagerly. 'When I was painting him, I was thinking about myself as a boy. I used to have terrible nightmares and I'd crawl into my parents' bed and snuggle down between them. All the time I was out there, I longed for that feeling of safety.'

Patricia said something which Elsie couldn't catch. She had moved closer to Stanley, responding more to him than to the painting, which she continued to view with a mixture of disappointment and bewilderment. As he often did when the subject was his work, Stanley seemed to speak with his whole body and the gestures brought a curious intensity to his words. 'There wasn't much room for any sort of emotion out there,' he explained. 'That's why the picture is so physical. See? The friends clasping hands or leaning against each other, the man stroking the tortoise. That's what *The Resurrection* is about: restoring the gestures which are natural to peace.' He pointed to the relevant parts of the painting and Elsie noticed Patricia looking at his hands. 'I used to think sometimes that the only way to stop the horror of the thing would be to set down our weapons and indulge in every sort of physical love we could think of.'

'All under the watchful eye of God?' Patricia asked wryly, looking at the tiny Christ figure at the top of the canvas.

'Why not? He's given us that joy. The least we can do is use it.'

Patricia looked uncomfortable. 'Why *have* you put Christ so far away up there?'

Stanley shrugged. 'He's got to go somewhere.'

She looked around for Dorothy, who was absorbed in the texture of the mosquito nets, then turned to the blank south wall. 'It's such a big undertaking for one person. How much longer will it take?'

'I've no idea. The Behrends are very good about it. They haven't rushed me.'

'If that's the case, perhaps you should divide your time between here and London and do some other work alongside it? Something that's more likely to attract the critics' attention and keep you in the public eye.'

To Elsie's embarrassment, Stanley ignored Patricia and came over to her instead. 'Are you all right?' he asked, touching her arm. 'You've been holding your side and you don't look well.'

'Just a touch of indigestion,' Elsie said quietly. 'I'm going back to the cottage now. I'll take something for it there.' She gathered her things and went outside. The pain in her stomach was suddenly much worse and it was an effort to get back to Chapel View. Somehow, she managed to smile and go about her business until the workmen left the house, then she bathed Shirin and settled her in her room with some toys. The indigestion powder had made little difference, except to increase her nausea, and she looked at the clock, wondering what to do. Hilda would be back soon and there was still plenty of cleaning to finish, as well as dinner to think about. The idea of facing anything to do with food was impossible, so she went upstairs to her room, hoping that she might at least dull the pain by resting. She hadn't been there long when she heard the back door open, and Stanley's voice called up the stairs. 'Elsie? Are you there?'

If he had brought Patricia and Dorothy back with him, that would be the final straw. She struggled from the bed but the pain was so acute now that it made her cry out, and Stanley was at her door before she could take more than a couple of steps. 'Elsie! What on earth's the matter? I knew you weren't right. Sit down.'

He eased her back on to the bed and she hadn't the strength to argue. 'What about the Preeces?' she asked.

'They've gone. Mary took them to the station after lunch.' Her priorities seemed to amuse him. 'Not too ill to be house-proud, then. We need to get you to hospital.' Elsie protested but he brushed her objections aside. 'Don't be silly. This could be serious. Let me help you down to the kitchen and I'll fetch the car.'

'That could be serious, too.'

'Desperate times call for desperate measures.' He smiled and supported her gently while she negotiated the stairs, then fetched her coat, scribbled a note for Hilda and picked up the keys.

'What about Shirin?' Elsie said.

Stanley's reassuring calm was temporarily flustered. 'What? Yes of course, I forgot. We'll have to drop her off at Mary's on the way. Rose can look after her, can't she?'

Elsie nodded and struggled out to the car. Stanley stalled three times before they reached the road, swearing under his breath, and Elsie tried – without much success – to use the perils of his driving as a distraction. 'I don't mind if we miss some of the potholes,' she groaned as the car bumped down the narrow track to Grey House.

'What do you think I'm trying to do? But there are more holes than road.'

They left Shirin with a worried Rose, promising that Hilda would collect her as soon as she returned from London, then

143

struck out for Newbury. Stanley kept up a constant stream of chatter, talking about anything that came into his head to take her mind off the situation, but he only succeeded in grating on Elsie's already fragile nerves. 'Can't you go any faster?' she asked, watching the needle on the speedometer hover at fifteen miles per hour.

'I don't want to make it more uncomfortable for you.'

'Uncomfortable?' she repeated, her self-control gone at last. 'I couldn't *be* much more uncomfortable. Just get us there, will you?'

He looked at her in surprise, but the gauge lifted to twenty, then to twenty-five. It was unbearably hot and she wound down the window for some air, trying in vain to stem the wave of nausea. 'Stop the car,' she shouted suddenly.

'What? You just said…'

'Stop the car. I'm going to be sick.'

Stanley pulled down hard on the steering wheel and the car made a graceless lurch on to the verge, stopping short of the hedge by a few inches. Elsie forced the door open and leaned out just in time, feeling a mixture of shame and relief. She heard him get out, and tried to wipe her face, but he was there before her, holding his own handkerchief gently to her lips. 'I'm sorry,' she said.

'Don't be. I've seen worse.'

And of course he had, far worse than she could ever imagine. He waited patiently while she composed herself, looking anxiously at the unnatural flush of her cheeks. 'Ready?' Elsie nodded and lay back in her seat, too weak to fight the dizziness but feeling suddenly safe. She thought of all the men he must have helped like this, the men who would live forever now on the walls of the chapel but whose last moments on earth had been made more bearable by something far more fundamental, by a brief reminder of kindness and trust and love. They were the true gifts, but they had nothing to do with the artist, and she wondered if he would ever understand how much they meant.

***

The voices were reassuringly familiar but they sounded distant and muffled, and for a moment Elsie felt like a child again, lying in her bed at home while her parents talked in the kitchen. With an effort, she shook off her grogginess and opened her eyes. The room was strange to her, and there was little in its plain white décor to help her get her bearings; from the window, framed by curtains which were the delicate blue of a spring sky, she could just make out the top of a horse chestnut tree and the roof of a building she didn't recognise; there was a door straight ahead but its glass was obscured and all she could see was the occasional dark figure passing along a corridor. 'You're in hospital, love.' Elsie tried to focus on the anxious faces by her bedside, and her mother took her hand. 'It was your appendix. They had to operate.'

That would explain the soreness in her side. As she took in her mother's words, the memory of that terrible pain came flooding back to her, and she welcomed this new, explicable discomfort. She tried to speak but her throat was dry, and her father poured a glass of water from the jug on the bedside table. 'Take it steady,' he said, holding it to her lips. 'You've had us all so worried.'

'How did you get here? Did Mr Spencer let you know?'

'He did more than that,' her mother said. 'He paid for a taxi to fetch us straight away. I think he was as worried as we were.'

'He thinks a lot of you, Else. He must to do all this.' Her dad waved his hand round the room. 'I can't say I'm happy about it, mind. He shouldn't be paying for the hospital. We'll have to find a way to give it back to him.'

On cue, Stanley appeared in the doorway carrying a bag of grapes, a bunch of yellow dahlias and a shoebox. 'Ah, the patient's awake,' he said. 'Good to have you back with us. How are you feeling?'

'A lot better than I was the last time I saw you.'

'Excellent.' Her father stood to give Stanley his chair, but he waved the offer aside and sat down on the bottom of the bed. 'Hilda sent these from the garden,' he said, looking round for somewhere to put the flowers. 'She says to watch out for the earwigs, but I think I shook most of them off on the way.'

Her mother took them from him. 'They're lovely,' she said, admiring the brightly coloured spikes. 'Elsie's always saying what a good gardener Mrs Spencer is. I'll ask the nurse for a vase.'

'Thanks, Edith,' Stanley said, and Elsie noticed how comfortable he and her parents seemed to be in each other's company. It didn't surprise her – Stanley had a knack of making himself at home with anyone of any class – but she had to smile when she remembered her parents' doubts in the early days of her job, when the word 'artist' was spoken with a suspicion usually reserved for crooks and foreigners. 'Now, I brought the grapes on Shirin's orders,' Stanley continued. 'Apparently all the children in her storybooks have them when they're in hospital, although why there are so many stories with sick children in them is beyond me. Whatever happened to Ratty and Brer Rabbit?' He grinned and took the lid off the shoebox. 'And these are from me.' Elsie looked down at the collection of framed family photographs. 'I brought a few from your room to make you feel more at home.'

Her pleasure at his thoughtfulness turned quickly to concern. 'I won't be here that long, surely?'

'You'll stay until you're better.'

'Mr Spencer's right,' her father said. 'You can't go scrubbing floors and filling coal scuttles straight after an operation. And when you're out of hospital, you'll come to us for a bit. Your mother insists on it.'

'But how will you manage?'

'It's all arranged,' Stanley said. 'The Behrends know a girl in the village who helps Rose out occasionally, so she's going to come in three mornings a week until you're back on your feet.' Elsie tried to smile, but the realisation that she was not after all indispensable piqued her, and she wondered what Rose had to say about the girl from the village. He stood up and put the photographs on the bedside cabinet. 'I'll be going now I know you're all right.

They're putting the scaffolding up by the north wall today and camp scenes don't paint themselves.'

Elsie's father held out his hand. 'We can't thank you enough for your kindness,' he said. 'Edie and me are very grateful, and we'll find a way to make it up to you.'

'There's no need,' Stanley said seriously. 'Your daughter does that simply by putting up with us.'

'Mind you don't manage too well without me,' Elsie said, touched by his words. 'I'll be back as soon as I can.'

'We'll hold you to that.' He headed for the door but turned back at the last minute. 'I almost forgot. You had a visitor this morning, Elsie. He turned up at the cottage just as I was leaving. Nice chap, name of Kenneth Beckford. Said he knew you from Cookham.' There was a twinkle in his eye as he added: 'He asked if he could come and visit you. I told him I didn't think you'd mind at all. In fact, I said I thought you'd be delighted.' Elsie blushed and Stanley waved his hand, leaving her to explain her new acquaintance to her parents.

21

Elsie chose an outfit carefully for her afternoon off. She had been as good as her word, making a speedy recovery and returning to work far sooner than expected, and for the first couple of weeks she gladly forfeited her half day to get the household back to normal – but this Thursday Ken had promised to finish his deliveries early and take her to a matinee in Newbury. It would be their first trip out and she found herself looking forward to it more each day. A hospital bedside didn't lend itself to romance, but she liked this man who made her laugh and let her tease him, and she wanted him to like her. The dress wasn't her newest, but it was her favourite: high-waisted and V-necked, and in the colours of the time of year – splashes of orange and yellow patterned the top like a curtain of falling leaves, and the background was a rich chocolate brown which brought out the colour of her eyes.

She added the pendant that Stanley had given her and her best felt hat, then popped her head round the sitting room door to say goodbye. 'I've laid everything out for supper, Mrs Spencer. The pie's ready to eat, but just stick it in for an hour if you want it hot. And there's stewed apple for dessert. I've kept Shirin's separate and put extra sugar on it.'

'Thanks, Elsie.' Hilda looked up from the jigsaw puzzle she was doing, a formal portrait of the king and queen with too many sequins to be interesting. 'Gosh, you look lovely. Going somewhere nice?'

'Just the pictures,' Elsie said, reluctant to admit to a rendezvous.

'Just the pictures sounds perfect to me. I wish I were coming with you.' She sighed heavily and pushed the colour-coded pieces into one jumbled heap in the middle of the table, undoing an hour of work. 'I'm so bored I could scream. It's too miserable to go for a walk and the garden's crying out to be dug, but Stan will be livid if I touch a spade in my condition.'

'What about some painting? A brush shouldn't be too heavy.'

'What is there to paint round here? A muddy field and a railway track. Hardly the most inspirational of landscapes.' She thought for a moment, then brightened. 'Wait a minute, that's not such a bad idea. Put your coat down and stand by the fireplace. Just there, at the edge of the hearth.' Elsie stared at her in bewilderment. 'Humour me, and put your hand on the mantelpiece.' Elsie did as she was asked, careful not to get coal dust on her clothes. 'No, that's not right. It's too forced.'

'What is?' Hilda didn't answer, but took her arm and led her through to the kitchen. 'Try by the range.' Elsie stood awkwardly in front of the fender and waited while Hilda looked her up and down. 'Yes, that's perfect. Stand exactly where you are and don't move a muscle. I'll be right back.'

She left the room and Elsie glanced anxiously at the clock. It was already a quarter to two and her heart sank when Hilda returned with a sketch pad. 'I've got to get my bus, Mrs Spencer. I'll miss the film if I don't go soon.'

'I won't keep you long.' She settled down on a chair, the pad on her knee. 'Now, turn your head slightly to the left and look out of the window. Yes, that's it.' There was a long silence as Hilda began to transfer what she saw on to the paper. Elsie looked round, trying to guess how much of the kitchen was included in the sketch. The washing above the range looked untidy, and there was a nasty scuff mark on the skirting board which she had been meaning to remove all day. 'Stop fidgeting!' Hilda said irritably. 'And keep your hands still.'

'I don't know where to put them when I'm not working. It feels wrong, just standing here.'

'Try one on your hip and the other down by your side. Better?'

Elsie nodded, although the stance still felt unnatural. Behind her, the clock whirred into motion, ready to strike the hour, and its two perfect notes – bright and chipper – seemed to mock her plans. The bus was due at twenty-past and it was a good ten minutes to the church in these shoes. She began to feel that her afternoon was fated, and it was hard not to read a more general warning into her fading chances of meeting Ken on time. She stood as still as she could, hoping that the muse might respond more efficiently if she co-operated, and then, when another five minutes had passed, she tried again. 'I really should be…'

'Ssssh!' Hilda held up her hand. 'This bit's crucial. I need to concentrate.'

One day at school, Elsie had been made to stand on a chair all morning with her back to the class, a punishment for calling one of the boys rude names. It hadn't been her fault – the boy in question was a bully who had picked on her for weeks, and her outburst was the final straw – but she had never forgotten the searing sense of injustice that had overwhelmed her, a blind, raging anger which was as impotent as it was intense. Now, as the minutes ticked past, she felt the frustrated tears of a child pricking at her eyes and she blinked them back, ashamed that a grown woman should still feel the urge to stamp her foot and say it wasn't fair. Hilda worked on, oblivious to the resentment she had caused, and when the clock spoke again, and then again, Elsie conceded defeat.

Long after three, Hilda finally put her pencil down. 'There! I hope I haven't kept you too long.'

It was probably just as well that Elsie needed to rub the feeling back into her legs or she might have been tempted to do something else with her hands. She should be gracious when the Spencers were so good to her, but she was too disappointed to pretend it didn't matter. 'The film will have started by now,' she muttered. 'I don't expect my friend will wait.'

'You were meeting a friend? Oh Elsie, you should have said.' Hilda looked down at her work and made a slight adjustment to something in the bottom left-hand corner. 'I won't show it to you yet if you don't mind. There's a long way to go.'

Elsie shrugged, hardly caring if she never saw the drawing that had ruined her afternoon. 'I'll be off, then, if that's all right?'

'Yes of course. Have a good time.'

There was no point in waiting for another bus. She went upstairs to change her shoes, then found her gaiters and went out to the motorbike, picturing Ken outside the cinema and wondering how long he would wait. He had probably given up already, but she had no intention of spending her afternoon off in Burghclere. Even the bike conspired against her. She turned the petrol tap on and tickled the carburettor, but on the fifth or sixth kick it still wouldn't fire. She tried again, sweet-talking the machine at first, then choosing her words more brutally, but it remained stubbornly silent.

'Your spark plugs are probably wet. Have you got a spare?'

She jumped and looked round. 'Ken! What are you doing here?' He looked nice, she thought. The suit had seen better days, but she was touched by the flower in his button hole and the diligently polished shoes. 'I'm so sorry. I was on my way to the bus when Mrs Spencer asked me to do something. She promised it wouldn't take long, but I've only just got away. I never dreamt you'd come looking for me.'

'Didn't seem like you not to turn up. I was worried you'd been taken ill again. If you've changed your mind, that's fine, but I just wanted to make sure you were all right.'

'I haven't changed my mind. Anything but.'

He looked relieved. 'Good, because it'd be a shame to waste that dress. You look lovely, Elsie.'

She smiled and took his arm. 'So Mrs Spencer said. That's what got me into trouble in the first place.'

22

The brown dress was worn regularly from then on, but not just for Ken. Sitting for her portrait became a central feature of Elsie's life at Chapel View, as much a part of her itinerary as cooking or chopping wood. Once a week, Hilda insisted that she change and stand for two or three hours at a time in front of the kitchen range, sometimes on her afternoon off, sometimes when she should have been doing the chores. Eventually, as she lost her self-consciousness, Elsie began to look forward to the sessions. She noticed that they were timed to coincide with days when Stanley was particularly engrossed in his work at the chapel, and although Hilda didn't ask her not to tell him about the painting, she understood that the sittings were a secret. When it wasn't in use, the canvas was tucked discreetly away behind the wardrobe and, by happy coincidence, Elsie's fixed pose by the range afforded her an excellent view of anyone coming across the field from the railway cutting.

'How are you getting on with Ken?' Hilda asked, when she was satisfied that the hat was worn at precisely the same angle as the week before. 'You'd obviously had a good time when you came in last night.'

'We did. Well, I did. He took me to a dance in the village hall, which was nice of him. He hates dancing.'

'Then it must be serious.' Elsie hesitated, wondering how to answer. These sittings were pauses in daily life, and the strange intimacy of the situation encouraged long conversations which would never otherwise have been had, but it was usually she who asked the questions, and she didn't feel the need to interrogate her own feelings in the way that Stanley and Hilda did. 'Well? *Is* it serious?'

'I like him,' Elsie said, 'and I know he likes me, so I suppose we'll see how it goes. Actually, that's one of the things I like most about him. He's good at living for the day. I wasn't really expecting to meet anyone, and I don't think either of us is in a hurry to change things.'

'That's good if it's what you both want. Unexpected meetings can make for the strongest marriages.'

'You and Mr Spencer met at a dinner party, didn't you?'

'That's right. He liked the way I served the soup. Don't ask me how you can see a life mapped out in the stroke of a ladle, but Stanley swears he did and I believe him. I wasn't thinking about us, though. We were inevitable, looking back. We had the same circle of friends and we both loved our work. It would have been more remarkable if we *hadn't* met.' She got up and moved the coal bucket closer to the hearth before Elsie could lift it for her. 'You really don't have to polish this every time, you know. I'll make sure it shines in the picture. No, I was actually thinking about my parents. Theirs was a real love story but they only met by chance.'

'What happened?'

'My father got a commission for a portrait in Essex and fell in love with the maid who answered the door.'

'Your mother was…'

'A servant, yes, although she might prefer the word "companion". You'd never guess, would you?' She smiled and shifted her chair round with the light. 'She was an orphan, and a family took her in to work for them. She knows nothing about her parents. The only memory she has is of a gypsy woman near Wales who might have been her grandmother.'

'No wonder you took to that caravan in the war. It's in your blood.'

'Yes, I suppose it is.'

'I can't imagine your father's family being too pleased about the match.'

'He proved them wrong and it *was* a strong marriage, but then my mother was dutiful and that had nothing to do with being rescued from service.' Hilda sighed, and Elsie watched as she coaxed the last of the dark brown paint from a squeezed and battered tube. 'She doesn't understand me, Elsie. We love each other, but my choices make no sense to her. She thinks I should work harder at my marriage.'

'But you and Mr Spencer have both been trying lately. And with the little one on the way…'

'I know, but my mother has a talent for seeing into the future. Perhaps it's that gypsy blood you mentioned.' She left the room for a moment and returned with more paint. 'What do you think of Patricia?'

It was said off the cuff, its relevance to the remark which preceded it almost coincidental. 'It's not for me to say,' Elsie began cautiously.

Hilda laughed. 'Since when have you *ever* been shy of telling us what you think?'

It was a fair comment and she acknowledged it with a smile. 'Let's just say I wouldn't want to work for the woman.'

'Really? It's strange, but I rather like her. And I do feel sorry for the two of them, rubbing around in that house to make ends meet. We've done that ourselves before Stanley made a success of things, and it's no fun.' She narrowed her eyes, concentrating on something in the lower half of the canvas, and Elsie wondered if she should be more explicit with Hilda about her concerns, but the moment was lost. 'What *do* you want from life?' asked Hilda. 'What do you dream about? I've been looking at that expression for weeks, and I've still no idea what you're imagining for yourself

154

when you stare out of the window.' Eighteen months ago, the answer would have been straightforward: marriage, somewhere nice to live, a home for her children which was as happy as the one she had grown up in; now, Elsie hesitated, torn between the life she had and the life she had always expected. 'I promise not to tell Ken how long it's taking you to answer,' Hilda said.

'It's not about him. I suppose it's about being here. I'm not sure I want to be rescued like your mother. Service is a bit easier than it was in her day.'

'Have we spoilt you?'

'Perhaps.'

'Well, I won't apologise for that.' Hilda stood up and stretched, her hand at her back. 'I don't know if it's the baby or the thought of moving on from here,' she said more seriously, 'but I've got a permanent knot in my stomach, just like I had when I was a child and my brothers were up to something. I feel like I'm bracing myself, and I have no idea what for.'

'Mr Spencer wants to move back to Cookham,' Elsie said quietly.

'I know he does. And I want to go to Hampstead. That sounds like stalemate.'

'It's natural that you should both want to go back to your roots.'

'Is it? I'm not sure about that. We were so happy in Hampstead when we were first married and I thought that would count for something. Anyway, my roots aren't in London. I grew up in Oxford, and I have no desire to go back.'

'Really?'

Hilda nodded. 'Our house was called The Shrubbery and there were trees everywhere. I know it sounds lovely, but I felt so hemmed in by them.' Elsie remembered the impenetrable wall of trees in Hilda's painting of Cookham Bridge; at the time, she had thought them beautiful but perhaps she had misread them. 'I shouldn't blame Oxford. I was the only daughter and it would have been the same anywhere – endless rounds of visiting and entertaining.

I think that's why I hate it so much. Stanley gets furious if I don't make an effort socially, but I've done my share of smiling at people who bore me. I don't see why I should have to do it now.'

Whereas Patricia made enough effort for both of them, Elsie thought uncharitably. 'So how did you all end up in London?'

'Dick and Sydney went first and I followed. You can sit down if you like. I've got what I need.'

'Then I'll put the kettle on. You don't mind if I move it?'

'Of course not. I've painted that bit. The idea was that I'd keep house for the boys and fit in art school around it. They rented studios down the road, and I got the corridor. I was fondly known as the passage artist.' She said it without the resentment it might have deserved, and Elsie thought consciously for the first time of how dominant the women were in her own family, led by her mother's example. She squabbled with her brothers and stuck up for herself when she had to, but theirs was a struggle of class, not gender, and the battle lines were never drawn at home. 'I clawed my way to London,' Hilda admitted, as if reading Elsie's thoughts, 'and I've always had to fight to be there.' She gave a rueful smile. 'I still do, it would seem, but for different reasons.'

'Is it so important now you've proved yourself?' Elsie set the tray down on the table and poured them each a cup. 'Mr Spencer values your work as much as his own. More, sometimes.'

'I know he does. Stanley doesn't have a chauvinistic bone in his body, but it's more than that.' She sipped her tea thoughtfully, and Elsie waited for her to find the right words. 'It's hard to explain, but in London I can find the space to be myself. Even in the bosom of my family, even married to Stanley, I can still remember who I am. I still *like* who I am.'

'And you wouldn't in Cookham?'

'I could never compete with her charms.' For a moment, Elsie was unsure whether she was talking about the village or Patricia. 'Ken lives in Cookham, doesn't he?' She nodded. 'Then it looks like I'm outnumbered.'

Before Elsie could argue, the back door opened and Stanley came in, shaking the rain off his clothes. 'What are you two up to? I'll have a cup if you're offering.' He stopped in his tracks when he saw the canvas and the expression of pure wonder on his face made Elsie long to take a look herself, but she had promised not to. There was a long silence in the kitchen, and she waited to see who would break it. 'Ducky, it's magnificent,' Stanley said eventually. 'Look at the way you've painted her skirt! And the tins on the mantelpiece – each one of those could be a painting in its own right.' If he expected Hilda to be pleased, he would be disappointed: her face was like thunder, and Elsie stood to fetch another cup, glad to have a reason to leave the room. 'Don't go,' he said, staring at her face as if seeing her for the first time. 'Stand back by the hearth, where you were.'

Elsie hesitated, not wanting to antagonise either of them, but Stanley was already unfolding his easel and setting it up behind Hilda's. 'What are you doing?' Hilda demanded.

'Starting a portrait,' he said, as if it were the most obvious thing in the world. 'You've inspired me, ducky. I can't imagine why I didn't think of it.'

'But that's just it. *You* didn't think of it. Anyway, we've finished for today. Elsie's got to get the supper on.'

The range betrayed the lie. 'It smells to me like she's already done that,' Stanley said. 'Steak and kidney, if I'm not mistaken.'

'Surely you've got plenty to do in the chapel?'

'Have you seen the weather? The light's almost gone. I can't paint a thing out there.'

Stubbornly, Hilda moved her canvas to the right, effectively blocking Stanley's view. 'You can go and get changed now, Elsie. I've done enough for today.'

'Stay where you are, Elsie.'

He shifted his easel in tandem with his wife's and began to unpack some pencils. Elsie hovered by the range, caught in an impossible position. Eventually she decided that a quick look at the hotpot would be the most natural compromise between staying in the room and getting on with her work.

'Why are you so contrary, Stan?' Hilda asked. 'You say you want me to work and pursue my own vision, but you can't stand it when I do something of my own. You have to do it, too.'

'I don't see why you should mind so much. I'd have thought it would interest you to paint the same things occasionally. It'll show us where our differences lie.'

'I think our differences are perfectly obvious without committing them to canvas. You've got a whole chapel to work in. Isn't that enough for you? Couldn't you leave Elsie to me?'

'I draw Elsie all the time. She's hardly your discovery.'

'So, *I'm* copying *you*? You really won't be happy until you've refashioned me in your own image, will you?'

'Will someone draw me?' Shirin stood in the doorway with a pencil in her hand, uncertain which parent to offer it to. Still engrossed in their own dispute, Stanley and Hilda stared at their daughter as if she were a stranger to them and it was left to Elsie to call a truce.

'Of course they will, sweet pea. Come here. You can take over from me.' She lifted Shirin on to the table and retied the bow in her hair. 'There, you look lovely. Mummy and Daddy have got all their painting things here, so why don't you let them both draw you and you can decide which picture you like best?' She glared at the Spencers and went upstairs to change, deciding that if they wanted to compete like children, they could at least do it with someone who deserved their attention.

23

The portraits of Elsie stood for weeks on either side of the dining room, sizing each other up like opposing armies in a war whose purpose was forgotten. Stanley had got his way in the end, and at first Elsie had missed the intimacy of those afternoons with Hilda, when they seemed to share an understanding which she had never expected to find with someone so different to her in every respect, but the sessions had thawed and the resentment set free by that first disastrous encounter had eventually been put back in its box.

There was no question which portrait she preferred, although the Spencers had been unusually tactful about asking. Hilda's painting was a magnificent full-length study which reminded Elsie of the pictures she had loved in her history books as a child, pictures of kings and queens in stately surroundings, with everything that mattered close at hand. The surroundings were more humble, but Hilda had kept her promise: the coal bucket was full and carefully polished; the fender shone; the washing was drying on the line; and the tea caddies had been neatly arranged on a diligently dusted mantelpiece. The picture boasted order and tranquillity, and she hoped it reflected what – in Hilda's eyes – her presence did for the household.

Stanley's picture was a head-and-shoulders view: Hilda had never relinquished her prime position, and he had always had to work with what he could see above her canvas. The image shocked Elsie when she saw it. At first glance it appeared to be a close-up version of Hilda's – the dress as carefully painted, the same ordered surroundings – and yet she looked so different: older, certainly, and there was something raw about her face, something in the twist of her mouth and the expression in her eyes that was much less gentle. Hilda's portrait showed her as she had been when it was painted – a young girl, dressed up for her afternoon off. Stanley's, she suspected, was less to do with what he saw in front of him than with the images he carried in his mind, and the title – scribbled hastily on the back – had upset her more than it should. Now, as the canvases stood opposite each other, it was as if Stanley's Elsie were looking back at Hilda's from a different, less innocent time. His notion had been to show the differences between his view of the world and his wife's, but to Elsie's eyes, the portraits only showed the changes in her. The contrast unsettled her. Whenever she looked at them, she felt that same knot in her stomach that Hilda had spoken of, the same sense of change ahead and the same fear of what it might mean.

24

Winter drifted imperceptibly into a half-hearted spring. Hilda's pregnancy was beset by a debilitating sickness and lethargy, and she made frequent trips to Hampstead to consult her Christian Science practitioner, taking Shirin with her and leaving Stanley at the mercy of his own moods. Whenever she returned to Burghclere, there was a brief moment of respite and the family reverted to normal, but the happy times grew shorter, the cycle of illness and departure more regular, and Elsie noticed that each absence seemed to fray the patched and mended fabric of their marriage. Despite what he had said about seeing things more clearly when they were apart, Stanley seemed to need Hilda's physical presence to believe in their union, even at the expense of her happiness. He begged her to find a practitioner closer to home, and, when that failed, offered to pay for the woman she trusted to be put up in the village, but Hilda remained immoveable on the subject, her stubbornness matching his selfishness stride for stride. Elsie had little patience with either of them, having come from a family that put its children first, and their arguments made no sense to her. What she did understand was how empty the cottage felt without Shirin.

'I've got friends coming to look at the chapel this morning,' Stanley said one morning as he sat down to breakfast. 'They're going straight there, so you won't be bothered.'

'Will they want lunch?' Elsie asked, assuming it was the Preeces.

'I'm not sure. Is that the last rasher of bacon? If it is, don't cook it.'

She stared at him in surprise, her fork hovering over the frying pan. 'Why not? You always have three rashers.'

'Then I'll make do with two. I need *that* for something else. Actually, wrap it up with one of the cooked rashers, will you, and do me an extra egg.'

She did as she was asked and sent him on his way, then set about her cleaning. Time passed quickly, and she had just begun to scrape some new potatoes when she heard a bicycle bell in the lane outside and the click of the garden gate. Her heart went cold at the sight of the telegram. She was of a generation which would never simply accept it as an efficient means of communication, and she hurriedly threw her apron aside and headed for the chapel. A dark green car was parked by the side of the road, and once inside she found a couple she didn't recognise looking closely at *The Resurrection*. Stanley was at the top of the scaffolding, small enough to blend into his latest painting. A young woman in a cotton print dress stood next to him, pointing periodically at the picture. Glancing at the visitors' book, Elsie could just make out the name 'Carrington' written three times. She cleared her throat, but Stanley was too absorbed in his conversation to take any notice. The couple turned around and the man smiled at her. 'I think someone wants you, Spencer,' he called, and Stanley looked down.

'A telegram's just arrived for you, Mr Spencer. I didn't think it could wait.'

'Thanks, Elsie. Bring it up, will you?'

Shaking his head in amusement, the man gallantly offered to take it for her, but Elsie refused. She climbed the ladder carefully, listening to the conversation as she neared the top. 'The canvas has to be woven in Belgium,' Stanley was explaining. 'There aren't any looms wide enough in England.'

His friend turned and smiled as she reached the top, and Elsie realised that she was older than she had looked from a distance – attractive, with an open, round face and big blue eyes, and a mop of hair that was the colour of wet straw. 'You've obviously done that before,' she said, nodding to the ladder. 'I made such a pig's ear of it.'

'This is Carrington, Elsie. We were at the Slade together.'

The use of a single name surprised Elsie but the woman seemed used to it. 'Very pleased to meet you,' she said. 'Cookham's been telling me about the portrait he painted of you.'

'Cookham?'

'Sorry. Old habits die hard. That's what we called Stanley at college because he went back there every evening on the train. He missed half the classes because he wouldn't leave his beloved village overnight.'

'It didn't stop me walking away with most of the prizes, did it?' Stanley retorted good naturedly. There was an easy affection between the two painters, and Elsie wondered why she hadn't heard Carrington's name before. She handed him the telegram, stepping over the bacon which lay on the boards between them, unwrapped but still in its greaseproof paper. 'Now you know why I needed it,' he said, pointing to the wall where a soldier was holding a pile of uncooked bacon between two pieces of wood. 'I had to get the difference between the fried and the unfried rashers. You've no idea how difficult it was.'

Carrington obviously did. She walked along the platform and stared admiringly at the detail in the picture. 'Only Cookham would do some of his best work thirty feet up where no one will ever appreciate it.'

It was true, Elsie thought. The wall was alive with bustling figures, tree-clad hills, and tents seemingly made from folded sheets of crisp white paper. Everywhere she looked, soldiers were cooking bacon or carrying vast cauldrons of tea, and in the foreground a figure with cockatoo hair wielded a rusty bayonet, using it for nothing more aggressive than collecting litter. The scene gave a vivid impression of life in the camps, but even on the brightest day the top of the chapel remained gloomy and difficult to see, and she doubted that anyone would ever look as she was at the dog eating from Fray Bentos tins or the care with which Stanley had recreated cast-off pages from the *Balkan News*.

'Is that you?' Carrington asked, picking out the man with the bacon.

Stanley nodded. 'I worked in the cookhouse and fried the bacon every morning.'

'Don't let Elsie hear that or you'll be cooking your own breakfast.'

'Two rashers each for sixty men, every single day. I remember one morning…'

He was about to start a story which might take anything from a few minutes to half an hour, and Elsie stared anxiously at the unopened telegram. 'Excuse me, Mr Spencer,' she said, daring to interrupt, 'but that might need an answer. Do you want to open it while I'm here?'

'What? Oh, I see.'

He slit the envelope and Elsie saw his face cloud over. 'What's wrong?' she asked. 'Is Mrs Spencer all right?'

'She wants you to go to Hampstead. The Carlines' maid has had to go off at short notice. Her mother's ill.'

'London? Mrs Spencer wants me to go to London?'

'That's where Hampstead was the last time I looked,' Stanley said waspishly, drawing a glance of surprise from Carrington.

'How long for?'

'You're to stay until the baby's born.'

'But I can't go all that way. How will you manage?' Elsie's true motives were more selfish. The idea of travelling to London on her own to look after the Carlines horrified her, but she didn't want to make a fuss on her own account and she knew that only Stanley's objections to the plan would keep her at home.

'My needs don't matter, you should know that by now.' He screwed the paper up and threw it on the floor. 'You'd better go and answer this. Hilda wants you there as soon as possible.'

Disappointed that he should give in so easily, Elsie tried to think of another argument that would save her but nothing suggested itself. She bent down to tidy some rubbish from the platform, reluctant to go while there was a chance that he might change his mind, but her efforts only brought her more trouble.

'Leave that paper where it is!' he shouted. She looked at him, bewildered, and he pointed angrily to the painting, using the same jabbing motion as the soldier with the bayonet. 'I'm painting lit-ter, Elsie. Don't you understand *anything* about what I'm trying to do here?'

'Cookham, that's hardly fair,' Carrington objected.

Somehow, being shielded from Stanley by a stranger made the assault even worse. Hurt and humiliated, Elsie left the chapel as quickly as she could.

25

The next day, she stood her suitcase inside the chapel door and looked up at the scaffolding. 'I'm off to the station now.' There was no answer, so she raised her voice and tried again. 'I've got to go. The train leaves in half an hour and I want to be there in plenty of time.'

Stanley turned away from his work and she felt rather than heard the sigh. 'Yes, I understood you the first time. Give my love to Hilda and Shirin. I'll see you when you get back.'

So that was that. She walked out into the orchard, trying to keep her temper. Stanley's mood since the telegram arrived had been insufferable, and as she crossed the railway bridge and took the turn to the station, she was almost glad to be leaving. The station house looked pretty in the morning sunlight, and she sat down on the platform bench to check through her bag one last time. This unexpected chance to see the capital would make her the envy of her siblings, and it should have been something she grasped with both hands, but it smacked too much of a dress rehearsal for something more permanent and she couldn't bring herself to view it as a treat.

The train ambled round the bend and ground to a halt with a flounce of steam. Elsie chose a seat by the window and settled down with the new *Woman's Weekly*, but was barely halfway through the first article when she heard someone calling her name. Glancing up, she saw Stanley riding Hilda's bicycle along the platform – slow and unsteady, like the first time she saw him. She waved and he braked alongside her, removing something from the bicycle basket and letting the ill-used machine fall to the floor. 'I forgot to give you these,' he called, gesturing for her to slide the window down. 'They're for Hilda.' He handed her bluebells wrapped in news-paper, and Elsie laid them gently on the seat beside her, wondering what state they'd be in when they reached their destination. 'Tell her they're from the garden,' he said. 'She planted some from the woods when we first got here and she's been looking forward to seeing them. Will you do that for me?'

'Of course I will. They're lovely.'

'And Elsie…'

'Yes?'

'I'm glad you're going to be with her. Look after them all, won't you, and yourself.' She had never known Stanley to apologise directly. Instead, he said or did something nice, expecting the ges-ture to stand for the words he couldn't bring himself to say, and she willingly forgave him. 'Let me know as soon as there's some news, and I'll come down and see you all.'

He waved until the train was almost out of sight, and Elsie watched his tiny figure turn and push the bicycle back up the slope to the road. She changed at Newbury and abandoned her magazine, dividing her attention between her fellow passengers and the unfamiliar countryside. The journey was much shorter than she had expected, and London – a world away in her imagin-ation – much closer. Its suburbs came as a shock to her, abruptly replacing the solid, rural landscape with a newness which bewil-dered her: factories made of glass and steel rather than the grim, blackened bricks she had envisaged, and small, modern houses with neat gardens which seemed to occupy a sort of no man's land between town and country. The train ran into a deep cutting and the daylight dwindled; by the time it returned, a guard was pass-ing down the corridor, announcing that they would shortly be in Paddington.

The station was vast and Elsie stared in amazement at the high glazed roof and motionless trains, waiting in their platforms like miniature streets of terraced housing. Everyone seemed to know exactly where they were going, and she moved closer to the wall to progress at her own pace without getting in anybody's way. Half-way along the platform stood a monument to railway employees who had given their lives in the war, and Elsie looked up at the bronze soldier, dressed in a greatcoat. Like most of the memorials she had seen, it was an impressive sight, sombre and dignified, but – having lived for so long with Stanley's uniquely personal trib-ute – she couldn't help but feel that these grand, imposing statues only distanced ordinary people even further from their dead. No woman remembered her husband or son like this; she remembered the man who ate at the table and shaved over the sink, who stood in his doorway looking out at the street he loved.

She made her way to the entrance, where she was due to be met by the Carlines' temporary help. Lizzie turned out to be a bonny, talkative girl, younger and less experienced than Elsie, but with a surfeit of cockiness that made up for any shortcomings, at least in her own mind. 'It'll be different to what you're used to,' she said, when they were settled in the back of a taxi to Hampstead. 'If I had a shilling for every time the missus had something to say about the way her daughter runs their household, I'd be a rich woman and you'd be scooting round after me.'

Elsie hid a smile and Lizzie seemed oblivious to the insult, chat-tering on as the taxi wound through a series of expensive-looking streets. 'We're nearly there now,' she said. 'That's Hampstead Hill Gardens, where the rich people live.' From the way Hilda spoke of her own home the Carlines were hardly poor, but the comment was delivered without irony. Elsie stared at the handsome, red-brick villas and tried to remember when she had ever seen a single house that was as grand, let alone a whole street of them. Downshire Hill was the next turning on the right, a wide, tree-lined road with an attractive variety of buildings on either side. The blossom was fading now, but Elsie could imagine how beautiful it must have looked in the spring, and she was surprised and pleased by how countrified the area seemed. Ahead of her, at the bottom of the hill, she could see the beginnings of a stretch of parkland which she guessed was Hampstead Heath, and when she got out of the car, the only noise to disturb the peace was the pure, flute-like song of a blackbird.

Hilda's family home was a solid, square house, with fresh, cream paintwork. Each of the windows in the upper storeys had a small wrought iron balcony, and the window boxes were filled with a profusion of lobelia and red geraniums, which suggested that Hilda's green fingers ran in the family. Even if she hadn't heard so much about the dinner parties and the conversations late into the night, Elsie would have said it was a welcoming house.

To her surprise, Lizzie headed brazenly for the front door rather than the side entrance, and Elsie had no choice but to follow. Inside, it was dark: the ground floor windows were all but obscured by two gnarled apple trees in the tiny front garden, and the contrast with the bright summer's day was disorientating. When her eyes had adjusted to the shadows, she saw that the hallway was decorated with heavily framed paintings, hung so close together that it was impossible to say what colour the walls were. A long case clock stood at the bottom of the stairs, marking time with a heavy, ponderous sound, and the floor was covered in a series of richly decorated rugs – souvenirs, probably, from the family's foreign travels.

'Ellie! Ellie! Ellie!' Shirin had never seen the need for the 's' in Elsie's name. She ran down the corridor, ignoring Lizzie's instructions to slow down, and flung her arms round Elsie's legs.

'Goodness, where did the whirlwind come from?' Elsie lifted her up, trying not to squash the bluebells, and kissed her on both cheeks. 'One's from Daddy and one's from me. He misses you, and he's promised to visit as soon as he can.'

'Elsie? Is that you? Come in here and say hello.' The familiar voice drifted out from the sitting room, and Elsie did as she was asked. Hilda was resting on a rose-pink chaise longue, although 'resting' hardly described the awkward position which her swollen belly had forced her to adopt, and she looked as if she hadn't been comfortable for weeks. Her face was pale and drawn, her eyes tired, but her welcome was as warm as Shirin's as she tried to struggle to her feet. 'It's nice to see you. You've got us out of a real hole, and we're all grateful.'

'There's no need, Mrs Spencer. Please don't get up.'

Hilda smiled apologetically. 'I'm not sure I could. You have no idea what I'd give to walk around like a normal person again.'

'Not long to go now.' An older woman sat in the chair opposite Hilda with an open bible on her knee, and Elsie guessed that she was a Christian Scientist. 'Mr Spencer sent you these,' she said, glad to relinquish responsibility for the bluebells. 'He picked them from the garden.'

Hilda's face lit up. 'That was thoughtful. How is he?'

'Difficult and bad-tempered, just like he always is when you're away. But he's tearing along that big wall, and he says he'll come as soon as the baby's born.'

'That's good.'

Elsie watched as Hilda selected one of the bluebells and pressed it carefully between the pages of the book at her side. 'I'd better get to work,' she said, hoping that the hint might encourage some guidance on the habits of the house and what her duties were to be.

'I couldn't agree more.' The voice came from behind her, and Elsie turned to see Mrs Carline standing in the doorway. 'I'm pleased you've arrived safely, Elsie. Elizabeth will show you to your room, then I'd like you to come to the drawing room and discuss the arrangements for the rest of the week.'

Remembering that Annie Carline used to be a companion, and wondering how quickly she had grown accustomed to giving orders rather than taking them, Elsie followed Lizzie out of the room. The paintings continued all the way up the stairs, and although she hadn't time to look at them properly, her impressions were of a series of beautiful women in long, white dresses, holding or surrounded by flowers. Her room was at the top of the house, small but comfortably furnished, and its proportions were more than made up for by the fact that she didn't have to share them. Lizzie left her to unpack, and she changed her clothes and tidied her hair as quickly as she could. The sound of laughter carried through the wall from the house next door, muted but companionable, and for the first time since her early days at Chapel View, Elsie felt a pang of loneliness.

When she went downstairs, the drawing room was empty and she tried to decide whether it was better to wait for Mrs Carline or to go in search of her. In the end, curiosity got the better of her and she was drawn to a collection of family photographs which stood on the mantelpiece. She picked one up to look more closely at the five young faces: Hilda with her brothers, the girl in a family of boys, a tabby cat in her arms and a black Labrador sitting loyally at her feet. The picture must have been taken when she was twelve or thirteen, but the determined expression on her face and those striking features – deep-set eyes, a strong mouth, and thick, tumbling hair – already hinted at the woman Elsie knew. The youngest boy – Dick, it must be – was the spitting image of his sister, with long, feminine curls which would mortify him now. The rest resembled each other but not their younger siblings, and it saddened Elsie to think that two of them were already dead.

She heard the door close behind her and dropped the photograph as if the frame had burnt her.

'Good grief, child, what on earth's the matter with you?'

'I'm sorry, Mrs Carline, I was just…'

'Dusting?' There was a twinkle in her eye as she sat down by a tall, arch-shaped window which looked out to the side of the house. 'I dare say Elizabeth's been filling your head with tales of how strictly the house is run and how difficult I am to please?' Elsie started to deny it, but her blush gave her away. 'Well, it's true enough that I like things done properly, but you can take at least half of what she tells you with a pinch of salt. She's young and she exaggerates to take up more room. We've all done it, but you strike me as having the sense to make your own mind up.' She beckoned Elsie closer and handed her a list. 'These are the menus I had in mind for the next few days. Obviously it's important that Hilda keeps her strength up, and I'm particularly keen that we have your pork with prunes in red wine as soon as possible. I've been trying to get Doris to make it, but it's been hopeless every time. You must leave her the recipe when you go. Actually, there are several recipes I'd like you to pass on to her. Elizabeth will give you the details of our suppliers and where we hold accounts, and if there's one thing I *really* can't abide, it's irregular mealtimes. We have breakfast at nine, lunch at one, tea at four and dinner between seven and eight. Is that clear?'

'Yes, Mrs Carline.'

'Good. We won't be entertaining now until after the baby's born, so you'll just be cooking for the household. Bear that in mind, because I hate waste. I'm sure you'll settle in quickly, but if there's anything you're unsure about, please ask. That way, we won't have any misunderstandings.'

'No, Mrs Carline.'

She ran through a few more of the house rules, then requested tea for herself and Hilda. 'And one more thing, Elsie…'

'Yes?'

Annie Carline paused, choosing her words carefully. 'It's no use pretending that I understand what goes on between my daughter and Stanley, and I dare say you know a lot more about their lives than I would ever want to. It was different in my day. You were either married or you weren't, and once you made the decision, you stuck to it.' She sighed and walked over to the mantelpiece to look down at her younger self, pictured with a snowy haired, kind-faced man. 'I hope another child will knock some sense into them, or at least give them less time to think about themselves, but the one thing I *am* certain of is how much you do to hold the family together. It requires patience and kindness to avoid taking sides in a marriage like theirs, and I appreciate your loyalty as much as they do. They're lucky to have you.' Touched and surprised, Elsie opened her mouth to speak but was interrupted before she could say a word. 'It's five to four,' Mrs Carline said, tapping her watch. 'Let's start as we mean to go on.'

26

Elsie looked forward to her afternoon walks with Shirin on Hampstead Heath, pleased to be out in the air and away from the waiting and worrying which had dominated the last days of Hilda's confinement. Rarely had she felt more exhausted or more helpless. As soon as the labour began, cries of pain from Hilda's room filled the rest of the house, and she could do nothing more than administer sticking plasters to the rest of the family, comforting Shirin at bedtime when no one would let her see her mother, and reassuring Mrs Carline. The strain of the waiting affected them both, giving their relationship a strange nocturnal life in which the conventional lines of servant and mistress were dissolved; in the early hours, when the cries were finally replaced by the harsh, indignant screams of a newborn baby, both of them were in tears. Later that morning, Elsie sent the long-awaited telegram to Stanley, imagining his joy when the news reached Burghclere. 'Girl arrived 3.10 a.m. Both splendid. Love. Writing. Hilda.'

'Can I choose her name?' Shirin asked, when she had finally decided where Elsie was to lay the picnic rug. 'I've been thinking about it, and I've got some very good ideas.'

She spoke so earnestly that Elsie had to smile. 'Mummy and Daddy will probably have their own ideas about a name, but I'm sure they'll ask you before they decide.' The spot Shirin had chosen was by the nearest of the Hampstead ponds, and Elsie smoothed the rug down so that they could sit and watch the world go by. 'Let's hear it then. What names would *you* choose for your little sister?' Like Rumpelstiltskin, she was treated to an imaginative stream of suggestions which had clearly been inspired by Shirin's most recent reading. With the possible exception of Alice, nothing seemed very suitable, and she doubted that any girl in later life would thank the flash of inspiration that had christened her Rapunzel. 'You're right, they are good ideas,' she said encouragingly, 'but we'll have to wait and see. Perhaps they'll decide when Daddy gets here.'

'Is he coming soon?'

'Later on today. That's why we've got to be home early.' Shirin took that as her cue to make the most of the afternoon, and Elsie watched, amused, as the little girl stalked a pigeon, moving from the base of one tree to another while the bird flitted about in the branches overhead. She had come to love the Heath during her time in Hampstead, partly as respite from the claustrophobic intensity of the Carline household, partly as somewhere which was genuinely different from anywhere she had ever been – a sprawling tumble of hills, meadows and ancient woodland, which kept the city landmarks at a determined distance and yet refused to be rural. Its character was different at weekends, she noticed. Usually when she was here, the paths and benches were dotted with women like her, caring with varying degrees of affection for children who were not their own. Today the children were in families of three or four, and Elsie looked on as the fathers – awkward and uncomfortable in their leisure clothes – made up for long absences during the week by flouting the discipline that their wives had worked so hard to establish. What sort of family would the Spencers make now, she wondered? Would the new baby bring them closer together, as Mrs Carline hoped, or would she be one more strain in an already delicate balancing act?

Exhausted with her nature trail, Shirin flopped down on to the rug and drank her lemonade. 'Is it nice to have a sister?' she asked, in tune with Elsie's thoughts. 'Mummy told me it was, but she hasn't got one so I can't be sure she's telling the truth.'

There was an indisputable logic to that, as there often was to Shirin's reasoning, and Elsie gave the question serious consideration. 'It's nice *most* of the time,' she said evenly. 'Sometimes you'll squabble, and sometimes you'll be jealous of each other, but the nice bits are more important than the annoying bits. Sisters look out for each other, even if they don't always get on. You grow up together and you always have that special family time in common. You'll understand how much that matters when you're older. And one thing I *can* tell you – it's much nicer than having brothers. I've got both, so you have to believe me.' She bent to whisper in Shirin's ear and the little girl giggled. 'The best bit is that you have someone to side with you against the grown-ups, but don't tell your mummy I said that or we'll both be in trouble.' In the distance, she heard the clock from St John's strike three. 'Well, sweet pea, that's our time up. I'll race you to the gate.'

She knew that Stanley had arrived as soon as she opened the front door. His tweed jacket was hanging on the rack in the hallway, too far gone now for any new paint stains to be particularly noticeable, and Elsie smiled when she saw it, surprised by how intensely it made her long for them all to be together again in their own home. Further down the hallway, Lizzie was on her hands and knees scrubbing a floor which should have been done hours ago. 'Ah, you're here at last,' she said, although the clock by the stairs confirmed Elsie's suspicions that they were back earlier than planned. 'You're to take her straight up. He wants to see her.'

Elsie took 'her' upstairs, stopping off to brush the little girl's hair and wash the grass stains from her knees. She knocked at Hilda's door and let Shirin go in ahead, cringing as her cries of delight woke the sleeping baby in Stanley's arms. She ran to her father, taking the most direct route across the bed, and he managed somehow to gather her up in his other arm. 'Hello, Elsie,' he said, his words muffled by Shirin's hug. 'Isn't she beautiful?'

'She's a dear little one, that's for sure.'

'I meant Hilda. I don't think I've ever seen her so radiant.' It was true, Elsie thought; Hilda was sitting up in bed, looking so relaxed and happy that the strain of the past few weeks might have been nothing more than a dream. Unusually, her hair was loose and it fell across her shoulders, catching the light from the window in a hundred different shades of red and gold, and reminding Elsie of the girl she had seen in the photograph. 'The baby looks awful at the moment,' Stanley added, as matter-of-factly as if he were discussing the weather, 'but she'll look lovely later.'

There was no answer to that, so Elsie busied herself in straightening the bedclothes that Shirin's joyful scramble had disturbed. 'We've decided on a name for her,' Hilda said, 'and we wanted you two to be the first to know.'

'Oh yes?' Shirin looked hopeful and Elsie waited for the announcement with the same childlike eagerness. If she'd been a betting woman, she'd have put her money on Annie, a name which was significant to both the Spencers and the Carlines; the choice, when it came, was as unexpected as some of the more outlandish suggestions on Shirin's list, and yet it seemed fitting.

'Hilda thought of it,' Stanley said proudly, 'and I think it's perfect. We're going to call her Unity.'

27

To Elsie's partial eye, Burghclere had never looked lovelier than it did that summer. The air around the cottage was filled with the sweet scent of new-mown hay, and all along Ox Drove the sun coaxed fronds of bracken from the dead leaves until they lined the path like tiny shepherd's crooks. As she walked up the lane from the main road, she noticed that Chapel View had finally earned its place in the landscape: the garden no longer looked bare and newly planted, and for the first time – much to Shirin's delight – a family of house martins had chosen to make its nest under the eaves.

She let herself in by the back door and found Stanley cooking dinner. 'Hello, Elsie,' he said, moving sausages round the pan with the handle of an old paintbrush. 'You're back early.'

'Ken's got to get up at the crack of dawn tomorrow so we called it a night.'

'But you had a good time?' She nodded. 'Good. Hilda's just gone to bath the baby.'

'Why don't you go and help her? I'll finish those off.'

'But it's your half day.'

'I don't mind. I'll bring them through when they're done.'

She swapped the paintbrush for something more appropriate, then gathered plates and a serving dish for the new potatoes. When everything was cooked, she set it to keep warm and took a tray of tea through to the dining room, noticing how cosy it looked. Hilda sat by the fire with Unity nestled in her lap, wearing a red dress with wide sleeves that made her wrists seem as slim and fragile as her daughter's. The baby had fulfilled her father's prediction, growing lovelier by the day and taking on a sunny disposition which seemed to Elsie to be a more innocent version of her sister's wry delight in the world. Her bath time was a family affair, and Shirin had been charged with fetching the grey bath mat from the airing cupboard. It began to unroll itself as she dragged it in, much to the delight of the beautiful, long-haired cat who had appeared from nowhere on their return from Hampstead and who now refused to leave. Stanley brought the bathtub in, and Elsie noticed that he had lost weight while they were away. The jacket of his suit hung loosely on him, and the lines of his face were more sharply drawn. He set the tub in place with great ceremony and Elsie went to fetch the water. She loved moments like this, the ordinary domestic rituals that defined a family's life, and she was glad to have come home early enough to be part of it.

'I'll take these two up now,' Hilda said, when Unity was bathed and Shirin had indulged in as much helpful splashing as she could justify. 'It's long past their bedtime.'

'Do you want me to take them while you have your supper?' Elsie offered, but Hilda shook her head.

'No. I've got to change anyway. I'm wet through. And Stanley's got something to tell you.'

She looked meaningfully at her husband as she left the room, but he busied himself with emptying the bath tub. 'Mary wants to buy my portrait of you,' he said eventually, when he had run out of other distractions.

'Why on earth would she want to look at me all day?' she asked.

'She's very fond of you, you know that. And anyway,' he added, slightly affronted, 'it's a very good picture. Why wouldn't she want it?'

'It'll be strange to go round and see myself on the wall. I wonder where Mrs Behrend will hang it?'

'In the drawing room, obviously. Pride of place.'

'In the kitchens, more like. Or the smoking room.' They went on in the same vein, trading possible locations until they ran out of rooms, then Elsie asked: 'What about Mrs Spencer's picture? What will happen to that?'

'Stanley won't let me sell it,' Hilda said as she came back into the room, and Elsie noticed that she hadn't changed after all. 'Have you told her?' she asked, glancing anxiously at her husband.

'I haven't had the chance yet.'

'Told me what?' Elsie looked at him questioningly, but she knew what was coming. She had dreaded this moment, the announcement of their departure from Burghclere, but she had known, too, that it was inevitable and she waited to hear if it would be Cookham or Hampstead, Stanley's victory or Hilda's.

'We're sending Shirin away for a bit,' Hilda said eventually. 'She's going to stay with my sister-in-law and her mother in Hampstead.'

The news was so unexpected that Elsie thought she had misheard. 'Sending her away?' she repeated stupidly. 'Why? What's she done?'

'She hasn't done anything,' Stanley said, with a hint of impatience in his voice. 'But Hilda needs some time to get used to the new baby. She hasn't been well since she got back, and we've all had colds that we can't shake off. It's not good for Shirin to be around illness, and Hilda can't be worrying about her on top of everything else.'

An image of her own mother passed through Elsie's mind, struggling to cope with a house full of children but making each of them feel that they were the only thing that mattered. She shook it off and looked pleadingly at the couple. 'Stanley needs to get on with the chapel without any interruptions,' Hilda said firmly, 'and he's not well, either. You know he had those terrible kidney stones while we were away, and it's bound to slow him down.'

Uncharacteristically, they were thinking of each other to justify the decision they had reached, and Elsie wondered whose idea it had been. 'Then I can do more,' she insisted. 'I can spend more time with Shirin *and* Unity.'

'You do so much already, far more than you should. And anyway, it will be nice for Shirin to have a change of scene. She loves Hampstead and the Harters will take good care of her. We mustn't be selfish about it.'

But Elsie did feel selfish, more selfish than she had ever felt in her life. 'Have they got children already, these people she's going to?'

'No. My brother's death was so unexpected, and Gwen hasn't been herself since it happened. They were denied the chance to have children of their own, you see.'

Elsie tried and failed to picture Shirin's sunny, joyful exuberance in a house of mourning strangers. 'How long is she going for?'

'We haven't decided yet. We'll see how things go.'

It was funny, Elsie thought, but Stanley and Hilda seemed more united on this decision than they had ever been before, and she noticed that they were breaking it to her gently, as though she were the one who would suffer most. She thought back to the periods of Hilda's first absence, when the house had felt so empty, and the memory of Shirin's joy at coming home struck her like a personal rebuke. 'But I promised her…' She tailed off, defeated by their solidarity and all too conscious now that she should never have promised Shirin anything.

'What did you promise her?'

She was silent for a moment, then told the first lie that came into her head. 'I promised to teach her to ride a bicycle. She'll be old enough soon and she wants one for her birthday.'

'You can still do that. She'll come back for visits.'

The final word was telling, and somehow the idea of Shirin as a guest in her own family was worse than her never coming back at all. 'Have you told her yet?' she asked, although she already knew the answer.

'No. We'll do it later this week, and we'd be grateful if you could be encouraging.'

So they knew in their hearts that Shirin would hate it. 'When will she go?'

Hilda glanced at Stanley. 'In a fortnight or so, when she's had the chance to get used to the idea.'

28

She threw the sheets off, unable to sleep in the heat. The images of the past few weeks played in her mind like a film she had never wanted to see: the hurt and confusion in Shirin's eyes when she learnt she was to be sent away; her efforts to be good each day, as if she could change her fate by becoming the child she thought her parents wanted; and then today, the car that had come to collect her and the older woman's hand on her shoulder, the strangely formal goodbyes and the small, lost figure in the back seat as it drove off down the lane. Every day, Elsie had expected Shirin to challenge her over that rash, foolish promise, but she never did – an acceptance, perhaps, that all adults were fundamentally flawed. The house was quiet after she left, and in the nursery – broken and abandoned on the little girl's pillow – Elsie found the doll she had given Shirin for her fourth birthday. There was no question that she had left it deliberately, a gesture more eloquent than any verbal accusations of betrayal, and Elsie made a vow to herself then and there that no child of hers would ever doubt her love. Now, everywhere she looked she saw the child she had cared for, and she felt her absence as a kind of grief. The Spencers felt it, too, that much was obvious, but their pain was tempered by a need to believe in the decision they had made. Even so, it took hours rather than days for their solidarity to twist itself into a mutual but unspoken sense of blame.

The room was stuffy and claustrophobic, in spite of the open windows, and suddenly she couldn't stand it any longer. She dressed quietly, finding what she needed with the help of a full moon, and slipped from her room to get some air. The staircase was dark but she knew the house so well now that it was easy to make her way to the kitchen without disturbing anyone, collecting her coat on the way in case the night proved chillier than it seemed. As an afterthought, because she could think of nowhere else to go, she took the key to the chapel from its hook by the door and let herself out into the garden.

The simple, stark outline of the building was even more pronounced at night. The silvered moonlight brought a magical, fairy-tale existence to the trees and fields, covering them with a delicate cloth of light which looked as if it might dissolve at a touch, but it had the opposite effect on the chapel, dulling the red of the brick until all that was visible was a plain, solid row of rectangular forms. She unlocked the door and went inside, unsettled immediately by how different the interior felt at night. Usually, when she closed the door behind her, the sudden dimming of the light made her think of an Egyptian tomb, but the effect was dramatic rather than frightening and the claustrophobia soon passed. This unfaltering gloom was altogether more threatening, strengthened as it was by a heavy silence. Sometimes, when the chapel was filled with the babble of visitors, Elsie had longed for a stillness such as this; now, it only unnerved her.

Familiar with the paraphernalia of Stanley's work, she quickly found the candles which he kept for emergencies, even though he rarely painted in artificial light. The strike of the match against the box sounded unnaturally loud, but she was glad of the friendly, dancing flame as she walked across to *The Resurrection*, feeling like one of the soldiers huddled round the campfire. The painted figures by the altar seemed more exaggerated than ever in the candlelight. Enormous, pale hands loomed out of the darkness, as if reaching specifically for her, and the faces – nightmarishly close to her own – transfixed her. Perhaps it was her mood, but in this light the joyful sense of being born into a new, more spiritual world was harder to find. In this light, these were the pale, blank faces of the dead.

There was a noise on the steps outside, and instinctively she blew out the candle. She heard the door open, and Stanley's voice echoed softly across the chapel. 'Elsie? Is that you?'

She breathed a sigh of relief. 'Yes. What are you doing here?'

'I couldn't sleep. I was standing at the window and I saw you go out.' He lit a candle of his own and she noticed that he hadn't bothered to dress, but had simply put a jumper on top of his pyjamas. 'I thought you'd come here and I needed to get out of the cottage.' He walked over to her and she watched the flames throw shadows on to his face. 'You're angry with us, aren't you?'

'It's not my place to be angry.' He had only used those words to her once, but they had stung at the time and she remembered them now.

'Perhaps not, but you are. You think we've done the wrong thing for Shirin.'

'Yes, I do. And not just for Shirin – for Unity, too. Sisters are important, and they'll need each other more than most.' He frowned, in puzzlement rather than anger, and his lack of understanding infuriated her. 'You don't have any idea how lonely it is to be a child of yours, do you? Having a sister could have made up for that – some of it, anyway – but it will be harder in the future if you make them strangers to each other now. You're both from close families, you and Mrs Spencer, and that's what I don't understand. How would you have felt if you'd been sent away? If you'd been separated from Sydney or Gilbert?'

'I was sent away and separated from Sydney, if you remember. The war managed that.'

'It's not the same thing and you know it.'

'You're right, it isn't.' He lifted his glasses and rubbed his eyes. 'I can't think of the war tonight,' he said, and it was hard to tell if he meant the one on the walls or the private battle raging within his own family. 'I'm too tired, and I'll be living with it all again tomorrow. Let's go outside.' He led the way to the door and sat down on the chapel steps. 'I used to come out here at dusk when you and Hilda were away,' he said quietly. 'It was too dark to paint and I didn't want to go home to an empty cottage, so I'd sit here and watch while the light disappeared. There's a single branch that sticks out from the rest of the trees over there by the cutting. I'd never noticed it in daylight, but a blackbird sits there every evening at the same time and sings its heart out. And the darker it gets, the louder it sounds. Then the owl starts further down the copse. It's just a few seconds, but it seems so momentous – the handing over of day to night, one life passing to the next. I've seen it time and again.' She assumed that he was referring now to the men who had died in his care, but she struggled to understand everything he said or to make the connections that he made; what was obvious, though, was a profound sense of melancholy in his thoughts which she had never seen before. 'There's still so much to do,' he said wearily.

It was the first indication he had ever given that the scale of the chapel daunted him. 'Does it worry you? You never show it.'

'Yes, it worries me. It's years of work and there's so much riding on it. Sometimes I see it all coming together like the most glorious piece of music. Sometimes I don't think the damned thing will ever be finished and I just want it to be over.'

There was something in the casual way he dismissed his achievements that riled Elsie, and the darkness gave her courage. 'I'm sure the Behrends would be delighted to hear you talk about it like that,' she said scornfully.

'The Behrends aren't painting it.'

'No, but they're moving heaven and earth to make sure that you can. The least you could do is finish it. I thought it was something you'd dreamt of for years?'

'It is, but that's just it. I *have* been living with it for years. I know what the whole chapel will look like, down to the very last stroke of the brush. The discoveries have all been made. Now I want something new.'

'Some*thing* or some*one*?' The question overstepped the mark, and only when she had asked it without any sense of regret did she realise that her life with the Spencers meant less to her now than it had done before Shirin's departure. Right now, she cared little for her position, and while she would probably feel differently when the household settled down again, the novelty of having nothing left to lose was liberating.

'Does it matter?'

'Of course it matters. One makes you an artist and the other makes you a fool.'

It was hard to say if the look he gave her was down to the comment itself or her temerity in saying it. 'Don't be so judgemental,' he snapped. 'Why shouldn't I love more than one person?'

'Because life's not like that.'

'Some lives are. Lots of Patricia's friends live with two lovers.'

'She told you that, did she?'

'Yes.'

'And are they happy, these friends of hers? Or is it all one big, miserable mess?' His silence encouraged her to go on. 'I don't understand what more you could want,' she said honestly. 'You spend your days doing work that you love. You've got patrons who respect you and pay you handsomely for everything you do, not to mention building a chapel to put it in and a lovely house for your family. You've got a wife you say you love and two children who worship the ground you walk on, God help them. Oh, and that reminds me – you've got God, too, or so you say, smiling benevolently down on anything you touch. I don't quite see what Miss Preece could add to that once the novelty wears off.'

She stopped to take a breath, bracing herself for the outburst she deserved, but his response wrong-footed her. 'I want what you've got. Why is that so wrong?'

'What *I've* got?' She stared at him in astonishment, wondering if he was mocking her. 'What do you mean?'

'I wish you could see yourself. Perhaps then you'd understand.' Tenderly, he touched her cheek. 'It's in your nature to be happy. I watch you going off on jaunts to your family or talking to the tradesmen or going about your work, and all the time you laugh and smile and live. That's what I want. The love songs you sing while you're working, the spring in your step when you go off for the afternoon with Ken and the smile on your face when you come home. Everything about you is looking to love, to a life ahead, and you're so full of joy that you don't even think about it. I walk into the house sometimes and I see Hilda looking tired or depressed or bored, and I feel as though I've been picked up and turned away from any sort of happiness.'

She listened to what he was saying, torn between an under-standing of what he meant and an anger at its selfishness. 'It's too easy to want what you haven't got,' she said. 'I could say the same about you and Mrs Spencer. Ken and I don't have things in com-mon like you do. You're both artists and it's the centre of your lives, so in spite of your differences you understand each other in a way we never could. Our marriage – if we have a marriage – will be full of compromises, and we just have to hope they'll be happy ones. And if we want that full life you talk about, do you know how hard we'll have to work for it? How we'll have to scrimp and save for years to afford a home of our own? How careful we'll have to be with every penny if we want to look after our children properly?'

'As opposed to giving them away, you mean?'

'I didn't say that.'

'No, but it's what you were thinking. You're going too far now.'

'Am I? Someone's got to tell you and it might as well be me. You expect too much, you *and* Mrs Spencer. Most people just want to be happy, but you're striving for some sort of harmony that doesn't exist, and the harder you try, the more you'll fail. If you carry on like this, you'll lose everything that matters most.'

He got up and began to walk away, but it was the moment for resentments to surface and Elsie had one more left. 'Why did you call that picture *Country Girl*?' she shouted after him.

'What?' He turned around, his fury cut short by the sudden change of subject.

'My portrait. You called it *Country Girl*. Mrs Spencer called hers *Elsie*, but you didn't use my name. It was as if I could have been anyone. Is that how you see me? Just a simple village girl like all the others?'

'No, but perhaps I was wrong if that's really what you think.' He took a few paces back towards her, and she was surprised by how upset he seemed. 'Is that who you see in the painting?' he demanded. 'Or in any other drawing that I've done of you? Just some girl who could be anyone?' Elsie said nothing, realising that she had been guilty of the same naivety and self-absorption that she criticised in Stanley. 'Or do you see the girl I've watched so closely, the girl whose neck I love, whose mouth, whose legs, whose whole demeanour – not because I love *them*, but because I love *her*. I called the painting *Country Girl* because it celebrates everything you and I have in common. If you're ashamed of that, if you think it was an insult, look to yourself, not to me.'

29

The seasons changed swiftly that year, ushered out by a fierce easterly wind that arrived before its time, stripping the last of the autumn leaves by mid-October and sending them scudding across the fields in brittle scraps of red and gold. Elsie walked to the chapel through a lingering mist, intending to give the place a much-needed tidy before Stanley returned from a trip to Cookham, but the door was already open when she got there. Hilda was standing in front of the painting called *Filling Tea Urns*, absent-mindedly jiggling Unity's pram with one hand, and she was such a rare visitor that Elsie found it impossible to hide her surprise. 'You've caught me red-handed,' she admitted. 'I know I'm sneaking in the minute his back's turned, but I can't concentrate when he's here. He will keep explaining things, and I just want to look at the paintings in peace.'

Elsie smiled. 'I'll come back later, when you've finished.'

'No, don't go. You won't disturb me.'

'All right, if you're sure.' They stood together and looked up at the wall in silence. It was complete now, the empty arch having been filled by Stanley's promised *Kit Inspection*, a painting of several soldiers laying out their belongings on groundsheets with varying degrees of efficiency: some struggled to straighten the blankets, one seemed to have fallen asleep and lay sprawled on top of his towel, and Elsie could only imagine how Stanley had fared in real life with a task that demanded such order and tidiness. It was by no means one of her favourite paintings – the flattened groundsheets looked too much like graves, a hint of what was to come – but she loved its detail and camaraderie. She stepped back, taking in the finished wall and *The Resurrection* combined, and the effect was so powerful, so breathtaking in its busyness, that it was hard to believe there was still more to come.

'Magnificent, isn't it?' Hilda said in a low voice, echoing her thoughts. 'It's the best thing he's done. The best thing he'll ever do, probably, although don't tell him I said that. Mind you, it *should* be good. It'll have lasted longer than the war by the time it's finished.'

Elsie laughed. 'And I dare say there'll be just as many celebrations when it is.'

'Amen to that.' She bent over the pram and stroked Unity's cheek. 'Anyway, I've got some good news for you. Shirin's coming home for her birthday and she'll stay until after Christmas. I had a letter from the Harters this morning.'

'Oh, that's wonderful!'

'Isn't it? I *have* missed her. You were right. We should never have sent her away, but I just couldn't cope. Sometimes my mind is so muddled that I feel like one of those snowstorm toys that's been picked up and shaken, and I have to get away from him until it settles again.'

Elsie had no idea what to say. She didn't doubt Hilda's anguish, but still she couldn't bring herself to endorse what the Spencers had done with any words of sympathy. 'It'll be nice to have her home.'

If Hilda expected anything more, she didn't show it. 'I'd better go,' she said, tucking Unity's blankets in against the cold. 'Stanley's bringing the Preeces back with him and Mary's expecting us all for lunch.'

Elsie watched her leave, wondering how long their marriage could continue like this without irreparable damage. She began to tidy up, her mind preoccupied by thoughts of the future. The scaffolding had been dismantled and moved to the other side of the chapel, ready for Stanley to start on the south wall, and all the detritus from the platform stood in a pile in the middle of the floor. Elsie filled one basket with rubbish and another with dirty plates and cups, then tidied the table which was always by his side when he worked, piled high with art materials: a sand-coloured leather pouch filled with pencils, sharpened until the tips were impossibly long; brushes of every size, their handles stained with trickles of colour; a fold-out measuring stick which he used to square up his canvases; and two small palettes, one for greens, greys and darker colours, the other for reds, yellows and creams. They looked like maps of foreign countries, with contours of paint hardened layer by layer across the years until it was impossible to guess at the pictures that could have been created. She ran her fingers across the rough, textured surface, looking for the paintings that might have been, and saddened by the sense of things discarded, things now lost.

30

Chopping firewood had rarely been such a pleasure. Elsie held the branch up in front of her, anchoring it with her foot, and deftly removed the twigs with a fruit pruner, watching them scatter like jackstraws at her feet. The argument had been raging for some time, and the voices drifted down to her from the bedroom, loud and clear even though the window was closed. The bone of contention seemed to be the car, but – as with other disputes in recent weeks – the subject was nothing more than an excuse for Stanley and Hilda to vent their sadness over Shirin. Her visit, though a joy while it lasted, had unsettled everyone, especially the little girl herself, and Elsie feared that it would be a long time before she returned to Chapel View.

She heard the sound of a car in the lane and saw the Behrends' chauffeured Daimler pulling up by the gate. The couple got out without waiting for the driver to open the doors, and Elsie hurriedly dropped what she was doing in the hope of heading them off, but they crossed the lawn at such a brisk pace that any interception was impossible. They seemed annoyed, which was out of character for both of them, and Mrs Behrend brandished a rolled-up newspaper as if she would dearly love to strike somebody with it. 'Good morning, Elsie,' she said. 'We need to speak to Stanley. Is he here?'

The answer came from upstairs, on cue and regrettably clear. 'I'd never have bought the bloody thing if I'd known it was just going to make it easier for you to go gallivanting here, there and everywhere,' he shouted. 'You say you hate the place, but I don't see how you can possibly know that when you're never here.'

'This isn't a very good time,' Elsie said nervously, hoping that the colour rising in her cheeks might be put down to her efforts with the wood. 'Perhaps I could give him a message?'

'I'm sorry but it can't wait. Please let him know we're here.'

Her expression deterred any more objections, and Elsie went inside. 'The Behrends are here to see you,' she said, as Stanley hurtled down the stairs. 'They don't look best pleased.'

'Neither am I. What the hell do they want?'

'An explanation,' Mary called from the kitchen, and Elsie cursed herself for leaving the back door open; she had assumed they would wait outside. 'There's an article on the chapel in this morning's *Times*, together with a very provocative editorial about people who fund extravagant private memorials while veterans are forced to live on the streets.' She threw the paper down on the kitchen table, open at the relevant page. 'This is exactly what we didn't want. We said no publicity, and we meant it.'

Stanley shrugged. 'Don't blame me. I haven't said anything.'

'So how did they hear about it? Someone must have told them. There are very specific details about the paintings.'

'The world and his wife's been through those chapel doors. Why on earth would I say negative things about my own work to *The Times*?'

He spoke with a weary, strained patience, but the Behrends refused to be placated. 'Mary's not suggesting you said anything negative,' her husband said, matching Stanley's tone with his own exasperation. 'They don't need any help with that when the country's in such a mess. All we're saying is that by alerting them to the chapel in the first place, someone has given them the perfect opportunity to put a negative slant on what we're trying to do. What we're *all* trying to do. It isn't just your reputation that's at stake here.'

'I know that, Louis, but *I* had nothing to do with this.'

Mary sighed. 'Very well, but something will have to be done about it.'

'Why? It'll blow over in a day or two.'

'I doubt that. No, we must take charge of the situation ourselves and make sure they have the facts – the real costs, for a start, rather than the ridiculous figures they're bandying round, and details of the almshouses. There's no mention here that we're providing homes for veterans and their families, so we need to set people straight.'

'What do you suggest?'

'A press day for the most important critics. We'll give them lunch at Grey House – you'll have to give Rose a hand with that, Elsie – then we'll take them over to the chapel and Stanley can talk them through the paintings.'

'But it's not finished! How can you expect them to understand the whole idea if half the paintings are missing?'

'You'll have to explain the scheme to them,' Behrend insisted, 'and we'll make it clear that it's a privilege to see you working on it. We can't afford to wait when we have no idea how much longer you'll be there. Well, do we?'

He looked pointedly at Stanley, who shook his head. 'We'll arrange it for next month, then,' Mary said. 'The weather will be better by the end of March and there'll be more natural light in the chapel.'

'We'll be in Cookham at the end of March. The house is already booked.'

'Then you'll have to come back specially,' Behrend said, glancing at his wife's worried face and finally losing his patience. 'This is non-negotiable, Stanley. We're relying on you.'

***

For once, Stanley gave in and the Behrends got their way. The press day was arranged for the last Friday of March, and much of Elsie's time was spent helping Rose with the preparations. As Stanley had predicted, her portrait – now re-titled *Country Girl: Elsie* – was hung prominently on the ground floor of Grey House, not quite in the drawing room but just outside, where her face greeted anyone coming down the stairs. She passed it several times as she carried a buffet lunch through to the dining room, and she hoped in vain that anyone attending the reception would be too preoccupied with Stanley and their own importance to recognise the servant.

The spring day was soft and warm, and the guests – chauffeured in twos and threes from the station – mingled happily on the terrace, content with their own conversation and a fine Tio Pepe. Elsie recognised a few visitors to the chapel among the crowd and most people seemed to know each other, making for a bright, convivial atmosphere which boded well for the success of the day. Despite professing no interest in such occasions, Stanley had made more effort than usual with his clothes and was now in his element, surrounded by people whose sole wish was to hear him talk about his work. 'Where's Hilda?' he asked, as Elsie passed by with another bottle.

'I'm not sure. I haven't seen her for a while.'

'She's gone back to the cottage to lie down,' Mary Behrend said, overhearing the exchange. 'Sorry, I was supposed to tell you. She said she wasn't feeling well, but she'd try to join us at the chapel.'

'What? This is a fine time for her to take to her bed. Why can she *never* support me when it matters?'

'It's unfortunate but she did look very tired. Pale, too. I wondered… well, I probably shouldn't say.'

'Say what?'

'It just crossed my mind that you might have some good news to tell us? Family news, I mean?'

'Chance would be a fine thing,' Stanley muttered, but the comment was mercifully lost in the babble of conversation. He drew breath for another tirade on Hilda's shortcomings, but she was saved from an unlikely quarter. Patricia appeared at the edge of the lawn, dressed in white and accompanied by a distinguished-looking gentleman in his sixties with a strong face and small round glasses. 'What's Roger Fry doing here?' Stanley asked irritably, watching as Patricia threw back her head and laughed at something her companion had said. 'He won't look at anything that doesn't have "Made in France" stamped on the back of it.'

'Patricia asked if she could bring him,' Mary explained patiently. 'We could hardly refuse. Be nice, Stanley.'

She went over to join her husband, and the conversation fell away at the chink of silver against crystal. 'Ladies and gentlemen,' said Louis Behrend, 'it gives me great pleasure to welcome you to Burghclere today, not just to meet one of our finest living artists, but to view the progress of his most ambitious work to date. Eight years ago, Mary and I visited Dorset and called in on our friend, Henry Lamb. It was to prove an auspicious afternoon, as Henry's guest at the time was Stanley Spencer. We had met Stanley before and already owned one of his paintings. On this particular day, which we remember very clearly, he was sitting at a table, drawing sketch after sketch for an extraordinary scheme of war pictures that had been in his mind for years. Those sketches made such an impression on both of us that we knew we had to do all we could to give them life, and we wrote to him shortly afterwards, offering to finance a building to house the paintings. His response, rather prophetically as we now know, was "What ho, Giotto!"'

A ripple of laughter ran across the terrace, and Louis continued. 'As I hope you'll agree when you see the chapel, it is not claiming too much to connect the Oratory of All Souls, Burghclere, with Giotto's beautiful Arena Chapel in Padua, both spiritually and technically. Stanley's work consists of nineteen large canvases in all: eight arches of seven feet by six; eight rectangular pictures of three feet by six; two long walls, each twelve feet by twenty-eight; and last, but certainly not least, a remarkable altar piece which measures twenty-one feet by seventeen and a quarter. Taken together, the paintings form a grand scheme of ordinary moments, and they defy all expectation. They are not propaganda, for or against the war. They are neither sentimental nor sensationalist, and many of them are not especially dramatic – and yet I challenge you to show me a more moving or intriguing interpretation of the war which casts its shadow over us all. First and foremost, they are a record of one man's experiences during four years of service to our country, and a tribute to our dear brother Hal, who – like Stanley – served in Macedonia, and who died shortly after his return.' He paused to look at his wife, who smiled and raised her glass. 'People will tell you that we commissioned this chapel. We did not. The idea was Stanley's, and Stanley's alone. It has been our great privilege to work with him to bring it to fruition and, in so doing, to build two new homes for veterans and their families. Later, when we get to the chapel, I'm delighted to say that Stanley has agreed to talk to you about the paintings and answer any questions you may have. In the meantime, please join us in the dining room for lunch.'

Elsie was too busy after that to notice much of what went on, but it was impossible to miss the frostiness between Patricia and Mary Behrend; according to the gospel of Rose, the Behrends suspected that it was she who had alerted the press to the chapel in the first place. As the guests finished their coffee, Mary walked across to the corner of the room, where Patricia and Stanley were deep in conversation, and Elsie chose her moment to collect the crockery within earshot.

'Time to make a move,' Mary said. 'We thought you could go in the first car, Stanley, so you can welcome people to the chapel as they arrive.'

'We were just talking about how well it's all going,' Patricia said. 'We must have days like this in the summer when Stanley moves back to Cookham. His paintings and Hilda's, mine and Dorothy's. It could be quite productive.'

'Back to Cookham?' Mary looked sharply at Stanley, and Patricia blushed.

'I'm sorry, I thought…'

'You're moving back to Cookham?'

'Yes,' he said brazenly. 'As soon as possible.'

'But, Stanley, you can't. What about the chapel?'

'It won't make any difference to the chapel. The south wall is nearly finished, and there's no reason why I can't paint the rest of the panels wherever I am.'

'But you'll be painting them out of context. You've done everything else *in situ*.'

'Is everything all right? People are ready to leave.' Louis looked anxiously at his wife.

'Stanley's just informed me that he's moving back to Cookham.'

'Cookham? Is that really the most sensible idea?' He waved his hand round the room. 'You've got all these people interested in your work. If you must move, wouldn't London be a better idea?'

'Louis, that's hardly the point…'

'No, my dear, of course not. I just meant that he doesn't want to be stuck in Cookham for the rest of his life.'

It was the worst thing that anyone could have said. Stanley squared up to him, barely able to contain his anger. 'I wish all the people who think they know what's best for me would consider for one moment that I might know my own heart. Now, do you want me to go and talk about these paintings or not?' He strode from the room, followed by an embarrassed Patricia, and Elsie was left to wonder if she now knew more about Stanley's plans than his wife.

31

'That wasn't so bad, was it?' Elsie took Ken's arm as they strolled across the fields behind her parents' cottage, pleased to be able to show him the countryside she had grown up in. 'You've got my mother eating out of the palm of your hand, and there's not many can say that.'

'I'm not sure your father's quite so keen.'

'You could be the Prince of Wales and still not be good enough for my father.'

He laughed, and stood aside to let her go ahead as the path narrowed. 'As long as I'm good enough for you.'

'You're that all right. And my dad will come round.'

She turned and kissed him, taking him by surprise. 'What was that for?'

'Lots of reasons, but mostly because I felt like it.' She put her hand to his cheek, tracing the creases at the corner of his eye with her thumb. 'It's nice for me to look across the family table and see someone who's there just for me. I always wondered who he'd be, and now I know.'

Ken smiled, and covered her hand with his own. They walked on in silence for a while, following the edge of a wood where trees in new leaf magnified the clap of pigeon wings. Up ahead, a row of cottages marked the boundary of the neighbouring village and Elsie paused, knowing that this was the moment she'd been waiting for. 'I've got some good news,' she said. 'At least,

I hope you'll think it's good news. The Spencers are moving to Cookham.'

'And you're going with them?' She nodded. Without warning, he picked her up and swung her around. 'I knew you had something up your sleeve. When are they moving?'

'As soon as he's found a house he likes. I don't think it'll be long.'

'But I thought Mrs Spencer wanted to go to London when the chapel was finished?'

'She did. She still does, even more so now that Shirin's there, but he was always going to get his way.'

'Well, I can't say I'm sorry.'

'No, me neither.' It wasn't a lie, exactly, but she still had mixed feelings about the move. She loved her life in Burghclere, but had come to realise that it was an interlude which could never last – and in spite of her sympathy for Hilda, she was relieved not to be going with the family to London.

'Will they get the little one back? I know how much you miss her.'

'I don't know. The Harters have grown fond of her, Mrs Spencer says. It's almost as if they don't like to ask for their own daughter back in case it offends someone, but I suppose it's hard to admit you've made a mistake. And the Harters have found her a good school in Hampstead now, so it's even harder.'

'I bet she misses you, too. You'll be a wonderful mum one of these days.' She saw him redden, and he led her over to a fallen tree trunk and sat down. 'Else, there's something I've been wanting to say to you. I've no right to ask yet and I swore to myself I'd wait until I had a bit more saved up, but now you're coming to Cookham and we'll be seeing a bit more of each other...' He tailed off and she waited for him to find the right words. 'Well, I hoped there might come a day when we'd be spending *all* of our time together. Eventually, I mean, when I can...'

Elsie laughed, and put him out of his misery. 'If that's a proposal, Ken Beckford, the answer's yes.'

32

It was the first time she had ever seen the sea, and she had expected more than this flat, grey expanse of water which sat sulkily under a cloud-streaked sky. Hilda paid for two deckchairs at the kiosk and they made their way down to the shoreline, scrunching over pebbles and shingle, with Shirin running ahead and Unity wriggling in Elsie's arms. Southwold beach was busy, but they found a spot by one of the groynes which stood at intervals along the strand, its wooden pillars marching in pairs out to sea. Hilda smoothed the blanket down and they struggled to unfold the chairs, eventually creating their own private encampment in stripes of blue and orange. Elsie looked round, daunted at first by the unfamiliar emptiness of the horizon. There was a stiff breeze from the sea, and most of the occupied deckchairs were gathered either side of a long windbreak which ran at right angles to the shoreline. Behind them, the promenade was dotted with brightly coloured beach huts, freshly painted for the season and obviously loved by their owners – a doll's house version of the pretty cottages which distinguished the rest of the Suffolk town. The ropes on either side of the esplanade served as a washing line, and a fitful sun did its best to dry the array of towels and bathing costumes that hung there, casting fleeting shadows on to the salt-and-pepper beach.

'It's a shame that Mr Spencer couldn't come today,' Elsie said, watching Shirin and Unity cover the blanket with sand. 'The girls would have loved it, and Shirin's not with us for long.'

'*Wouldn't* come, you mean.' There was an edge to Hilda's voice, which was often there now when she spoke of Stanley. 'At one time I would have danced for joy to see him working so hard to get the chapel finished, but it's Cookham that's made him do it. Nothing to do with his family or career.'

'He said you both liked the house, though.'

'Did he?' Hilda shrugged. 'It's nice, I suppose, and bigger than what we've been used to. But it's still in Cookham.'

'How much bigger?'

'Six or seven bedrooms.' She must have seen Elsie's expression change, because she added: 'No, I don't know why we need somewhere like that, either, but it suits Stanley's notion of a grand homecoming for the village's famous son.'

'And it's in the high street?' Elsie tried to recall the house from her visits to Cookham, but nothing came to mind.

'*Behind* the high street, just down from Fernlea.' Hilda rolled her eyes. 'In fact, you can see Fernlea from the back garden. I don't feel particularly encouraged by that.'

'How *do* you feel?'

Hilda waited for the squawk of gulls to die down before answering. 'Resigned to it, I suppose. Resigned, and a little frightened.'

'Of what?'

'Lots of things. How much I'll hate it there. How bored I'll be. How Stanley will change. He's changing already, you must have noticed that.' Elsie said nothing, but Hilda was right: in the past few months, the selfishness which had always been part of Stanley's personality had come to dominate all their lives, as if he genuinely believed that his wishes were the only thing that mattered. 'And I'm not a fool. I know he'll see more of Patricia when we live in Cookham.'

'What will you do if he does?'

'*When*, not if. I'll be sensible about it and try to make a friend of her. It's funny but I quite enjoy her company, so I'll let Stanley do exactly as he likes and pray that he'll get her out of his system and come back to me.' Hilda waited while Elsie hauled Shirin back from the shoreline, where she was getting far too brave with the tide. 'But there are times when I look at the family without him and think to myself that I might as well get used to it. Sooner or later, things will fall apart and there'll be no going back.'

'Surely it won't come to that?' Even as the words came out, Elsie knew that they were foolishly optimistic. Stanley was his own worst enemy, and while she desperately wanted Hilda to fight for her marriage, she knew somehow that she wouldn't.

'He told me the other day that he can't bear the idea of divorce, so he must be thinking about it, even to dismiss it.' The word shocked Elsie. She watched the waves lick at the shore and recede, their pattern laboured and unchanging like a music hall star performing the same tired sketch every night. 'But if anyone can stop it coming to that, it will be Patricia, not Stanley.'

'What do you mean?'

'Dick's been telling me what he's heard about her from friends.' She was about to go on but seemed to change her mind, and Elsie didn't feel she could press the point. 'Even if it's what Stanley wants, I don't think she'll marry him. But it will be better for both of us if he finds out once and for all how he feels about her, and he'll only do that if they spend more time together.'

'And you'll stand by while they do?' Elsie tried to put herself in Hilda's position, but she knew that she would never be able to accept such an arrangement. It would be all or nothing, on both sides.

'Not stand by, no. I'll have to spend more time away. I know that's not the answer, but I can't see an alternative. The stupid thing is, I don't think he ever means to hurt me. He's just thoughtless.'

'Sometimes that's worse. It's harder to change, at any rate.'

'Yes, I suppose it is.' Hilda sighed and joggled Unity on her lap, bringing forth the most irresistible of smiles. 'They don't deserve any of this, do they? Sometimes I wonder if we'll ever be able to look back at their childhood and find a moment that isn't tarnished with guilt and regret.'

33

'I've left my glasses in the chapel. Go and fetch them, Elsie, will you?'

She agreed willingly, glad to have an excuse to look at the long south wall painting that Stanley had recently finished. The first residents had moved into one of the almshouses and the key was now kept there so that builders and visitors didn't have to call at Chapel View. It added ten minutes to any visit: Mrs Bainbridge was a cheerful soul who had come from the city and missed her friends, but she was a nice woman and Elsie never minded stopping to chat. She admired the new curtains, gave advice on cooking beef, and collected the key, promising to drop it back as soon as she had finished.

It was the best time of day to visit, and the light filtered through the tall chapel windows. In some ways, the new painting echoed its counterpart on the opposite side, but the setting was a riverbed, not a camp, and it felt strangely empty. There was none of the detail that Elsie loved, and she wondered if that was a true memory or if Stanley had simply been in a hurry to finish? The sun chose that moment to emerge from a bank of cloud, illuminating the soldier nearest the window, the only human presence in that part of the canvas. He was returning from the river after washing his clothes – a small, dark figure, bare-chested and precariously balanced on two large boulders. He steadied himself with outstretched arms – one gesturing back to *The Resurrection*, the other pointing at the door – and he straddled two worlds, torn between war and peace, confinement and escape. Perhaps it was a coincidence, but it seemed an eloquent expression of Stanley's current dilemmas. She found his glasses on the altar step and turned to go, but there was a poignant finality in the act which held her back. Muffled noises came from the house next door as Mrs Bainbridge moved from room to room, but to Elsie it was the unmistakable sound of life moving on. Her time here was coming to an end. The scaffolding would be taken down and the final panels transported from Cookham as soon as they were finished, and the chapel would carry on without them for as long as people wanted to remember. She looked round at the faces she had lived with, the soldiers and the orderlies and the hundred different Stanleys, and knew how much she would miss them. For the first time, as she was about to leave the life she loved, she truly understood what Stanley's work here was all about and why it mattered so much to him. Memories of the past three years played in her head like a chapel of her own creation, the scenes so vivid and familiar that she trusted them now to stay with her.

34

The car drew up behind the removal van and Elsie looked at her new home for the first time, responding with a mix of emotions. There was no question that Lindworth was a handsome property, tucked away behind Cookham High Street. It was semi-detached and set in substantial gardens, which gave it both peace and privacy, but there was no hint of the cosiness that she had loved about the Spencers' home in Burghclere. The house seemed impossibly vast, bigger even than she had expected, with sprawling accommodation on three floors, and as the removal men began to unload the van, its familiar contents seemed woefully inadequate.

Inside, her fears were confirmed. Although the downstairs rooms were spacious and well-appointed, with high ceilings and elegant fireplaces, the décor was shabby and the house had a run-down feel, as if the previous occupants had struggled with its upkeep. In places, the wallpaper was peeling and the air smelt damp, and there were certainly none of the modern conveniences like gas or electricity which she had hoped a move to Cookham might bring. With a sinking heart, she went in search of the kitchen quarters and immediately felt as if she were stepping back in time by at least twenty years. As she came face to face with a stubborn-looking apology for a range, she realised how spoilt she had been in Burghclere. Unlike the newly built Chapel View, Lindworth had plenty of dark corners in which dust could gather, not to mention a bewildering number of stairs and more draughts through loose-fitting windows than could ever be effectively plugged. It was the sort of house which – before the war – would have had two or three servants to run it.

Stanley was directing the removal men from a vantage point on the stairs, so Elsie went in search of Hilda to check that Unity was safe. She found them both in a large, oval-shaped sitting room which overlooked the lawn at the side of the house, the pram having been placed in a shaft of welcome light from the French windows. To Elsie's amusement, Hilda was preoccupied in arranging a bunch of snowdrops that she had brought from the garden at Burghclere, utterly oblivious to the chaos in the hallway and the larger task at hand. The vase – obviously the only one she could lay her hands on – was far too big for the flowers, but she had managed to make the combination work and now stood back to admire her efforts. The gesture reminded Elsie of the early days at Chapel View, when Hilda's refusal to address the unpacking had infuriated her, but she also found it strangely endearing. Suddenly, with that collection of delicate, white-green flowers, so lovingly grown and transported, the room felt like home. 'They're beautiful,' she said, joining Hilda to admire them. 'I thought I'd make some tea if I can find the kettle.'

'That would be lovely. Do you want me to go for milk?'

'If you don't mind.'

There was a crash from the hallway, followed by some choice words from Stanley, and Hilda winced. 'On the contrary. I'd be glad to escape.'

She pushed the pram out through the French windows and headed for the high street, leaving Elsie to make sense of the kitchen. Once she had resigned herself to the scale of the job, she began to enjoy the challenge and spent a pleasant few minutes planning the changes she would make once they had all settled in. 'Elsie! Elsie, where are you?' She traced Stanley's voice to the sitting room and found unexpected company. 'Patricia and Dorothy have dropped in to welcome us back to the village,' he said, and she noticed that he was holding a bunch of exotic flowers. 'Isn't that kind of them?'

'Very kind.'

Before she could stop him, Stanley took Hilda's hint of spring from the vase and dropped them on to the hearth, replacing them with the grander flowers. 'Make us some tea, will you, while I give the girls a tour?'

He led Patricia and Dorothy out of the room, as if he were showing the house to prospective clients, and Elsie stooped to collect the discarded snowdrops.

'What happened?'

Hilda was standing at the French windows, a bottle of milk in her hand, and Elsie looked at her apologetically, unable to think of any explanation other than the real one. 'Miss Preece and Miss Hepworth are here.'

'Of course they are.'

Hilda left the milk on the step and wandered out to the garden with Unity in her arms. Elsie longed to follow, but there was nothing she could say to repair the damage, so she found a jam jar for the snowdrops and warmed the pot with a very bad grace. Before the tea had time to brew, a loud knock called her back to the hallway. Swearing quietly under her breath, she wrenched the door open with no attempt to hide her impatience. 'Ken!' she said, delighted to see him. 'What are you doing here?'

'I thought I'd make sure you've got everything you need, but I've obviously picked a bad time.'

'I'm beginning to think there'll never be anything else,' she said, guiding him round the boxes to the kitchen. 'And we've only been here an hour.' She shut the kitchen door behind her and gave him a hug. 'You have no idea how pleased I am to see you.'

'Not too grand to speak to me yet, then,' he laughed. 'This is one hell of a house, I must say. Here, I've brought you a few things from the van. Just some cheeses and a bit of cooked meat, and a fresh loaf of bread. I thought you'd have enough on without worrying about the shopping.' He put the basket on the table, and his kindness was so welcome that she could have cried. 'What's up, Else?' he asked, putting a hand on her shoulder.

'Nothing, really. It's just all so different. I suppose I'll get used to it.'

'Of course you will. You'll be queen of your own castle again before you know it.'

She nodded, unconvinced. 'It's gone to his head, this success,' she said, unpacking the groceries. 'When I first met him, he wasn't bothered about anything as long he could work. Now we've got to have this great big house and the new piano's due at three.'

Ken squeezed her arm and looked at her, concerned. 'Why do you stay with him? You could have your pick of households, and they'd all give you a lot less trouble than this one.'

Elsie hesitated, unsure of how to justify her affection for Stanley to herself, let alone anyone else. 'I couldn't leave them now, not when they've just moved, and Unity's had enough disruption as it is.'

'Well don't get too upset about it. Things will settle down, and it's not forever, is it?'

'No, it's not.'

He looked at his watch. 'I'd better be off. Will you be all right?'

'Course I will.'

'And we're still on for Thursday?'

'If I haven't run away by then.'

'Don't do that, not when I can give you a lift.' He winked and left her to it, and she took a tray of tea through to the sitting room, scarcely caring if it was cold by the time Stanley and his guests came to find it. Her own suitcases still stood at the foot of the stairs and she picked them up, one in each hand, to take them to the second floor. Her room was at the back of the house, overlooking the garden. It was twice the size she was used to, and while she was pleased with the extra space, she would willingly have swapped it for another pair of hands around the kitchen. She walked over to the window and looked down at the gardens and rooftops. Terracotta tiles provided the only splashes of warmth and colour in a world of muted greys, and every garden looked tired and faded, held in limbo by the winter. Next door, swathed in scarves and mittens, a little girl with red hair was dancing on the lawn.

A knock at the door made her jump. 'You might as well have these,' Hilda said, holding up the snowdrops. She joined Elsie at the window and put the jar on the sill.

'Thank you. They're lovely, and they'll last a lot longer than orchids in a house as cold as this.' Hilda smiled and Elsie gestured down to the garden. 'I was just thinking, there's plenty out there to keep you busy.'

'I know. That's what I missed at Burghclere – those lovely surprises you get from an older garden when you spend your first year with it.' Stanley emerged from the house with Patricia and Dorothy, and they watched as he pointed to the far corner of the lawn, where a pergola stood. 'That's where he's going to have his studio built,' Hilda said, as if it were the thing most worthy of comment.

There was a long silence, broken only by a pair of rooks bickering in the nearby trees. 'Why won't you put up more of a fight?' Elsie asked eventually, as bewildered by Hilda's passive role in the destruction of her marriage as she was by Stanley's stupidity. 'For the kids, if not for yourself? You know he loves you. Is it just pride that's stopping you? Because you might come to regret that.'

'No, it's not pride.'

'Then what?'

Outside, Stanley touched Patricia's arm and Hilda looked away. 'I've never known a village with as many walls as Cookham,' she said, staring out across the gardens. 'Just look at them. They're everywhere.' She was right, although it had never occurred to Elsie before. 'Still, we're here now. I suppose we'll just have to make the best of it.'

'Love is the essential power in the creation of art and love is not a talent.'

Stanley Spencer

1

Dorothy stood at her bedroom window and watched as the removal van made its way slowly along the edge of Cookham Moor, cautiously avoiding the dregs of winter flooding. She traced its progress towards the village, past the Crown Hotel and the war memorial, pausing briefly by the blacksmith's to allow a horse and cart to pass, then moving off again only to disappear among the taller buildings at the head of the high street. Long after there was anything left to see, she stared out across the Moor, her landscape indistinct through the leaded, rain-splashed windows; the day had come, and she didn't need to keep the van in sight to know where it was heading. The vague unease which had taken root slowly but surely in recent months hit her hard now, fist-tight and spiteful in her stomach – a kind of grief, she supposed, although nothing as yet was lost. In the cold, damp room, she shivered.

And there it was, as if summoned by her fears – the familiar maroon car on its way to Lindworth. She imagined the Spencers in the front seat, bickering as they always did, each taking pleasure in the other's discomfort. It was something that she and Patricia had begun to do more often, she noticed, and it saddened her. When she thought back to those early days in Cookham – carefree and united, never doubting Patricia's love – it was as if someone else had lived them.

She heard footsteps on the stairs and Patricia's voice, light and animated. 'They're here, darling. I've just seen the car across the Moor.' Dorothy turned to the door and caught her breath, scarcely more trusting of Patricia's beauty now than she had been when they met. She remembered that first glimpse of her, standing in a narrow corridor at the Slade, leaning against a pile of crates which held the drawing boards and talking to one of the tutors as though only he and she existed. The passage was dingy and claustrophobic, depressingly quiet at the end of the war, but even those drab surroundings were transformed for Dorothy by the life which seemed to spill from the woman in front of her. Patricia had turned and smiled, curious to be gazed at so intently by a stranger, and it was as much as Dorothy could do not to look back over her shoulder for someone more deserving of such attention. Now, standing in the doorway, Patricia had that same vitality, sharpened by age into something more worldly, and for a moment Dorothy was that shy, insecure girl of nineteen again. 'Dorothy, did you hear me?' Patricia asked impatiently. 'Why are you looking at me like that?'

'Yes, I heard you.'

'Then don't just stand there. It's time we were going.'

'If we must.'

'Come on, darling. We agreed to go over and welcome them.'

'Yes, but I don't see why we need to go panting round to Lindworth as soon as they arrive. How will that look, Peggy? The neighbours find enough to talk about as it is.'

Patricia sighed. 'It's none of their damned business what you and I do. Anyway, what's so scandalous about visiting friends?'

'Absolutely nothing. But whenever Stanley Spencer's in Cookham these days, he spends more time at Moor Thatch than he does with his family – and that *is* worth a raised eyebrow and a sly remark, don't you think?' Dorothy shook her head in frustration. 'I can't understand why you're encouraging him.'

'I'm not encouraging him, at least not in the way you're implying. But he might be useful, to both of us.'

'I don't see how.'

'He's on the up, Dodie. Look how well the press responded to the chapel when they were finally allowed inside it…'

'As I recall, that was *you* being useful to *him*.'

'And he's convinced that the Academy is going to offer him membership at any minute,' Patricia continued, ignoring the interruption. 'It can't hurt to have someone like that talking about our pictures.'

'But that's just it. He doesn't even talk about our pictures when he's here, in our company, so I doubt he gives them a second thought when he's anywhere else. He's selfish, Peggy. The only thing he truly cares about is his own work, nobody else's.'

'But he can still introduce us to people.'

'Can he? When he's spent the past five years in the middle of nowhere? And you've got your own contacts. We do all right.'

'But we could do better.' The phrase was so like a spoilt child's that Dorothy half expected Patricia to stamp her foot. 'Anyway, he's amusing enough and I like Hilda very much. You did, too – at least you said you did.'

'It's not Hilda who's going to sit in our kitchen every afternoon for weeks on end, though, is it? Now that they're moving back here, we'll never be rid of him.'

'Oh, don't go on so, darling. You're wearing me out, and you know you're being ridiculous.' It was Patricia's practised response to any situation she found difficult, and – as far as she was concerned – it always settled an argument in her favour. She looked Dorothy up and down, making it clear that the conversation was closed. 'You're not going round to Lindworth like that, are you?'

Dorothy glanced over to the full-length mirror and saw her own shabbiness reflected back in the heavily repaired shoes and a tweed suit which had seen more winters than she cared to remember. 'Why not?' she snapped, ashamed of the contrast between her own outfit and the chic woollen dress that Patricia had chosen. 'What do you want me to wear? No one will be looking at me. He barely notices if I'm in the room.'

'Even so, you need to make more effort.' Patricia went over to the wardrobe and rummaged briskly through the hangers, making Dorothy feel like a fading chaperone who was about to embarrass her ward at a party. 'You're being awfully unfair, you know. Stanley *is* intriguing. I've never met a man quite like him.'

If she was trying to be provocative, she had succeeded. 'What do you mean?' Dorothy demanded, hating the note of uncertainty in her voice which she had noticed more often of late. 'Just how much *do* you like Stanley Spencer?'

'As much as it takes to get what I want. What *we* want.' She chose a dress which was far too flimsy for the season and laid it out on the bed. 'I don't know why you won't just let the subject drop. Stanley's perfectly harmless and you're making much more of this than you need to.'

Any hint of reassurance was lost in the weariness of Patricia's tone, and she left the room without another word. Dorothy followed her downstairs, tired of the bickering and keen to reach a truce before they had to face the Spencers, but all her good intentions disappeared when she saw a large spray of orchids on the table in the hallway, elaborately dressed with ribbon. 'Where on earth did they come from?' she asked.

'I had them sent up from London. They're a house-warming present.'

'But you know we can't afford that sort of gesture. They must have cost a fortune.'

Patricia shrugged defensively. 'We can't go round there empty-handed, and one little extravagance won't hurt.'

'One little extravagance that would have fed us for a week.' The row opened up before her and Dorothy was helpless to stop it. Somehow, regardless of his physical presence, Stanley always seemed to be in the house with them these days, chipping away at their happiness and widening the cracks in their relationship that money worries had already opened up. For the thousandth time, she wondered what had happened to those carefree days in Paris, when they had survived on so little and needed only their freedom and each other to be happy. Perhaps it was age, perhaps familiarity, but Patricia was no longer content to make do – and neither, if she was honest, was Dorothy. 'We sit here night after night in the cold because we can't afford the heating,' she said bitterly. 'We're not eating properly and neither of us is truly well, and yet you spend our money on hothouse flowers. Now who's being ridiculous?'

Patricia glared at her. 'All the more reason to improve our situation. Don't nag so, darling. Think of these as an investment. A considerably more reliable investment than your father's, I might add.'

'Don't you dare throw that in my face. If it weren't for my family, we wouldn't have a house to lose in the first place.' Dorothy bit her tongue, cross with herself for having risen to the bait. Her father had financed the mortgage on Moor Thatch through the family business, but the business was now threatened by liquidation, and she still felt unjustly responsible for their precarious financial situation. 'I can't work any harder,' she admitted, unable to keep the emotion out of her voice. 'I'm painting here, day in, day out, because it's the only thing I know how to do, and still we're in this mess.'

Defeated, she sat down on the stairs, her head in her hands, and Patricia came over to comfort her. 'I'm sorry. That was mean of me. I know how hard you work, but let's face it – our pictures don't carry much of a price at the moment. We need something else.'

Dorothy took Patricia's hand, feeling trapped by the truth of what she said. 'But does it really have to be this?'

She had expected the remark to usher in another round of objections, but Patricia's expression changed to one of intense sadness, all traces of anger suddenly gone. 'I wish we'd never come here,' she said quietly, and Dorothy felt the familiar sense of being blown off course. 'Why didn't we choose somewhere else? Somewhere more anonymous, where we could have been on our own?'

'We could move,' Dorothy suggested. 'We don't have to stay in a place that makes us unhappy.' Once spoken, the idea astonished her with its simplicity, ushering in the possibility of a new beginning for them both, and she realised that all she had needed to allay her fears was Patricia's tacit acknowledgement that they were still united.

'And sell the house for less than we paid for it, with an even bigger debt round our necks? How would that help?' She put a hand gently to Dorothy's cheek, forcing eye contact. 'I'm trying to make things better for us, darling, but only by sticking to what we agreed. You paint the pictures and I make the contacts. We're a team, and we just have to do what we're good at. It's always worked for us before.'

Dorothy nodded. 'Yes, it has.'

'Then trust me now and everything will be fine.' Patricia smiled. 'You do owe me an apology, though.'

'Do I? What on earth for?'

'I *never* pant.'

They both laughed, relieved that the crisis had passed. 'Promise me you won't let him suck you in,' Dorothy said. 'I couldn't bear it if he came between us.'

'When has anyone ever managed to do that?' Patricia asked, and it was true. Since those first days of friendship at the Slade, the outside world had been kept firmly at bay, with the only threat to their unity coming from their own insecurities. 'But I *do* promise. This is for us, nothing more. And you'll be there to look after me.'

As always, Dorothy thought, but she let the truce stand. 'We'd better get it over with. Give me a minute to change.'

She went back upstairs and put on the dress that Patricia had chosen for her, compensating with the warmest coat that she owned. Patricia picked up the flowers, as delicate and fragile as she was in the biting February cold, and they set out together towards the high street. People glanced curiously at them as they passed, and Dorothy was glad to turn into the enclosure at the back of the King's Arms, away from the busy main thoroughfare. Lindworth stood at the far end of the yard behind a discouraging brick wall, and there was something about the salvo of bare windows and sharply angled walls that Dorothy found instantly depressing. The removal van was parked where the drays usually unloaded, and three men in brown overalls were losing patience with a sofa which seemed to defy all their efforts to cajole it through the garden gate. They heard Stanley before they saw him, shouting instructions from inside the house, his voice quavering slightly as it always did when it was raised. 'Just turn it on its side and bring it into the sitting room. We haven't got all day, and I need you to get the paintings safely indoors before the rain starts again.'

The men did as he suggested, and Dorothy and Patricia followed the convoy up the garden path. Stanley beamed when he saw them, and fought his way past the sofa to give Patricia a kiss. 'We've brought these for Hilda,' she said, holding up the flowers. 'A splash of colour until you get yourselves sorted.'

'How thoughtful of you. I've no idea where she's gone, but she'll love them. Come into the sitting room.' He stood aside to allow Patricia through the front door, guiding her towards the first room on the left-hand side of the hallway, and Dorothy followed on behind, resigning herself to a day of being invisible. It was a curious space, oval shaped and dark, and in serious need of decoration. 'Elsie!' Stanley called, making Dorothy jump. 'Elsie, where are you?' The maid arrived, red-faced and unusually flustered, and greeted the visitors with a mixture of surprise and displeasure. 'Patricia and Dorothy have dropped in to welcome us back to the village,' he said. 'Isn't that kind of them?'

'Very kind.' There was an edge to Elsie's voice, the words just the right side of civility, and her mood wasn't helped when Stanley took a bunch of fresh snowdrops from an outsized vase and replaced them with the spray of orchids. 'Make us some tea, will you, while I give the girls a tour.'

The term grated on Dorothy and she objected more firmly than she had intended, earning a warning look from Patricia. 'There's really no need. You've obviously got a lot to do and we don't want to hold you up.'

'Don't be silly. It's no trouble at all, and it won't take Elsie long to get the place sorted. Come on, we'll start on the first floor.' He chattered constantly as he led them up the stairs and into a succession of empty rooms, seemingly interchangeable except for their size and outlook. Somehow, Patricia found something new and enthusiastic to say about a fireplace here or a dado rail there, and Dorothy marvelled at her ability to ingratiate herself in any company, especially one as inclined to be flattered as Stanley. He basked in the praise as if he had built the house himself, happy to accept Patricia's assessment of its status and his obvious right to it, and Dorothy found that she was almost beginning to enjoy herself. 'It's quite an investment,' he said, when they were half-way through the delights that the first floor had to offer. 'Seven bedrooms in all. Far too much space for just the three of us and Elsie.'

Dorothy looked sharply at him, trying to work out if his words carried a subtext or if her paranoia was simply getting the better of her, but it was impossible to tell. There was a noise on the gravel below, and from the landing window she could see Hilda guiding the pram round the side of the house, talking all the time to Unity, with a bottle of milk nestled in the child's blankets. 'Then you'll be bringing Shirin home, I suppose,' she said, turning back to Stanley. 'You must miss her.' Patricia's face had that sharp, strained expression which threatened an outburst as soon as the situation allowed for one, and she took Stanley's arm before he could answer, encouraging him to move on.

The rest of the upstairs rooms were spacious but drab, with draughts that made Moor Thatch seem tropical, and, while the tour ploughed relentlessly on, Dorothy tried not to imagine Patricia making herself at home here. As they reached the last room, she heard angry footsteps on the stairs to the attic, presumably Elsie going up to the servant's quarters, and when they got back downstairs there was a tray of tea and biscuits waiting on one of the packing cases in the sitting room. The milk was now in a jug and someone had tidied the discarded snowdrops from the hearth, but there was no sign of Hilda. Ashamed of how hungry she was, Dorothy poured the tea and ate the biscuits, listening while Stanley outlined increasingly extravagant plans for the house and garden, apparently oblivious to his wife's absence. After a while, he set his cup down with an air of finality and she hoped that they might be allowed to leave, but instead of showing them to the front door he opened the French windows and led them across the lawn to a pergola which had seen better days. 'And this,' he said, with the flourish of a conjuror who had saved his best trick till last, 'is where I'm going to have my studio.' He must have seen Dorothy's eyes stray back towards the redundant rooms in the house because he added: 'There's not enough light inside. Hilda says she'll make do, but I can't.'

'How many paintings have you still got to do for the chapel?' Patricia asked, looking doubtfully at the corner of the garden in which the work would be completed.

'Four. Then I can move on.'

'To what? You'll do some landscapes, I suppose?'

'If I must,' he muttered.

'The house won't do itself up.'

'No, and we could do with a bit more comfort.' Stanley looked at Patricia and smiled, and Dorothy wondered if either of them knew how much like a married couple they sounded. She opened her mouth to say something that would hasten their departure, but Stanley had been encouraged to expand on plans for his work and he was there ahead of her. 'I've been thinking about the next big project,' he began. 'Something even more splendid than Burghclere. Something to celebrate Cookham, and everything that's dear to me.'

He touched Patricia's arm and Dorothy turned away, scared by what she might see in her lover's face. A movement at the top-floor window caught her eye, and she saw Hilda and Elsie standing together, looking down at them. The maid moved back into the room – embarrassed, perhaps, to have been caught watching so intently – but Hilda remained at the window, staring out across the rooftops. Eventually she looked down to the garden again and met Dorothy's gaze, a silent observer of the shipwreck that threatened them both, and a fleeting moment of understanding seemed to bring them together. Dorothy raised her hand, half in acknowledgement, half in supplication, and prayed to God that Hilda Spencer loved her husband enough to fight for him. It was the only sliver of hope that she had.

2

Despite an unpromising start, life at Lindworth settled into a routine that suited everyone. While his studio was being built, Stanley busied himself lining the sitting room walls with bookshelves which he and Hilda filled together, surrounding themselves with the volumes of art and poetry that they both loved. The gramophone and record collection were soon unpacked, and their evenings were spent listening to music or taking regular trips to the Regal in Maidenhead. Elsewhere, furniture in the house was sparse but the walls were covered in paintings, and at Stanley's insistence most of them were Hilda's. Her portrait of Elsie, still one of the couple's most treasured possessions, took pride of place in the hallway, where Stanley could see it through the open door whenever he played the piano. To Elsie's surprise, Hilda showed no inclination to go to Hampstead but welcomed her mother and friends from London for occasional weekends. And she was as good as her word where the Preeces were concerned, gracious to both Patricia and Dorothy; if anything, she seemed to get on better with them than Stanley, who became difficult and quarrelsome with the women if his opinions were ever questioned.

'Can I borrow some photographs?' he asked one morning while Elsie was washing up.

'What sort of photographs?'

'Anything really. Something of your family. Pictures that you like to have around you.'

'I dare say I could find you some.'

'Good. Leave them in the studio when you've got a minute. I'll take good care of them.'

She finished the morning chores, then went up to her room to find what he wanted, choosing half a dozen of her favourite photographs: a family portrait and one of her parents on their own; a snap of Ken, which he had given her recently; a picture of her brothers in naval uniform and the photo of their ship that went with it; and one of herself as a little girl, just to see if he would recognise her. The studio was empty, so she laid them on the table next to his easel and took advantage of the peace to look at the latest chapel painting. It was almost complete and showed patients in a ward at Beaufort – dressed in blue suits, with pale, convalescent faces, sitting round a table having tea. The picture made her smile, so ordinary on the surface but filled with all the things that its creator most loved, and it reminded her of how much she missed her daily visits to the chapel. She had no idea where this new canvas fitted into the overall scheme, and she knew that only when a painting was seen with its neighbours did it acquire the full significance that Stanley intended. He, too, was obviously having to work hard to keep the unity of the chapel in mind: the studio was covered in detailed sketches of every image, those planned and those already executed, but she doubted that even Stanley's miraculous memory could match the peculiar, highly charged atmosphere of being there.

He had recently been working on a number of landscapes, and the small space was filled with views of Cookham. A set of brightly coloured canvases stood neatly against the wall and she knelt to look through them, but what struck her most vividly was a sketch rather than a painting. It was a drawing of a man – obviously Stanley – separating two fighting swans on the river bank while three angels looked on. A woman sat in the foreground, holding a book and staring into the distance, and Elsie assumed it was Hilda, but on closer inspection she saw that she was wrong. She had never known Stanley to include Patricia in a painting before. The setting was a part of Cookham where he had talked of playing as a child, and the combination of the birds with such a special place reminded her of *Swan Upping*, the painting that had sustained him through four years of war. To Elsie's eyes, Patricia's presence in the work was jarring and ill-omened, a figure far more significant than those faint pencil lines suggested.

Raised voices from the house confirmed her fears. She put the sketch back and headed across the lawn in her now familiar role as peacemaker, but this time she was too late. Hilda was outside with the car, putting Unity gently into the back seat, and Elsie's heart sank when she saw the suitcase on the pavement. 'Where are you going?' she asked, although she already knew the answer.

'Home, to Hampstead. I've got to get away. I can't believe what he's suggesting. No wonder he wanted such a big house. The idea that we could all…' She tailed off, unable to bring herself to finish the sentence. 'Well, it's disgusting. I'll need you to send some things on, but I can't think straight now. I'll write when I'm settled.'

'How long are you going for?'

'I don't know this time. I'm sorry, Elsie, but he's left me no choice.'

3

'He's still there. I thought he'd have given up by now.'

Dorothy glanced past Patricia to the stile on the edge of the Moor, where Stanley had been sitting for the past hour, hunched and watchful like a self-appointed gatekeeper to the village. 'That's the rub of a beautiful spring day. At least rain drives him in.' She took a step back and squinted at the canvas in front of her. 'I thought you asked him not to come here so often.'

'I asked him not to call at the house every day. I didn't know he'd sit outside instead.'

'Then just ignore him. He'll have to go home sooner or later, and I'll never get this picture finished if you keep turning round to look at him.'

'Sorry.'

Dorothy worked on in silence, but Patricia wasn't the only person distracted by the motionless figure beyond the window and she was glad when the portrait was as finished as it would ever be. She examined her work critically, wondering why she could never quite capture the Patricia she loved. The woman who reclined on the chaise longue was instantly recognisable, skilfully painted with the instinctive understanding of form that had earned Dorothy an invitation to the Slade from Henry Tonks himself, and yet there was something missing, something fundamental.

'Can I see?' Patricia pulled a dressing gown around her shoulders, and Dorothy nodded. They looked at the painting together, and the more Dorothy stared at it, the more dissatisfied she became. 'It's lovely,' Patricia said, looking down at the stylised, one-dimensional version of herself. 'Thank you, darling. You always make me look so much better than I really am.'

Perhaps that was it, Dorothy thought. There was no rawness in the image, nothing lurking below the surface except her own desire to please. 'You'd better sign it.' She picked up one of the finer brushes and Patricia used it with a flourish at the bottom right-hand corner of the picture.

'What shall we call it? *Self Portrait* doesn't seem very honest somehow.'

'*Self Portrait* is fine. It's nobody's business who does what in this house.'

'I suppose it's no worse than putting my name to a still life when I've done nothing but arrange the fruit.' Patricia gave her a wry smile and stood the painting gently in the corner with three other canvases of a similar size. 'I'll take them up to town tomorrow and see what I can get for us. Come with me. We'll have lunch to celebrate.'

'Anything to get me away from here. It's like being under siege.' Stanley had moved from the stile now and was pacing up and down in the lane outside, his eyes fixed on the house. Dorothy watched as two women left the Crown Hotel and headed in the direction of School Lane; as they drew closer, she saw one nudge the other and point towards Moor Thatch. 'People are staring,' she said angrily. 'You'll have to let him in.'

'But you said his voice was driving you mad and you couldn't tolerate him in the house.'

'It's better than watching him hang around outside, humiliating us in front of the whole village. I'd like to hold my head up in the high street. If I have to pay with my sanity, so be it.'

'All right. Thank you, darling.'

Patricia kissed the top of Dorothy's head, dispelling any illusions that an afternoon with Stanley would be purgatory for both of them. She stood in front of the mirror, and Dorothy watched in surprise as she tidied her hair and tightened the belt on her dressing gown. 'Surely you're going to get dressed first?'

'I'm perfectly respectable as I am,' Patricia insisted, hurrying out into the hallway. 'And be nice!' she called back over her shoulder.

'Aren't I always?'

Dorothy heard the bolts sliding back on the front door, and Stanley's voice – raised in complaint – spilled immediately into the house. She braced herself against a tide of recriminations for making him wait so long, but surprisingly the source of his resentment lay elsewhere. 'I can't believe that Mary's been sending reproductions of the chapel paintings out to all and sundry behind my back,' he grumbled, flinging himself into the nearest armchair without so much as a glance at Dorothy. 'I had to hear from Gil that there were crits in the papers. Didn't it occur to her that I might be interested in what people are saying about my work?'

'Outrageous,' Patricia said soothingly. 'You should have the final say on that sort of thing. I'd insist on it if I were you.'

'I think I will. In fact, after the chapel's been open for a bit, I've a good mind to send the moveable pictures down to London for an exhibition. If Mary wants reviews, let's see what that does for her.'

'Would you be allowed to do that?' Dorothy asked innocently. 'After all, the paintings aren't really yours any more, are they? I imagine the Behrends would prefer to keep them in the chapel they've paid for.'

Stanley glared at her and Patricia poured oil on troubled waters. 'Talking of galleries, we're going up to town ourselves tomorrow. Dorothy's done some beautiful sketches, and I've got a few new oils to show.' She picked up the nude 'self portrait' and showed it to him, perching on the arm of his chair. 'I'm rather pleased with how they've turned out.'

Stanley took the canvas and put it on the floor by his feet, as if it were nothing but an irritation. 'I'm having a devil of a job with the latest chapel painting,' he admitted. 'It's far too busy and the scale of the figures is all wrong. It won't sit with the rest of the pictures.'

'What's the subject?' Patricia asked, and Dorothy noticed how much more interested in the chapel she sounded now that she wasn't obliged to visit it.

'It's a route march with an officer reading a map. His men are at the bottom, resting by the side of a road, but the map takes up most of the canvas. When I've finished, it will show all the places I was sent to in Macedonia. I'm going to have to rethink the whole thing, though, and make the officer smaller. It's such a nuisance, when I want to get on to other things.' He took Patricia's hand, suddenly animated by thoughts of the future. 'Being back here has energised me,' he said. 'Sharing Cookham with you, seeing it again through your eyes – it's brought back all those feelings that I thought the war and marriage had knocked out of me.'

How easily he linked love and conflict, Dorothy thought, although from what she had seen of his relations with Hilda, the comparison was not inappropriate. He began to hark back to the days when he and Patricia had first been in Cookham together, ignorant of each other's presence and yet – in his eyes – mysteriously and profoundly linked. Dorothy listened, hoping to find something in his words that she could use as a weapon against Patricia's apparent infatuation, but every half-remembered reference seemed to bring them closer together. 'Whenever I'm with you, I know I can do great work again,' he continued. 'The other day, when we were on Cockmarsh Hill, I suddenly saw the landscape I wanted to paint – the thistles and the sunlight, and you in the middle of it all, as much a part of it as the trees and the rabbits.'

Dorothy stared out across the Moor to the gentle green slope that she and Patricia had climbed together so often, laughing and talking about nothing in particular, picnicking there in the summer or taking bracing winter walks to think clearly whenever a decision had to be made. Cockmarsh Hill was a place they both

231

loved, symbolic of the settled life they had chosen in Cookham, but all she saw walking there now were the ghosts of a more joyful time. Patricia laughed, and Dorothy noticed how intently Stanley was looking at her lover, how frequently his eyes travelled to the pale, bare skin of her shoulder, tantalisingly visible where the dressing gown had fallen loose. His foot caught the canvas and knocked it flat to the floor, and the carelessness seemed more important than it was. Before she said something she would regret, and for which Patricia would never forgive her, Dorothy left the room.

She set the kettle to boil on the stove and walked out into the garden. Five years on, the shrubs that she and Patricia had planted in the empty soil of their new home were finally beginning to look as if they belonged there, cared for and flourishing. The lilac was her particular joy and she lifted the young flowers gently to her face, using their sweet, haunting fragrance to smother her anger. It was becoming harder to tolerate Stanley. She could put up with his physical presence and the constant chatter, infuriating as it was, but she and Patricia were different now even when they were on their own, and it was the way that he reached into their most private moments that she most resented. The meadows they loved were little more than a backdrop to his paintings, and even their past was vulnerable, rewritten by her own fears. These days, whenever she thought of the Slade, it wasn't that magical first meeting that came to mind, nor the excitement of her own achievements; it was Stanley's painting of the nativity, hung on the wall to celebrate one of the school's most brilliant pupils and recast now in Dorothy's imagination as an ill omen, created specifically to taunt her. Ironically, she had loved the picture more than Patricia, admiring its strong colours and carefully painted detail. It was set at the height of spring in Cookham, but in Stanley's confident hands the placing of the miracle felt natural and exuberant, as if God had been mistaken in his original choice of season. An artist with such an individual view of the world would be someone worth knowing, or so she had thought at the time. The quirk of fate would be funny now, if only she could remember how to laugh.

The whistle of the kettle called her inside, and she made the tea. Back in the sitting room, she found Stanley and Patricia in earnest conversation. 'I've put up with her humiliations and contrariness for long enough,' Stanley was saying. 'No man could try harder to please someone, but it's never been enough – for her, or her family. They're welcome to each other. She all but coerced me into marriage in the first place, and the whole thing has been a waste of time. It's a relief to me that she's gone.'

'What's happened?' Dorothy asked.

'Hilda's left Stanley,' Patricia said, refusing to meet her eye.

'But she's coming back?' Dorothy looked at him defiantly, as if by speaking the words firmly enough she could force them to be true. 'She can't have gone for good.'

'We were completely unsuited in every way,' he grumbled, hardly acknowledging the interruption. 'I don't know why it took me so long to see it. When I first began to think of marriage, it was always to someone so completely different from Hilda. She has no understanding of the things that please me, no understanding of what a man needs to live and work.'

'You do seem very different…'

'Peggy!' Dorothy stared at Patricia in horror, scarcely able to believe that she would encourage Stanley to end his marriage. What had begun as a harmless mockery of one man's selfish vanity suddenly threatened everything that she held most dear, and she was at a loss to know how to protect it. 'Think about what you're saying,' she continued more guardedly. 'Love should be treated with respect, not thrown away at the first sign of trouble.'

'She's right, though,' Stanley said, oblivious to the more veiled conversation that ran alongside his own. 'Why shouldn't I have the happiness I deserve?' He turned gratefully to Patricia. 'You've saved me from the muddle I've been living in. I always think so clearly when I'm with you.'

At least she had the decency to look embarrassed, but Dorothy wondered what turn the conversation would take if she left the room. She stood her ground and waited for Stanley's new muse to declare her loyalties, one way or the other. 'Then you'll know it's time you were leaving,' Patricia said breezily, pulling Stanley to his feet. 'Dorothy and I need to get ready for London, and you've got a chapel to finish.'

He scowled like a petulant child, sent to bed early. 'But I haven't finished what I was saying.'

'Then tell me another time.' Patricia ushered Stanley out into the hallway, still protesting. She closed the front door behind him with a bang and smiled at Dorothy, but it was far too late for conspiratorial glances. The damage had already been done.

4

Elsie shut the front door behind her and headed for the high street, already too hot by the time she reached the shade of the pavement. Usually, she loved the bustle of a weekday morning in Cookham, but today it was a trial: even the most genial of locals found it hard to smile in the heavy heat. She stopped outside the chemist's, annoyed to find that the ginger beer which she was taking to Stanley had leaked from its bottle, and set her basket down to sort out the mess. The shop was one of the most popular stores in the village, not least because it was as easy to pick up gossip there as it was a cold, and today was no exception; she didn't recognise either of the voices drifting through the open doorway, but she knew exactly who they were talking about. 'His wife's been away for months,' the first speaker said. 'I never liked the woman, but I can't help feeling sorry for her. And I don't know what Ken Beckford's thinking of, letting his fiancée go on working under the same roof as that man with no one there to keep an eye on things.'

'Ken Beckford's not thinking anything because he's a decent man who doesn't go round spreading spiteful rumours,' Elsie called, too angry to care if half the street heard her. 'Carry on like that, and you'll be glad you're in a chemist's.'

The women turned to face her, and the shopkeeper looked mortified. 'Can I get you something, Miss Munday?' he asked diplomatically, but Elsie moved on without another word, more upset than she cared to admit. She shouldn't have been surprised by the gossip: nothing went unnoticed in a village the size of Cookham and Stanley was hardly the soul of discretion himself, but she couldn't stand by and let him be insulted, particularly when her own reputation was at stake. She was still fuming when she got to the churchyard.

It soothed her, as it always did, with its peace. The sun shone down on the stone angel which stood just inside the gate, giving its bowed form an appropriate luminosity and making the memorial even more striking than usual. A pair of magpies chattered against the sweeter birdsong, but everything else was harmonious and she could understand why Stanley loved working here. There was no sign of him, so she wandered among the graves for a while, following a butterfly as it fluttered from stone to stone. The Spencer graves – Stanley's grandparents and various aunts and uncles – were to the left of the path, and she walked between them to some of the older, more elaborate headstones. From nowhere, a familiar head popped up in front of her, making her jump, and she realised that Stanley had been lying on the grass behind one of the vaults at the edge of the churchyard. He smiled when he saw her, and she went over to join him. 'Gosh, you gave me a fright. I thought that painting of yours made sense after all.'

'It makes more sense than ever on a day like this. Would you like me to explain it to you again?'

'No, you're all right. I've brought some ginger beer.'

'Good. Come and have it with me.'

She put the basket next to his sketchbook and sat down with her back against an old silver birch. 'Mary Behrend telephoned this morning,' she said, handing Stanley a glass. 'They'll be here at midday to pick up the final two panels.'

'She's quick off the mark. The paint's barely dry.'

'Perhaps she thinks they've waited long enough.' Elsie gave him a wry smile. 'Anyway, she sounded very excited. She kept saying that she didn't know how she could ever thank you. I told her

I thought a house, a chapel and wages for five years was a good start.'

'Did you really?'

'Of course not, but I was tempted. She was worried about getting the canvases back safely, so they're bringing the landaulette.'

'They'd better get a move on, then. It's black over Widbrook Common.'

She followed his gaze and saw that he was right. The storm which would inevitably break the intense heat of the past few days was hours away at most. 'Wouldn't you rather have taken the paintings yourself and seen them in place? There's something not quite right about waving them off down the street and someone else being the first to see it finished.'

'I don't really mind.'

'Well you should.'

There was something in her tone that made him smile. 'Are you put out, Elsie Munday?'

'I am a bit.'

'Then we'll go to Burghclere next week and look at the chapel. You can make us a picnic.' She agreed eagerly, wondering at the same time how it would feel to return without really belonging. 'Come on,' he said, getting up. 'We mustn't keep the Behrends waiting.'

He tossed the sketchbook into her basket and they walked back to Lindworth. There was a pile of post on the doormat, and Stanley quickly isolated a letter addressed to him in Hilda's hand. 'Why don't you just go and see her?' Elsie asked. 'All these words you keep flinging at each other don't seem to be helping.'

'Why should I?'

'Because it might save your marriage.' She spoke firmly, fighting now for the family she loved. Over the past few weeks, she had felt it fracture irretrievably as Stanley insisted on reading her the flurry of recriminating letters which passed between Cookham and Hampstead. It was funny, she thought: most couples needed to be together to tear themselves apart, but the Spencers seemed to manage it perfectly well from a distance. 'You haven't lost her yet,' she added, although the words were less assured than they would have been three months ago.

'Haven't I? Then why am I here on my own? She's deserted me, Elsie.'

'Are you sure that's the right way round? Or is it just a convenient excuse to behave badly?' Elsie glared at him, happy to defend him in public but loath to feed his self-pity when it was just the two of them. 'You don't have to leave a house to desert someone. Mrs Spencer would be here now if she felt you really wanted her, but she knows you've had your head turned.' Elsie's anger at Stanley's behaviour had been simmering for weeks, but she had managed to keep it in check and remember her place. Now she realised she had nothing to lose: if his future was to be with Patricia Preece, then she wanted no part of it, no matter how much she cared for him. 'If you really think the grass is greener, why don't you just let Mrs Spencer go instead of tormenting her with those letters you keep sending? What's the point of hanging on to something you can only find fault with?' Stanley remained stubbornly mute, so Elsie answered for him. 'You still think you can have them both, don't you?'

'Just because I love one landscape doesn't mean I can't love another.'

The argument was so ridiculous that Elsie didn't bother to refute it. 'What do you think the view from Moor Thatch gives you that the view from here can't?' she asked.

'People take me seriously when I'm with Patricia. Don't I deserve that after all this work? A little charm, a little elegance? Someone who can socialise and talk to people properly. Someone who doesn't contradict everything I say in company and delight in showing me up.'

'You're doing all this because you want somebody to flatter you?' As disappointed as she was with Stanley, Elsie had never expected his explanation to be quite so shallow. 'What about love and understanding? What does flattery get you when you close the front door and it's just the two of you?' Her frustration brought her close to tears, but she fought them back. 'I don't understand why you crave all this nonsense when it's not who you are. What happened to the country boy you claimed to be the last time we had this conversation? You said we were alike, Mr Spencer, but we're not – not if you can behave like this.'

Behind her, Elsie heard the sound of a car turning in from the high street. 'That'll be the Behrends,' she said, half-relieved and half-disappointed to be pulled away from a conversation which she had never intended to go so far.

'They're early.'

'I told you she was excited. You'd better go and greet them.'

Without another word, Stanley went to the studio to fetch his canvases and Elsie watched him go, sad not to have seen the final paintings which were about to leave the house with very little ceremony. The chapel that he had worked so hard at seemed to mean more to her now than to him. It was childish of her, but suddenly she longed to keep those pictures here, as if by holding on to them she could hold on to the man he had been when he first began to paint them. But that man was lost, even to himself, and to wish for him was pointless and naïve. Burghclere was in the past. What the future held was anybody's guess.

5

Dorothy heard the letterbox clatter and pictured the daily delivery of bills and final demands. Their post was predictable these days: reminders from grocers and coal merchants which differed only in the sum at the bottom of the page and the degree of courtesy with which it was requested, and she had come to dread picking the envelopes up off the mat each morning. The hot summer had been a blessing, but they had nothing saved for winter fuel; Patricia, as usual, had adopted the Micawber principle, believing firmly that something would turn up without actually doing anything about it. With a sigh, Dorothy walked down the hallway and sorted the post into two piles, one more desirable than the other. There was only one proper letter, postmarked London and addressed to Patricia in purple ink by a distinctive hand.

She put the envelope on the breakfast tray and took it upstairs. Patricia was sitting up in bed, looking slightly recovered from the septic throat which had laid her low for several days. 'How are you feeling?' Dorothy asked, pulling back the curtains to let sunlight into the room.

'Better, I think.'

'Well enough to go out? It's a beautiful day and I thought we might take a stroll down to the river if you're up to it? We haven't done that for ages.'

Patricia nodded and opened the letter while Dorothy poured the tea. 'Who's that from?' she asked, noticing the look of surprise on Patricia's face.

'Virginia Woolf.'

'Virginia *Woolf?* Why on earth is she writing to you?'

Patricia shrugged and read on. 'She wants a friend of hers to sit for me,' she said when she had finished. 'Ethel Smyth.'

'The composer? But that's wonderful news. How did she hear about you?'

'Through Roger Fry, apparently. He and Vanessa Bell were talking about my work and they encouraged her to buy a painting. If this drawing's successful, she wants to publish it in *Time and Tide*.'

Dorothy threw her arms round Patricia. 'See? What did I tell you? You don't need Stanley Spencer to get commissions when you've got people like that taking notice of you. This could be just the stroke of luck we need. Who knows what doors it might open?' She looked at Patricia's pale face. 'Why aren't you more excited? It's the best news we've had in ages.'

'You know why. Virginia Woolf hasn't bought one of *my* paintings, has she? She's bought one of yours, with my signature. How can I turn up in London and draw Ethel Smyth? They'll see through the whole charade.'

'But, darling, it's not as if you *can't* draw. You were at the Slade, after all. I enjoy it more than you do so I have more practice. That's why my pictures sell, nothing more.'

'That's nonsense, and you know it. You're the one with the talent.'

'But surely you can manage a basic sketch, something you can bring back here for us to work on together? There must be photographs of the woman, for God's sake. We can use those as well.'

'And if Virginia Woolf asks to see what she's paying for while I'm there? Don't be silly, Dorothy. It would make fools of us both.'

'But you can't refuse Virginia Woolf. It's too important. Why don't you ask Miss Smyth to come here to sit for you? Tell her you can't work in an unfamiliar studio and we'll sort it out between us.'

'That's a ludicrous suggestion.' Patricia flung the bedclothes aside and collected her dressing gown from the back of a chair. 'I can't believe you're hiring me out like some tuppenny-ha'penny street artist for the sake of a few pounds. It's too demeaning.' Dorothy couldn't help but think that there were more demeaning ways to get money out of unsuspecting admirers, but she bit her tongue. 'I'm not doing it, and that's my final word on the subject. Anyway, I won't be here on the dates Mrs Woolf suggests so the whole thing's impossible.'

'What do you mean? Why won't you be here?'

'I'm going to see Stanley in Switzerland. One of his patrons has taken him out there for a month or so to paint some landscapes. I had the most charming telegram from him the other day while you were out, asking if I could spare the time to join them. I've been meaning to mention it.'

'But we can't just swan off to Switzerland. We haven't got the money and I won't accept charity from Stanley Spencer *or* his cronies.'

Patricia turned to face her and Dorothy was shocked by the hostility in her eyes. 'You're such a hypocrite, Dodie. You don't mind Stanley's charity when he's paying our bill at McKay's or adding our framing costs to his own, so why should this be any different? Anyway, you don't have to trouble your conscience. I said he'd invited *me*, not us, and I've already accepted. Some fresh mountain air is just what I need. I'm leaving on Monday.'

The ground had shifted so unexpectedly that it took Dorothy a moment to catch up. 'You're going on holiday without me?' she repeated stupidly.

'Just this once, yes. It'll do us both good to spend some time apart. I can't stand it when you're possessive like this, and I won't be bullied.'

'Is Stanley there on his own?' Dorothy demanded, caring little now if she was proving Patricia's point. Hilda had returned to Cookham earlier in the summer, but had come and gone so often since that it was impossible to say if the couple had actually separated, and Patricia was always conveniently vague on the subject.

'I told you. He's with his patron.'

'That's not what I meant and you know it.' She repeated the question, but Patricia refused even to acknowledge it. 'Peggy, I'll ask you one more time before I go over to Lindworth and find out for myself. Will Hilda be in Switzerland while you're out there with Stanley?'

'No,' Patricia said defensively. 'She's gone back to London.' Seeing that defiance was getting her nowhere, she tried another approach. 'Dodie, darling, surely you don't grudge me a little break? It's very mean of you. You know I haven't been well and my throat still isn't…'

'Damn your throat! And how can you say I'm mean? I've put up with that man fawning all over you for months, right under my nose. Now I have to wait here while you disappear to Lindworth for hours on end to sit for him when I know there's no one else in the house except his maid. What else do you get up to while you're there? I haven't seen any paintings to justify all the time you spend with him.'

'Don't be silly. I've had enough of this. I'm going to run a bath.'

It was the last straw. Suddenly, Dorothy was sick of her love being dismissed as ridiculous or silly or foolish. A wave of uncontrollable anger flooded over her, and she caught Patricia by the wrist as she tried to leave the room. 'Have you slept with him? Is that it? And don't you dare lie to me.'

'Dodie, let go. You're hurting me.'

'Good. Now you know how it feels.' She tightened her grip and pushed Patricia against the bedroom wall, ashamed of how gratified she felt when a look of genuine fear passed across her lover's face. 'Have you let him touch you?'

'No,' Patricia insisted, beginning to cry. 'No, I haven't let him anywhere near me. Now please – let me go.'

Dorothy knew she was telling the truth. Her anger dissolved as quickly as it had come, and she did as she was asked. Patricia pushed her away and left the room, and Dorothy heard the bathroom door slam on the other side of the landing. Mortified by her own behaviour, she went to make amends but the door was locked and Patricia wouldn't answer. 'Please, Peggy, let me in,' she called. 'I'm sorry. I don't know what came over me. I just can't bear the thought of you and him together.' The only reply was a stifled sob, and Dorothy realised that she had gone too far. 'I promise I'll never do anything like that again, but I'm begging you – please don't go to Switzerland with Stanley. It'll change everything.' The silence only confirmed what she already knew. By losing control, she might as well have handed Patricia her passport and waved her to the door.

6

Hilda paused on the narrow footpath and gazed down at the familiar red-brick cottage where she and Stanley had spent their honeymoon. The farmhouse was exactly as it had been seven years ago: a neat, no-nonsense building surrounded by a productive garden, settled and at peace with itself under the vast Suffolk skies. A curtain billowed gently from an upstairs window, but otherwise the scene was so still that she might have been looking at the landscape painting which Stanley had begun shortly after their return to Hampstead. The countryside was at its most glorious now, in the late-August sun, and she had to shield her eyes to look at the gently sloping fields behind the house, where small piles of hay ran in rows towards the trees, straight and true, like a line of fate in the palm of a hand.

She turned to move on before the view could crowd her with memories of a happier time, but the back door opened and she hesitated, recognising the couple who had made them so welcome at the start of their married life. Mrs Lambert carried a basket, waiting expectantly while her husband went to the shed to fetch a spade, and Hilda considered going to speak to them, but something in their obvious companionship made her reluctant to face the inevitable questions about her own marriage. Instead, she watched as they gardened quietly together, working side by side and taking pleasure from a common endeavour; it was how she had always envisaged her life with Stanley – the two of them bonded by their painting, finding joy in each other's successes and spurred on to greater achievements by the very fact of their union. And it *had* been that way at first, beginning here with the ordinary miracles of a shared life, all the more precious because she had never expected to find a soul that mirrored her own. Everything so leisurely, so uncritical, so pure.

'Come on, Mummy! We're waiting.' Unity's impatience rescued Hilda from her thoughts, and she acknowledged her younger daughter with a wave. She gathered up the picnic basket and followed her children along the hedgerow path, noticing how protective Shirin was towards her little sister whenever she strayed into the fields, smiling at the grown-up gestures which Unity had begun to adopt in an attempt to close the gap between them. It had been her greatest fear that the girls would grow to resent each other for the separation imposed on them by their parents, but nothing could be further from the truth; there was no awkwardness between them, no jealousies or spite, and she hoped that the bond would stand them in good stead for the future; they would need each other if they were to survive the folly of their parents, and no one outside the family could ever understand. In that respect, they had been lucky with Elsie; she had made her mark on both children in their early years, always good-natured and firm, protecting them from pain without ever selfishly absorbing their affection, and it was a gift – unconsciously given – for which Hilda would be forever grateful. There were times in the early days when she had resented Elsie for the way that she coped and loved without effort, but those feelings seemed foolish now, and she knew that her marriage would have reached this stalemate much earlier without the sticking plaster of Elsie's kindness and common sense. But even Elsie had no answer to Stanley's obsession with Patricia.

An ancient oak tree, its trunk spectacularly split and bleached with age-old sunshine, marked the beginning of a stretch of woodland. Hilda caught up with the children and took Unity's hand in hers as the path meandered through the trees. The shift from light to shadow was sudden and disorientating, an assault on all her senses as the hot, sweet smell of corn gave way to green pine and a faint scent of autumn. Until it was muffled by the canopy of leaves, she hadn't realised how loudly the birdsong had filled the open fields. There was a clearing up ahead, where the trees were young enough to let a pleasant, dappled light filter through, and the terrain was a sufficiently varied mix of grass, sandy hillocks and rabbit burrows to keep her young explorers amused. It was still too early to eat, so she lay back in the grass and listened to their laughter as Shirin attempted to teach Unity a particularly complex tune that she had learnt at school. The beauty of her daughter's voice always delighted Hilda; when the solo became a tentative duet, she was filled with a sudden, intense sadness which had nothing to do with the music, and she longed for her children as she never had before. Why hadn't she listened to Elsie, or asked for more help from her family? The sort of help that would have kept them together, rather than farming out her first-born to a relative they hardly knew. How could she have allowed her own daughter to be raised by another woman, handed over like an unwanted gift? The simple truth was that she had not been strong enough to cope emotionally with Stanley *and* two children, and when she felt herself going under, she had chosen him. A part of her would always blame Stanley for the decision she had made, for demanding so much of her that she had very little left for anybody else – but she was also honest enough to admit that her loss was so much harder to bear without him.

The church clock struck noon, loud and clear across the fields, and she wondered how something so simple could bring back so many memories. Her wedding outfit, a brown velvet coat that she had made herself, warm against the February cold; Stanley at her side as they walked to the church for the ceremony, happy now, with all his doubts forgotten; waving the handful of guests off in a taxi after the wedding breakfast, and then the first night at the Lamberts' house, the two of them finally alone together in that small bedroom with the forget-me-not wallpaper. Everything was still so vivid in her mind, although she rarely allowed herself to revisit the joy she had felt when she was sure of Stanley's love; it was too dangerous, too unsettling, and she needed all her strength to face this current crisis. She couldn't remember a time when she had felt more alone, at odds with everyone around her because she genuinely wanted Stanley to have what was best for him, even at the expense of her own happiness. Elsie reproached her as sternly as she dared for being nice to Patricia, while her mother was constantly urging her to fight for her husband, but neither of them understood what seemed so obvious to her: unless Stanley truly believed in their marriage like she did, there was little point in coercing him or punishing Patricia. If they were ever to be happy, he had to come back to her of his own free will, or not at all.

And there was still hope. Stanley had talked to her for hours about Patricia, trying to work out how he felt and complaining that she blew hot and cold, teasing him one minute and sending him away the next. Hilda recognised those doubts all too well from her own broken engagements and blissful reunions, and she knew now – as then – that the only thing she could do was wait for Stanley to make up his mind. His frankness with her wasn't deliberately cruel, just thoughtless. They had always been able to hurt each other without meaning to, ever since that first, careless mistake she had made in inviting Gilbert to join them here on their honeymoon. She still wasn't sure why she had done it: a misguided belief that Stanley would be pleased to see the brother he loved, or a fear of being alone as a couple, away from the safe camaraderie of friends and family. Perhaps, even then, she had sensed that the intensity of his personality could overwhelm her, that she might lose herself in his orbit. As long as Gilbert was there, she knew she would always be visible.

Whatever her motivation at the time, it seemed ironic now that Stanley should still feel so slighted by her innocent introduction of a third person into their marriage. She reached for her bag and took out the post which had been forwarded from Hampstead. Stanley had written to her constantly while he was in Switzerland, full of the pictures he was painting and the generosity of his patron, and she had recently received a card from Patricia with the same Saas-Fee postmark. It was hard to say how much artfulness was in the note. Amid the improvements to her health and her gratitude for Hilda's understanding, Patricia had seen fit to include enough detail to show how close their daily lives had become – the peace and romance of the mountain villages, the wildflowers that filled her room, the shirts that they had chosen together at the market. It was a new stage in their relationship, one from which it would be very difficult to return, and the implied intimacy hurt Hilda far more than if Patricia had brazenly claimed to be sharing Stanley's bed. But that, she thought, was unlikely.

She put the letters back and called the children over for lunch, finding solace in their company. The afternoon drifted away from her, as much as she would have liked it to go on for ever, and all too soon it was time to go back to their lodgings in the centre of the village. Hilda swung a sleepy Unity into her arms and put Shirin in charge of the empty picnic basket, then chose a different route home which would take them past Muttet's farm, where she had worked as a land girl. The narrow lanes became increasingly familiar as she walked, and she remembered the hundreds of journeys that she and her friend, Cora, had made, returning at dusk from hedging or ploughing, so exhausted that it was as much as they could do to prop each other up on the horse's broad back. Those dreamlike evenings, coming home to a caravan in the corner of a field, the silence broken only by the sound of hooves on the lane, had bonded her to this small Suffolk village, where she had no history, no family ties and no responsibilities except to work until she dropped. She had been wary of returning this time, afraid that visits with Stanley might have clouded its uncomplicated magic, but she wanted the children to have a summer in a place that she

249

regarded as hers, and it hadn't let her down. She still found peace here – peace, and a clarity of mind which was rare and precious.

'Mummy! What's that? Can we go and look?'

Shirin paused by the gate to the farmyard, and Hilda walked back to see what had caught her attention. There was a collection of stables and outbuildings just beyond the fence, and Shirin was pointing to a flash of coloured paint, visible through an open door on the far side of the yard. Hilda smiled, grateful to her daughter for spotting what she would otherwise have missed. There – broken and left to rot in the corner of the farmer's barn, but still beautiful to her – was the old Romany caravan which had been her home for three years. 'That's where I lived when I stayed here for the first time,' she said. 'Do you remember? I told you that Aunt Cora and I camped out while we were working on the land? We had so much fun.' Shirin giggled and shook her head, obviously doubtful of her mother's story. 'Well, it was out in the fields in those days, not tucked away here. I thought it would be long gone by now.'

'So *can* we go and look?'

Hilda nodded. 'I don't see why not, but don't touch anything. There's probably some old machinery lying around, and I don't want you to hurt yourself.'

She pushed open the gate and they walked across the yard to the barn. 'It's like the one Toad has,' Shirin said excitedly, and she was right; the caravan was indeed a washed-out version of the canary-yellow cart from *The Wind in the Willows*, a story that Stanley had read so often to the children that they virtually knew it by heart. Up close, it was even more dilapidated: the carvings around the windows were still striking, but the red and green paint which had made them stand out was chipped and faded, and the bunks, cooking stove and pans had been removed altogether, leaving just a shell. The caravan had come off its wheels completely, and they lay in a pile on the floor next to it, missing most of their spokes.

'Could we have it?' Shirin asked, all scepticism gone. 'If you explain that you lived there, the farmer might think that was nice and let us buy it. Daddy could fix it up, and Unity and I could play in it when I come to visit.'

The words stung Hilda all the more for their innocent acceptance of the situation. 'Daddy doesn't fix things,' she said, hoping that her daughter couldn't detect the edge in her voice, 'and even if he did, I don't know how we'd move it all that way now.' She knelt down and looked at Shirin, conscious of her disappointment. 'It's sad, I know, but some things go too far to be mended, and we have to be grown up and leave them behind. It doesn't make them any less special, does it?' The little girl shook her head, and Hilda would have given anything to see less understanding in her eyes. She held her close with Unity, who was still fast asleep in her arms, oblivious to the excitement of their discovery. 'Come on,' she said. 'We can come and look again tomorrow if you like, but we'd better go now or we'll be late for tea.'

7

London was unbearable in the heat, and Dorothy half-wished she hadn't come. The tube train was crowded with an uncomfortable muddle of seasoned commuters and summer visitors which only grew worse as they approached the more fashionable stops; the stifling crush of bodies made her anxious and claustrophobic, and she began to regret her decision not to waste money on a taxi, but it had seemed an absurd extravagance in their current circumstances. She shifted the portfolio awkwardly under her arm, drawing irritated glances from the passengers on either side, and cursed Patricia's selfishness for the hundredth time that day. After their most recent row, which had shaken them both with its violence, the trip to Switzerland wasn't mentioned again and Patricia had left early on the Monday morning without a word of apology or farewell. For reasons which she couldn't entirely fathom, Dorothy had been cast in the role of villain; over and over, she had longed to reach out and heal the rift, but something inside her had shifted, and each time she tried the words stuck in her throat. The tension at Moor Thatch over the weekend was so bad that she was glad when Patricia finally left, but the relief didn't last long. The house felt empty without her, and Dorothy was horrified to realise how much of her everyday life, how many small routines and looked-forward-to moments, were wholly reliant on another person. It was as if her entire sense of purpose had been packed away neatly in Patricia's suitcase, while she sat at home and waited for them both to return. When the postcard arrived to say that the trip had been extended until the hotel closed at the end of the season, Dorothy had no choice but to face the truth: she could no longer rely on Patricia to be part of her future, financially or emotionally. The prospect bewildered and frightened her, but somehow she had to build a life of her own.

Her train slowed down at Green Park, and she was glad to fight her way to the door and up into the sunshine. The gallery was a few minutes' walk away in King Street, St James's, and she set out along Piccadilly, past The Ritz and the tiny French café where she usually waited while Patricia conducted their business. She found Mayfair intimidating at the best of times, but the first sight of her destination made her stomach tighten and she almost turned back; the gallery building was by no means the grandest in the street, but it was still an imposing four-storeyed Victorian house, stucco-faced and designed in the Italianate style to chime with some of the larger houses in nearby St James's Square. The premises had a shallow porch and iron railings, and Dorothy headed for the door to ring the bell, but she lost her nerve at the last moment and walked straight past. She stopped at the end of the street, loitering on the corner like a criminal, then retraced her footsteps to try again, but her palms were sweating and her throat was dry, and she would have to compose herself if she stood any chance of making the right impression. A man was watching her from a first-floor window on the opposite side of the street, and she knew how foolish she must look; spurred on by what Patricia would think of her behaviour, she took several deep breaths and approached the gallery again. To her relief, two men and a woman overtook her, obviously with the same intention; Dorothy quickened her pace as she saw them heading for the bell and was admitted with a smile on their coat-tails.

As soon as she was inside, she wished that she had done this before instead of allowing Patricia's charm to speak for her work;

that way, she might not feel so daunted by the imposing pillars and expensively polished floor which would have graced any celebrated museum. A man sat behind a vast leather desk at the far end of the room, and an air of masculine entitlement seemed to hang about the pictures on display, although perhaps that stemmed less from reality than from her own sense of inadequacy. He bid her a discreet good day and cast a glance at the battered portfolio which dated back to her time at the Slade; to be professional, she should have gone straight to the desk and stated her business, but the people who had entered with her were in earshot and she didn't want to draw attention to herself. Instead, she allowed the paintings to calm her. It was a mixed exhibition, a collection of lesser-known Impressionist works with one or two famous gems sprinkled in. She loved the work instantly, partly because of its inherent quality, partly because it reminded her of her days in Paris with Patricia, the happiest of her life. One painting in particular drew her in, an oil by Degas whose subject was two women seated at a table in a Parisian café, seemingly in deep conversation. Who they were and what they were discussing was impossible to know – and that, perhaps, was the picture's appeal. The woman on the left – half cut off by the edge of the canvas – was looking earnestly at her friend, who stared down at her hands, absorbed in her own troubled world. The mood of the painting was one of melancholy resignation, and something in it – something that Dorothy would have found difficult to acknowledge – reminded her of her own relationship with Patricia. No matter how long they had known each other, or how hard she tried to make her happy, there would always be something about Patricia that remained hidden and secret, a mystery as unfathomable as the women in this painting.

The door behind her closed softly, and she realised that the other visitors had left. She glanced over to the desk, giving the man the opportunity he had been looking for to engage her in conversation. 'Can I help you, madam?' he asked, looking again at the portfolio.

'Yes, you can. I'm sorry to trouble you,' she said, beginning instinctively with an apology, 'but my name is Dorothy Hepworth. You've been good enough to take one or two of my drawings in the past, and I wanted to show Mr Reid what I've been working on recently.'

Even to her own ears, the last comment sounded desperate and immature, more like a child seeking praise than an artist whose work was worthy of display. 'I'm afraid Mr Reid isn't here today,' the man said politely. 'I'm his assistant.'

'Mr Miller?'

'That's right.'

'I telephoned yesterday to ask if it would be convenient to call in. The lady I spoke to said she'd be sure to let you or Mr Reid know.'

'Yes, of course. Please forgive me.' Miller recovered quickly, although he obviously hadn't the faintest idea what she was talking about. Either he had forgotten, or the message wasn't important enough to be passed on. 'I'm sorry, what was the name?'

'Dorothy Hepworth.'

'Ah yes. And you say you've dealt with us before?'

'Yes. Well, no, not personally. My friend usually brings our work in, but she's away on a painting trip at the moment. Patricia Preece? She was last here about six weeks ago.'

'Oh, Miss Preece! Yes, of course. Always such a pleasure to deal with.' He looked at her curiously, and Dorothy was suddenly conscious that her unadventurous dress sense and lack of confidence was utterly at odds with Miller's idea of the circles that Patricia moved in. 'We sold one of her paintings only last week, the most charming oil of some gardens in Cookham. Two red-brick houses and...'

'...and a field of wildflowers. Yes, I know it.'

'Of course you do,' Miller said, looking embarrassed. 'Have you brought some more for us?'

'No. I'm afraid these are all mine.'

'Oh well, as you've taken the trouble to bring them in, by all means let me take a look.'

Dorothy opened the portfolio on the desk, feeling like a common salesman offering cheap lingerie. Miller carefully removed the contents, a mixture of drawings on paper and oil panels like the one he had sold, and began to look through them. 'I don't know how much Patricia told you about our training,' she said, filling in the silence, 'but we both graduated from the Slade just after the war, and went straight to Paris.' Miller paused at one of the panels, a still life of peonies in a terracotta vase, and Dorothy looked critically at the picture with him, finding it strange to see her own name in the corner instead of Patricia's. 'I was at the Atelier Colarossi for four years,' she added redundantly, knowing that he was barely listening.

'Very good,' he said, flicking quickly through the rest of the drawings. 'Right, we'll take these two to try. The others aren't really strong enough for us, I'm afraid.'

'Not strong enough?'

Dorothy's disappointment made her sound argumentative, when all she really wanted to do was flee her humiliation without another word. 'No,' Miller clarified, obviously feeling that his judgement was in question. 'It's hard to put into words, perhaps, but if you were to compare these with the oil we've just sold, you'll see that there's a confidence about Miss Preece's brushwork that is missing here.'

'But I painted that,' Dorothy said, overwhelmed with a sudden sense of injustice which was impossible to hide.

Miller looked at her, and it was hard to say if he was more disconcerted by her words or by the outburst which threatened the sanctuary of his gallery. 'I beg your pardon?'

Her anger dissolved in an instant. Miller was right, she knew that. Her heart hadn't been in any of the work she had done recently, and the pictures here were nothing but poor imitations of the ones that Patricia had delivered with a flourish. 'I painted that with such care,' she clarified. 'I'm sorry you don't like it.'

'It's not a question of personal taste,' he said, more kindly this time. 'If I bought only what I liked, these walls would look very different, but we have to think of the future, of what will last. We have to be a step ahead. And as I said, I'm more than happy to try these two. Shall we take it from there and see how we go?'

Dorothy nodded and put everything else back into the portfolio, scarcely caring if she tore the paper as she did so; it hardly mattered, when she knew that it would all be destroyed the minute she got home. 'Thank you for your time,' she said, her face scarlet with embarrassment.

'Not at all. And do give Miss Preece my regards. We'll look forward to seeing her when she's back from her trip – and the fruits of her labours, of course.'

Dorothy left before she could say anything more damaging and walked in a blur to St James's Square. She sat down on the first bench she came to and stayed there until all the tears caused by Patricia's betrayal had been spent. It was early evening by the time she felt ready to leave, and she was glad of the soft, refreshing rain which accompanied her journey home, where she would wait, as she always did, for Patricia to come back to her.

8

Since the move to Lindworth, Elsie had come to dread the winter. The house was devoid of comfort in the colder months and her days were filled with drudgery simply to keep it going, an endless round of cleaning fires, filling coal buckets, and wrestling with an out-dated kitchen that fought her at every turn. Stanley had made some improvements to the rooms and general décor, but a home the size of Lindworth demanded more than his finances or his inclination had to offer, and the rainy, dark days of November ushered in a bleakness which would last until the spring. The work was second nature to her, but its cheerlessness was not. She longed for Shirin and Unity, who would have brought this shell of a house to life, and missed the understanding that she and Hilda had shared, despite their differences in class and temperament. Most of all, she mourned the loss of Stanley's company, which she had enjoyed since that very first meeting at Palmers Hill Farm. He never talked to her about his paintings now, and there was none of the easy banter which had been such a feature of their life at Burghclere; if he noticed any absence of the joy which he had once professed to love, he did nothing to rekindle it. In her heart, she tried to hold on to the man she had been so fond of, but his foolishness over Patricia made it difficult. It was silly of her, she knew that: what she had now was what any maid could expect, and she should be grateful for the unconventional happiness of earlier days – but those days had spoiled her, and now she found it hard to settle for less. She sighed as she poured dried fruit into a mixing bowl, trying to remember a time when the preparations for Christmas had been made with so little heart. It couldn't come quickly enough for her this year, and she cherished the prospect of a few days with Ken and her family, miles away from Cookham.

The front door slammed, and she heard voices in the hallway. Stanley and Patricia went through to the drawing room and the gramophone started up, playing a now-familiar tune which Elsie guessed was a favourite of Patricia's because it seemed to have arrived with her more frequent visits to the house. After a while, Stanley called her name and she pretended not to hear, dreading the prospect of waiting on them both, but eventually he came to the door and she had no choice but to respond. She looked at the bags and boxes in the hallway as she passed, branded with the names of the most exclusive dress shops that Maidenhead had to offer, and wondered how much Stanley had spent this time.

'We've been shopping,' he said, although the explanation was hardly necessary.

'So I see. It's a wonder you could carry it all. Someone's in for a good Christmas.'

'Oh, they're not for Christmas. Why wait until then?' He beckoned her into the drawing room, where more boxes had been piled on to the piano and footstool. One of them was open, the tissue paper pulled aside to reveal expensive black silk lingerie. Elsie felt herself flush and looked away. She remembered the interest that Stanley had always taken in Hilda's clothes, so innocent now by comparison – a pattern on a dress that he liked, or a jumper he would ask her to wear until it was threadbare simply because he loved the way its sleeve fell against her arm. This shameless desire to dress Patricia was sordid by comparison, another empty gesture towards the social status he craved; even Patricia, she noticed, had the decency to look embarrassed. 'We had to come home in the end,' he said petulantly, putting the lid back on the box. 'Patricia wouldn't let me buy anything else.'

'I didn't have the energy to try it on.' Patricia sounded weary, as if she had already had to justify herself several times. 'If you wanted to keep going, you should have let the shop girl model them like she offered to.'

'What's the point of that? The shop girl isn't going to be wearing them.'

For a moment, Elsie thought that Patricia was going to answer back, but she thought better of it and squeezed Stanley's hand instead. 'Don't sulk, darling. We can go another day. And we had fun in the jeweller's, didn't we?'

Stanley grinned, his irritation gone in a second. 'Put the green dress on for me now,' he said, 'and the shoes I chose to go with it.' Patricia left the room, selecting a handful of bags as she went, and the look of longing on Stanley's face as he watched her go disgusted Elsie. She headed back to the kitchen without waiting to find out why she had been summoned, but he followed her down the passageway. 'I wish you'd be nicer to Patricia,' he said.

'I'm perfectly civil to her.'

'I didn't say you weren't, but you have a way of being civil which most people would recognise as the opening of hostilities. What's for dinner?'

'The rest of the rabbit stew. And I need to have a word with you about that.'

'About the rabbit stew?'

'In a manner of speaking, yes. I was at McKay's today and he asked me about the account. It's more than sixty days late, apparently, and he wants to know when you'll be settling it.'

'When I'm ready.'

'That's not good enough, Mr Spencer,' Elsie said, still smarting from the humiliation of having to apologise for the debt in front of other customers. 'What am I supposed to do if he refuses me the next time I go in? It's hard enough as it is to make the housekeeping stretch, but everything costs more at Christmas.'

Stanley sighed. 'I really don't want to be bothered with this. Tell Mr McKay he'll get his money at the end of the month. How you manage the housekeeping is up to you.'

'But I can't perform miracles.' Her frustration was about more than money: wherever she shopped in Cookham now, she was met by awkward silences and curious stares; there was a noticeable hostility towards Patricia and Dorothy in the village, not all of which could be traced back to Stanley's behaviour, and she knew that her own reputation was suffering because of the comings and goings at Lindworth and Moor Thatch. For the first time since joining the Spencer household, Elsie was seriously considering handing in her notice and finding another position until she and Ken had enough put by to marry.

Stanley must have sensed that she was at the end of her tether. 'I'll see what I can do,' he said. 'Perhaps Hilda could manage on less than I send her at the moment, say thirty shillings a week. Would that help? It's high time she took some responsibility where money's concerned. She never did when we were married, and her allowance just limits what I can spend here.'

Elsie longed to point out that he and Hilda were *still* married, and that there were other, more obvious, economies that he could make, but she daren't overstep the mark when he was in this mood. She hated the way that he continually slandered Hilda. To her credit, Patricia never encouraged him to do it and even stood her rival's corner on occasions; there seemed to be an unspoken etiquette between the two women, although it might have served Hilda better to lose her dignity and return some of the home truths with which Stanley was so liberal. 'The money you send Mrs Spencer is for the children, too,' Elsie said, as reasonably as she could. 'They shouldn't have to miss out. That wasn't what I meant.'

'Then what did you mean? It's my money. Why shouldn't I spend it on the things that I like rather than the things I'm obliged to pay for? I'll write to Hilda about it.'

'There's no need. You can discuss it with her in person. She telephoned earlier to say she was coming for a visit with the children. Shirin's with her for the holidays, so they'll be arriving the day after tomorrow and staying for Christmas.'

'Oh good. She can come to the Guinnesses' party with us.'

How easily the triangle turned, Elsie thought, with Hilda now the guest in her own marriage. She saw Patricia standing at the bottom of the stairs and nodded to the door. 'I think you're wanted. Will Miss Preece be staying for dinner?'

Stanley looked hopefully at Patricia, but she shook her head. 'Sorry, darling, not tonight. Dorothy's expecting me.' She looked theatrically at her watch, and Elsie wondered if that had been part of the 'fun' at the jeweller's. 'I'm already later than I promised to be.'

'But I haven't had a proper look at you in that dress.'

'Another time. I'll wear it to the party on Friday.' She put her coat on over the new outfit and filled the bag with the clothes she had arrived in. 'Be a sweetie, will you, and drop the rest over tomorrow?' Stanley nodded and went to kiss her, but Patricia had already walked out into the night.

9

Hilda pulled her chair closer to the easel and stared intently at Patricia. Perhaps she should have been more surprised by her husband's suggestion that she paint a portrait of his mistress; perhaps she should have refused – but Stanley's insensitivity to her feelings had lost its power to shock, and there was a part of her which relished the opportunity to study the woman who had replaced her in his life, if only to try to understand. Patricia had made an effort for each of the sessions, her blonde hair expensively permed, her make-up immaculate, yet still she sat awkwardly in the pose she had chosen, looking away into the distance, reluctant to meet Hilda's eye. There was something in the relationship between artist and subject that put Patricia at a disadvantage, just for a few precious hours, and although she would have been ashamed to admit it, Hilda had enjoyed having the upper hand. She looked again at the carefully defined eyebrows and small, rosebud mouth, and saw to her satisfaction that the expression of endurance in those disarmingly blue eyes had been captured to perfection on the canvas; already, there was an air of strained patience about the woman in front of her, and Hilda wondered if the charade of the portrait had made Patricia begin to question what other foolish schemes she might be expected to put up with if she pursued a relationship with Stanley.

It was quiet in the house, and all neutral topics of conversation had been exhausted in the first few sessions. A feeble winter sun had little comfort to offer this cold, north-facing room, and Hilda noticed Patricia give an involuntary shiver. 'I can't help feeling that Stanley could have chosen something more practical for you to wear,' she said, looking at the delicate emerald dress that he had insisted on for the portrait – green, the colour of envy, although Patricia could surely have very little to be jealous of. 'I don't mind if you want to get up and move around.'

Patricia did as she suggested, clinging gratefully to the room's one inadequate radiator. 'I did argue, but we both know how stubborn he can be when his mind's set on something.' She smiled, and Hilda tried to ignore the implication of a solidarity between them. 'And he was very particular that I should wear something that *he* had bought.'

'It's funny, but I don't remember Stanley ever having an appetite for shopping.'

'He's always been very generous.'

'Yes, I'm sure he has.' The words came out before she could stop them, heavy with sarcasm. Stanley's intention to cut her weekly allowance hurt her deeply, even more so because he had made no secret of why he wanted the money himself. They had argued bitterly on the subject, and Hilda cringed whenever she recalled herself begging for her livelihood, insisting that she spent nothing on herself. More than anything, she resented having to justify every penny she spent on their children, as if Shirin and Unity were a luxury for which she alone was responsible.

Her tone of voice wasn't lost on Patricia. 'I'll talk to him,' she said sympathetically. 'It's mean of him to withhold quite so much. He told me about the arguments you've been having. Why shouldn't you buy Unity the shoes she needs?'

If the comment had been waved as a white flag, it was sorely misguided, and Hilda felt a surge of resentment; there was only one thing she feared more than being beholden to Stanley, and that was owing Patricia a debt of gratitude. 'He's discussed all this with you?' she said, keeping her voice as level as possible.

'Of course. We have to go over each conversation the two of you have, analysing it from every angle. And when you're away, he reads your letters to me continuously, over and over again.' She laughed, but there was a forced quality to it, and Hilda's sense of betrayal was tempered suddenly by the realisation that Stanley's continued obsession with his wife's words and feelings threatened Patricia far more than it did her. 'It's as if you've never quite left the room.'

She sat down again to resume the session, and Hilda tried hard to bury her emotions in the portrait. Patricia's likeness emerged from a dark, sombre background, filling most of the canvas so that only the hint of a chair and the corner of a picture frame were visible at her shoulder. Hilda had wilfully refused to paint her rival in surroundings which she still regarded as her own: the books that she and Stanley had read together; the furniture they had chosen when they first moved into Chapel View. Her training had left her with a deep respect for the tradition of portraiture, and she knew all too well how symbolic the background to any subject could be; she wasn't yet ready to anoint her successor by making Patricia's occupation of Lindworth as unquestioned on canvas as it seemed in reality. She certainly didn't covet the house, which she had loathed from the moment she first walked into it, and she had long ago abandoned the hope that she and Stanley might once again be happy with their daughters in a true family home, but it was impossible not to contrast her own situation with Patricia's. Her mother meant well, but living under the same roof again with routines and priorities which were not her own felt more like a prison than a refuge. Even if she had been ready to remove her belongings from Cookham, she would have had nowhere to put them in the bedroom that she shared with her younger daughter, a room too small to unpack her painting things, and where Unity had to be tidier with her toys and books than any small child should know how to be. And yet here was Patricia, flitting between Lindworth and Moor Thatch, while someone made a home for her in each and waited for her to make up her mind. 'Does Dorothy mind you spending so much time here?' she asked, before any more pity could be sent her way.

The sudden change of subject wrong-footed Patricia. 'Of course not,' she said, rather too defensively. 'Why should she?'

Hilda shrugged. 'Oh, I don't know. Change can be hard when you've been so close all these years.' She looked at Patricia, but her face was impossible to read. 'You must care for each other a great deal. When someone comes along and upsets a strong relationship...'

She left the sentence unfinished, allowing Patricia to make the comparison. 'Dorothy's not like that,' she insisted. 'She wants me to be happy, and we all get along very well. In fact, we were think-ing of inviting you both for dinner at Moor Thatch on Saturday, but we weren't sure how long you were staying. None of us quite knows where we are with all these comings and goings.'

Her voice was pleasant, belying the rudeness of the words, and somehow Hilda managed a smile. 'We'll be leaving the day after tomorrow. Shirin needs to get ready for school.'

'That's a shame. Still, all the more reason why you shouldn't be wasting time on this. Stanley's already done a portrait of me in this room. He must have shown it to you?'

'Yes, he has.'

'Well, then. I can't imagine why he wants you to do it all over again.'

'He's always been keen for us to paint the same subjects,' Hilda said, remembering the bitter rows they had had over Elsie's portrait at Burghclere. How long ago all that seemed, she thought; a different life, and she would give anything now to go back to the problems which had seemed so insurmountable then. 'He thinks it sheds some light on what we have in common and where our differences lie.'

The suggestion that each portrait said more about its creator than its subject seemed new to Patricia. 'I would have thought the differences were perfectly obvious in this case,' she snapped.

It was the first slip, a crack in the veneer of courtesy which hid the tensions between them, and something in Hilda screamed to wrench it open. 'Stanley and I argue all the time about our work,' she continued. 'It used to drive me up the wall, the way he'd involve himself in whatever I was doing. Does he try that with you?'

It was obvious from the expression on Patricia's face that Stanley showed no interest in her work. 'No, and I wouldn't let him if he did,' she said. 'There's very little point in discussing anything to do with our paintings when we look at art so differently. I don't understand what's happened to him. His early work was so sensuous, but some of the figure paintings he's done recently...' She shrugged her shoulders. 'Well, they're beyond me.'

It saddened Hilda to think that the woman to whom her husband had turned as his muse seemed to have so little understanding of his soul. Patricia began a long critique of the faults in Stanley's work and her voice filled the room, self-assured and unrelenting, until Hilda longed to shout and holler simply to drown it out. The more she thought about it, the more surreal the last few days became: opening Christmas cards with Patricia in between the sittings; listening to the gramophone and talking about the children while Stanley looked on, insufferably pleased with himself, as if the peace of the season were a gift that he had personally bestowed. Could he really be so utterly oblivious to what she was feeling, while she struggled to keep it hidden for the sake of the children? And why was she allowing it to happen? Patricia's words wrapped themselves around her, mocking her with their certainty until they felt like a tangible force, beating her into submission. 'Do you think we should have a serving hatch?' she asked suddenly, unable to bear it any longer.

'What?' Patricia broke the pose, turning to look at her in bewilderment.

'A serving hatch, between here and the kitchen. I think it would make things so much easier for Elsie, but Stanley says it will spoil the flow of the room. What do you think?'

'I really don't know. It's not my house.'

The words hung in the air and Hilda continued to paint, adding some detail to the silver bracelets that lit up the bottom of the canvas. The painting was nearly finished and she considered it critically, noting the thick, heavy brushstrokes across Patricia's forehead and neck, the only physical evidence of the anger which had consumed her as she worked. 'I can't decide if all this makes us civilised or quite simply insane,' she said, as much to herself as Patricia.

'What do you mean?'

'This charade of ours. Playing at happy families, as if it's perfectly normal for Stanley to have everything he wants, no matter what the cost.' In the dark days of Burghclere, whenever she felt trapped by her marriage, she had always assumed that the one consolation for losing Stanley would be her freedom, but she had been wrong. There was no freedom in this half-life, neither here nor in Hampstead; just a suffocating obsession with the past. And in her heart, she had always believed that Stanley would come back to her.

An unexpected rush of grief disorientated her, and she stood up and walked over to the window, the brush held tightly in her hand. Outside, the garden seemed suspended in the failing daylight and the winter-blackened trees were as still as death, their branches brittle and exposed against a spiteful air. It would take so little to make them snap, she thought. Everything had its limits.

'Are you all right?'

The question was hesitant, uneasy, and Hilda was shamed by the satisfaction she took from Patricia's discomfort. 'It's finished,' she said, and only when the words were spoken did she see in them a significance beyond the portrait. Behind her, she heard Patricia get up and leave the room. It was a relief to be on her own, and yet still there seemed too little space for her in the world, too little space in her mind for thoughts that she could not control. There was no peace any more, not even in her faith, and she longed for a mental oblivion in which she could stop trying to make sense of Stanley's behaviour or reason with her own feelings. It was so exhausting, always to be remembering their happiness, and suddenly she craved the nothingness of the world beyond the glass.

The paintbrush snapped between her fingers, and there was a sharp, stinging pain as a splinter dug into her palm. She walked back to her easel and looked long and hard at the portrait before putting the brush down and picking up another, dipping it into the alizarin crimson, which she had changed her mind about using. It had found its place now, she thought, and bent low to sign her name, Hilda Carline, in vivid red paint along the bottom of the picture.

10

'Surely he wasn't serious?'

Patricia shrugged and lit another cigarette. 'That's what he said.'

The morning sunlight streamed in through the bedroom window, and Dorothy tried to make sense of what Patricia had told her. 'But why would he sign his house over to you? I know he's a fool, but even Stanley Spencer can't be that ridiculous. He's got a wife and two children to think about.'

'A wife who hasn't shown her face in months, not one visit since Christmas. The marriage is obviously over.'

'Perhaps it is, but even if Hilda *does* divorce him, he'll still have to support them.'

'All the more reason to sign the house over. It would mean fewer assets to consider when they weigh up the alimony.'

Dorothy stared at Patricia, scarcely able to believe what she had just heard. 'Please don't tell me that this was your idea.'

'Of course it wasn't.'

'But you've encouraged him?'

'I've simply pointed out what any good friend would advise under the circumstances.' She put the breakfast tray down on the floor and rearranged her pillows. 'If they get a divorce, the courts will force him to pay Hilda a damned sight more than he does at the moment, so he should be taking precautions now, before it looks too obvious. He's got no concept of money, you know that.'

The clothes and jewellery which filled Patricia's room were testament to that much. 'This isn't a game, Peggy,' Dorothy said cautiously, 'and it's not just about Stanley and Hilda. There are the children to consider. That house might not be their home, but it *is* their future. Surely you wouldn't want them to suffer?'

'Of course not,' Patricia said, a note of exasperation in her voice. 'I'm not trying to make *anyone* suffer, but there's got to be fairness on both sides. You're not telling me that the Carlines will take all this lying down, no matter how friendly they seem towards Stanley? He needs an ally, and there's no one else to speak up for him.'

'Since when has he needed help in that department? There isn't enough room in the conversation for anyone else.' Dorothy regretted the words as soon as they were out: the subject was too serious to lapse into a tit-for-tat argument. 'What are you expected to do in return?' she asked, acknowledging what really concerned her. 'Stanley's offering you a house. What are you offering him?'

'Nothing more than I do already.'

The answer was deliberately ambiguous and did nothing to dispel Dorothy's fears. 'Isn't that a little unprincipled?' she said.

'And isn't *that* a little hypocritical?' Patricia gestured to the bracelet which she had given Dorothy for her birthday, bought with the exchange of some of Stanley's gifts, but her anger was short lived. 'Don't you see, darling? This could be the security we've longed for. Your parents were always so generous to us when they could afford to be, but your mother has had her own concerns since your father's death and we can't rely on family any more. We have to stand on our own two feet, and...'

'But this is hardly standing...'

Patricia reached across the bed and put a finger gently to Dorothy's lips. 'Listen to me, Dodie. I know this is hard for you, and I'm sorry if I've hurt you by taking up with Stanley. That's the last thing I would ever want to do. But you've always been so strong for us. You're the one who found the house and persuaded your father to buy it; you're the one whose paintings keep the wolf from the door; you're the one who gets us through every single day, solid enough to face the next. Name one meaningful thing that I've ever done for you.'

'You've loved me,' Dorothy said, without a moment's hesitation. 'You've given me what no one else ever has or ever could.'

Patricia kissed her, long and hard, with an intensity which the years of bickering and jealousy had drained from their relationship; when she finally pulled away, Dorothy was moved to see tears in her lover's eyes. 'I'll always love you,' Patricia said. 'You believe that, don't you?' Dorothy nodded. 'I know this isn't the way that either of us would want to get our freedom, but it's the freedom that counts, and at last it's something that *I* can do for *us*. If it works, if Stanley really does sign the house over, anything is possible. We could borrow against it and go back to France like we've always longed to…'

'Or lease it and pay our way with the rent.'

The words made her complicit and Patricia took her hand, sensing the change. 'Whatever you want to do, as long as we're together.'

'You have no idea how I've longed to hear you say that.' Dorothy pulled Patricia close, and caught the faint but familiar smell of Tabac Blond on her skin. She breathed it in, remembering how seductive she had found Patricia's perfume when they first met, bold and uncompromising like the woman she was falling in love with. The scent of cedar and musk had somehow stood for freedom, and today it brought back an earlier happiness with such immediacy that Dorothy dared to believe in it again. 'Do you remember that awful boarding house we had on the Rue Saint-Romain?' she said softly into Patricia's hair. 'No furniture and a permanent smell of fish and garlic from the café across the road. Oh, and that student couple in the room upstairs who argued all night and made up all day. God, I loved that room.'

'I loved everything about Paris. The light on the rooftops, and the way the sun fell on those beautiful gardens near the

Colarossi. I can still see it now, that house with the iron-grated windows and the high ceilings. There always seemed to be music and laughter coming from those rooms, no matter what time of day or night we passed. We vowed we'd own it one day.'

'We've made sillier promises.'

'Yes, I suppose we have.' Patricia looked up at her and smiled. 'Make me one now.'

'If I can. What?'

'Our first night back in Paris. Promise me we'll go dancing again at the Bal Bullier, just like we used to.'

Dorothy laughed. 'Of course, if you like, but I'm not sure I've got the stamina to last all night any more. We were so much younger then.'

Patricia put her hand to Dorothy's cheek, serious for a moment, and Dorothy felt herself blush. 'We haven't changed that much,' she insisted. 'Not deep down. We've just let other things get in the way. Once we're away from here, we can be ourselves again.'

'I still can't believe he'd really go through with it,' Dorothy admitted, frightened now by how badly she wanted something which – just half an hour before – had repelled her. 'You told me that buying Lindworth meant so much to him, the fact that he could come back to Cookham as someone who mattered. He might well be prepared to sell his wife and children down the river, but why would he give that up?'

'Because he knows I need something tangible to make up for the trouble he's causing me. All the gossip in the village, the filthy looks and the poor service whenever we walk down the high street. I swear the waitress at the Copper Kettle would have turned all her chairs to the tables the other morning if she'd seen us coming in time. As it was, she probably spat in our coffee.' Dorothy tried to smile, but the atmosphere in the café had mortified her at the time, and she found the humiliation hard to shake off. 'I think it's the least he can do. Lindworth is a small price to pay for the sake of my reputation.'

'But Stanley doesn't care about gossip. He starts most of it.'

'Darling, does it really matter *why* he's thinking of giving me the house?'

'Of course it matters.' She saw that Patricia had misread her concerns and tried to explain. 'Peggy, I'm not going back on everything I've just said or looking for reasons to doubt you. On the contrary. I need to understand Stanley's motives because I need to believe in them. Our plans, our future – well, I need to be able to hope, and I can't do that if this is just another wild scheme that will never come to anything.'

Patricia hesitated, and Dorothy wondered what she was considering. 'I told him about your father's business,' she said eventually. 'I said that the company was going to be liquidated and that your mother wouldn't be able to keep up the mortgage payments on Moor Thatch. If the mortgage is called in, we'll have no choice but to sell up and leave.'

'So he's giving you his house to keep you in Cookham?'

'Among other things, yes.'

'When actually it's going to be your escape?'

'*Our* escape.' Patricia looked at her anxiously, waiting for her to speak. 'Can you bear that? Have I gone too far?'

In truth, a knot of fear had tightened in Dorothy's stomach, fear of something vague and undefined which refused to step out from the shadows, but Patricia had always made her brave, and now was no different. Tenderly, she lifted Patricia's nightgown and ran her hand across her skin, tracing the contours of her breasts and feeling the nipple harden against her fingers. Her touch was hesitant at first, made shy by the distance between them which had seemed so insurmountable, but Patricia's response surprised her with its intensity. 'Yes, I can bear it,' Dorothy thought, exhilarated by the forgotten joy of her lover's touch. 'I shouldn't, because we both know it's wrong, but I can bear anything except being without you.'

****

In the evening they walked over to Lindworth, taking a meandering route down Berries Road and back along the river. Patricia seemed in no hurry to get to the house, and Dorothy savoured every step that took them further from their destination, reluctant to break the spell of a perfect day. The May sunlight was beginning to fade, but still it drew a green-yellow radiance from the trees on the horizon, sharp and fresh as the oaks came into flower. It was her favourite time of year in the countryside, a fleeting moment of clarity between the pink and cream indulgence of spring and the sober greens of an older year, and today it resonated more strongly than ever. Not even the prospect of several hours in Stanley's company could dampen her spirits.

They turned into the yard by the King's Arms, but stopped in their tracks at the sight of the maroon car parked by Lindworth's garden gate. 'Did you know Hilda was going to be here?' Dorothy asked.

'No, of course not. Stanley said it would be just the three of us.'

'Then why has she come?'

'I've no idea.'

They stood under the arch that separated the yard from the high street, uncertain of what to do next. 'Do you think she's come back to him again?' Dorothy asked eventually, unable to disguise the fear in her voice. 'If she has, that's the end of all our plans.'

'Not necessarily,' Patricia said, squeezing her hand. 'But there's only one way to find out. Come on.'

She strode confidently towards the house, and Dorothy followed. The bell was soon answered and Elsie showed them into the hallway. Stanley's voice drifted out from the drawing room to meet them, angry and obviously in no mood for interruption. 'I hope you've got your tin hats with you,' Elsie said, unusually conspiratorial as she took their coats. 'It's like the war never ended in there.'

'Have we come at a bad time?' Patricia asked. 'We don't want to interrupt if Mr and Mrs Spencer are in the middle of…'

'Oh no, he's perfectly capable of having an argument with himself,' Elsie said, and Dorothy smiled; she was wary of the Spencers' maid, who had never masked her dislike for Patricia's relationship with Stanley, but she had to admire the way that Elsie could sum up her employer in a few carefully chosen words. 'Someone's rejected his paintings, apparently, and you can imagine how that's gone down.'

'But Mrs Spencer *is* here? We saw her car outside.'

'Yes, but she's not staying.' If Elsie had added the words 'more's the pity', her feelings could not have been clearer, but Dorothy had to struggle to hide her own relief. 'Go through to the drawing room. Dinner won't be long.'

They did as instructed and found Stanley pacing up and down in front of the fire, clutching a piece of paper so tightly that it threatened to disintegrate in his hand. 'Oh, there you are,' he said, his face as black as thunder. 'I thought you were never coming. I need to talk this through with you.'

'What is it, darling?' Patricia asked, ignoring the issue of their late arrival. 'What's happened?'

'The Academy's sent two of my pictures back.' He flourished the letter in front of them, and Dorothy suspected that he knew its contents well enough by now to quote them verbatim. 'The Hanging Committee has requested that I withdraw *Saint Francis and the Birds* and *The Lovers*. Apparently they're not of advantage to my reputation or the Academy's. How dare they talk to me like that!'

'But you sent five paintings, didn't you? So you'll still have three in the show.' Patricia took the letter from his hand and scanned it. 'Yes, it says here that the Committee has pleasure in placing your other works in good positions.'

'Over my dead body. It's all or nothing. If they don't want *Saint Francis* and *The Lovers*, they're damned well not having the other three. I shall demand they send them back.'

'I'm not sure they'll do that,' Dorothy ventured. 'It's Royal Academy policy not to change the position of any painting once the Council's made its decision.'

Stanley glared at her. 'I don't give a damn about "policy". I'm the artist, and I won't be bound by rules and regulations. Those are *my* pictures and I want them back. If they don't do as I ask, then it's tantamount to theft and I'll have no choice but to resign. In fact, I'm going to resign anyway.'

Patricia threw Dorothy a weary, apologetic look. 'But is that really wise? Think about how pleased you were when they elected you.' Dorothy remembered the day all too well. Stanley had come over to Moor Thatch with the news while she and Patricia were polishing the painting room floor, and they had been forced to listen while he read out his telegrams of congratulation. He had been thrilled at the time, but it was so typical of him now to sacrifice the achievement for a point of principle. Rather than worrying about Hilda's return to Lindworth, she began to wonder how the marriage had lasted so long.

Patricia's words of caution were a waste of breath. 'Whose side are you on?' Stanley demanded, rounding on her with a renewed sense of slight. 'If you're not *for* me in this, you're against me.'

'Of course I'm for you. That's entirely my point. You need to do what's best for your future. It's all I'm thinking of. The Academy won't be damaged by this. You will.'

Her advice was common sense, but Stanley refused to be mollified. 'We'll see about that,' he said. 'I've got right on my side and I'm not going quietly, either. I think I'll write to *The Times*. Let's do it now, while I'm still riled about it. You can help me.'

The exercise in self-righteousness had no role for Dorothy, so she excused herself and went to find the bathroom. In the drama of Stanley's indignation, she had almost forgotten that there was anyone else in the house; when she reached the first-floor landing, it came as a shock to glimpse Hilda through the Spencers' open bedroom door. She paused on the top step, watching as Stanley's wife took some clothes out of the wardrobe and folded them carefully into a suitcase. Hilda moved like a ghost about the room, quietly unravelling her life until there was nothing left but her absence, and Dorothy felt her eyes fill with tears. Perhaps it was pity for Hilda, perhaps just the knowledge that this could so easily have been her own fate, but she found it unbearable that Stanley should be downstairs, raging against something that hardly mattered, while the greatest sadness of his life was unfolding in another room, unseen and unopposed. Without warning, Hilda looked up from her task and Dorothy flushed, ashamed to have intruded on the most private of moments. She waited for a rebuke but Hilda said nothing, simply walked across the room and closed the door.

She found the bathroom further down the landing and took her time in freshening up. The house was quiet enough for her to hear footsteps on the stairs as she dried her hands, and she guessed that Hilda had finished her solitary task and was taking her cases down to the car. She headed back to the drawing room, hoping to avoid an awkward meeting before she got there, but her attention was caught by another open door at the end of the corridor. In the half light, she could see the outline of a picture on an easel, covered by a blanket, and another group of canvases stacked against the wall; it was, she guessed, where Stanley stored his paintings when his studio was full and she walked down to look, curious to find the portrait of Patricia that she had heard so much about but never seen.

The room was bleak and chilly, with two stripped single beds pushed against the far wall. Dorothy lit the lamp on the table by the door and walked over to the easel, smiling when she recalled Patricia's indignation at the unflattering way in which Stanley had depicted her, leaning awkwardly against the dining table and looking straight ahead so that the cast in her eye was obvious to anyone who saw it. She lifted the blanket, and immediately wished that she hadn't; the portrait *was* of Patricia, but it wasn't the one she was looking for. The woman she loved stared back at her from the canvas, dressed like a tart in a black lace camisole and velvet headband; she lay with her knees drawn up towards her chest on a bed of crumpled sheets, one hand stretched out by her side, palm upwards as if in supplication, the other playing idly with her toes in a gesture so painfully familiar that Dorothy could scarcely breathe. There was an air of taut sexual anticipation about the picture which disgusted her – the nipple tantalisingly visible through the lace, the material tucked suggestively between Patricia's legs – and she fought against her imagination, but a vision of Stanley slipping the straps from Patricia's shoulders, of his mouth on her skin, was so strong that she could almost hear his breathing.

Instinctively she closed her eyes, but it was impossible to draw back now. Somehow, she forced herself to look at other canvases. The first two were also of Patricia, but this time she was fully nude. In one, her head lay awkwardly twisted, as if Stanley had forgotten to leave room for it in the composition, but it was her body that dominated – the shifting patterns of light and shade on her thighs, the glimpse of pubic hair. The other painting was more conventional in its pose but no less revealing; Patricia's breasts hung low against her stomach, painted in such meticulous detail that Dorothy could see a web of blue veins contrasted against the pale skin – or flesh might have been a better word for something so clinical and devoid of human emotion. Under Stanley's relentless gaze, everything that Dorothy had cherished as private and sacred was irredeemably cheapened, and she could stand it no longer.

There was a small washbasin in the corner of the room and she reached it just in time, bending low over the bowl as the sharp, sour smell of revulsion rose up to greet her. If she could have trusted what her head was telling her, she would have known that the portraits were not about desire but its absence. She would have noticed how awkward Patricia looked and understood the expression of blank resignation on her face, but her sense of betrayal was too acute to see reason. She retched again as the memory of the morning became inextricably linked with what she had just seen, the tenderness of their lovemaking now twisted and distorted until she no longer believed in it as real.

Her cheeks burned with shame and she splashed cold water on her face, knowing that somehow she must go back downstairs. When at last she felt ready to leave, she was horrified to find Hilda watching her from the doorway. 'I'm sorry,' she said, despising the instinct to apologise. 'I know I wasn't supposed to see these.'

'Really? Then Patricia must be much kinder than Stanley, or perhaps she just loves you more than he loves me. She's obviously shielded you from this. I've lived with every blow since it started.' She walked across the room and stood by Dorothy's side, looking down at the canvases. 'Didn't you know she was modelling for him?'

'Yes, but not like this.' The admission made her feel both stupid and angry, like a naïve child who had failed to grasp what was obvious in an adult world. None of this was Hilda's fault, but her pain compelled her to retaliate and she was past caring where the blows fell. 'Why didn't you fight harder?' she demanded furiously. 'You could have saved us both from this misery, but you just stood there and let him walk away.'

'I could ask you the same thing, but we both know that it would never have made any difference.'

'It might have done,' Dorothy insisted. 'You still love him, don't you?' Hilda nodded. 'Then how can you be so calm about it?'

'I'm not calm. That's really the last thing I am.' She shook her head and smiled sadly to herself. 'Stanley was pure when he came to me, I imagine you know that. He'd never known anyone before we married, and that felt precious, the greatest gift he could have given me. So, every brush stroke here…' She gestured towards the paintings, and the expression of pain in her eyes made the rest of the sentence irrelevant. 'These last few years have been like a slow form of death, and I can stand anything but his hatred. Stanley turns so easily against something he's once loved.'

'That must make for a simple life,' Dorothy said quietly. 'I wish I could do it.'

'You and me both. But as I can't, and never will where Stanley is concerned, leaving is the only option – before I go under, and for the sake of the children.'

Dorothy nodded, surprised that Hilda should speak so openly to her. 'I'm sorry for what I said just now.'

'Don't be. You love her, and you're frightened.'

The need to disown her love for Patricia in public was so engrained in Dorothy that she opened her mouth to argue, but there seemed little point in denying something that lay smashed and broken at her feet. 'Why does he make everything ugly?' she asked instead, looking at the emptiness in Patricia's eyes which made her seem so much older in the paintings than in life.

Hilda thought for a long time before answering. 'It's ironic, isn't it? I've no doubt that you know Patricia a thousand times better than Stanley ever will, and yet you could never paint her like he does.'

'Why would I want to? It's disgusting.'

'Perhaps, but it's honest.'

'That's easy for you to say. You're not staring at someone you love.' In the silence that followed, Dorothy knelt down by the nearest canvas and brushed Patricia's cheek. 'I don't know what to do,' she said, her voice barely more than a whisper. 'Everything keeps changing.'

Hilda looked at her sympathetically. 'I know how it feels to have no control. You sit around and wait, hoping that something will change, knowing in your heart that it won't. But we're not in the same situation, you and I. Patricia isn't lost to you in the way that Stanley is to me.'

'Isn't she?' Dorothy laughed, a hollow sound that she barely recognised as her own. 'Then what are these? I'm not interested in how honest they are. You surely don't expect me to stand here and admire the brushwork?'

'That's not what I…'

'All I see when I look at those paintings is Patricia alone in a room with your husband, with his eyes on her for hour after hour after hour. I see them together, in one of those beds, when she swore to me that she wouldn't. That's not honesty. It's betrayal.'

'Don't torment yourself.' Hilda replaced the blanket over the easel, then took a less provocative canvas from the stack by the wall and used it to cover the nude. The gesture was meant in kindness, but her choice was ill-fated and Dorothy found herself looking at another image of Patricia, this time on Cockmarsh Hill. It was the picture that Stanley had vowed to paint in celebration of their shared love of Cookham, and he had achieved all he set out to: Patricia appeared as a natural extension of the landscape, her hair golden against the grasses, her necklace echoing the jewel-like flowers which dotted the gentle slope. 'What's wrong?' Hilda asked, as Dorothy continued to stare in horror at the bottom of the painting. It was the smallest of details, innocent by comparison with the overt sexuality of the other paintings, and yet far more devastating. Suddenly, Hilda seemed to realise her mistake, but by then the damage was done. Dorothy turned and walked out of the room without another word.

****

Left alone, Hilda looked through the rest of the pictures. Whenever Stanley had written to her about them, he had emphasised how different the nudes were from his figure paintings, taken from nature rather than his imagination, and he was right: the detail was unflinching, like nothing she had ever seen before, and the confusion of grief and resentment which it stirred in her couldn't prevent her from admiring its courage. Even in his torment, Stanley was original.

And torment was the only word she could think of. She looked at the paintings closest to the wall, double nudes in which Stanley had painted his own naked form alongside Patricia's. In one, he knelt by the bed, facing away from the viewer, his head framed by Patricia's breasts and hips, while she lay on her side, staring blankly past him. The other was more provocative still: Patricia sprawled on her back, her arms above her head, her legs parted, while Stanley squatted at her side, dejected and impotent, his head hung in shame. The image was ruthlessly personal, and yet there was no intimacy in it, no hint of passion or fulfilment; if anything, it bore witness to the death of desire, emphasised by the sallow grey sheen on their skin and the raw piece of meat that Stanley had inexplicably placed at the bottom of the picture. Only she would ever truly understand why he had done it: the leg of mutton, seemingly so incongruous, was a reference to their courtship, to the Leg of Mutton Pond by his Hampstead studio where they had often walked, and a time and place that had made them happy. It was Stanley's way of honouring their marriage while in the very act of destroying it. An apology of sorts, although perhaps that was going too far.

She turned the canvas to the wall but the image stayed with her, desperate and bleak. Even now, as she wrenched her life from his, Hilda had never felt as distant from Stanley as these two naked forms seemed from each other, physically touching but spiritually a thousand miles apart. Perhaps she should have found comfort in that, as any spurned wife might, but she could take no pleasure from Stanley's unhappiness. All she felt as she left the room was a gnawing, unredeemable sadness that their marriage had been sacrificed for this.

****

The walk back to Moor Thatch was a blur of tears and humiliation. Dorothy slammed the door behind her and went straight to Patricia's room, tearing the drawers open one after another, searching for proof of what she had seen in the painting. She rifled through the underwear that Stanley had bought, feeling like a voyeur in her own life as she found the black lace camisole and the velvet headband, but there was nothing more tangible than silk and satin. The wardrobe was equally fruitless but still she persisted, going through each and every pocket before throwing the clothes on to the bed – hundreds of pounds worth of coats and dresses and accessories, a vast pile of vanity and excess. By the time she had finished, the room looked as if a tornado had passed through it, an uncanny reflection of her own emotions, but still there was no sign of what she was looking for.

She looked round again, asking herself where she would hide something so incriminating, daring to hope now that it existed only in Stanley's imagination, but her eyes were drawn to Alfonse, the teddy bear on Patricia's pillow. They had bought him together from a tiny shop in Paris and he had travelled with them ever since, battered but still loved. Whenever they were apart, Patricia would leave Alfonse on Dorothy's bed – covered with her perfume, a letter concealed beneath his faded blue jumper. Now, Dorothy picked up the bear and noticed that one of the felt pads on his feet had some stitches missing; inside, tucked safely among the straw and cotton, she found the ring that Patricia had been wearing in Stanley's portrait.

This time, her rage left no room for tears and grew stronger with every passing moment. Calmly, she put the ring in her pocket and gathered up as many of the clothes from the bed as she could carry, taking them out into the garden. She dumped them in a heap by the fence, as far from the thatch as possible, then went to fetch the paraffin from the shed. When she was sure they were burning safely, she returned to the house for the rest and watched as Stanley's money – Stanley's lust – went up in flames. In just a few minutes, the jealousy of months was reduced to ash, and she went back inside to wait for Patricia.

It was shortly after ten when she heard the front door. 'Dodie, where are you? You might have told me you were leaving. Hilda decided to stay until the morning, so I've had the most excruciating time.'

'I'm in here.'

Patricia switched on the drawing room light and looked at Dorothy in astonishment. 'Why are you sitting in the dark? And what's that smell of smoke?' She put her bag down on the table and took off her gloves. 'Jesus, you look terrible. What on earth's been going on?'

'You lied to me.'

'About what? Darling, I haven't…'

'Don't try to deny it. I've seen the paintings.'

'Oh.'

Patricia sat down on the chaise longue and Dorothy waited for her to speak. 'Well? Is that all you've got to say?'

'Those paintings don't mean anything, really they don't. It's not as if he'll ever be able to exhibit them. There'd be an outcry.'

Dorothy glared at Patricia, scarcely able to believe that she could be so stupid. 'Is that the only thing that matters to you? Your public reputation? Can't you stop to think, just for a second, of how I might have felt when I found them? They're done, Peggy. They exist, no matter who sees them. And because of that, Stanley Spencer can have you whenever he likes. He owns a piece of you now. Don't you understand that?'

'Of course he doesn't.'

'You swore to me that he hadn't touched you. Even today, when we were making love…'

'It's not the same thing. I *love* you. With him, it's just sex, and if you saw the paintings you should know that. They're hardly an homage to a beautiful woman by her lover.'

Patricia's vanity incensed Dorothy. 'When did it start?' she demanded.

'Does that matter?'

'*When*, damn you.'

'After we got back from Switzerland.'

'So all this time…'

'It's not like it sounds. We haven't… well, it never really worked. I couldn't pretend, not when I thought about you, and even Stanley can't persist with a woman who finds him repellent.'

Patricia reached out to take her hand, but Dorothy snatched it away. 'Don't touch me,' she said. 'I can't bear to be near you.'

'Please, Dodie, at least try to understand. Yes, I took my clothes off, but the rest is in his head. Don't let those pictures spoil everything. What about France? What about our plans?'

'And what about this?' Dorothy held up the eternity ring, imagining Patricia carefully removing it each time she left Lindworth to come crawling back to Moor Thatch. 'Is that in his head? He painted you wearing it, so it must mean something.' For the first time, Patricia looked genuinely shocked, but Dorothy found no pleasure in the victory. 'You've said you'll marry him, haven't you? That's why he's giving you the house. That's what you couldn't bring yourself to tell me.'

'Only because you would never believe me when I say it makes no difference.'

'Of course it makes a difference. You're going to leave me.' The words broke Dorothy, giving a reality to her greatest fear. She tried to fight as Patricia held her close, but her rage had given way to despair and she had no resistance left. 'You're going to leave me and marry him.'

'No.'

'You've been planning it all along.'

'*No.* I haven't, Dodie, you're wrong.'

'You said it would always be *us*. Life and death, always together.'

Her sobs – raw and violent – shook them both, and Patricia clung to her. 'And it will be, I promise. This won't change things.'

'How can you say that?'

'Because it's true.' She took Dorothy's face in her hands and made her look up. 'Listen to me. I *have* to marry Stanley. You think I care too much about my reputation and perhaps you're right, but I feel just as naked when I walk down the high street as I am in those pictures. You've heard the things that people are saying about me, never quite behind my back – calling me a vamp and a slut, looking at you with such pity because you breathe the same air as a whore.'

'Don't, Peggy…'

'But it's true. You know it is.' Dorothy looked at the pain in Patricia's eyes and understood for the first time that the indifference at which she seemed so practised was nothing more than a mask, brittle and easily destroyed. 'If it were just Cookham, I could bear it, but I can't even show my face in London now.'

'Why? Has something happened?'

Patricia nodded. 'The other day, at the gallery. We'd finished the meeting and I left in a hurry because I couldn't wait to get back and tell you that they'd agreed to give us an exhibition. I was so excited that I left my gloves behind…'

'You told me you'd lost them on the train.'

'That was a lie. When I went back, I heard the men laughing and one of them was talking about me and Stanley.'

'What did he say?'

'I can't…'

'Tell me, Peggy.'

'He said if I painted like I fucked, Spencer might take more notice of my work instead of hiding in the taxi whenever I bring my pictures in. And it's true. That's exactly what he does. He doesn't even make a show of supporting me.'

'You don't need his support. We'll make a success of that exhibition and prove him wrong.'

'But it won't stop them talking, will it? And it won't stop me feeling filthy all over. That was the last straw. I don't think I can face it any longer.'

'Why didn't you tell me you felt like this?' Dorothy asked quietly.

'Because I'm never more ashamed of myself than when I'm with you. I've let this thing with Stanley get out of hand, when I should have listened to you right from the start. I wish I had, but there's no going back and I'm too involved now to walk away – people will crucify me. If I marry him, the scandal will die down and we'll have some sort of security, but it will only ever be a legal arrangement. I'll never be his wife in the true sense of the word, and I swear to you – I will never, ever leave you.'

With the contrariness of someone in love, Dorothy longed to believe Patricia without conceding the argument. 'You'll still be vilified,' she said. 'People will take Stanley's side. He has a talent for rousing sympathy, and the man is never at fault when there's a woman to blame.'

Patricia shrugged. 'I'd rather be a money-grabbing bitch than a penniless whore.'

She smiled, but Dorothy saw something in her lover's face that reminded her of Hilda's words: there *was* something truthful in the way that Stanley had painted Patricia, and its presence disturbed her. 'You frighten me sometimes,' she said. 'I never know quite what you're capable of.'

Patricia touched her cheek, wiping away all traces of her tears. 'If it's any consolation,' she said, her face suddenly more serious, 'I frighten myself as well.'

11

Hilda slept later than she intended and, when she awoke, it took her a few moments to recognise the peeling Japanese print wallpaper of Lindworth's smallest bedroom. She drew the curtains back and looked out on the sort of day she most loathed. An unyielding stretch of cloud had settled heavily over the Cookham rooftops, draining the colour from everything it touched and shrouding the garden in a half-hearted, depressing mist. Beyond the wall, in the back yard of the inn, a man was unloading barrels from a brewery dray and she watched as he rolled them methodically over to the cellar. It must have gone nine and she would have to go down eventually, but the prospect of another row with Stanley made her linger. The evening had descended into more bitter recriminations over money, inflamed by Patricia's early departure, and she hadn't the energy to start again this morning.

Downstairs, she heard the front door slam as if in answer to her prayers. Stanley emerged from the house, dressed in an overcoat and his favourite hat, pulled low against the drizzle. He walked quickly towards the high street, struggling to balance a canvas and painting materials with his easel and a large, ungainly umbrella which threatened to open of its own accord at any moment. As soon as he was out of sight, Hilda dressed quickly and checked that she had all her belongings, then closed the door behind her and hurried downstairs.

Elsie was waiting for her in the hallway, and Hilda was moved by the look of sadness on her face. 'Do you want some help with your bags?' she asked.

'Thank you, Elsie, but no. I've got all I need for now.'

'Then at least let me make you something to eat before you go?'

Hilda hesitated, and Elsie read her thoughts. 'He'll be gone for hours,' she said. 'She's got him out painting in all weathers. You won't have to see him.'

'All right, then. That would be lovely.'

Hilda followed her through to the kitchen. 'Sit down, Mrs Spencer. I've just made a fresh pot.'

'Of course you have.' She took two cups from the dresser and poured tea for them both while Elsie cracked some eggs into the pan and fried the bacon. The smell was so familiar, the company so easy, that Hilda was reminded of the early days at Chapel View, when Elsie's uncomplicated kindness had meant more to her than she would ever be able to explain. 'So Patricia's cracking the whip?' she asked, spreading butter on a piece of toast.

'I don't think there's an inch of Cookham that he hasn't stood in front of these past few months.'

'That makes sense. She knows his landscapes will sell.'

'Doesn't mean he's happy about it, though. He comes home in a foul temper and all he can talk about – when he does talk to me these days, which isn't often – is doing another building like the chapel, except this one will be about the people he loves.' She gave Hilda a long-suffering smile as she piled her plate high. 'We'll all be in it, apparently, whether we like it or not.'

Hilda thought about the paintings she had seen the night before and tried to imagine the reaction if they ever saw the light of day; if Stanley thought he would find a patron like the Behrends to support this new scheme, then he really was deluded. 'Tell me honestly, Elsie – is Stanley in *serious* trouble with money? You'll know better than anyone, and I trust you. If he is, then I'll happily sell some of my pictures rather than press him about the allowance.'

'That's very generous of you, but it's more than he deserves. There'd be plenty of money to go round if he thought a bit more about his priorities.' Elsie sat down at the kitchen table and began to drink her tea. 'Can I say something, Mrs Spencer?'

'Yes, of course.'

'It's really not my place…'

Hilda smiled. 'We didn't always stick to that arrangement, if my memory serves me correctly, so I don't think we should start now. Say whatever you like.'

'Be careful over the money. Miss Preece seems to handle all that now. He takes his landscapes over to Moor Thatch for her to sell as soon as they're done, and she comes round here every morning to sort out his post.'

'She reads his letters?' Elsie nodded. 'But not mine, surely?'

'I think so. Like I said, I shouldn't be saying any of this, not when Mr Spencer still pays my wages, but I thought you should know. And soon it won't matter what I say, so I might as well warn you while I can.'

'What do you mean?'

'He's told me he'll have to let me go. He's here on his own for most of the time, so he can make do with a woman coming in for two or three mornings a week. That's what he said, anyway.'

The down-to-earth tone of her voice hadn't changed, but Hilda saw the hurt in Elsie's eyes and wondered how Stanley could be so reckless with someone who had served him faithfully for years. 'He doesn't mean that. You've been a good friend to him, and he's always listened to you – more than anyone, I think. He can't do without you. Me, yes. Patricia, in time. But not you.'

'I think he *does* mean it, Mrs Spencer.'

'Then he's his own worst enemy. What will you do?'

Elsie shrugged. 'Look for some work nearer home, I suppose, and see Ken when I can. We haven't saved enough to get married and find a place of our own, but we can get by. We could move in with his parents for a bit if it comes to that, although I'm not sure there's a kitchen big enough for me *and* his mother.'

'I wish I could do something to help,' Hilda said, 'but I've got no influence with Stanley any more. All hell breaks loose whenever we try to reason with each other, as you well know.'

'That's kind of you, but you've got troubles of your own.' Elsie poured them both more tea, then refilled the pot. 'And if I'm honest, a part of me will be glad to leave now. It was hard when he first told me, but it's never been the same without you and the children, and if he's giving the house away it's probably just as well I'm not here. I won't hang around to get my marching orders from her.'

Hilda stared at her in astonishment. 'If he's *what*?'

Elsie flushed, mortified to have said more than she should. 'I'm sorry, Mrs Spencer, but I thought you knew. I assumed he'd *have* to tell you if he's having paperwork drawn up.'

Hilda's rage made her numb, and it took her a moment to speak. 'Are you sure about this? Stanley's really making legal arrangements to have this house signed over to Patricia?'

'Yes. He told me the other day. He was so definite about it, as if it was done and dusted. That's why I assumed you knew.'

'How dare he!' Hilda slammed her hand down on the table and blinked back tears of anger. 'Does he really think I'll stand by while he squanders our children's future for a woman who will never love him? It's not happening, Elsie. I'll fight him every step of the way over this.'

'I'm sorry, Mrs Spencer.'

'Don't be. It's not your fault.' She bit her lip and made an effort to calm down. 'Who knows when I'd have heard about it if you hadn't told me? When I tried to get in and found that Patricia had changed the locks, I suppose.'

They fell silent, while Hilda tried to come to terms with the way in which Stanley could still surprise her by the depth of his betrayal. 'He hasn't stopped painting you, you know,' Elsie said quietly. 'They're so tender, those pictures. Scenes of us all at Burghclere, and private portraits of you that he probably shouldn't have shown me. There's so much love in all of them. It's as if his art's got more sense than he has.'

It was an insightful comment, true of the nudes she had seen the night before – the artist acknowledging a futility which the man refused to see. If Elsie had meant to comfort her, she had chosen the wrong information to disclose. The idea of Stanley living in a past of his imagination while she carried on alone was more than Hilda could bear. 'You see what I mean?' she said. 'He'd be a fool to lose you. You're still loyal to him, even now.'

She had meant it as a compliment, but Elsie shook her head. 'No, it's not that. I'm being selfish, really. Those pictures give me hope – hope that those days might not be lost.'

Hilda hesitated, touched by the affection in the words. 'They *are* lost, though. That's if they ever existed, at least for me. I'm going to divorce him, and it's only fair that you should know that. I've hung on for as long as I can in the hope that whatever this is would burn itself out, but there's no going back now. I dare say Stanley will marry Patricia as soon as he's free.' How bitter that word tasted, she thought, whenever it belonged to someone else.

'I won't work for that woman.'

Hilda smiled. 'No. I can't see that being a happy arrangement.' She pushed her plate away and got up from the table. 'It's time I was going. Thank you for…'

'You don't have to thank me.'

'Yes, I do, and not just for this morning. For everything, from the moment you came to us.'

Elsie began to tidy up, giving a little too much attention to brushing some crumbs from the table. 'Give my love to Shirin and Unity when you see them,' she said, and Hilda could hear the emotion in her voice. 'Tell them I still miss them, every single day. I expect I'd hardly recognise them now, they'll have grown so fast.'

'I dare say you'll have children of your own soon.' She picked up her bag and squeezed Elsie's hand. 'Be happy, and make sure Ken treats you well. Make sure he's kind.'

'I'll do my best.' Hilda turned to go, surprised by the tears which threatened to overwhelm her, but Elsie's voice called her back. 'Why does he do it, Mrs Spencer? He's a nice man, and he loves you.'

She paused in the doorway, struck by the familiarity of a question which she had asked herself a thousand times. 'I don't think any of us will ever know that, Elsie,' she answered truthfully. 'Stanley least of all.'

****

Elsie finished her chores and went upstairs to her room. She sat at the small writing desk that Stanley had fetched from Fernlea when they first moved to Cookham, and looked round at the familiar walls, hoping to find something which would change her mind – but to her surprise, all the small mementoes of a life she had loved only strengthened her resolve. It was important to leave now, while the memories were still precious; if she continued to waver, her present unhappiness would tarnish everything that had gone before. She took some notepaper from the drawer and found the right tone on her third attempt: brief, and without sentiment. When it was done, she waited for the sadness and anticipation of those last few days at Burghclere to return, but this was a different sort of ending, a fracture rather than a turn in the road, and all she felt was resentment.

Downstairs, she heard the slam of the front door and Stanley's voice, calling her name. 'Find me some dry clothes, will you?' he asked, when he saw her on the landing. 'I'm soaked to the skin, and all for the sake of the gardens in Cookham Rise.' The easel clattered to the floor, and he threw the umbrella down on top of it. 'What a waste of time. I hope the art-buying public will be satisfied when it reads that the heir to Giotto caught his death while painting bloody lobelia.'

'I don't doubt that someone at Moor Thatch will be,' Elsie muttered to herself, 'as long as Giotto made his will first.'

'What was that?'

'Nothing. I've laid some clean clothes on your bed.'

'Thank you.' Stanley handed her his overcoat and she collected the umbrella from the floor, where it was leaking a pool of water on to the tiles. 'Is Mrs Spencer still here?' he asked.

Elsie looked at him in bewilderment, wondering why he would expect Hilda to drag out the agony any longer than she had to. 'No, she isn't. She left straight after breakfast.'

'That's a shame. I wanted to talk to her about the house. Never mind, I'll write to her later. I'd better get changed and take this over to Patricia.'

He gave the canvas a disparaging shove and headed upstairs, but Elsie called him back. 'Before you go, Mr Spencer, I wanted to give you this.'

She held the resignation letter out and he looked at it impatiently. 'Whatever it is, can't it wait?'

'Not really,' she said, reluctant to give herself the chance to change her mind. 'It's my notice, see. You'll want time to get someone else in.'

He began to smile, then realised that she was serious. 'Don't be ridiculous, Elsie. You can't possibly hand in your notice. What on earth would I do?'

'But you said you'd have to let me go. I'm saving you the trouble.'

'When did I say that?'

'The other day, when you came in from…'

'You must have misunderstood. Whatever I said, I certainly didn't mean this.' He held up the letter, relieved to put it down to a simple mistake. 'If that's what this is about, if you're feeling snubbed…'

'No, that's not it.' She held his eye, shivering a little as the rainwater from his coat soaked into her sleeve. 'Please open it. My resignation stands, and I won't be talked out of it.'

'But you can't leave.'

'I have to. Things have changed. I need to think about the future.'

Stanley sighed and scratched his head, as if he were trying to solve a problem in his painting, and the gesture was so painfully familiar that Elsie had to look away. 'Of course you do,' he said. 'I know you'll be getting married soon, but you'll stay in Cookham, won't you? Ken's here, and I assumed you'd still come in, even if it's only for one or two days a week.'

'That's the trouble, Mr Spencer, you assume too much.' She expected him to take offence, but he simply stood on the stairs like a lost and frightened child. Elsie stared at the letter in his hand, watching tiny rivulets of water bleed across the envelope and smudge his carefully printed name, and suddenly all her anger disappeared. 'I want a family of my own,' she said, speaking frankly, like they used to. 'It's meant a lot to me to be part of yours, but I need more than that now and I haven't got all the time in the world if Ken and I are to have kids.' She was about to add that things had changed in the Spencer household, but she realised with a stab of relief that what she had said already was more important: she had a new life to look forward to, one which put her in control of her own happiness. 'I'll stay until you marry Miss Preece,' she promised, 'but that's all.'

12

Time passed, and it seemed to Dorothy that her life was in limbo. There were endless negotiations between Stanley and Hilda over money and bitter recriminations about the house, which, at his second attempt, Stanley had signed over to Patricia. If Dorothy had had her way, they would have borrowed against the property and left for France immediately, but Patricia was determined to rescue her name from the dirt and insisted they stay to see the plan through, however long it might take. And so they lived on at Moor Thatch, with one month seeping into another, their future a hostage to fortune. Rarely had Dorothy been so conscious of her life slipping away.

The winter had been spiteful and long, with heavy snowfalls that soon outlived the magic of their first appearance. In March, when the thaw finally came, it was sudden and extreme, flooding the Moor and Causeway and leaving the southern side of the village entirely cut off. From Moor Thatch, for as far as the eye could see, the meadows were glassy with standing water, reflecting the light in a weaving together of earth and sky which Dorothy tried repeatedly to paint, but its subtleties always eluded her. Storms followed, biblical in their intensity, and they watched anxiously from the windows, using a bench on the opposite side of the Moor as a marker for the flood's ebb and flow. On the third day, the water entered the cottage. Stanley arrived by punt like a sou'westered angel, helping them to move the most precious items of furniture, rugs and antiques to the safety of the first floor, then returned each day by the same eccentric method with coal and other provisions. Supplies were limited, as half the businesses in the high street were damaged by the flooding, but he had been characteristically generous and it seemed to Dorothy that the water brought with it a welcome suspension of hostilities; despite their differences, Stanley's kindness touched her.

At the beginning of the second week, just as their confinement to the cottage was taking its toll, the sun appeared suddenly through a tear in the cloud. The water sparkled in response, bringing a welcome source of light to a world that had seemed dreary and forgotten, and Dorothy felt her spirits lift. 'It's definitely receding,' she said, watching a flock of geese in chevron flight across the sky. 'The level's dropped by a few feet. You can see the path now. We might as well start clearing up.'

She found them both some old clothes and they ventured downstairs. At its worst, the water had been more than ankle-deep throughout the ground floor, as the dirty grey tidemark above the skirting testified. 'We'll have to decorate again,' Dorothy said, looking at the damage.

'At least that's one paint job I *can* manage.' Patricia shivered in the bone-cold damp of the hallway. 'It's the smell I hate most,' she said. 'It hangs around for weeks, like the house is slowly rotting and taking us along with it.' She walked over to the cupboard under the stairs, cringing as her boots sank into the thin film of silt that the water had left behind, and took out a variety of mops, buckets and old towels. 'We'd better get on with it. The sooner we start, the sooner we can forget it ever happened.'

Dorothy followed her through to the kitchen, picking up a trail of miscellaneous oddities that they had forgotten to remove to safety – shoes, gardening gloves and magazines, stranded haphazardly like litter brought in on the tide. 'Thank God this doesn't happen every year,' she said. 'At least we get a chance to recover.'

Her sanguinity faded when she looked out of the back window and saw close-up what she had been trying to avoid. The garden was a scene of devastation, more reminiscent of Flanders field than a quiet corner of Berkshire. Patches of mud and murky brown puddles still sat wherever the lawn dipped, and the plants in the borders were crushed and bent as if someone had trampled them into the ground. Except for one small patch of primroses, a miracle that sat defiant and untouched at the end of the path, all the spring flowers were destroyed.

Her silence drew Patricia's attention. 'Come on,' she said gently, putting her arm round Dorothy's shoulders. 'It's worse than it looks, and we got through it last time. We'll make it beautiful again, I promise.'

'All that work.' Dorothy looked at the flattened and dirty crocus petals, trying to shake off her despair. 'You can never get a spring back once it's lost, and this will be our last one here. I wanted it to be precious.' Patricia said nothing, but turned away and began to fill the kettle. Dorothy watched her, concerned by her silence. 'What's the matter? You've been so quiet lately whenever I mention France.'

'Have I?'

'Yes. Is there something you're not telling me?' Patricia shook her head, but the gesture was unconvincing. 'Have you changed your mind?'

'Of course not…'

'But?'

'But I don't want to tempt fate.' Patricia pulled a chair out and sat down at the kitchen table. 'It's just something that Stanley said about the divorce. It worried me.'

'What was it?' Dorothy asked, beginning to panic. 'Is there a problem? I thought everything was going smoothly.'

'It is, but the other day he was saying how much he hated not being able to write to Hilda. The lawyers have put a stop to any sort of communication between them and it's driving him to distraction. He told me how much he was looking forward to the divorce going through so that things could go back to normal and he'd be able to see her again.'

'I don't understand. What's that got to do with France?'

'Isn't it obvious? He wants Hilda back, and he's made that perfectly clear. What if he changes his mind about the wedding?'

'Of course he won't change his mind. Stanley wants you both, you've always known that. He's been like a dog with two wives on the rare occasions that he's had you both under the same roof at Lindworth.'

'What's to stop him leaving things as they are?'

'You've told him you won't accept that. He knows it's marriage or nothing.'

Patricia sighed. 'I don't know, Dodie. Six months ago I'd have agreed with you, but something's changed. I used to be able to wrap Stanley round my little finger, but a part of him is always somewhere else, somewhere in the past.'

'Isn't it just the old cliché of not knowing what you've got until it's gone? We're all guilty of that.'

'Perhaps you're right.' She took two cigarettes out of the case and lit one for each of them. 'I *hope* you're right, but it's not just the things he says about Hilda. He's started to paint her again. I went into his studio the other day and there were some new pictures. Stanley obviously didn't want me to see them or he'd have shown them to me. You know how he likes to share his work.'

'What were they?'

'Scenes from Burghclere, all very cosy and domestic. Stanley and Hilda going to bed, with the children clambering all over them. Hilda dusting a shelf. Even the bloody maid doing the washing up. It made me think that he hasn't really let that life go.'

'It's just nostalgia, Peggy. Perhaps the finality of the divorce has made him think about his life with Hilda, but it was never that idyllic, no matter how he chooses to paint it. Deep down, Stanley knows that.'

'But what if he *is* having doubts? If he gets cold feet and pulls out of this wedding, I'll have no legal standing whatsoever, and where would that leave *us*?'

Dorothy was tempted to say 'free', but she knew that Patricia would never be satisfied until she had a ring on her finger and the right to call herself Mrs Stanley Spencer. 'If you're really worried, you should insist on fixing a date,' she said. The irony of encouraging her lover to hasten a marriage to someone else hadn't escaped Dorothy, but now that she had resigned herself to its inevitability, she wanted it done as quickly as possible; perhaps then they could move on with their lives. 'When does the decree absolute come through?'

'Late May, I think.'

'Well that's not long to wait. Book the registry office for the end of the month and get it over with.' Patricia stared at her in surprise, and Dorothy took her hand. 'To answer the question you were about to ask – no, I'm not happy about that at all. But I *am* sick to the back teeth of having our emotions dangled on a string that can be pulled by the Spencers whenever they feel like it. It's time we took control. I can't live like this much longer. We panic whenever there's water at the door, but I don't really see what difference it makes. Flooding or no flooding, we're trapped.'

'I know, and I'm sorry.'

'I don't want you to be sorry. I want you to fix it. I've put up with Stanley Spencer round here for months on end. I've waited alone night after night for you to come home to me. I've made love to you when you've left his bed feeling cheap and dirty all over. It's gone on for so long and I've put up with it because I love you, but now it's time you did something for me. Do whatever you need to do to get a marriage certificate, then just walk away and come back to me. *All* of you, just like it used to be.'

'Life and death, always together?'

Dorothy nodded, encouraged by the tears in Patricia's eyes. 'We've come this far. Now I'm relying on you to finish it. Fix the date, buy a hat if you must, and stop worrying about Hilda. If she and Stanley get back together afterwards, then good luck to them, but it really won't matter to us any more.' Patricia looked at her and seemed ready to argue, but Dorothy interrupted her before she could say anything. 'Think about it – what could be better? If Stanley goes anywhere near Hilda after you're married, you'd be the wronged woman. You could leave him whenever you like, with no recriminations.'

'So, you think I should cheer him on?'

'I think it's a way out, and God knows we need one. You said Stanley was naïve to think that Hilda would ever agree to share him, but she still loves him desperately, there's no doubt about that. It might not take much to bring them together, especially if she thought she had your blessing.'

'How do you know she still loves him?'

Dorothy thought back to their brief exchange in front of the paintings at Lindworth, when both she and Hilda had been in mourning for what they thought was lost. 'She told me. It was the night I found those paintings. She caught me looking at them and we talked. It's strange, but she was much less shocked by them than I was. I didn't understand that at the time, but perhaps I do now. You can put up with most things for the person you love.'

'You never told me you'd spoken to Hilda.'

'As I recall, I had more important things to discuss with you that night. Hilda was kind to me, though, when she didn't have to be. She told me to fight for what I loved, and she was right. At the time I could only think of myself, not of what she was going through, but perhaps there's more to be salvaged from this than you and I. If she *did* go back to Stanley, nothing would be destroyed. We could stop feeling guilty.'

'Do you feel guilty?'

'Yes, all the time. Don't you?' Patricia shrugged, avoiding the question, and Dorothy tried to read the expression on her face.

'Peggy, are you sure the wedding is the only reason you've been worrying about Stanley and Hilda?'

'What do you mean?'

'You're not jealous, are you? Jealous because he still cares for her?'

Patricia laughed. 'Of course I'm not jealous. Hilda's welcome to Stanley's affections. I've got no use for them. You're right about everything else, though. I'll speak to Stanley later about a date. He's bound to come over today.'

She got up from the table and Dorothy joined her in the clearing up, feeling as if her concerns had been brushed to one side along with the mud and any belongings which were too wet to salvage. 'Talk of the devil,' Patricia said, when they had been working steadily for most of the morning. 'Stanley's now leaving the far distant shore.' They watched as the punt made its way gracefully across the Moor, steered by one of the village gardeners, who – in the absence of land to work – had offered their services as boatmen. 'It's just as well that he won't have to do this for much longer,' she added wryly. 'I've never had much luck with water. Three men have saved me from drowning and one of them died in the process. Now I *do* feel guilty about that.'

'But it wasn't your fault. You were just a girl, and it was an accident.'

Dorothy had lost count of the times she had used those words, but still Patricia was haunted by the incident in her youth, when W. S. Gilbert had dived into a lake to help her out of trouble and died in the attempt. 'A lot of people weren't so forgiving at the time,' she said. 'I killed one of the most famous men in England, and I don't want to do it again. Twice would look like carelessness.' The words were light and mocking, but they masked a sense of shame. 'I've been dreaming about it recently,' she admitted, 'except in the dream it's you who swims out to save me, not him. It's always the same. I have my hands on your shoulders and I'm safe, then suddenly you're not there and I feel myself sinking. That's how this whole business with Stanley feels. I'm frightened, Dodie. What if I marry him and I'm trapped? What if you can't keep me safe?'

'Of course I'll keep you safe.' She held Patricia tight, trying not to think of all that could go wrong with the promise. 'But you need to be strong. Sometimes it feels like we'll die in this cottage, and nothing will ever have changed. I'm relying on you to finish this once and for all. Please don't let me down.'

'I won't,' Patricia said, clinging to Dorothy as if her life depended on it. 'A few more weeks and this will all be over.'

13

Hilda felt as if she were living a double life in the months that followed her final departure from Cookham. One was made up of things that were tangible and familiar, like her mother's routines and the grasp of Unity's hand in hers, things that had no more mystery than the food on her plate and the necessity to eat it. The other was defined by absence, by the endless questions to which she had no answer and the dark uncertainty of her future, by moments of feeling herself lost or out of reach, unwanted and unneeded. The lives existed in tandem, but neither made sense of the other and there was no meaningful pattern to her days, at least none that she could see.

The gardens at Downshire Hill were never more beautiful than in the early summer. She wandered aimlessly for a long time that morning, feeling as if she had strayed into one of her own portraits. She had painted her mother at this time of year, just a few months after her father's sudden death. They were staying with friends in a tiny Hampshire village, and Hilda had watched every morning as her mother walked lost and alone in her grief, gazing longingly at the sunlit fields which lay beyond the gate but never leaving the dark green shadows of her own mourning. The painting was tangled with memory, one no less real than the other, but it seemed to her now that the small, melancholy figure in a landscape of joy and promise had been a premonition of things to come; for the first time, more than fifteen years later, she truly understood the emotion of the picture.

She went back inside and up to her room. Downstairs, she could hear Unity's laughter as she played with her grandmother in the drawing room, but she wanted no part of that joy today. The room seemed full of paper: letters and diaries and legal documents, rustling in the draught as she closed the door behind her, as if the written words had found a voice. She walked over to her desk and put Patricia's note to one side to deal with when she cared. Her long-neglected daybook eluded her at first, but eventually she found it amid a pile of half-finished sketches and turned to the next blank page. 'Saturday May 29th,' she wrote, astonished by how commonplace the words looked. 'Stanley married again.'

14

The bus was hot and stuffy, and Dorothy took a handkerchief out of her bag, relieved that the registry office was only a few miles away in Maidenhead. It was the one blessing in a day which had surpassed her worst nightmares. Neither she nor Patricia had slept properly until the early hours, and they were both tired and irritable when they finally awoke, much later than planned. Patricia, in particular, was a bag of nerves, threatening at regular intervals to pull out of the ceremony altogether, and eventually finding the strength to get dressed at the bottom of a gin glass. In the absence of other comfort, Dorothy had joined her, but the headache which was just beginning to throb at her temples made her regret her own weakness. There was very little air to be had in the crowd of Saturday shoppers, and she fought off a wave of nausea as the bus swerved sharply to avoid a pothole in the road. For the thousandth time, she wondered why Patricia hadn't insisted on taking a taxi.

The small wedding party which alighted in Maidenhead High Street must have provided a curious spectacle. Stanley had chosen to finish off an otherwise respectable suit with his favourite felt hat, floppy and weather-beaten, and conspiring with his general air of excitement to give him the look of an over-animated pixie. His best man, Jas – an old friend from Hampstead – wore a flat cap and carried a walking stick, and the two men talked constantly, mercifully oblivious to the bride's lack of enthusiasm.

Patricia grew paler by the second, and Dorothy looked at her lover with concern. She hadn't eaten properly for days and the stress of the wedding had brought on a recurrence of the septic throat which regularly laid her low; a light summer dress only emphasised how painfully thin she had grown, and no amount of make-up could mask the shadows under her eyes. At times over the past few weeks, Dorothy had seriously considered Patricia to be on the verge of a breakdown.

The registry office was in the Town Hall, just a few minutes' walk from the bus stop. It was a new building, harsh and geometric, and to Dorothy's eye it looked uncannily like a much bigger version of the chapel at Burghclere. They were directed to the first floor, where a man in a sober grey suit was waiting for them at the top of the stairs. 'Mr Spencer? And Miss Preece, splendid. My name is Ronald Sibley, and I'm your registrar. Please let me offer my congratulations. This must be a very happy day for you both.'

'The first of many,' Stanley said, beaming at Patricia.

'Indeed. Are you expecting other guests?'

'No, it's just the two witnesses.'

'Excellent. Then let's get under way. Please follow me. The room is at the end of the corridor.'

Patricia hesitated like a prisoner on her way to the gallows. She clutched at Dorothy's arm for support, but Stanley – looking peevish – immediately seized her other hand and Dorothy let him take her, reluctant to make the bride look like a doll in a playground tug of war. She glanced at the registrar, but he had the air of a man who was rarely surprised. 'There's absolutely nothing to worry about,' he said, smiling reassuringly. 'It's a very straightforward service.'

The room was an uncomfortable compromise, essentially formal but with an effort here and there to transform the atmosphere into something more celebratory and memorable. They walked past three rows of empty chairs and stood in an awkward group by a table at the head of the room, where a vase of pale pink roses, wilting in the heat, gave off the faint scent of cloves. 'Do we stand or sit down?' Dorothy asked, conscious of being both maid of honour and congregation.

'Entirely as you wish. All we need from you is a signature afterwards, so you're welcome to sit for the vows if you prefer.'

She stayed standing, because it felt less like abandoning Patricia to her fate, and Jas did the same, periodically checking his pocket for the ring. There was something faintly adolescent about the whole thing, she thought, something faded and pathetic; even if she hadn't known the extent of the charade, she would have sensed instinctively that this odd collection of people was ill-fated, chasing a happiness that each in his heart knew was hollow. The ceremony – such as it was – got under way, and Sibley made the obligatory request for any lawful impediments to be declared. Next to her, in the silence, Dorothy heard Patricia catch her breath. As Stanley began to repeat his vows in a clear, determined voice, the situation suddenly felt so surreal that she could have been watching a badly acted play. When Patricia's turn came, she stood stiff and awkward, her hands clenched tightly at her side; as she began to speak the words which would tie her to someone else, Dorothy's sense of loss and desolation was so great that it was as much as she could do not to scream. She knew the vows were a lie and she had expected to remain untouched by them, but as she listened to the woman she loved talking of better and worse, richer and poorer, she had never in her life felt so alone. They had made a terrible mistake, she knew that now. Nothing was worth this, and in her heart she sensed that they would pay with their own happiness, no matter how far they ran.

Suddenly, Patricia faltered. Stanley glanced at her and she tried again to complete the line, but the words love, cherish and obey seemed to stick in her throat. The silence stretched out, intense and accusatory. Dorothy moved a little closer until her hand brushed Patricia's, and she felt her fingers relax and respond; it was

309

the subtlest of gestures, imperceptible to anyone else in the room, but it was enough to give Patricia strength. She finished the vows with no more hesitations, her hand resting lightly against Dorothy's until it was almost possible to believe that they were speaking to each other.

The giving of the ring and the final declarations passed in a blur, and the registrar looked curiously at Patricia as she turned away from her new husband, dropping his hand as if it had burnt her. They signed the register as directed and Dorothy looked at the clock, wondering how something so momentous could have taken place in less than twenty minutes. 'Now, I expect you'd like some photographs?' Sibley asked, when he had checked that everything was in order.

'Yes, of course,' Stanley said enthusiastically.

Patricia looked at him, and Dorothy was pleased to see that she had regained her composure now that the ceremony was over. 'I'm so sorry, darling, but we didn't bring a camera,' she said. 'It was stupid of us, but in the excitement of getting ready…'

'Not to worry,' the registrar interrupted. 'It's all part of the service. There's so much to think about on the day, and we always have a camera standing by. My colleague will take care of it, and we'll post the photographs on to you.'

'Excellent,' Stanley said, putting his hat back on. 'We can send one to the papers. People will want to see the new Mrs Spencer.'

'In that case, would you like to go outside? You're lucky with the weather, and I never think this room does justice to the occasion.'

They followed the registrar back down to the entrance hall, where he wished them well and left them in the hands of a keen young man with a camera, who seemed much more enthusiastic about the photographs than anyone destined to be in them. They left the Town Hall by the back entrance and he struck out ahead of them, obviously with a destination in mind, but they had only got as far as Park Street when Patricia's patience ran out. 'Let's do them here,' she said, stopping suddenly on the pavement.

The photographer looked doubtfully at the dark flint walls and dilapidated shutters of T. W. Stuchbery and Son, Solicitors. 'Are you sure?' he asked. 'There's a nice park just around the corner and couples usually like to…'

'Here will do. It's sunny. What more could we ask for?'

'We're a bit pressed for time,' Dorothy explained, taking the edge off Patricia's sarcasm, which was as far from the euphoria of a newly-wed as it was possible to get. 'We've booked a table for lunch and we don't want to be late.' It was a lie, as far as she knew, but it served its purpose and they lined up along the pavement with Stanley and Patricia in the centre, awkwardly straddling a grating.

'Aren't you going to take that damned hat off?' Patricia asked, as the photographer tried to move them closer together.

'Are you talking to me or to Jas?'

'You, of course. I haven't married Jas.'

'Ah, be careful about that. I remember a time when he wanted to marry Hilda, but she chose me instead.' If there was a remark less appropriate to the occasion, Dorothy struggled to think what it might be. She looked at Jas, feeling his embarrassment, but he smiled and raised his eyebrows, gallantly resisting the temptation to retaliate.

'Right then, everybody, eyes towards me please.' Stanley and his best man did as they were asked, but Dorothy glanced sideways at Patricia, who was staring off down the street, her attention focused on anything but the camera. She waited with a fixed smile while several shots were taken, holding her handbag self-consciously in front of her and wishing that she'd chosen to wear something more memorable than a familiar cardigan and a tweed skirt, something worthy of Patricia's elegance. If Stanley got his way and a photo-graph appeared in the papers, what on earth would people make of it in years to come, she wondered. Would they be able to tell who was the bride and who the groom? Would they say, with all the false wisdom of hindsight, that the marriage had been doomed from the start? With the exception of Jas, who had his hand companionably on his friend's back, there was no physical contact in the picture, no hint of closeness or joy. In fact, the distance between the married couple was so marked that it would be easy to cut the photograph in half, leaving Stanley abandoned with his best man, while she and Patricia escaped to another scrapbook, another life.

Eventually the ordeal was over and they walked to the high street to find a café. Stanley was euphoric, ordering a lavish wedding breakfast and telling anyone who would listen that this was the day which would inspire the greatest pictures he had ever painted. Patricia picked at her food, and it was left to Dorothy and Jas to hold the occasion together with something resembling a normal conversation. She seethed throughout the meal, resenting Stanley for his high spirits but knowing that it was she and Patricia who were out of kilter with the day, not the groom. Stanley's behaviour was perfectly natural in a man who thought he had all he wanted, and it wasn't entirely his fault that he was wrong. A different strain of guilt began to gnaw at her, seamlessly replacing its predecessor, and she was glad when it was time to leave.

Back in Cookham, it seemed as if the eyes of the whole village were on them when they climbed down from the bus. Stanley took Patricia's arm as they walked along the Causeway and Dorothy hung back, keen to make things look respectable. Jas had caught the train back to London from Maidenhead, so she walked alone with nothing to distract her from her thoughts except the locals out strolling on the Moor and the occasional whispered aside. She stared them out whenever she could, but for every snatch of open-air gossip there would be at least three more twitching curtains. If Patricia had ever truly believed that a ring on her finger would stop people talking, she would soon be disappointed.

At the war memorial, Patricia withdrew her arm from Stanley's and patted his hand. 'It's been lovely, but I must go and get some rest,' she said, overtly stifling a yawn. 'The excitement has quite worn me out.'

Stanley stared at her in surprise, wondering if she was making fun of him. 'But surely you're coming to Lindworth for the evening? I've got everything ready for you.'

'Not tonight, darling. We agreed I wouldn't move in until we got back from St Ives.'

'But I thought you might change your mind.' He smiled, and looked appealingly at her. 'Elsie's been spring cleaning like there's no tomorrow. She's even got rid of those curtains you hate and made us some new ones.'

'That's very sweet of her, but there's no point in my hauling everything over just for one night, is there? Save the surprise for when we get back. We'll have more time to enjoy it then.'

She turned towards Moor Thatch but Stanley caught her arm. 'It might just be *one* night, but it's our *wedding* night, for goodness' sake. Doesn't that mean anything to you?'

'It means we're starting out on a whole new life together and there's plenty of time to wait. Come on, Dodie.'

Patricia shook herself free and began to walk home, but Stanley wouldn't be so easily discarded. 'Don't you dare walk away from me like that,' he shouted, drawing curious stares from the tables outside the Crown Hotel. 'For years you've led me on, vamping me whenever it suited you and teasing me when I didn't respond, but I'm your husband now. I have rights.'

Patricia seemed frightened and on the verge of tears. She stared at Dorothy, imploring her to intervene. 'People are staring, Stanley,' Dorothy said, standing in front of Patricia so that her husband couldn't touch her. 'Don't be ridiculous. This village has enough to gossip about already.' Surprised, he took a step back and she spoke more calmly. 'We agreed on a plan, and I'm asking you to stick to it. Patricia is exhausted and she needs her rest. We're leaving early for Cornwall and there's still plenty of packing to do, including all the things you brought over yesterday for us to take on your behalf.'

'Then let me come and help.'

'Absolutely not. We'll go ahead and get the cottage ready, just like we said we would, while you stay here and tie up all the loose ends. You've got to finish that landscape, or we won't be able to pay for the holiday,' she added, unable to bring herself to call the trip a honeymoon. 'And you promised to encourage Hilda over to collect the last of her things from Lindworth and sort out the remaining finances, so shouldn't you telephone her? By the time you've done all that, we'll have settled in and made everything comfortable for you.'

Stanley nodded reluctantly. 'I'll send a telegram to let you know I'm coming.'

'Good. As I said, we're leaving early so I doubt we'll see you again before we go. We'd better say goodbye now.' She turned away as he kissed Patricia, wondering how much longer either of them would be able to endure this.

15

'I'd forgotten how much I love this journey,' Patricia said, looking out of the carriage window as the train pulled slowly out of Exeter. 'You get this far and you think you're nearly there, but the best part's still to come.' Despite the early start, she was animated and in good spirits, and Dorothy was pleased to see that she had some colour in her cheeks, brought on by the sheer exhilaration of escape; for the first time in months, the woman in front of her looked more like the Patricia of old than the ghost who had replaced her. 'We had some good times down here, didn't we?'

'Yes, we did,' Dorothy agreed, thinking back to the months they had spent in the west country before settling in Cookham. It was the first place they had tried after leaving France, hoping to find a milder climate than most of England could offer, and they had been happy there for a while, renting a series of houses around Newlyn and St Just. 'And I intend to make sure that we have some more now.' The cottage in St Ives where they were headed belonged to a friend of Patricia's and they had taken it for six weeks, keen to give Stanley – who had exhausted every corner of Cookham – the time and inspiration to paint some new landscapes. His arrival would dampen their holiday spirits, no doubt, but Dorothy was determined not to let him cloud the handful of days between now and then. She smiled at Patricia. 'What was it you used to say? We need to collect as many happy memories as we can and not waste the flying years. Well, now's our chance.'

The train laboured up a steep incline, talking to the rails in a dogged, clipped rhythm. 'Do you think Hilda *will* go to the house while he's there?' Patricia asked.

The strain had returned to her face, and Dorothy tried to reassure her, in spite of her own waning patience. 'I don't know, but you have to put that out of your mind for now,' she said firmly. 'We've done all we can. You've written to Hilda, inviting her to collect her things while we're away, and you've encouraged Stanley to speak to her, which I've no doubt he'll do. You've even invited her to join us down here, for God's sake, although I'm not sure that was a good idea.'

'I just thought it might show there was no ill feeling.'

'Well, it's done now. But whether or not she goes to Lindworth and what might happen between them when she gets there is entirely in the lap of the gods. We can't do anything from three hundred miles away except hope.'

'No, I don't suppose we can.'

They lapsed into silence, struck by the magnificent spectacle of the Royal Albert Bridge as the route took them over the Tamar and into Cornwall. Beyond Truro, woodland gave way to gorse-clad hills and low stone walls, an attractive patchwork of browns, yellows and purples. The *Cornish Riviera Express* lived up to its name, making steady work of the countryside and ticking off the stations one by one. 'I'm sorry, Dodie,' Patricia said out of nowhere.

'You don't have to be sorry.'

'Yes, I do. I could have ruined everything. I could have destroyed us.'

Dorothy would have found it hard to put her finger on the moment when she and Patricia had reversed their roles, and even harder to say why it had happened. All she knew was that the emphasis was now on her to drive this ludicrous situation with Stanley to some sort of conclusion, pushing things along and trying to see the bright side, while Patricia remained helpless and shell-shocked. She had hated standing by while Patricia directed their lives, but this new situation was every bit as exhausting as the other had been humiliating. 'You haven't destroyed us, though,' she said calmly, stepping up to the part. 'We're still here, still together, and you've got the legal protection and financial security you wanted. Whatever happens now, Stanley has obligations to you as his wife.'

At St Erth, they changed trains for the final leg of the journey. The connection was half an hour away, so they had tea in the tiny station buffet, then crossed the footbridge to the other platform, where Dorothy left Patricia with the first batch of luggage while she went back to fetch the rest. Within a few minutes of boarding, they were skirting Lelant Saltings and looking out over the Hayle Estuary. The tide was coming in, pulling with it a stretch of grey, low-hanging cloud, and the breeze rippled the water so that some areas shone and others were left matte, like wet and dry paint on a canvas. The train went into a cutting, a long tunnel of sharp green, and when it emerged, the first glimpse of the sea came as a relief. Without warning, the sun broke through the cloud and Patricia smiled. 'It might be all right after all,' she said.

The sides of the cutting closed in again, and low, unruly branches hit the carriage window, challenging her optimism. At the grand Carbis Bay Hotel, the line began its gentle descent into the familiar curve of St Ives Bay, and Dorothy felt a strange mixture of excitement and wistfulness, surprised that a place which had never been home should still be capable of stirring up such strong emotions. There was no sign of the famous Atlantic light today, and nothing really to suggest that the town was a haven for artists and writers, yet still she found it hard to think of anywhere which she regarded with such uncomplicated affection. They found a taxi among the clutch of cars gathered on the platform, and waited while the driver did his best to fit their luggage neatly into every nook and cranny. Their accommodation was on the other side of town, and the journey was a blur of whitewashed cottages and stone staircases, with cobbled streets so narrow that pedestrians had to step into doorways to allow the vehicle to pass.

Here and there, a few straggling, forgotten flags still hung from the shops and lamp posts, faded reminders of the recent Coronation.

The taxi pulled over in Back Road West, opposite a short passageway leading down between two houses. 'Harry's Court,' the driver announced, although the slate above the entrance proclaimed as much. 'Which cottage is it?'

'It's called The Cobbles,' Dorothy said, 'but you can leave our luggage here. We'll see ourselves in.'

He did as she asked, and Patricia tipped him for his trouble. Left alone, they looked despondently at their temporary home. Harry's Court was a clutch of six stone- and slate-fronted cottages, gathered round a small, communal yard. It was still the middle of the afternoon but most of the courtyard was already in shadow, and even something more generous than the feeble sun they had arrived to would surely struggle to penetrate the gloom. The walls were draped with fishing nets and the smell was overpowering, made worse by a large drain in the middle of the yard, littered with seagull feathers. A couple of the doors stood open, and it was immediately obvious to Dorothy that privacy was a luxury which they wouldn't be afforded. Everything could be overheard from here. Every word, every row, every secret.

'This wasn't how I imagined it,' Patricia said, staring round in horror. 'When James said a cottage by the beach, I thought it would at least…'

She tailed off as a young woman came out of one of the houses, her expression a mixture of welcome and curiosity. 'Can I help you?' she asked, wiping her hands on a tea towel.

'Thank you. We're looking for The Cobbles.'

She nodded towards the left-hand corner. 'It's the one at the front there. You here for the summer?'

'For six weeks, yes. We've come to paint.'

The woman smiled and nodded towards the paraphernalia in Dorothy's arms. 'Thought as much. I didn't have you down as the fishing type, and it's always one or the other here. Just the two of you?'

'No,' said Dorothy, just as Patricia nodded. 'Well yes, at the moment, but my friend's husband will be joining us in a few days.'

The phrase felt awkward and alien, but she must have carried it off because the woman simply smiled. 'Well, I'll let you settle yourselves in. I'm just across the court if you need anything. Don't hesitate to ask. Bye now.'

'She seems nice,' Dorothy said, as their neighbour went back into her house.

'Thank goodness. We're going to know each other *very* well by the time six weeks is up.' Patricia looked round again, and a second glance only served to confirm her worst fears. 'I never dreamt it would be quite so confined.'

All Dorothy could think about was how much more claustrophobic the small cottage would be when Stanley arrived, but she put it out of her mind, determined to be positive. 'Let's go in. Have you got the key?'

Patricia nodded and opened the front door. Inside, the cottage was transformed by light flooding in from the front, and the view across Porthmeor Beach and out to sea was breathtaking. 'This is more like it,' Dorothy said, looking round in delight at the simple but comfortably furnished sitting room. 'Once we get our things in place, it'll soon feel like home.' They dragged the cases in from the yard, leaving the more cumbersome easels and painting stools in a sheltered place by the door. There were two bedrooms upstairs, both with sea views, and Dorothy took the smaller one. The sleeping arrangements for when Stanley arrived was an issue which neither of them seemed keen to address.

'What would you like to do?' Dorothy asked when they'd finished unpacking. 'Have a rest after the journey?'

'That's the last thing I want.' Patricia took her hand as they stood by the window. 'Suddenly I don't feel in the least bit tired. I thought we might go for a walk. It's warm and there's plenty of daylight left. We could take our sketchbooks and see where we end up.'

The beach was bracing and exhilarating. They headed for the grassy hill which was visible from the cottage and climbed the footpath to the top, where an old seafarers' chapel stood lonely and defiant against the elements. 'Well, that was worth it,' Patricia said, panting a little from the climb. She looked across the bay to Godrevy Lighthouse, shrouded in smoky mist. 'This is beautiful. I haven't felt so free in years.'

They settled down on a slope of springy turf and Patricia took out her sketchbook and a selection of pencils. Dorothy glanced at her curiously, but said nothing; it was unusual for Patricia to show any interest these days in the passion which had brought them together, and she didn't want to spoil it by making her self-conscious. She chose a book for her own entertainment but soon let it fall from her hand, lulled into sleep by the early start and the rhythm of a troublesome sea as it broke on the rocks below. When she woke, Patricia was looking intently at her. 'Don't sit up. I've nearly finished.' She completed a few more strokes with the pencil, then tore the page out and passed it over. Dorothy looked down at the sketch of herself sleeping. It was hesitant in some places, idealised in others, but she was moved beyond words by the love which was the drawing's defining feature. 'It's lucky that you were out for the count,' Patricia added, suddenly shy of her silence. 'That's my fourth attempt, and we'll be lighting a fire with the others.'

'It's beautiful,' Dorothy said, meaning it. She leant forward and gave Patricia a kiss. 'You really ought to take this up for a living.'

Patricia laughed. 'I love you. You know that, don't you?'

'For my shameless flattery?'

'Not *just* for that.' She touched Dorothy's cheek, suddenly more serious. 'Most people would have thrown me to the lions for what I've done. I could have woken up this morning in his bed, but you didn't let me down.'

'Of course I didn't, and I never will.' She put the drawing carefully between the pages of her own sketchbook and stood up to go. 'Come on,' she said, holding out her hand. 'Let's go home.'

16

The weather deteriorated steadily over the next few days. In Harry's Court, the cobbles which gave their cottage its name were treacherously slippery, and outside, whenever they looked up from the courtyard, all they could see was an oblong of leaden grey sky. Patricia had packed all the wrong clothes, which forced a series of shopping trips to replace her summer wardrobe with something more robust, and Dorothy flinched when she saw the bill; the days when Stanley could spend money like water were long gone. But not even the rain could dampen their spirits. They made the most of the town, exploring the antique shops and lunching each day in Curnow's Café, then retreating to the cottage to read or paint. In the evenings, they lit a fire in the cosy sitting room or occasionally ventured out to see a film, walking back in the dark through crooked, dimly lit alleyways that could easily have belonged to a different age. Looking back later, it seemed to Dorothy that they had laughed and talked more in that brief interlude than ever before, but the days passed quickly, as happy times always do, and the telegram arrived at the end of the week. Stanley would be joining them on Monday.

In contrast to their mood, the day dawned bright and fair, and Back Street West was draped with drying laundry as they walked to the Norway Stores to pick up groceries. Stanley's train wasn't due until late afternoon, but it was impossible to make the most of the day when they were both anxious and irritable, and at half past four, after several hours of bickering, Patricia set out for the station to meet him. Dorothy busied herself with preparations for a dinner that she didn't want to eat, but in no time at all she heard a familiar voice calling through the open front door. 'Why are my things outside? They'll be ruined if it starts to rain.'

She clattered some pans and pretended not to hear, but Stanley followed the noise through to the kitchen and repeated his question without any further greeting. 'Because there's not enough room in here,' she replied. 'Our easels are there too if you look closely.' She glanced behind him, but the hallway was empty. 'Where's Patricia?'

'I've no idea. I assumed she'd be here waiting for me.'

'But she went to meet your train.'

'Oh, I got an earlier connection at St Erth. She must have missed me. How annoying.'

'I'm sure she'll be back as soon as she realises.' She nodded towards the small case in his hand. 'You might as well settle in while you're waiting. Your room's the one on the left.'

He went upstairs, but came back down again almost immediately. 'Why are we stuck with the twin beds?'

Dorothy sighed, cursing the punctuality of the train which had left her to deal single-handedly with Stanley's arrival. 'Because the room is bigger and Patricia preferred it. It's got views on two sides and lots of light. Anyway, she hasn't been well and she didn't want to disturb you in the night.'

'Chance would be a fine thing. When is she *ever* well?'

'That's hardly fair, and she's only being considerate. You don't want to be ill when you have to go out and paint.'

'No, I suppose not.' He seemed on edge, and she tried to imagine what mood he might be in if he had taken the first step towards a reconciliation with Hilda, but it was impossible to know. 'So, what have you two been up to?' he asked.

'Not much. The weather's been foul and we haven't really been able to get out.' She began to peel some potatoes and changed the subject, keen not to dwell on the happiness of the past few days in case she couldn't hide it. 'Have you finished the landscape you were working on?'

'Yes, of course.'

'We expected you earlier. Was there a problem?'

She hoped he would say that the delay was down to Hilda's visit, but he was uncharacteristically reluctant to talk. 'I'm sure you haven't missed me,' he said, drumming his fingers on the table and looking sulkily at the clock. 'Where *is* Patricia? This isn't much of a welcome.'

'She should be back by now,' Dorothy admitted, getting worried. 'I'll go and look for her.'

'No, you won't. *I'll* go.' They glared at each other across the kitchen table, but Dorothy was saved the humiliation of backing down by the sound of the front door.

'Dodie?' Patricia called. 'He wasn't on the train. It looks like fate might have given us…' She faltered when she saw him. 'Stanley! You're here already. How lovely.' He moved to kiss her and she threw her arms round his neck, summoning more enthusiasm than usual to make up for her *faux pas*. 'We thought you were never coming.'

'Why don't you two go through to the sitting room while I get the supper together?' Dorothy suggested, looking pointedly at Patricia. 'You must have a lot to talk about.'

'Good idea. We'll have a sherry and Stanley can tell me what's been happening in Cookham while we've been away.'

She rolled her eyes at Dorothy and ushered Stanley out of the kitchen, closing the door behind her. Resisting the temptation to take a glass to the wall, Dorothy put the fish pie in the oven and set to work on the washing-up. She made herself scarce for as long as she could bear it, managing almost an hour of tact before curiosity drove her next door. Stanley was sitting close to Patricia on the sofa, obviously in a much better humour. 'Supper's ready,' she announced, tidying away her book and the spectacle case which had been moved to the single chair. 'But if you want to freshen up after the journey, there's just about time.'

'Excellent.'

He went down the passageway to wash and Dorothy waited until she could hear the splashing of water. 'Has he said anything about Hilda?' she whispered.

'Not yet.'

'Haven't you asked?'

'Don't you think that would be a bit obvious?' Patricia snapped through gritted teeth. 'How do you suggest I broach it? "Darling, I just need to check if you've slept with your ex-wife, because if you have I needn't sully myself?" Christ, Dodie, it's not that simple.'

'Sorry.'

'We're just going to have to be patient.'

Stanley was the only one with any real appetite for the meal. Patricia picked at her food, eventually relinquishing her knife and fork in defeat. 'I'm sorry, Dodie. It was delicious, but I'm just not up to it tonight. That walk to the station really took it out of me.'

'Dorothy says you've been ill?' Stanley said, clearing the plates and refusing any help with the washing-up.

'It's my throat again, and I feel so tired all the time.'

'Then you need to rest.'

'I will, darling, I promise.'

He began to hum as he wiped the dishes, filling in the words when he knew them. '"When you're lying awake with a dismal headache, and repose is taboo'd by anxiety."' The performance would have grated at the best of times, but it didn't help Patricia's mood that he had chosen a tune by Gilbert and Sullivan, for whom he had an unfortunate liking.

'I think I'll go for a walk,' Dorothy said, unable to bear it any longer. 'It's the first beautiful evening we've had.'

Patricia looked up eagerly. 'I'll come with you.'

'That won't help your throat,' Stanley said waspishly. 'You've just promised to rest.'

'All right, but only if you choose a different song. Light opera isn't very soothing.'

Dorothy left them to it and fetched her coat. She walked aimlessly down the valley of little streets, sorry to leave Patricia's side but fearing for her own sanity if she stayed. There was a relaxed air about the town tonight, a shared relief in the change of fortunes that had brought finer weather and calmer seas. Wet oilskins and heavy boots had finally dried in the sun, ready for the night's fishing, and women stood gossiping in doorways, apparently without a care in the world. At first, the warren of lanes had seemed unfathomable to Dorothy, but now she could find a route to anywhere in five or ten minutes and she headed for the harbour, eager to see the ocean at sunset. She sat on a wall by the Sloop Inn and watched as the townsmen emerged from their houses, joining together in small groups and slapping each other on the back as they made their way down to the boats. Gradually, in twos and threes, the vessels drifted out to sea, forming a procession that grew smaller by degrees until the first to leave was nothing but a black dot on the horizon. Still there were more to come. The stragglers unfurled their deep-red sails, taking to the water like birds leaving a nesting place, and the soft evening light graced everything with a gentle nobility that Dorothy found intensely moving. It was one of the most beautiful sights she had ever seen, and she wished that Patricia could have shared it; already, she missed her desperately.

When the last boat had been swallowed up by darkness, she walked reluctantly back to Harry's Court. The lamps were still on in the sitting room and she stood across the street from the cottage, waiting for Patricia and Stanley to go up to bed. Before long, her patience was rewarded and the light downstairs disappeared to be replaced almost immediately by the lamp in Patricia's window. Dorothy held her breath, hoping that somehow Patricia might have found an excuse to retreat to the second bedroom, but the window remained stubbornly dark, and soon even the other light was extinguished. When she was sure it was safe, she went back inside and climbed the stairs as quietly as possible. She paused outside Patricia's bedroom door, listening like a dirty voyeur for the creak of a bedspring, but there was nothing, only silence, and she crawled exhausted into her own bed. Her mind refused to rest and she lay awake for a long time, shamed by her need to know the worst, but all she could hear was the ticking of the grandfather clock and the welcome chime of midnight. Somehow, the first day was over.

17

One day became two, then three, and Dorothy was surprised to find that a week had passed without anything more serious than a squabble. All Stanley would say about Hilda was that everything had been sorted satisfactorily, but there was no talk of the future or what it might hold. Patricia continued to keep him at bay with talk of her health, but he remained cheerful and took pleasure in the change of scenery, leaving early each day to paint and coming home full of enthusiasm for his work. He got on well with the locals, finding an instinctive affinity with the routine of their lives and falling easily into conversation; by return, they were happy to show him the best views to paint from in unseasonable weather, lashing stones together to anchor his easel and taking as much interest in his craft as he did in theirs. In fact, despite their differences, all three of them seemed to value something solid and reliable in this simple, structured life so far from Cookham.

On Monday morning, Stanley and Patricia decided to walk to Carbis Bay, but they were back by early afternoon. He had begun work on an atmospheric picture of the harbour at low tide and was keen to continue, so Patricia and Dorothy gathered their painting things and followed him down. Dorothy set up her easel at a discreet distance, but Stanley surprised her by beckoning her over and they painted together in companionable silence, while Patricia wandered along the shoreline collecting shells. The day was clean and fresh after overnight rain, and Dorothy breathed in the now familiar smell of salt, seaweed and wet sand, pungent and earthy, and somehow symptomatic of this harsh, physical world. The harbour was bustling today, and the night had obviously been kind to its fishermen. Shoal after shoal was lifted from beached boats and packed efficiently into vast wicker baskets, and some of the grander prizes had been laid out on the lifeboat slipway to be admired and haggled over.

'Look at that,' Stanley said, fascinated by the carts that were bringing the catch ashore. Slime from the fish was running down to the wooden spokes and, as the wheels turned, the breeze caught it up and created bubbles along the sand. 'It reminds me of when I was a boy. We used to blow bubbles from the nursery window and off they'd go in the wind. It's so vivid still, that memory.' He seemed lost in the happiness of his childhood, and at moments like this she understood the innocent charm which had first attracted Patricia to Stanley, no matter how fiercely Patricia denied it now. She had seen a different side to him over the past few days, and although she could never bring herself to like him, his art and observations appealed to her; occasionally, she caught a glimpse of the man he must have been without the jealousies and selfishness which both Hilda and Patricia seemed to arouse in him.

He strolled down to the shoreline to share the memory with Patricia, and Dorothy watched as he took her arm and walked with her, occasionally bending down to add a shell to her collection. Patricia laughed at something he said and Dorothy looked away, distracted by a cacophony of noise to her left, where a flock of seagulls was descending on the boats in a whirlwind of wings, fighting over fish that were too small to sell. When she turned back a moment or two later, the mood between Patricia and Stanley seemed to have changed. Their conversation was more urgent, and Stanley was waving his arms about and shouting. His words were still no match for the guttural cry of the gulls, but although Dorothy couldn't hear what was being said, she sensed that this was the moment they had been waiting for. Patricia looked upset, and Dorothy got up and moved closer, ready to step in if the row got out of hand.

'But you encouraged me,' she heard Stanley say, and there was bewilderment rather than anger in his voice. 'You told me to go to Hilda. You said you wouldn't live with me until she agreed to come back. You *understood* that I wanted you both. I've never kept that a secret, not from you.'

'Do you really hate me so much that you can humiliate me like this? My God, Stanley, we've only been married a week.' Noticing that people were beginning to stare, Patricia moved further down the beach, where they wouldn't be overheard except by Dorothy. 'I told you to keep Hilda on side,' she said. 'I told you to invite her to Lindworth and make your peace. I did *not* tell you to sleep with her the minute my back was turned.'

'But you implied it.'

'Only in your twisted little mind. No sane person would ever accept that. You can't possibly carry on sleeping with her when you're married to me.'

Telling Stanley what he couldn't do was a red rag to a bull, and his rage exploded. 'I'll sleep with Hilda whenever I feel like it,' he shouted. 'You can't stop me. No one can.'

'Perhaps not, but I *can* stop you touching *me*. Sleep with Hilda by all means, but don't come knocking at my bedroom door any more. As far as I'm concerned, you've made your choice.' She turned to Dorothy, obviously believing that the conversation was over, but Stanley wasn't ready to give in so easily.

'I'll sleep with Hilda, I'll sleep with you, I'll sleep with as many women as I damned well want,' he said, catching her arm. 'As many as my art needs.'

'Your *art*?' Patricia laughed in his face. 'Don't blame this on your art. This is about *you*, Stanley — nothing else. And even if it was about art, do you honestly think you can walk all over ordinary, human emotions just because you want to paint a picture? Do you ever stop to think about how Hilda or I might feel? Your bloody art always comes first, but do you really think that justifies everything? Do you think that gives you the right to hurt me whenever you feel like it and tarnish everything I touch?'

'No, I don't.'

'Then what does?'

'*She* does.' He gestured towards Dorothy, and Patricia looked at him in astonishment. 'You've got *her*. You've always had her, and you always will, so why shouldn't I have Hilda?' Patricia opened her mouth to speak, but stopped when she saw that Stanley had tears in his eyes. 'Don't lecture me about loving two people,' he said. 'At least I'm honest about it.'

He stormed off in the other direction, leaving Patricia staring after him. Dorothy led her back up the beach and they collected their things and went home. 'He's really done it?' she asked, when the door was safely closed behind them, and Patricia nodded. 'I can't believe it. Hilda actually slept with him? I never thought she would.'

'Well, she did. They had a blissful night, apparently. Just like old times.'

There was a hollow note in Patricia's voice, and Dorothy looked at her curiously. 'Aren't you pleased?' she asked. 'It's more than we could have hoped for. Now you never have to let that man come near you again.'

To her surprise, Patricia burst into tears and her sobs tore through the peace of the cottage. Dorothy took her gently upstairs and helped her fetch her things from the room she had so briefly shared with Stanley. 'You're coming in with me now, and that's where we're staying. Go and lie down. You need some rest.'

Patricia nodded, and Dorothy helped her get undressed. 'I don't want to see him, Dodie. Please don't let him in here.'

'Of course I won't. You're safe now.' She held Patricia until she slept, playing the conversation over and over in her mind. Downstairs, the front door opened and closed and she slipped out of the room to wait for Stanley at the top of the stairs.

'I need to talk to Patricia,' he said, and Dorothy was relieved to see that his anger had disappeared.

'She doesn't want to see you.'

'Please, Dorothy, just let me speak to her.'

'Perhaps in the morning, but not now.'

'She's my wife, damn it. We need to talk.'

'You gave those rights up when you betrayed her. Now go to bed, Stanley, and leave Patricia in peace. She'll be staying with me from now on.'

'Yes, of course she will.' He spat the words out and tried to get past, but Dorothy barred his way. They struggled for a moment, until Stanley lost his footing and nearly fell backwards. He grabbed at the handrail just in time and glared up at her. 'You must really be enjoying this.'

Dorothy looked at him sadly, remembering the emptiness in Patricia's voice and the beautiful, spirited woman she had fallen in love with. 'No, you're wrong about that,' she said. 'There's no pleasure whatsoever in this for me. We've all lost something, Stanley. Now we just have to learn to live with it.'

18

The rain began early, a soft but insistent presence at the window. Unable to sleep, Patricia heard the clock strike six and slipped quietly from Dorothy's bed, making sure not to wake her. She took a handful of clothes down to the sitting room to dress, then let herself out into the wet St Ives morning, crossing Harry's Court and heading right towards the beach. The fresh, salty air was invigorating, and she walked along the promenade until she found a sheltered place to sit and watch while the light slowly strengthened across the sea. After everything that had happened, she needed to be on her own.

The bay was strangely deserted in the early part of the day. Two boats were sailing back to harbour after a long night's fishing, and the vessels that had beaten them to it were secured safely halfway up the beach, leaving lines in the wet sand where they had been dragged ashore. The paving stones shone in the rain, reflecting the benches and mooring posts that dotted the seafront with a glass-like precision. There was something faded and melancholy about those empty benches, waiting forlornly to be filled, which chimed with her mood.

By seven o'clock, the day was as bright as it was going to be. The grey sky blended with the hills on the horizon, and the only hint of colour came from a thin band of metallic blue which teased the very edges of the water. She sat there for a long time, staring at the sea through a mist of rain and tears; eventually, still trying to make sense of her emotions, she walked back across the beach to the woman who loved her.

19

'You're quiet tonight.' Ken put a gin and tonic down on the table and squeezed Elsie's hand. 'Something on your mind?'

'Not really.'

'If there's one thing I've learnt these past few years, it's "no" means no and "not really" means yes.' Elsie laughed, but didn't deny it. 'Come on, sweetheart. What's the matter?'

She sighed. 'They're back from their honeymoon this evening.'

'Ah. So that's why you chose a night at the Crown instead of a slap-up meal in Maidenhead.'

'We can't afford a slap-up meal. We're saving for the wedding.'

'And that's why we've had to sit outside…'

'It's a lovely summer's night.'

'…with a decent view of Moor Thatch.'

She held up her hands. 'All right, you've got me there. Guilty as charged.'

'It's your evening off, Else, and like you said, it's a lovely summer's night. Can't we just enjoy it and forget about the bloody Spencers?'

'Ken!'

'Sorry. I know you've been dreading them coming home but your notice is up at the end of the month. You've only got to put up with it for another couple of weeks.'

She looked across the Moor to where the thatched cottage sat, deserted and in darkness. 'A fortnight of newlyweds, especially those newlyweds, can be a very long time.'

Ken grinned. 'You'll manage. I know who I'd put my money on.' He took a healthy swig of his beer and spoke more seriously. 'I'll be as pleased as you are when you can leave and get a normal job.' Elsie opened her mouth to object but he wouldn't be interrupted. 'I know you always defend him and I admire you for it, but he doesn't deserve your loyalty, really he doesn't. I don't know who he thinks he is, cutting off his wife and kids with hardly a penny, then spending the night with her again the minute they're divorced.'

'Ken, be quiet!' Elsie cried, looking round anxiously at the other tables to see if anyone was listening. 'I told you that in confidence. If anyone gets wind of it I can wave goodbye to a reference.'

'At least it would solve your problem about working two more weeks.'

'I'm serious. You can't go round telling people that sort of thing. It's private.'

'Of course I won't tell anyone, but you know I'm right. You don't like this other woman, and with good reason by the sound of it, but she doesn't deserve that. No one does.'

Elsie hushed him again, but not out of tact this time. 'Look! They're here. There's a taxi pulling up outside Moor Thatch.'

'Why's it going to Moor Thatch and not Lindworth?'

'They'll be dropping Miss Hepworth off first.'

'I forgot she'd gone with them. I can't make head nor tail of that one. I hope you're not thinking of bringing Rose on *our* honeymoon.'

She and Rose were hardly the same thing as Patricia and Dorothy, but Elsie wouldn't have known how to explain that to Ken. 'There's Stanley,' she said, watching as he leapt from the front seat and opened the door for Patricia. 'He's behaving like her chauffeur already.' Dorothy got out the other side and went ahead to open the front door, and Elsie saw the lights go on downstairs. The driver attempted to take something out of the back of the car, but Stanley shooed him away and carefully carried a stack of well-wrapped canvases into the house. 'The new Mrs Spencer will be pleased with that,' Elsie observed wryly. 'That's her wardrobe for the next couple of months.'

'A lot's happened since the last time we watched him come back here in a car,' Ken said, and Elsie smiled, remembering the day of their first meeting. 'Elsie, I just wanted to say…'

'Why's the taxi leaving?' she demanded, interrupting Ken as Stanley paid the driver and disappeared into the house.

'I suppose they'll walk to Lindworth. It must be all of two hundred yards.' He took an envelope out of his jacket pocket and slid it across the table. 'That's why I wanted to take you into town.'

'What is it?'

'Open it and see.'

Intrigued, she picked it up and took out a postcard with a date and nothing else. 'I don't understand.'

'It's our wedding day, if you'd like it to be. I've had a promotion and I reckon by then we'll be able to afford a place of our own.' She got up and threw her arms round him and he held her close, delighted by her reaction. 'Can I take that as a yes?'

'You know you can. It's perfect. I love you, Ken Beckford.'

'And I love you, too. There is one thing, though.'

'What's that?'

'The new job's in Reading. We'd have to move.' Elsie hesitated, and Ken looked at her with concern. 'Is that a problem?'

She shook her head, looking back towards the high street. 'Of course it's not. I came to Cookham for work, and other than meeting you, it hasn't been the happiest of places. It's time to move on.'

He grinned and picked up the empty pint glass. 'Another drink to celebrate?'

'Go on, then. It's the least I can do. I feel awful about turning down your meal when there was such a good reason for it.'

'Don't be daft. Like you said, this is where we met, so it's special, and the look on your face is enough of a treat for me. Hey up…'

'What's the matter?'

Ken nodded to Moor Thatch again. 'He's leaving. On his own.'

Elsie followed his gaze, and saw Stanley walking down the garden path with a small suitcase. He stopped by the war memorial and turned back to look at the cottage, waiting and watching until someone drew the curtains across the sitting room window, then he lowered his head and walked off in the direction of an empty house. 'What on earth's gone on there?' Elsie said, bewildered.

Ken shrugged. 'Who knows? Could be anything.'

He sounded suddenly despondent, and Elsie looked at him. 'What's the matter?'

'Nothing, really. It's just…'

He tailed off, struggling to find the right words, and Elsie put a hand gently under his chin, forcing him to look at her. 'What is it?'

'If he's on his own again… if they've all told him what to do with his offers, I'm worried you might change your mind and go back to him.'

'Why would I do that when I've got our wedding day to look forward to?'

'Because I know you care about him and I know he's been good to you, in his own way.'

She smiled and leant across the table to kiss him. 'All that's true, and those years at Burghclere were the happiest of my life – at the time. But there are happier days to come, I know that. And you'd better believe it, too, Ken Beckford, or you'll be standing at that altar on your own.'

20

The house in Pond Street was barely a mile from Downshire Hill, and yet it felt like a new start. It was bigger than the Carlines' previous family home – a handsome, cream-stuccoed villa spread over four storeys – and Hilda had liked it from the moment she stood on the pavement outside and looked through the cool, dark rooms to vivid green gardens beyond. There was something settled about it, something reassuring and permanent. From her window, she gazed down on the wide, leafy roads that she loved, peaceful in the warm July sunshine, and felt a tremendous sense of gratitude for the second chance that Hampstead was offering her.

Her room was in disarray after the move, with boxes of books still to be sorted and too many paintings lining up for a place on the wall. Stanley's request to come and see her so soon after his return from St Ives had taken her by surprise and she half-wished that she had put him off until the house was tidier, but really that was just an excuse, more palatable than acknowledging her nerves. It would be their first meeting since the night she had spent at Lindworth, and no matter how hard she tried to reason with herself, she felt like an awkward young girl again, desperate to make a good impression. Her renewed intimacy with Stanley wasn't something she had ever intended, but the joy of it was overwhelming and she had found it impossible to hide her happiness when she got back from Cookham. If her mother or brother had guessed its cause, they had been discreet enough not to ask.

The doorbell rang and their maid went to answer it. Hilda paused on the landing, watching as Stanley dropped his suitcase in the hallway, making himself at home just as he always had from the moment her brothers first asked him to stay. Even now, whenever he came to Hampstead, it was as if he brought their early years with him, invoking happier times until she could almost believe that Burghclere and Cookham had never existed. Those days became more precious as the years passed, resurrecting forgotten emotions and people she had lost until the images in her mind were more valuable to her than anything she had ever painted. There was a magic to those long summer evenings on the terrace at Downshire Hill: Dick and Jas arguing about art; the charades and the laughter; Stanley lounging by the door in his crumpled suit. She had thought him beautiful then.

He looked up and saw her, and his face broke into a smile. 'Grand house, ducky. Quite the toff, aren't you?'

Hilda laughed. 'I hoped you'd like it.' They kissed, and the texture of his old tweed jacket felt rough and familiar against her hand. 'As you can see, Mum's desperately trying to turn it into the last house by moving in as much of the old furniture as possible, but we're hanging on.' She looked more closely at his face. 'You've caught the sun. The West Country air must have been good for you.'

Stanley shrugged the compliment away. 'It's windburn, not sun. The weather was awful but the pictures got painted, so I suppose the trip was a success.' His voice was heavy with sarcasm, but he changed the subject before she could reply. 'Here, I've brought you something.' He rummaged in his suitcase, turning clothes on to the hallway floor, and took out a small pile of letters. 'You wanted these back when you came to Lindworth, but with everything that happened you forgot.'

She took the bundle, noticing again how carefully he had arranged them – his most recent letters and her replies, all numbered and tied with ribbon. 'I didn't forget,' she said, handing them back. 'I just didn't have the heart to separate them. Keep them together. I know you still read them.'

Pleased, he put the letters in his pocket and patted his jacket. 'Some things can't be separated.'

The love in his eyes unsettled her. Upstairs, she heard her brother moving about and knew that he would soon be down with a flood of conversation, and their privacy would be lost. She didn't want to share Stanley today; she had done that for too long. 'Let's go for a walk,' she suggested. 'Lunch won't be for a while.'

The Heath shone in the morning sunlight, and its atmosphere of lazy bustle symbolised what Hilda loved most about Hampstead. They slipped easily into their old routes, she noticed, both instinctively heading for the Vale of Health, and for once Stanley seemed content in her company, without the need for conversation. 'Elsie said you helped her spring clean the house while we were in St Ives,' he said, when they had been walking for a while. 'That was kind of you.' Kindness had had less to do with it than guilt, but Hilda kept her silence. 'Not that Patricia appreciated it, of course. She went straight back to Moor Thatch.'

'Does she know you're here?'

'Yes, of course. I'm not hiding anything from her. I don't see why I should.' Stanley was all too egalitarian in that regard, Hilda thought. He had written to her constantly from St Ives, giving a detailed account of the situation with his new wife, and while she felt nothing but remorse for the way that she had betrayed Patricia's position, she couldn't help but feel that Patricia herself now had everything she wanted. In hindsight, the invitation to visit Stanley at Lindworth had been absurdly transparent. 'She was shocked when I told her what had happened between us,' Stanley admitted, 'and I suppose I was more brutal with her than I should have been, but we're perfectly friendly now. She understands that our marriage will never stop me seeing you.'

'Yes, I'm sure she does.'

Something in her tone made Stanley look sharply at her, but he didn't argue. 'This is exactly like it was when we first met,' he said, and she realised suddenly that he actually believed it. 'And speaking of the early days, I thought we might go to Wangford together this summer. We could get the Lamberts to give us our old room again and relive our honeymoon. Perhaps the children could come with us this time. You said you wanted to take them, and I…'

'No, Stanley, I can't,' Hilda said, before the vision of their family – whole again and happy – could seduce her. 'Actually, that's not true. I *could* come to Wangford with you, but I don't want to.'

He stared at her. 'Why not? If you're worried about Patricia, you needn't be. She sees the sense in our being together. She says I can have as many women as I want and it won't change the way she feels about me.'

'It's got nothing to do with Patricia.'

'Then what is it?'

She took his hand and led him over to a bench, where they could talk properly. 'It's too late, don't you see that? I used to be your *wife*. I can't be your mistress.'

'You're as bad as Patricia, always so worried about what people think. Who says we can't love more than one person? The sin is *not* to love.'

'I don't care about other people. It's what I feel in *here* that stops me.' She put her hand to her heart, suddenly furious with him. 'You still don't know me at all, do you? Even now, after everything we've been through and the thousands of words we've written to each other, you still don't understand.' She wrenched the letters from his pocket and threw them in his lap, but the breeze caught the paper and suddenly the Heath in front of them was littered with their words, dancing across the grass in a flurry of ink, as if the wind were making light of their feelings. Stanley rushed to save them, eventually collecting the final pages from the tangle of a hawthorn bush, and Hilda's tears as she watched him were a mixture of laughter and despair. 'This is as hard for me as it is for you,' she said, when he returned to the bench. 'I thought our marriage was forever.'

'It is, I'm certain of that.'

They walked on, crossing East Heath towards the Vale of Health Pond. 'You should try to make it work with Patricia,' Hilda said earnestly.

'It's working perfectly on paper.'

The sharpness in his tone was back, and she tried to work out when it had become so habitual; he had never sounded bitter when they first met, not even when he talked about the war. 'But you won't be content unless it's a marriage in the truest sense.'

'I would if I had you.'

'You'll try harder with Patricia if you don't.'

Stanley pulled some low-hanging branches aside and let her go ahead on the narrow path. 'That side of things has never been any good between us,' he admitted. 'Not even at first.'

'They might improve. Get her to see a doctor. Someone might be able to help her.'

He sighed, dismissing her suggestion. 'Come back to Cookham with me. Patricia's not living at Lindworth, and I doubt she ever will be, not unless I move out. You can stay as long as you like.'

Hilda shook her head. 'I don't want to live anywhere but in London.' He opened his mouth to argue again but she put her finger to his lips. 'Don't think that night meant nothing to me. I loved it, every single moment of it. Just to know that you don't hate me any more, that we still have feelings for each other... well, that was enough for me. I feel as if things have been laid to rest between us. We can look back on our last night as something that was perfect and unspoilt. Let's leave it there.' He took her hand in his and kissed her fingertips. 'Don't look so despondent,' Hilda said. 'You know you can come here whenever you want to see me.'

'It's not the same. I hate being welcomed to your house and barred from your bedroom.'

She cupped his face gently in her hands, willing him to understand. 'You made me learn to cope without you, and now I've done that I can't go back. I love you – I'll always love you – but I don't *need* you.'

He turned away without another word, and she followed him along the edge of the path, watching as he kicked stones into the undergrowth, deep in thought. 'I thought I'd paint you with Unity while I'm here,' he said after a while.

'She'd like that. She misses you.'

'I miss her, too. And Shirin.'

'Well, they're both doing well at school. Unity dances so beautifully now and Shirin was a page boy in *Richard of Bordeaux* last term. She played the lute. I've got some photographs to show you when we get back to the house, and…'

He turned abruptly, stopping Hilda in her tracks. 'I'm not giving up, ducky. I'll never give up.'

'But you *must*, Stan. I want your happiness more than anything else in this world, and you'll never be happy until you do.'

21

Elsie took one last look across the rooftops from her bedroom window, fixing the details in her mind as best she could. She doubted that she would be quick to return to Cookham. Stanley had gone out after breakfast without saying goodbye, and she wondered if he would be back before Ken came to fetch her. He had avoided much conversation over the past few days, managing to imply with his silence that Elsie, too, was deserting him, but the thought of leaving his house without a chance to make peace saddened her. In spite of everything, she wanted them to part friends.

She took her final suitcase downstairs and went through to the kitchen to make some tea. Stanley's latest series of sketches was scattered all over the table, and she picked up the pages one by one, as keen as ever to find his heart through his work. One in particular drew her attention, a pencil and watercolour sketch of Stanley and Hilda in their bedroom at Lindworth. The drawing was far from finished, with the faintly drawn squares still visible beneath the image, but its fragility seemed to chime somehow with its sense of forlorn longing. Stanley – a tiny figure, dwarfed by the vast bed – struggled to put on a pyjama jacket while Hilda reached for a book from the shelf above her head. Her hair – the hair that Stanley loved – hung down in two thick plaits, and Shirin and Unity scrambled in delight over the mountain of legs beneath the sheets. The sketch was in stark contrast to the portrait that Stanley had brought back from his trip to Hampstead. It was magnificent, even she could see that, but when he had first shown her the image of Unity on her mother's lap, cradling her doll, Sonia Rose, Elsie had been so upset by the grief and isolation of the picture that she could hardly bear to look at it. She tidied the sketch and its memories away, wondering why it had never been enough for him. Instead, he had two wives, neither of whom would live with him; two daughters, who loved their parents but were wrenched apart; and a list of debts and financial responsibilities which he could ill afford to meet. Deep down, Elsie feared for Stanley and his future, and no matter what she said to Ken, her loyalty wouldn't let her leave him lightly.

A vehicle drew up outside, as if Ken had arrived just in time to save her from herself. Elsie went to the window to wave, but it was a car, not a van, and one she didn't recognise. To her surprise, Stanley got out of the driver's seat and bounded up the path, and she heard him whistling as he let himself in. 'Elsie?' he called. 'Are you ready for the off?'

It hurt her that he could be so cheerful about it. 'Ken should be here in a bit,' she said. 'I thought you were him.'

'Oh, I've put him off until tomorrow. I hope you don't mind. He was very good about it.'

'Why have you done that?'

She glared at him, angered by his arrogance, but Stanley simply smiled. 'Because you and I have somewhere to go.' He walked over and put his hands on her shoulders. 'I'm sorry, Elsie. I made you a promise years ago and I didn't keep it, so today I'm putting that right.'

'What do you mean? What promise?'

'We never did have that day out at the chapel, did we? You were there for almost every stroke of the brush but you haven't seen it finished. I've borrowed a car for the day. Get your coat and cross your fingers.'

'You're serious, aren't you?' Elsie said, delighted by the gesture. 'You're driving all the way to Burghclere?'

'It's not that far.'

'It is at ten miles an hour.'

He laughed and held out the keys. 'Then perhaps you'd like to do the honours.'

'I think I'd better,' Elsie said. 'The last time you drove me somewhere, I ended up in hospital.' She looked at him and felt herself blush. 'Thank you, Mr Spencer. You've no idea how much that means to me.'

'I think I have,' he said earnestly, 'and it's Stanley from now on. We're friends, Elsie.' She turned to get her coat, but he caught her arm. 'We *are* friends, aren't we?'

'Of course we are. How else would I have got away with answering back so often?' The clock in the hallway struck the hour, and she glanced towards the kitchen. 'Have I got time to pack us up something to eat?'

'It's already taken care of,' Stanley said, opening the front door for her. 'I called in a favour from Mrs Buckpitt at the Copper Kettle. She liked the way I painted her roses, so she agreed to make us a picnic. It won't be a patch on yours, of course, but beggars can't be choosers.'

'I bet that set tongues wagging in the high street.'

'Let them talk. It's nothing I haven't heard before.'

For Elsie, the journey back to Burghclere was a peculiar jumble of emotions – comfortably familiar, and yet something she had conditioned herself so strictly not to want that a part of her felt guilty for making it. They entered the village from the western side, and she had forgotten how quickly the chapel appeared, dignified but still a little alien against its rural backdrop. She parked the car by the hedge on the opposite side of the road, and they looked in silence for a moment or two at the building that had brought them together. 'I still think they were wrong about the roof,' Stanley muttered eventually, and Elsie burst out laughing.

'When will you ever learn to count your blessings? Come on, I want to see inside.'

The apple trees between the chapel and the road had matured considerably in five years, and Elsie breathed in the rich scent of freshly cut grass as they walked up the path, avoiding the butter-flies which were sunning themselves against the warmth of the brick. The chapel door was locked, so they knocked at one of the almshouses for the key. The Bainbridges must have moved on, because the woman who answered was a stranger; she showed no sign of recognising the artist whose work she was guarding, and for once Stanley didn't announce himself and was content to behave like a tourist. As he opened the door, Elsie felt a knot in her stom-ach, just as she had on her very first visit, but her nerves this time had nothing to do with walking into an unfamiliar world; more than anything, she feared disappointment, the sudden realisation that her love for this building and all it stood for was an accident of time and place, something that by now she had grown out of. The sunlight pushed through the door and flooded the altar wall, and Elsie knew instantly that her doubts were unfounded.

She began to look around, but Stanley stopped her. 'There are two paintings you haven't seen, aren't there?' he asked, and she nodded. 'Yes, I thought so. Come here, this one's called *Making a Firebelt*.' He pointed to the final arched panel on the right-hand wall and Elsie stared up at a group of bare-chested, muscular soldiers using spills made from newspaper to burn off the grass around their camp. The tangle of tent ropes and the busyness of the men was disorientating and it took her a moment to get her bearings, but what struck her immediately was the firelight play-ing over the naked skin of the figure in the foreground; it gave the painting a raw, primitive feel which was quite unlike any of the others. 'But this is the picture I really wanted you to see,' Stanley added, moving her on. 'You should have seen it years ago, because I painted it for you. This is *Bedmaking*.'

At last, Elsie understood why he had wanted to borrow her photographs in those early days at Lindworth. The final rect-angular panel was set in a cosy hospital ward. In the centre, an orderly was shaking out a sheet while the evacuated patients stood wrapped in patterned blankets, one with his feet on a hot water bottle. Along the back wall, behind the beds, the men's family pictures and postcards were pinned to the striped wallpaper, all painstakingly recreated in paint from Stanley's own photographs and the ones she had lent him. She stepped closer and stared at them in delight, remembering how much it had meant to her to have pictures while she was in hospital, and how surprised she was that Stanley had brought them. Now, two of her brothers – dressed in naval uniform – stared cheerfully out from the chapel wall, and next to them was an image of their ship. On the right-hand side of the painting, half-eclipsed by a patient making his bed, a framed photograph of a dark-haired young woman stood on a chest of drawers, and Elsie caught her breath as her own face looked back at her. 'That was one of the first things you told me when you walked in and signed the visitors' book,' Stanley said quietly. 'You wanted people to know that you were here. Well, now they always will.'

'Fancy you remembering that.'

'Of course I remember. Isn't that the point of all this?' Elsie nodded, scarcely able to believe what he had done. The gift was so precious and so unexpected that she didn't know what to say. 'I want these walls to mean something to all of us,' he added, his voice barely more than a whisper. 'A living memorial, if you like. Remembering shouldn't just be for the dead.'

'Thank you,' she said, knowing how inadequate the words were. 'I can't believe this has been here all the time and I had no idea.'

'You'd have seen it sooner if you'd been at the press opening. I wanted you there, Elsie. Why were you so determined not to come?'

'Because you'd fallen out of love with it by then,' she said, without hesitating. 'It seemed to mean nothing to you at all, but it was still special to me. *Very* special, and I didn't want it spoilt.' She looked at some of the other images that he had chosen to recreate: his father standing in the porch of a church and his brother, Percy, in an army cap; Unity in her pram, looking unnervingly like the black-eyed doll in the portrait he had just painted; and at the heart of it all, the photograph of Hilda that he most loved, leaning forward in a deckchair in the garden at Downshire Hill.

Stanley followed her gaze and brushed his fingertips lightly across Hilda's face. 'Perhaps you were right not to come. I do spoil things.'

'Yes, you do.' She looked at him, finding it easier than she had for years to see the man she loved. Perhaps it was the surroundings playing tricks on her, but something had changed in Stanley, as if he were a patient recovering from an illness and waking to a new morning with the fever passed. 'What are you going to do?' she asked.

He shrugged his shoulders. 'Paint my pictures. Wait for Hilda to come back.'

'And if she doesn't?'

'She will. I know she will.'

Elsie shook her head, exasperated by his stubbornness. 'You could have a thousand and one wives, but there'd still only be one person in the relationship.'

He smiled ruefully. 'You're right, Elsie. Letting Hilda go was the worst thing I ever did.'

'I didn't mean Hilda,' she said, with a final glance up at the chapel walls. 'I meant the man staring back at you from the mirror.'

'All things seem to have to be memorials for me to love them.'

Stanley Spencer

Cookham Rise to Pond Street
May, 1958

Dear Ducky,
The morning is sunny and beautiful, but already it's far too hot in the house, so I have stopped painting my Crucifixion to spend the afternoon with you.

On the platform at Cookham station the light hurt my eyes and it was impossible to write, but now I have an empty carriage where I can speak to you in peace. I have brought no book or newspaper so I can think only of you and this letter. The happiness, ducky! The sheer, endless happiness as the little train pulls out of the station and I see Cookham growing smaller and know I am on my way to you. Every minute brings us closer and I imagine what you might be doing. You are in your favourite chair, perhaps, enjoying the breeze from the window. I can see you now, propped up on piles of cushions, with your orange dress caught up in bunches around your legs and your feet turned in a little. Adorable to me, of course. You are soaking up the quiet of your room and listening to the blackbird in the garden, and I wonder if you've guessed yet that I'm coming?

Closer, ducky, ever closer. You are with me as I look out of the window at Maidenhead. All the fine folks are getting on, with their loud voices and their laughter, but we cling together, you and I, and there is nothing here but our love and this page. I shall soon be at Pond Street.

Stopping and starting, stopping and starting, and my pen refuses to behave. Inky scratches everywhere, all over you and me and our thoughts. Inky scratches like the ones that went scampering off over Hampstead Heath, chasing each other in the wind, spreading our precious love to the trees but still we had more. Always more love, you and I.

I am at Paddington now, pushing through the crowds to get to you. I am on the bus, loving the number twenty-seven because it carries me to you, loving the buildings in Marylebone Road and Euston Road and Hampstead Road, loving you. Now we are in Ferdinand Street, and then the long haul down Malden Road, where our bus feels the urgency and picks up speed. I am looking out for the first sign to the Heath now and the very word fills me with joy. There is the cinema. There is the hospital where I held your hand and you read your love to me. There is Pond Street. There is number seventeen.

I sense you turn your head when you hear me open the gate, the creaky iron gate that no amount of oil can ever hush. You hear me knocking on the big, red door beneath the rowan tree. You know I have come, like I always do. Come to kiss my ducky and my girls. Come to you.

Ever and ever, your loving
Stanley

The bus dropped her by Cookham Moor, just across the road from the war memorial. She straightened her clothes in the June heat, wishing now that she had worn her favourite summer dress rather than clinging sentimentally to the two-piece simply because he had always liked her in blue. The wool felt rough where it touched her skin, and she tried to ignore the urge to fling the jacket away as she squinted against the sun, taking in the long dry grass and pink summer sedge, the crooked rooftops curving away down School Lane. Sunlight danced playfully against the memorial's clean white stone, brushing the names of the fallen before leading the eye further down the road, and it pleased her to find that she still saw things as he had seen them. The past tugged at her like a child seeking attention, effortlessly wiping away the years until she half-doubted their existence. Only the Jubilee oak – a sapling when she first came to Cookham – gave any indication that time had moved on.

Behind her, laughter spilled out from the Crown Hotel's open windows and she caught the faint smell of beer and cigarette smoke. The village idled away its Sunday under strong, blue skies, asking nothing more from the world than to be left alone, and it occurred to her that any newcomer to Cookham would instantly sense its childlike innocence in every nook and cranny. She smiled to herself when she remembered her mother's warning about crossing the Moor at night, its name having conjured a bleak and lonely place, home to the demons and trolls of her storybooks. As it turned out, Ma had been right about the demons and the darkness, but they were hidden somewhere else altogether, and they were never the stuff of make-believe.

The broad expanse of grass gave way to a bottle-necked high street – the village breathing in, she had always thought. She walked slowly, counting off the stores that she recognised, acknowledging cautious smiles from those who knew her face but couldn't quite place her after twenty years. Most shop windows had found room for the bright-yellow poster which advertised the exhibition, and she followed the trail to the end of the street. Up ahead, she could see crowds of people crossing from a makeshift car park, moving in a steady stream beneath the heavily wooded horizon. With a final glance at her own reflection in the window of the chemist's, she joined the throng and turned left towards the riverside church.

The queue for entry stretched back from the vicarage gates and she waited patiently in line, soaking up snippets of conversation and hoping that no one would know his paintings well enough to recognise her younger self in them. People milled round in the churchyard, smelling a flower or climbing the stile to the river path; a woman stood with her baby in the shade of the rose-covered porch, another gave her husband's jacket a brush before going inside, and the light on the church walls seemed to soften and animate the stone, making it more than just a backdrop to each tiny human drama. The scene appeared to her now as a living, breathing version of the painting which she had never really understood, in spite of his efforts to explain it. Perhaps she had never tried hard enough, because today – later in his life, and in hers – this joy in ordinary moments made sense. She paid her two-and-six at a temporary box office converted from the vicarage summer house, and nodded to the ladies in charge of refreshments: tea, sandwiches and jugs of lemonade laid out with military precision on long trestle tables; crisp, white tablecloths which rippled like sails in the breeze.

The vicarage was busy, so she headed for the church to look at the paintings there. Pendrill, Nott, Worster – the moss-covered names on the headstones were as familiar to her as friends she had lost touch with, learnt unconsciously on warm afternoons while he painted and she talked. She was remembering those conversations when she saw him, standing under a stunted elm tree at the edge of the churchyard. It was a shock, even though she had known he would be there, and she paused by a gravestone to gather her thoughts. He was talking to a child about a half-finished picture and his energy played tricks with time, giving him a youthfulness which belied his sixty-odd years. His hair was white now but as unruly as ever, and he fiddled constantly with the paintbrush in his hand. The gesture floored her with its familiarity and she turned away, too flustered yet to speak to him.

Inside, the church was cool and quiet, and she closed her eyes to adjust to the half-light. When she opened them again, it was as if she were standing once more in a world entirely of his making. She walked over to the choir stalls, where eight small pictures of Christ were hung together, each offering a different scene from His days in the wilderness, but it wasn't Christ she saw; it was an ordinary man, the man she had worked for and in whose house she had lived for almost a decade – rising from his bed, protecting an animal, kneeling to smell the flowers in the grass, just as his daughter had done when she was a toddler. Saddened for reasons which she would have found hard to explain, she turned away and walked towards the altar, where the largest painting in the exhibition was hung. It was a crucifixion, although the cross stood not on Calvary but on the rooftops of Cookham, and she looked up, trying to make sense of it. Mary lay prostrate on a pile of earth, dressed in a summer frock whose pattern was familiar; she had washed and ironed a similar one many times, but it was the only part of the picture to which she could relate. Christ had his back to the viewer and the focus of the painting was on His tormentors, who hammered in their nails with a cruel, frenzied pleasure. The violence shocked her, and she realised that she had never seen anger or hatred in his work until now, not even in the images of war. She looked for the date and saw that it was a new picture, painted that year. If she thought he had laid his demons to rest, she was obviously wrong.

Wondering now what to say when she spoke to him, she made her way back outside but his easel had been cleared away. Disappointed, she wandered through the vicarage, looking at the pictures there, but they seemed to belong to a different artist, someone more like the harmless man she had seen on her way in. There were flower paintings, views of Cookham, and the occasional portrait of a village dignitary, but nowhere – here, or in the church – could she find images of the women he loved. Only now, when she felt so let down by the absence of the world she had been part of, did she realise how badly she had wanted to see it again.

'You always did love the potboilers.' His voice was warm and affectionate, if gently mocking. 'How many times have I told you, Elsie? It's the people who make a landscape. They don't mean anything if they're empty.'

She turned around, scarcely knowing whether to embrace him or shake his hand. In the end, she did neither, but simply refuted his argument. 'It's not empty, though, is it?' She looked again at the painting that had caught her attention, a colourful display of geraniums with the river and boatyard in the background. 'How can it be empty when you're in every inch of it?' He smiled, and she noticed how unlined his face was, how bright his eyes. 'It's nice to see you, Stanley. How have you been?'

The question sounded trite, even to her, but she was saved from a response in kind by the arrival of the vicar and a distinguished-looking lady whom she took to be his wife. 'Another busy day,' the woman said, nodding to Elsie. 'We'll have that roof fixed in no time.'

Stanley ignored the comment and put his hand gently on Elsie's shoulder. 'Michael, Rachel, I'd like you to meet our little maid, Elsie Munday. Elsie, this is the Reverend and Mrs Westropp.'

A flicker of confusion crossed the vicar's face as he tried to reconcile the description with the middle-aged woman in front of him. Elsie was no longer little in any sense of the word, but she knew from Stanley's expression that he still saw her in his mind as the girl he had first met thirty years ago, and that it was more than a trick of memory: he had always been able to retreat to a moment that suited him better than the present. 'Elsie Beckford now,' she said, shaking hands with the couple. 'It's nice to meet you.'

'The pleasure's all ours. How lovely that you've come.' Mrs Westropp seemed genuinely delighted. 'Stanley's told us so much about you, and we feel we know you already from the paintings. You're famous in Cookham.'

Elsie smiled, embarrassed to see that the nearest bystanders were taking an interest. 'It was a long time ago now,' she said, 'and my family would laugh to hear you say that. I'm a wife and mother these days.'

'How many children have you got?'

'Two. Irene and Gordon.'

'Are they here?' Stanley asked.

'No. They're out at work.' She didn't say so, but she hadn't wanted company when she came to Cookham. She had never really been able to explain her feelings for Stanley to Ken, and her children – with all the selfishness of youth – were as yet untroubled by any curiosity about her life before they arrived.

'Then you've got a bit of time?' Stanley asked. 'There's something I'd like to show you.'

She nodded, expecting him to take her back to the church, but he led the way to the gate, collecting his painting from behind a gravestone on the way. There was a pram waiting outside and he balanced the canvas on top of the brushes, palette and paint-stained umbrella already inside. In its younger days, she had used the pram to push Unity along these very streets and the memory made her smile. 'How are the children?' she asked.

'Flourishing. Shirin's teaching out in Africa now.'

'Really?'

Stanley nodded. 'She's turned out to be a splendid musician. Unity's down in Kent, but we see a lot of each other. She's done some wonderful paintings, Elsie. I'm so proud of them both.'

'Give them my love when you speak to them.' They walked slowly back up the high street, drawing curious glances from strangers. 'Where are we off to?' Elsie asked.

'Home. I'm living at Cookham Rise now, in Annie's old house. I moved in just after she left us.' His choice of words was ambiguous and she wondered if his sister had died or simply moved to another village. 'They put her away,' he added more quietly, sensing her uncertainty. 'A policemen caught her trying to dig her own grave on the Moor one night during the war. We didn't have any choice.'

'I'm sorry,' Elsie said. She remembered how gentle Stanley had been with his elder sister and knew that the small shrug he gave belied a deep grief.

'I go and see her whenever I can.'

He changed the subject, talking instead of his surprise at the thousands of people who had flocked to see his paintings in the current exhibition. They crossed the road by the war memorial, and she saw his eyes stray automatically to the pretty thatched cottage at the edge of the Moor. 'Do you see much of Patricia and Dorothy these days?' she asked casually, knowing that she was treading on dangerous ground but too curious not to ask.

Stanley shook his head. 'We communicate by cheque. As you can imagine, it's a very one-sided conversation.' There was a bitterness in his voice, and she tried to decide if it was genuinely new or if she had simply forgotten it in an idealised version of the past. 'Patricia bleeds me dry, but there's no change there. Still, I manage, and all I really need is an empty room, peace and quiet, and a fire in the grate.'

Elsie said nothing, but thought privately that a lot of pain might have been saved if he had only realised that sooner. They walked over the bridge and into the Pound, where a profusion of flowers blurred the careful symmetry of the chequered footpaths. The character of the village changed as they approached the railway station: the houses were newer here, and more uniform. After a few minutes, Stanley turned without warning into a quiet street and pointed to a pert, red-brick house which stood alone on the corner of Worster Road. 'Cliveden View,' he said, and grinned. 'Of a fashion, and only from the first floor.'

As he dumped the pram by the front door and ushered her inside, she wondered how he felt about living on the outskirts of his beloved village, away from the larger, more attractive houses that had once meant so much to him. 'It suits me well enough,' he said, noticing her expression. 'I had hoped that Hilda and the children would join me here one day, but it wasn't to be.' A kitchen and two other rooms led off from the hallway, small but arranged in the simple, uncluttered way which he had always preferred, and a faint smell of bacon lingered in the air. 'Come up and see what I've been doing.' She followed him up the lino-covered stairs to a small bedroom at the front of the house which he had obviously adopted as his studio. There was a plain metal army bed in one corner, but it was so covered in sketchbooks, canvases and tubes of paint that it would have been hard to say if he ever slept in it. More drawings covered a table by the window, and the only other furniture consisted of a small paraffin stove, a trestle table with a stool perched on top and a couple of old crates.

'It looks like our lounge when Ken's about to decorate,' she said, using the joke to give herself time. This sudden immersion in a world so familiar and yet so changed was not what she had expected, and she felt again the jarring awkwardness of her first few months in the Spencer household, when everything had seemed too close, too intimate. 'He's as dangerous with a paintbrush as you are.'

'Never mind that,' Stanley said impatiently. 'This is what I want you to look at.' He gestured to a canvas which had been taped to the wall, and Elsie moved closer to look at it. The work was still in its early stages and only the top left corner had actually been painted, but the figures sketched in pencil were clearly Stanley and his first wife. 'We're outside the house in Downshire Hill. Do you recognise it?' She nodded, remembering the Hampstead street. 'I've been doing lots of pictures for the chapel I told you about,' he added, as if the conversation had taken place yesterday rather than years ago. 'Have a look at the sketches. You're in some of them.' He picked up a pile of papers and Elsie hastily moved a half-drunk cup of tea from one of the crates before he put them down on top of it. She listened while he talked about the paintings in his head, recalling his extraordinary energy. The vitality was unchanged, but his plans had a desperation about them now, as if he were terrified of what might be left unfinished, and the thought depressed her so much that she was relieved when a knock at the door called him downstairs.

She looked around the room again. A navy- and gold-checked dressing gown hung on the back of the door, braided on the collar and sleeves, its tasselled belt brushing the floorboards. There was something unaccountably sad about its proximity to the drawing of Hilda, and she got up to put it out of her mind. Curious to see more of the house, she wandered through to the back, treading as lightly as possible on the boards. The sun had moved round and the small bedroom which overlooked the garden was pleasantly cool. She pushed the door open further and looked at the unmade bed, a pile of pillows at its head, the blankets bunched up in a heap at the side. His bible was on the bedside table, marked in several places with letters or postcards, and a copy of *The Wind in the Willows* lay open on top, the same edition that she remembered him reading to his daughters. The book seemed appropriate, because there was something nest-like about the bed: everything he valued was pulled close around him, as if he were still in a trench or a dugout. It would have been impossible to venture far into the room, even if she had wanted to, because the floor was a sea of blue notepaper: sheet after sheet, all covered in Stanley's distinctive handwriting and annotated with tiny drawings; hundreds of unsent letters, beginning 'Dear Ducky' and ending with love. 'I write to her every night when I get in,' he said quietly from the landing. 'I always hated it when she went away. You know that.' Elsie turned around, embarrassed to have been caught intruding on something so private, but it was Stanley who seemed to feel the need for justification. 'I can be myself with Hilda,' he added. 'I always could.'

'You don't have to make excuses to me. There's nothing wrong with saying the things you wish you'd said. We'd all like that chance.' He nodded and walked past her into the room, scattering the pages and stopping in front of a photograph above the tiny fireplace. It was of Hilda, leaning forward as if she were listening intently to the words strewn beneath her on the floor. Elsie looked at the strong face, adding colour and life to the features from her own memory, and found it hard to believe that eight years had passed since

Hilda's death. 'It seems to me that she can hear every word you say,' she continued gently. 'Come on, I'll put the kettle on.'

He closed the door and they went back downstairs. 'I don't think much of your daily woman,' Elsie said, running her hand down the banister and examining the dust on her fingers.

'You can't get the staff these days.'

At last he smiled, and she left him in the sitting room while she went to make the tea, falling easily into an old routine. The kitchen was tidy in comparison with the first floor, and she guessed that the time he spent here was negligible. The frying pan and a single cup and plate had been washed and neatly stacked on the drainer, and there was an egg ready to be boiled in a saucepan on the stove. It was a life of habit, monastic in its simplicity, and she would have been troubled by the sparseness of it all had she not known that Stanley rarely bothered with material things. She found what she needed and took a tray through to the sitting room, guided by the first few notes of a tune which she recognised but could not name. Stanley was sitting at the piano and she looked round for somewhere to put the tea, then stopped in surprise as she came face to face with the full-length painting of herself in the kitchen at Burghclere. 'You've kept it all these years,' she said, as much to herself as to him.

'Of course I have. Hilda's was so much better than mine.' He closed the piano lid and came over to where she was standing. 'I often wish we could have stayed there forever, don't you? Just the three of us and the children in that house by the railway cutting. We could have been so happy.'

Elsie looked at the girl in the portrait, trying in vain to share his sense of longing. She thought about the life she had now, with a husband she loved and two children who meant the world to her, and realised with a surge of happiness that she would not have changed a moment of the past twenty years. But the lie cost her nothing and she offered it willingly. 'Yes,' she said, knowing what he wanted to hear. 'Yes, Stanley, I do.'

Endnote

There is, of course, more to the story.

Hilda died in November 1950 after a long battle with cancer, during which Stanley was almost constantly at her side. He continued to write to her for the rest of his life, and many of his finest paintings from the 1950s – *Love Letters*, *Hilda With Bluebells*, *Hilda Welcomed*, *Hilda and I at Burghclere* – recall scenes from their marriage during happier times.

Stanley was knighted in July 1959, with Patricia taking the title of Lady Spencer. He died the following December at the age of 68, cared for by family and friends, and his ashes were laid to rest at Holy Trinity Church, Cookham. His vast canvas, *Christ Preaching at Cookham Regatta* – together with many planned paintings of Hilda, Patricia and Elsie – was left unfinished at his death, but it can be seen on display at the Stanley Spencer Gallery, the old Methodist Chapel in Cookham which was secured by the Sir Stanley Spencer Memorial Trust in 1962. The Gallery (stanleyspencer.org.uk) holds regular exhibitions of Stanley's work, and is a wonderful tribute to an extraordinary man at the heart of the village he loved.

Patricia and Dorothy lived on together at Moor Thatch until Patricia's death in 1966. Dorothy outlived her by twelve years, and they are buried together in Cookham Parish Cemetery; the inscription on their headstone reads 'United in life and in death'.

Louis and Mary Behrend continued as generous patrons to the arts and gave the chapel at Burghclere to the National Trust in 1947 (www.national trust.org.uk/sandham-memorial-chapel). Elsie may have been unique in witnessing its creation, but the emotions which Sandham Memorial Chapel inspires in her are universal: it is a deeply moving and beautiful place – once seen, never forgotten.

Elsie Munday enjoyed a long and happy marriage to Ken Beckford, and – with all the zest for life that Stanley so admired – was dancing well into her eighties. She was characteristically modest about her service to the Spencer family; only after her own children were married did she tell them about her early life, subsequently travelling with them to Burghclere, Cookham and Brighton to show them the paintings that she had inspired. Hilda's portrait of Elsie, which Stanley kept until he died, now hangs resplendent in the Brighton Museum & Art Gallery.

Acknowledgements

Stanley and Elsie is supported using public funding by Arts Council England, and I'm indebted to a Grants for the Arts award for its research and writing.

My thanks go to Jane Munro, Keeper of Paintings, Drawings and Prints at the Fitzwilliam Museum in Cambridge, whose exhibition, *Sargent, Sickert & Spencer* first introduced me to Elsie and led me to Burghclere; to Duncan Robinson, for his insights into Spencer's life and work; to Ann Danks, Archivist at the Stanley Spencer Gallery, for guiding me so patiently through a vast amount of material, and to Chrissy Rosenthal for making additional interviews available; to Alison Paton and Paul Grist from the National Trust for their help in the research on Sandham Memorial Chapel; to Alan and Robina Cassie for an insight into life at Moor Thatch; and to everyone at the Crown Inn for their fabulous hospitality.

I'm especially grateful to Elsie's son, Gordon Beckford, for trusting me with precious memories of his mother; to Carolyn Leder for her knowledge, advice and counsel – given so generously throughout this project – and for her close and sensitive reading of the manuscript; and to Shirin and John Spencer for allowing me to quote from Stanley Spencer's writings.

Many other writers – on the period in general and Stanley Spencer in particular – have contributed to the background for the novel: Keith Bell; Amanda Bradley; Richard Carline; Andrew Causey; Maurice and Louise Collis; Adrian Glew; Kitty Hauser; Alison Light; Fiona MacCarthy; Kenneth Pople; Jean Rennie; John Rothenstein; Gilbert Spencer; John Spencer; Unity Spencer; and Denis Winter. Paul Gough's *Journey to Burghclere* was indispensable, and Alison Thomas's *The Art of Hilda Carline* is a rare and valuable study of an artist too often in the shadows.

Thanks also to my agent, Véronique Baxter, for her enthusiasm and loyalty to *Stanley and Elsie*; to Rose Cooper and everyone at Duckworth for creating such a beautiful book, and in particular to my editor, Abbie Headon, for nurturing the manuscript at every stage and answering all the difficult questions before I'd even asked them; and to Helaine and Yorick Blumenfeld for helping this book on its journey, and for twenty years of very special friendship and encouragement.

My grandmothers – both wonderful women – had much in common with Elsie; although they're no longer here to see it, their lives have filled in the details of her character where history could not, and I'm grateful to them and to my parents for all the years of love and stories.

And to Mandy, who has had such faith in *Stanley and Elsie* from the beginning and made it better in every way, thank you. This one is definitely for you.

Supported using public funding by
ARTS COUNCIL ENGLAND

LOTTERY FUNDED

About the Author

Nicola Upson was born in Suffolk and read English at Downing College, Cambridge. She has worked in theatre and as a freelance journalist, and is a regular arts contributor to a number of radio networks. Her non-fiction works include *Mythologies: The Sculpture of Helaine Blumenfeld* (Overlook Press) and she is the recipient of an Escalator Award from the Arts Council England.

Nicola's debut fiction, *An Expert in Murder*, was the first in a series of novels to feature the real-life author and playwright Josephine Tey, one of the leading figures of the Golden Age of crime writing. The book has been dramatised by BBC Scotland for BBC Radio 4, and was praised by P.D. James as marking 'the arrival of a new and assured talent'; taken together, the seven novels published to date paint an atmospheric picture of England between the wars, and have been critically acclaimed on both sides of the Atlantic.

Nine Lessons, Nicola's most recent novel, was chosen by *Publishers Weekly* as one of the Best Books of 2017, and shortlisted for the 2018 CWA Historical Dagger. Nicola lives with her partner in Cambridge and Cornwall.